James Burks

BiRD & SQUiRREL

ALL TANGLED UP

graphix

An Imprint of

SCHOLASTIC

To Steph McHugh for always facing the audience and sharing your love of books with kids big and small.

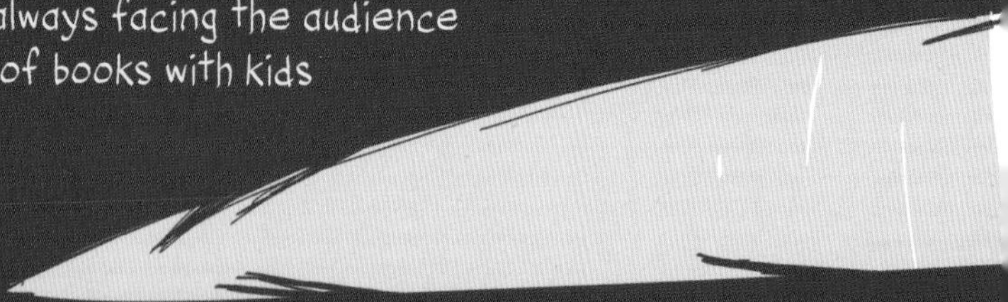

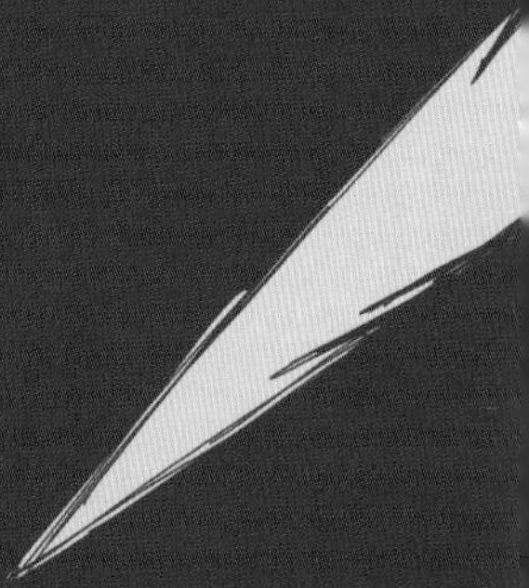

Library of Congress Control Number: 2016947440

ISBN 978-1-338-25183-8 (hardcover)
ISBN 978-1-338-25175-3 (paperback)

10 9 8 7 6 5 4 21 22 23
Printed in China 62

First edition, February 2019

Edited by Adam Rau
Book design by Phil Falco
Creative Director: David Saylor

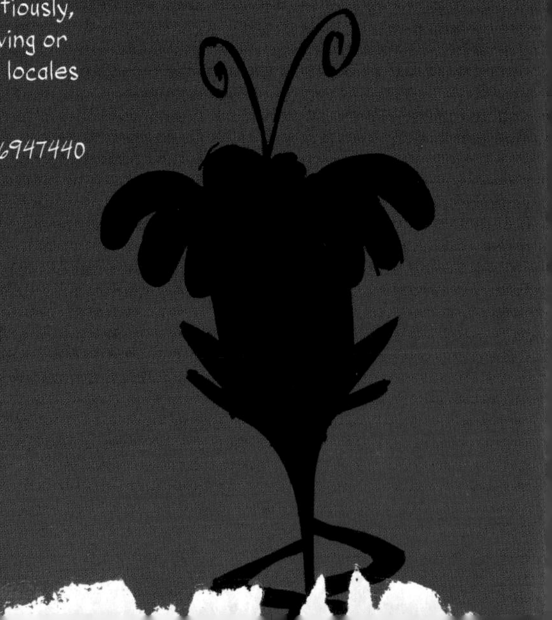

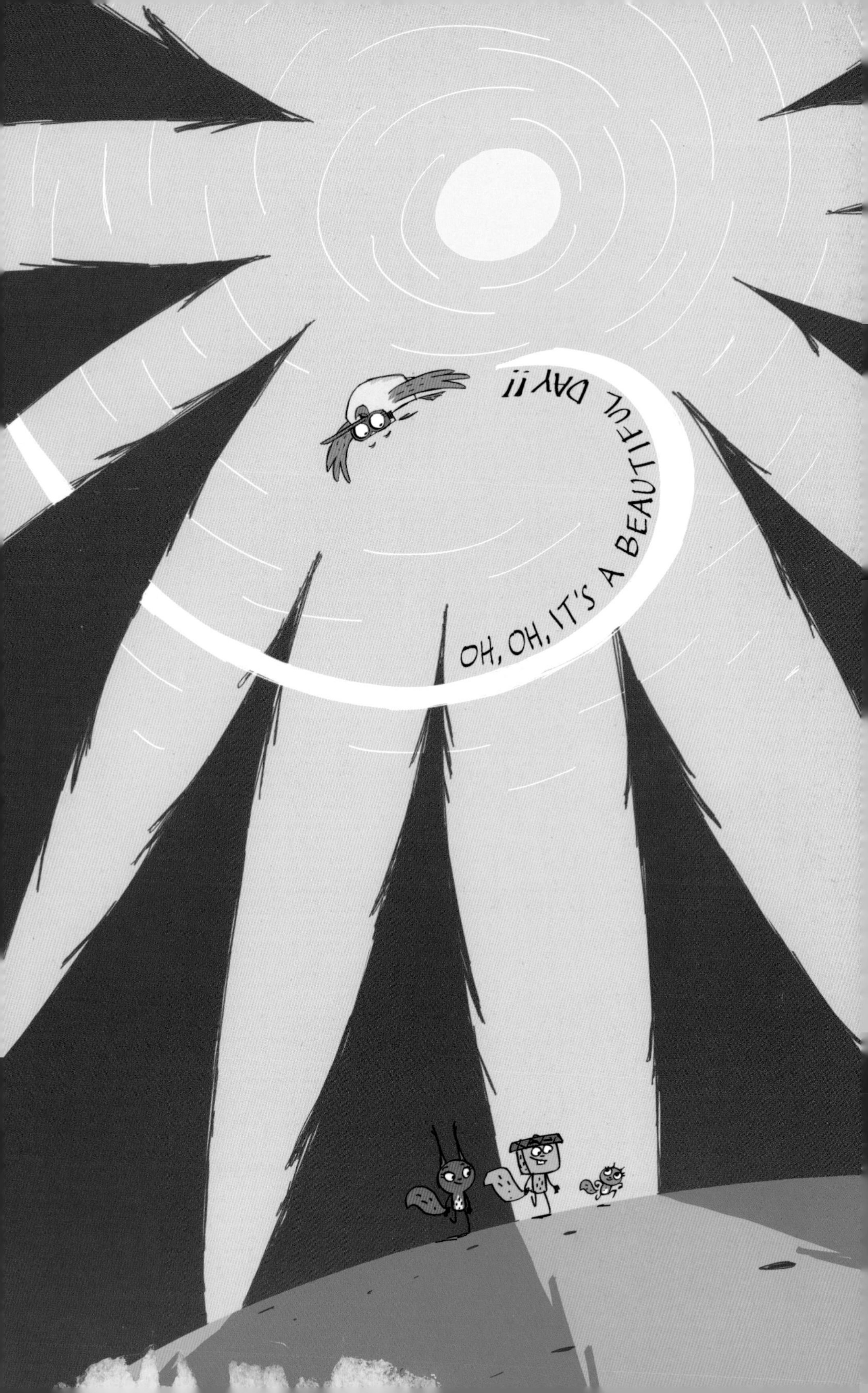

OH, OH, IT'S A BEAUTIFUL DAY!!

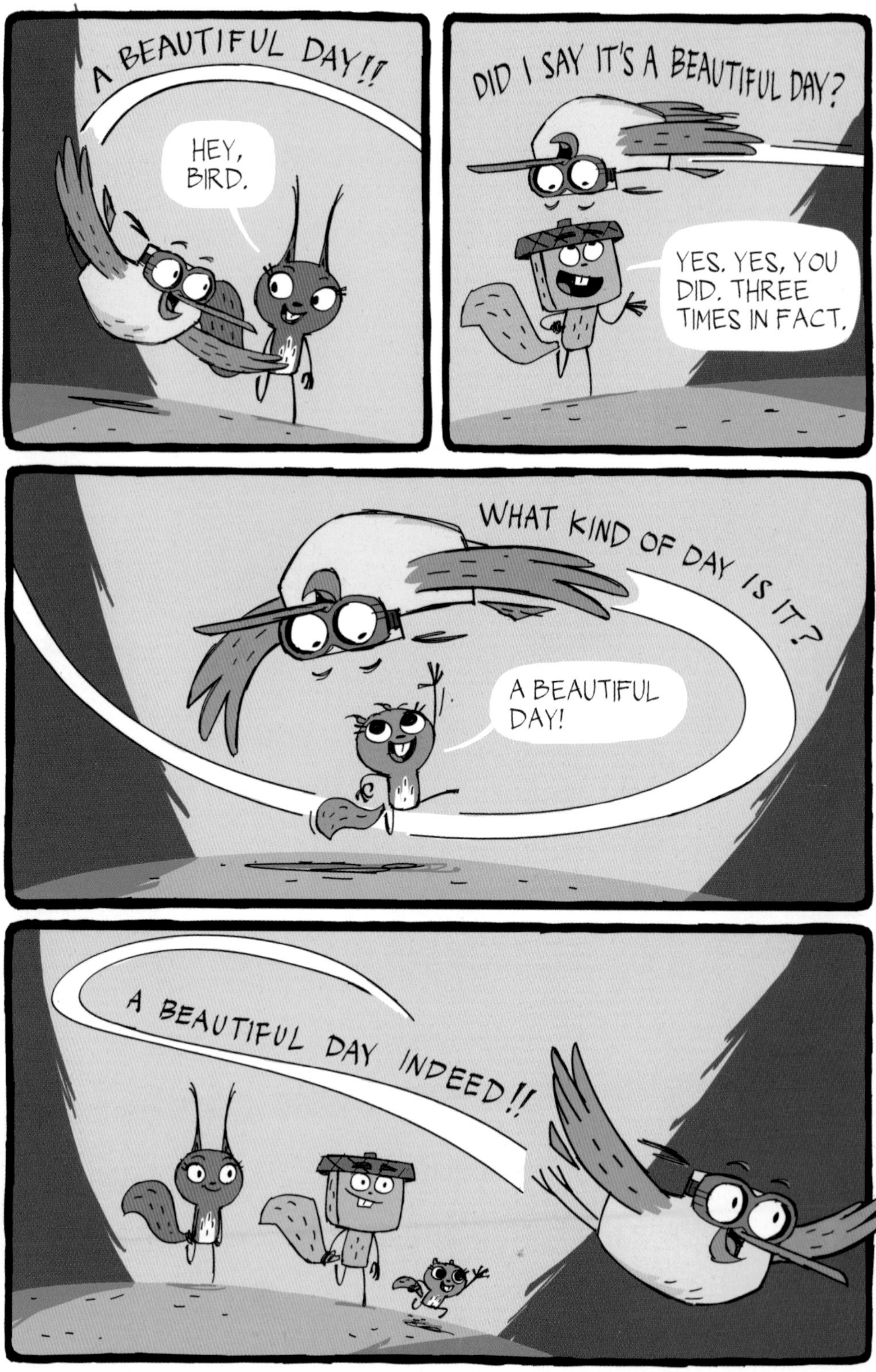
A BEAUTIFUL DAY!!
HEY, BIRD.
DID I SAY IT'S A BEAUTIFUL DAY?
YES. YES, YOU DID. THREE TIMES IN FACT.
WHAT KIND OF DAY IS IT?
A BEAUTIFUL DAY!
A BEAUTIFUL DAY INDEED!!

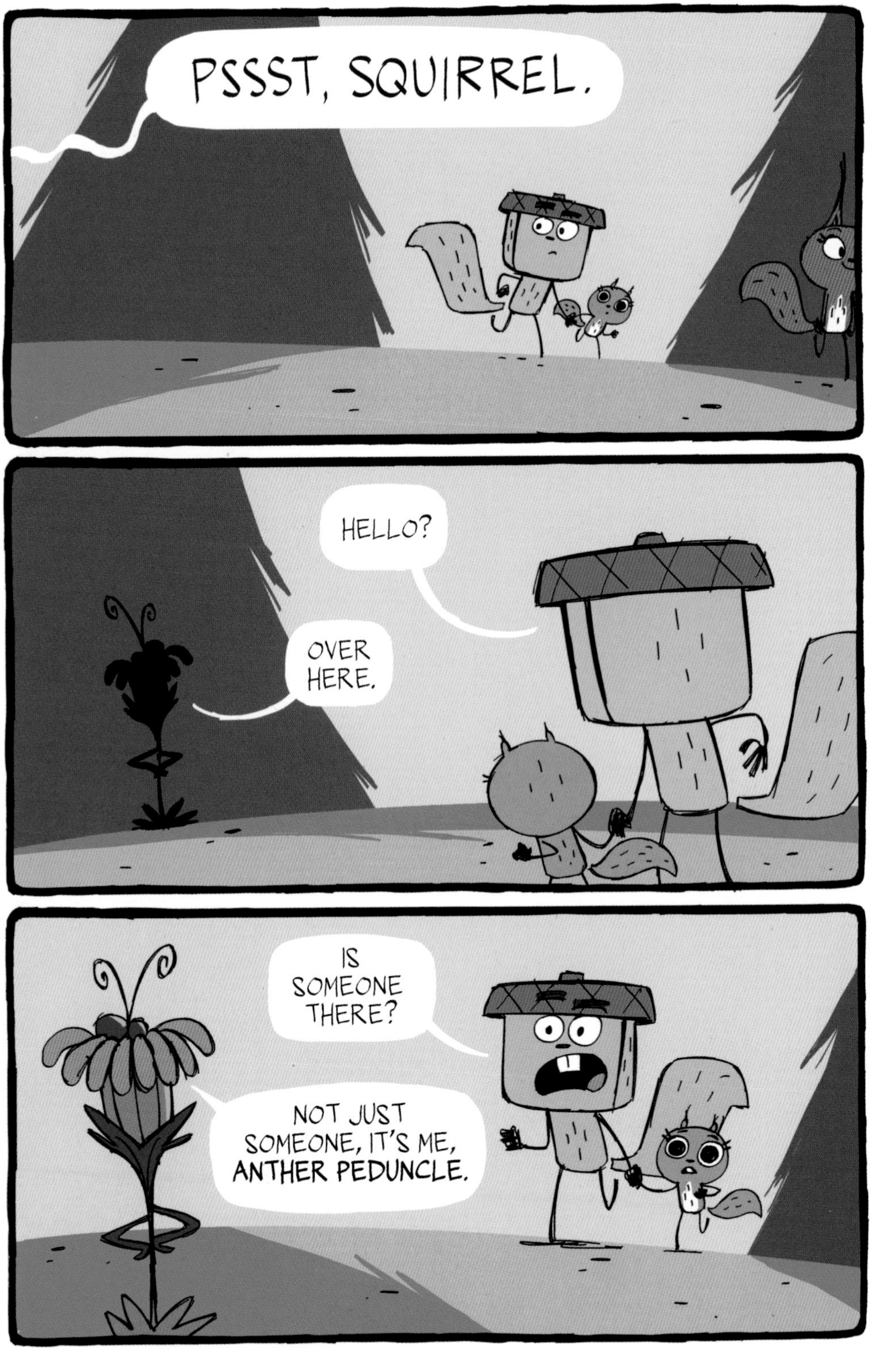
PSSST, SQUIRREL.
HELLO?
OVER HERE.
IS SOMEONE THERE?
NOT JUST SOMEONE, IT'S ME, **ANTHER PEDUNCLE.**

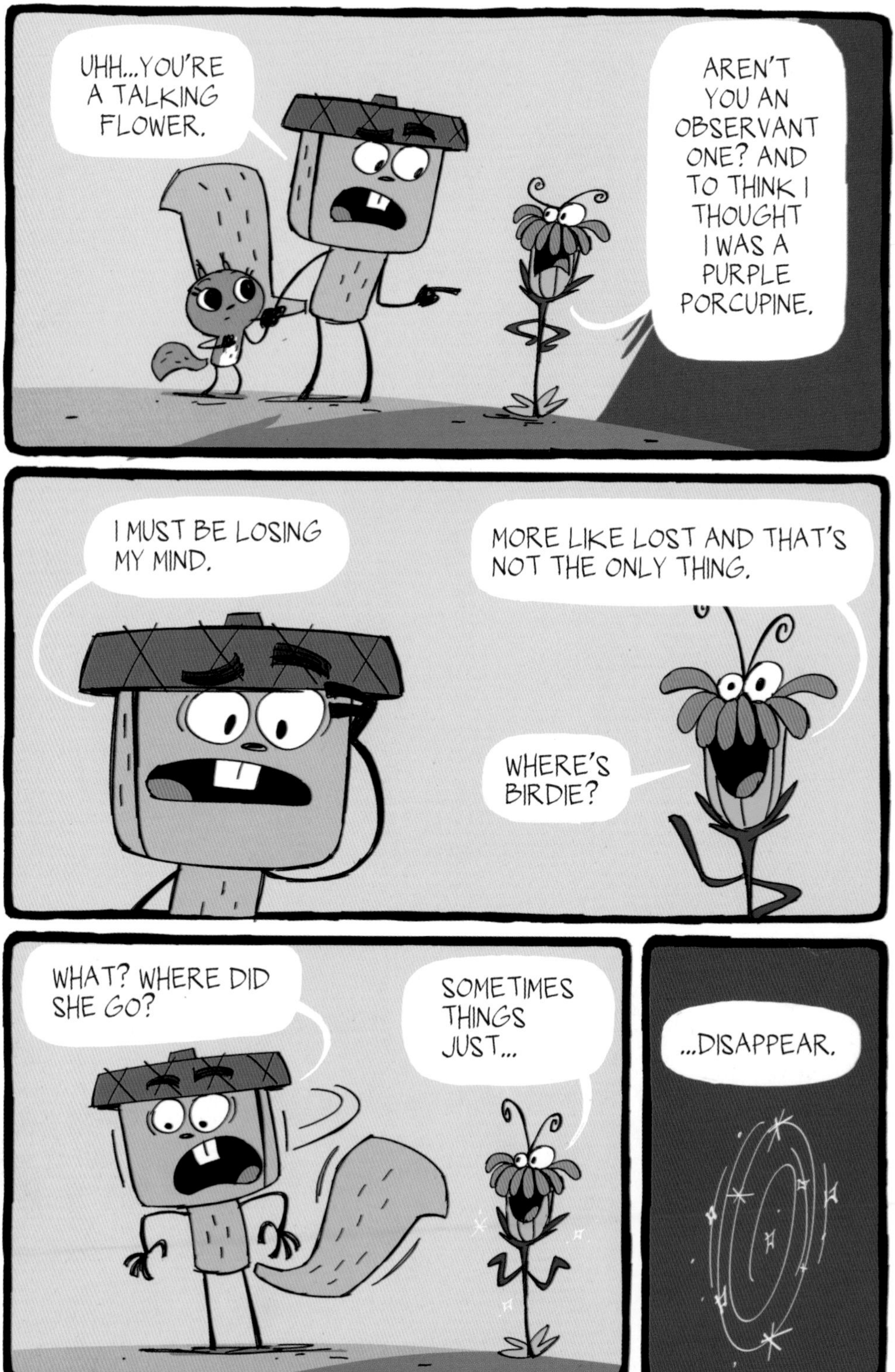
UHH...YOU'RE A TALKING FLOWER.
AREN'T YOU AN OBSERVANT ONE? AND TO THINK I THOUGHT I WAS A PURPLE PORCUPINE.
I MUST BE LOSING MY MIND.
MORE LIKE LOST AND THAT'S NOT THE ONLY THING.
WHERE'S BIRDIE?
WHAT? WHERE DID SHE GO?
SOMETIMES THINGS JUST...
...DISAPPEAR.

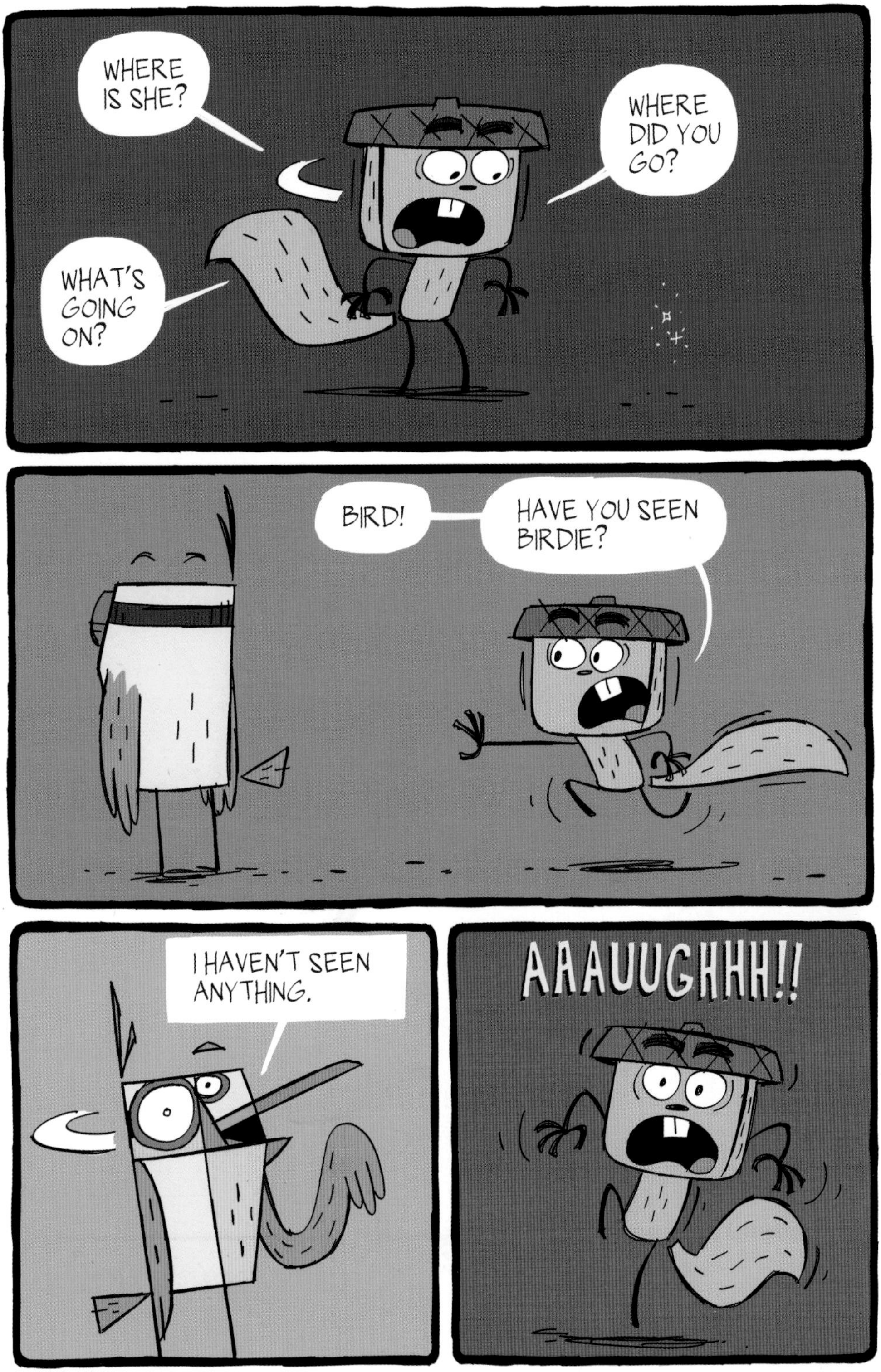
WHERE IS SHE?
WHERE DID YOU GO?
WHAT'S GOING ON?
BIRD!
HAVE YOU SEEN BIRDIE?
I HAVEN'T SEEN ANYTHING.
AAAUUGHHH!!

RED! WHERE'S BIRDIE?!!!!
WHERE'S BIRDIE?
WHERE'S BIRDIE?
WHERE'S BIRDIE?
THIS CAN'T BE HAPPENING!!
DADDY!!

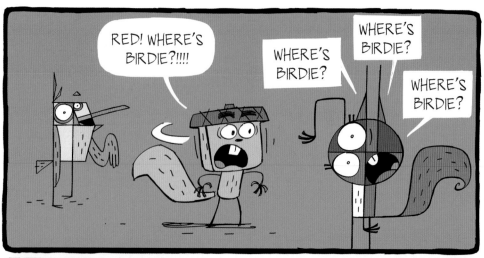

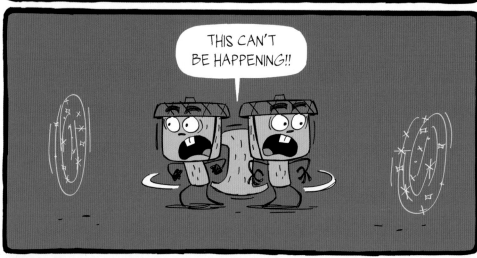

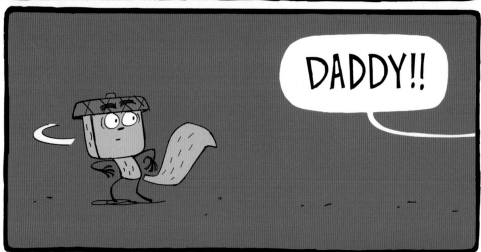

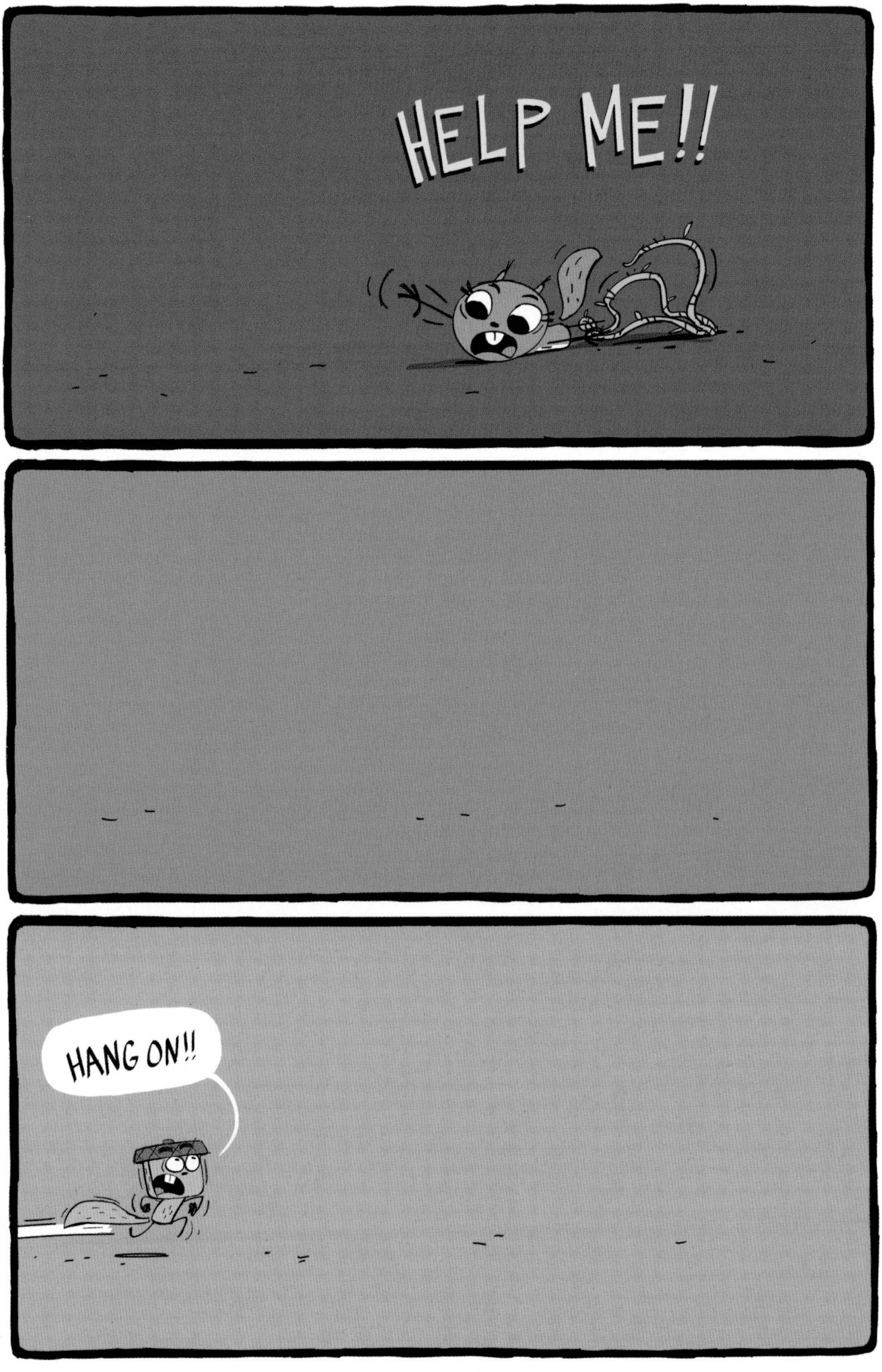
HELP ME!!
HANG ON!!

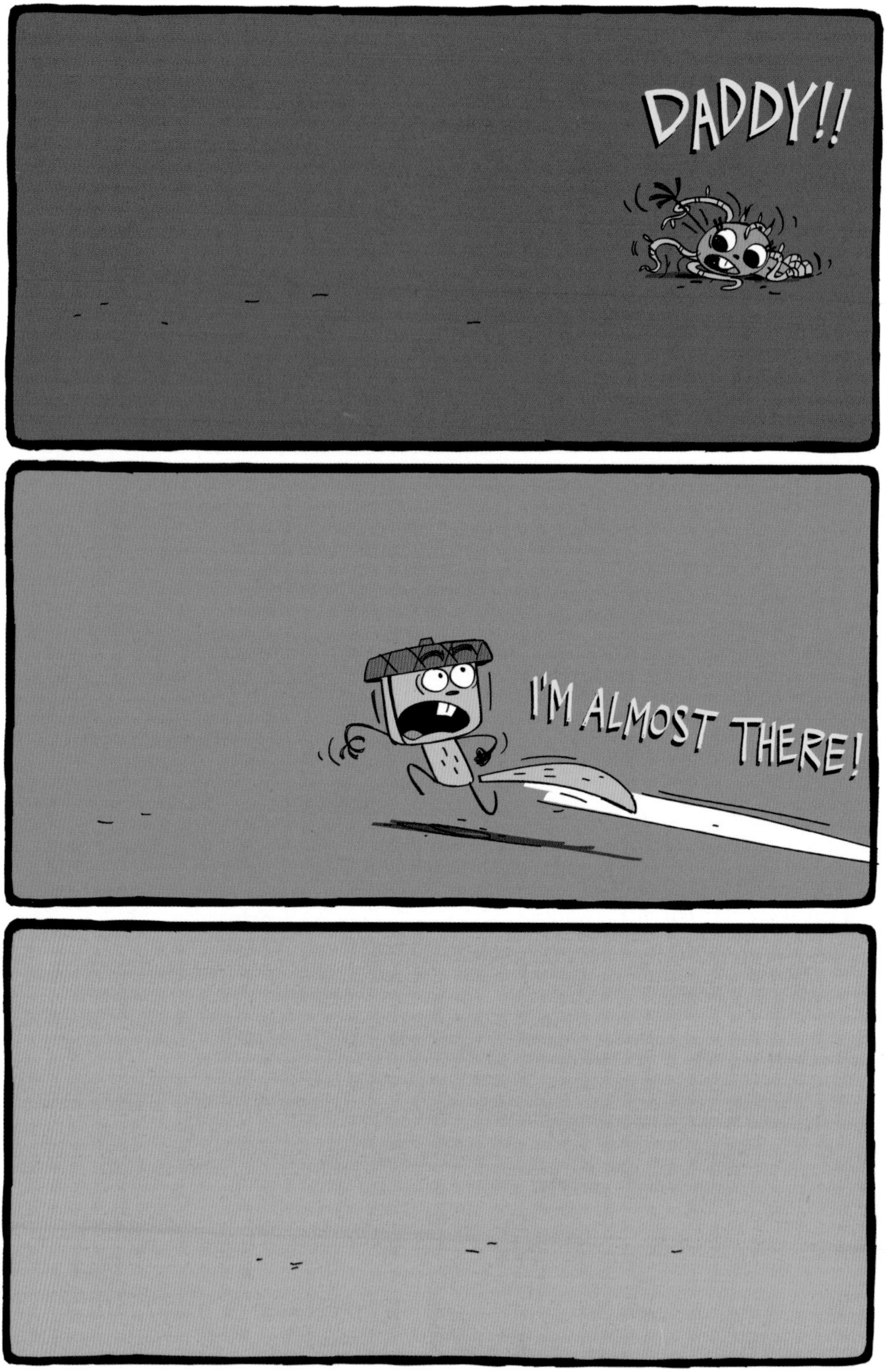
DADDY!!
I'M ALMOST THERE!

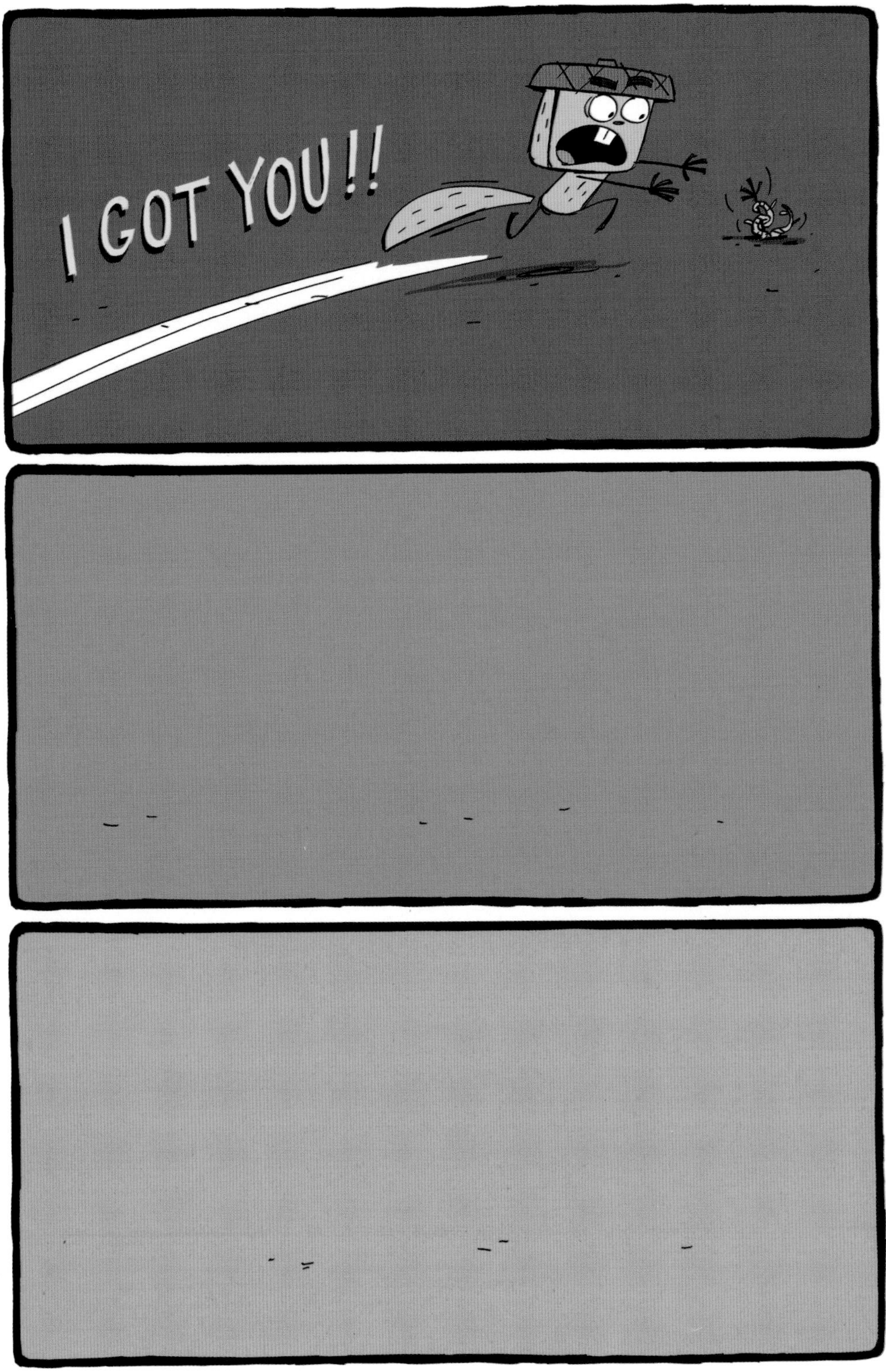
I GOT YOU!!

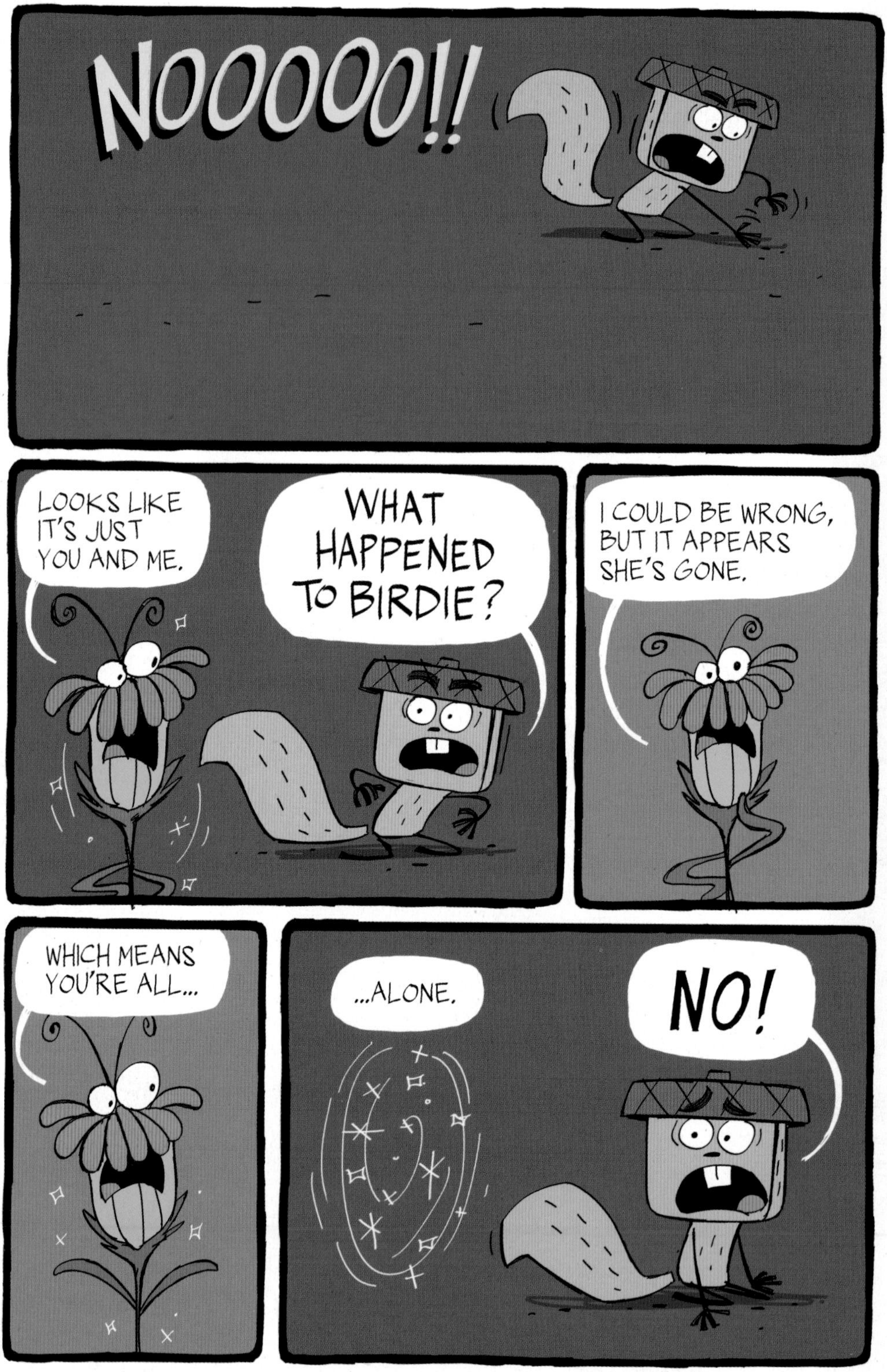
NOOOOO!!
LOOKS LIKE IT'S JUST YOU AND ME.
WHAT HAPPENED TO BIRDIE?
I COULD BE WRONG, BUT IT APPEARS SHE'S GONE.
WHICH MEANS YOU'RE ALL...
...ALONE.
NO!

NOOOOOOOO!!!

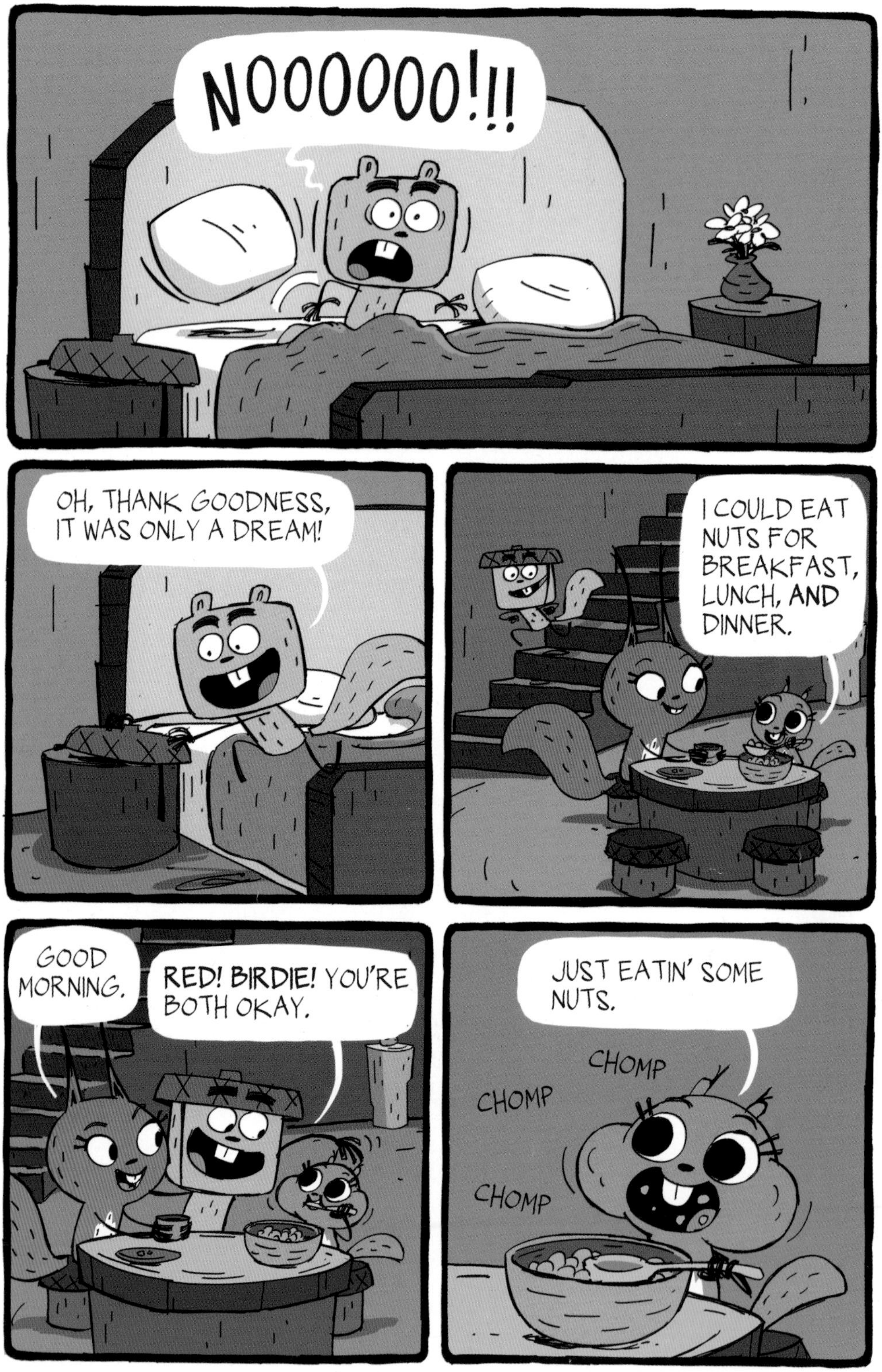
NOOOOOO!!!
OH, THANK GOODNESS, IT WAS ONLY A DREAM!
I COULD EAT NUTS FOR BREAKFAST, LUNCH, AND DINNER.
GOOD MORNING.
RED! BIRDIE! YOU'RE BOTH OKAY.
JUST EATIN' SOME NUTS.
CHOMP
CHOMP
CHOMP

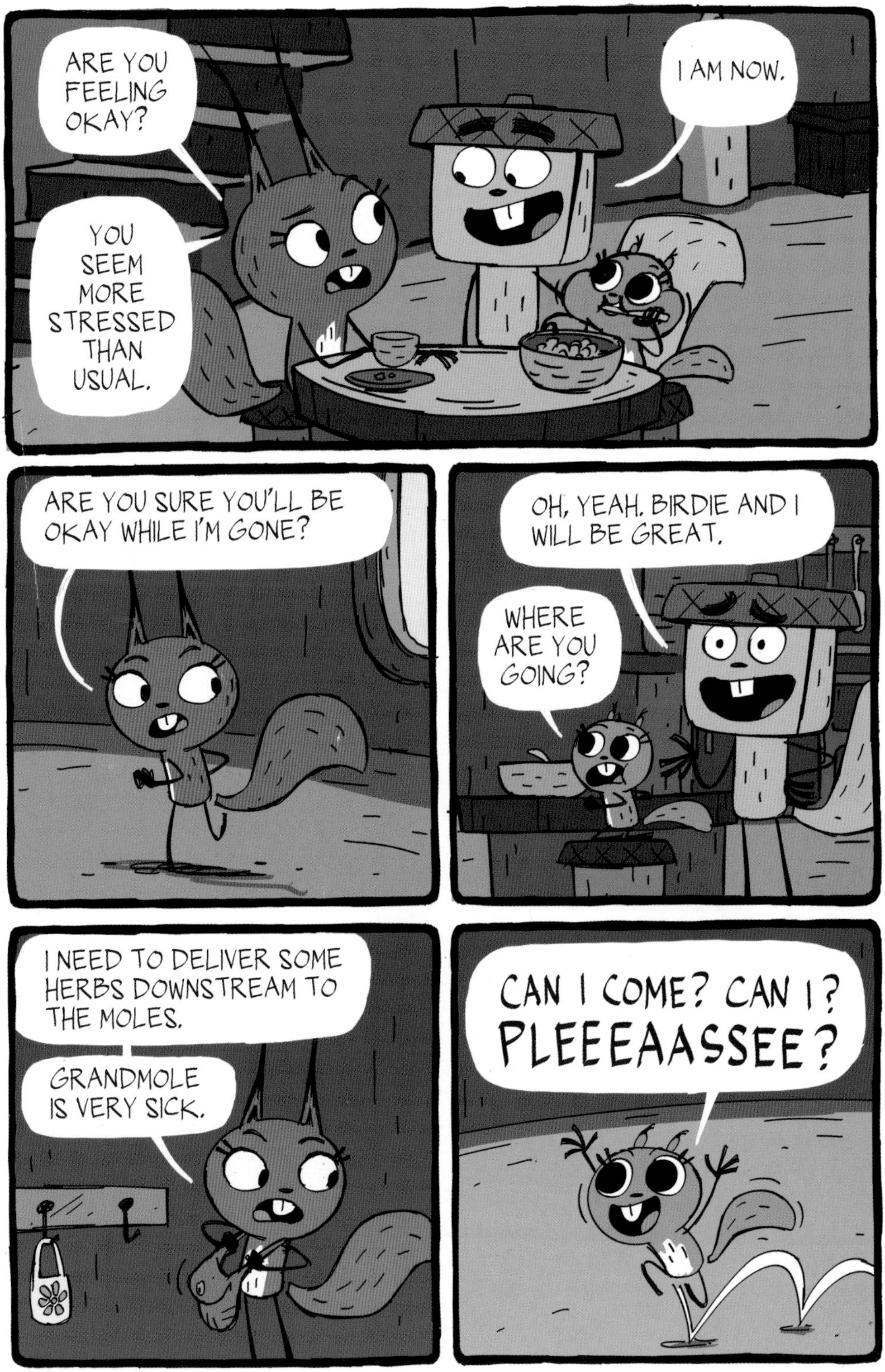
ARE YOU FEELING OKAY?
I AM NOW.
YOU SEEM MORE STRESSED THAN USUAL.
ARE YOU SURE YOU'LL BE OKAY WHILE I'M GONE?
OH, YEAH. BIRDIE AND I WILL BE GREAT.
WHERE ARE YOU GOING?
I NEED TO DELIVER SOME HERBS DOWNSTREAM TO THE MOLES.
GRANDMOLE IS VERY SICK.
CAN I COME? CAN I? PLEEEAASSEE?

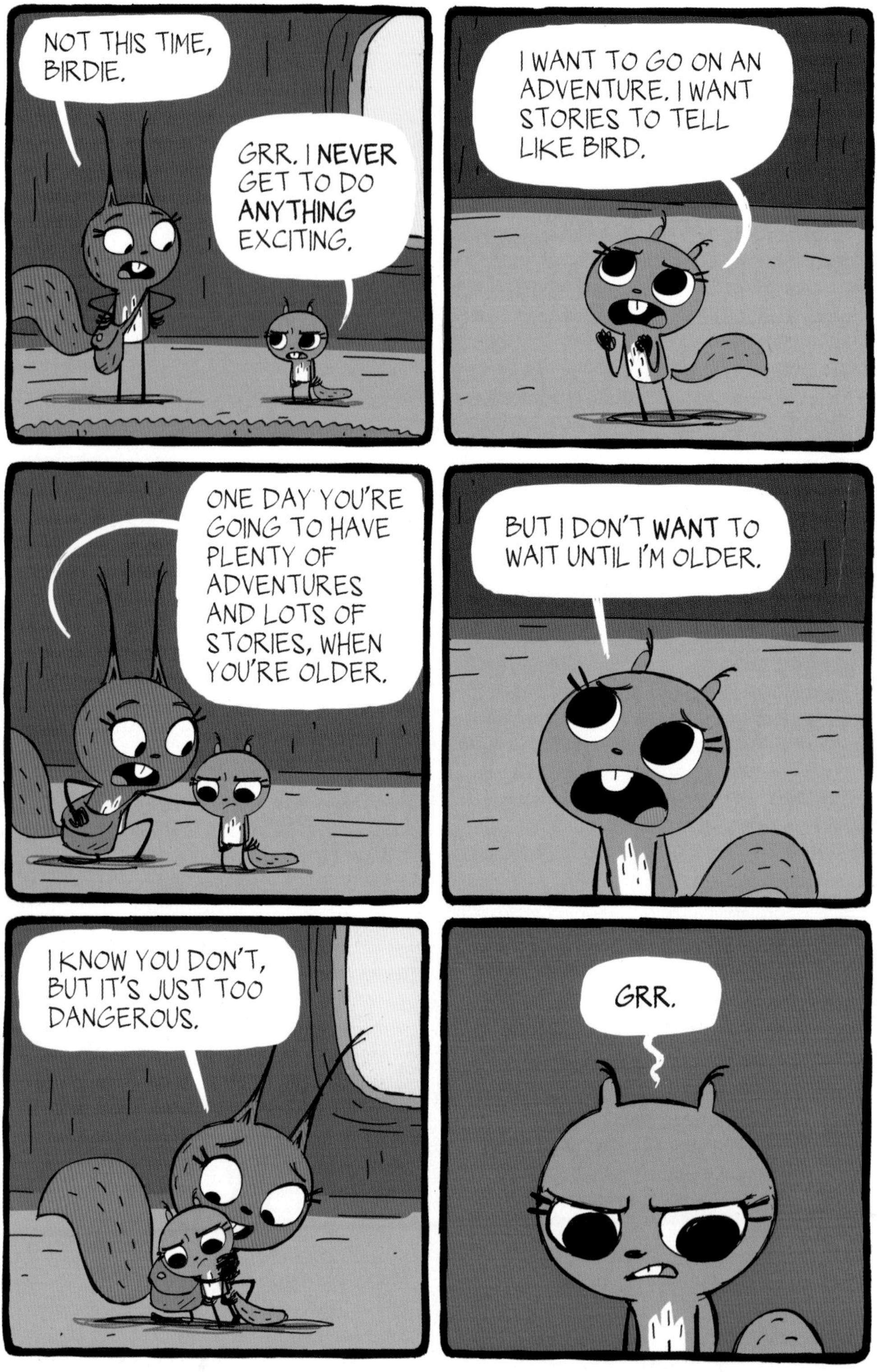
NOT THIS TIME, BIRDIE.
GRR. I **NEVER** GET TO DO **ANYTHING** EXCITING.
I WANT TO GO ON AN ADVENTURE. I WANT STORIES TO TELL LIKE BIRD.
ONE DAY YOU'RE GOING TO HAVE PLENTY OF ADVENTURES AND LOTS OF STORIES, WHEN YOU'RE OLDER.
BUT I DON'T **WANT** TO WAIT UNTIL I'M OLDER.
I KNOW YOU DON'T, BUT IT'S JUST TOO DANGEROUS.
GRR.

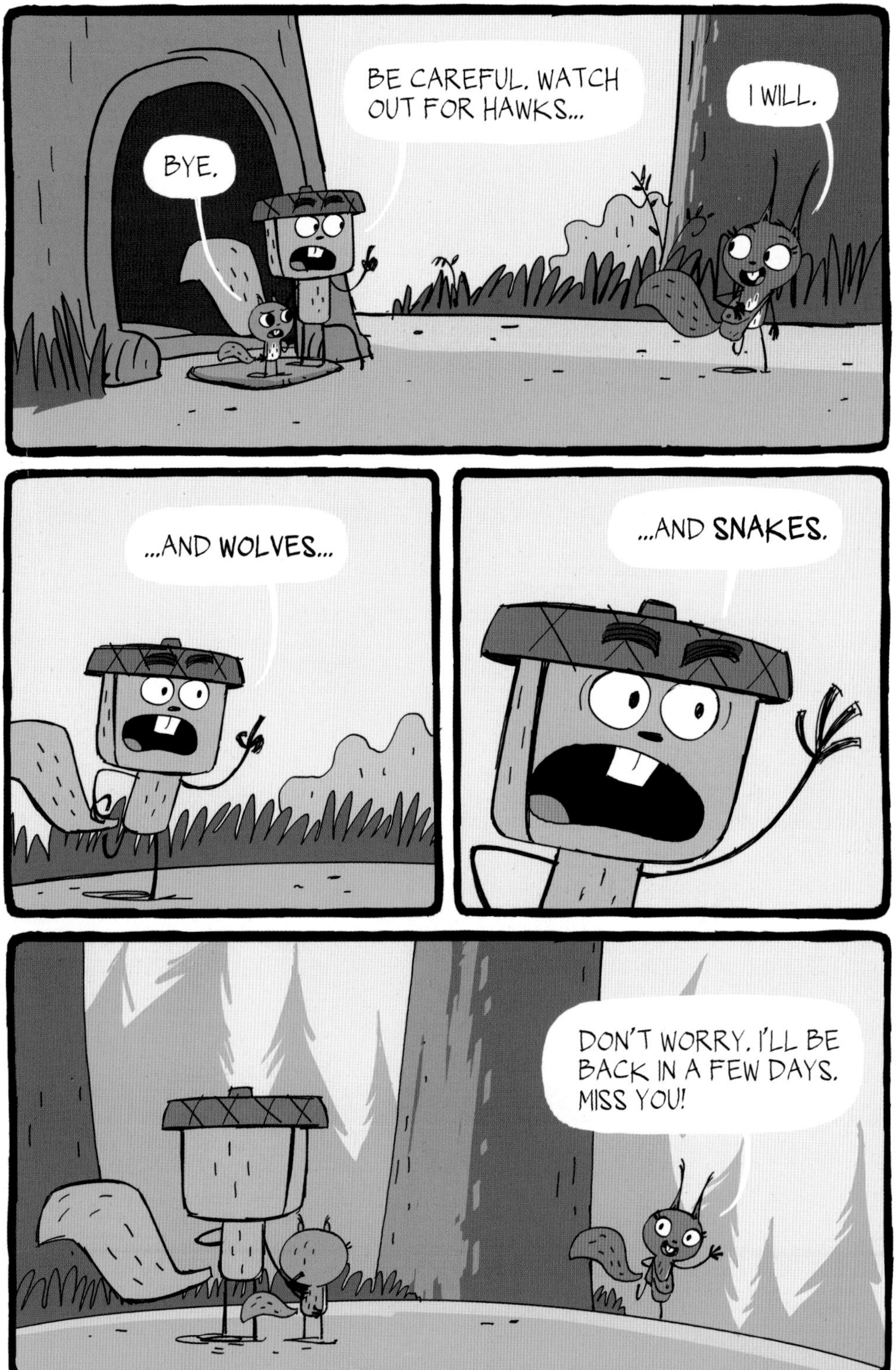
BE CAREFUL. WATCH OUT FOR HAWKS...
BYE.
I WILL.
...AND WOLVES...
...AND SNAKES.
DON'T WORRY. I'LL BE BACK IN A FEW DAYS. MISS YOU!

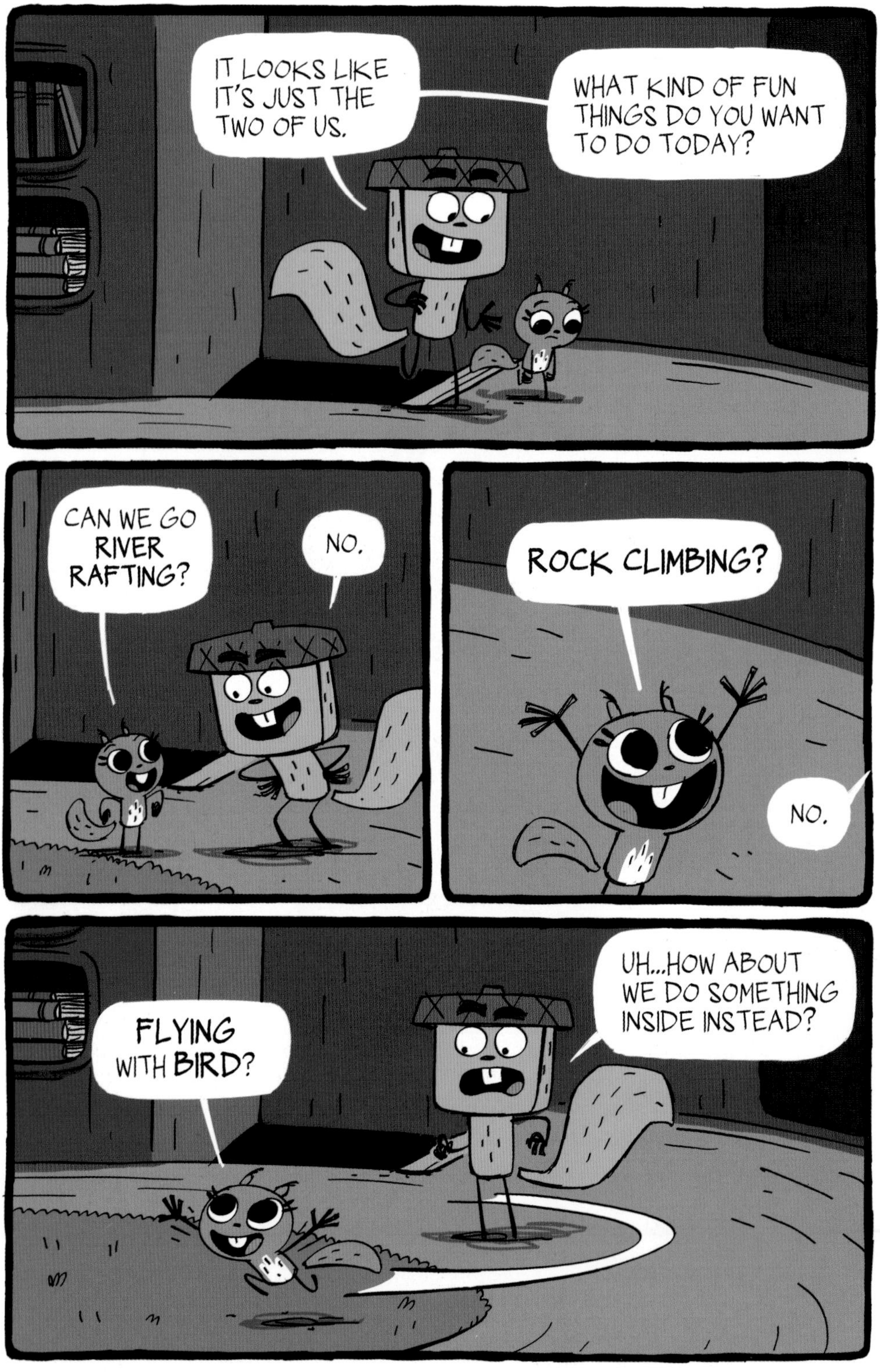
IT LOOKS LIKE IT'S JUST THE TWO OF US.
WHAT KIND OF FUN THINGS DO YOU WANT TO DO TODAY?
CAN WE GO RIVER RAFTING?
NO.
ROCK CLIMBING?
NO.
FLYING WITH BIRD?
UH...HOW ABOUT WE DO SOMETHING INSIDE INSTEAD?

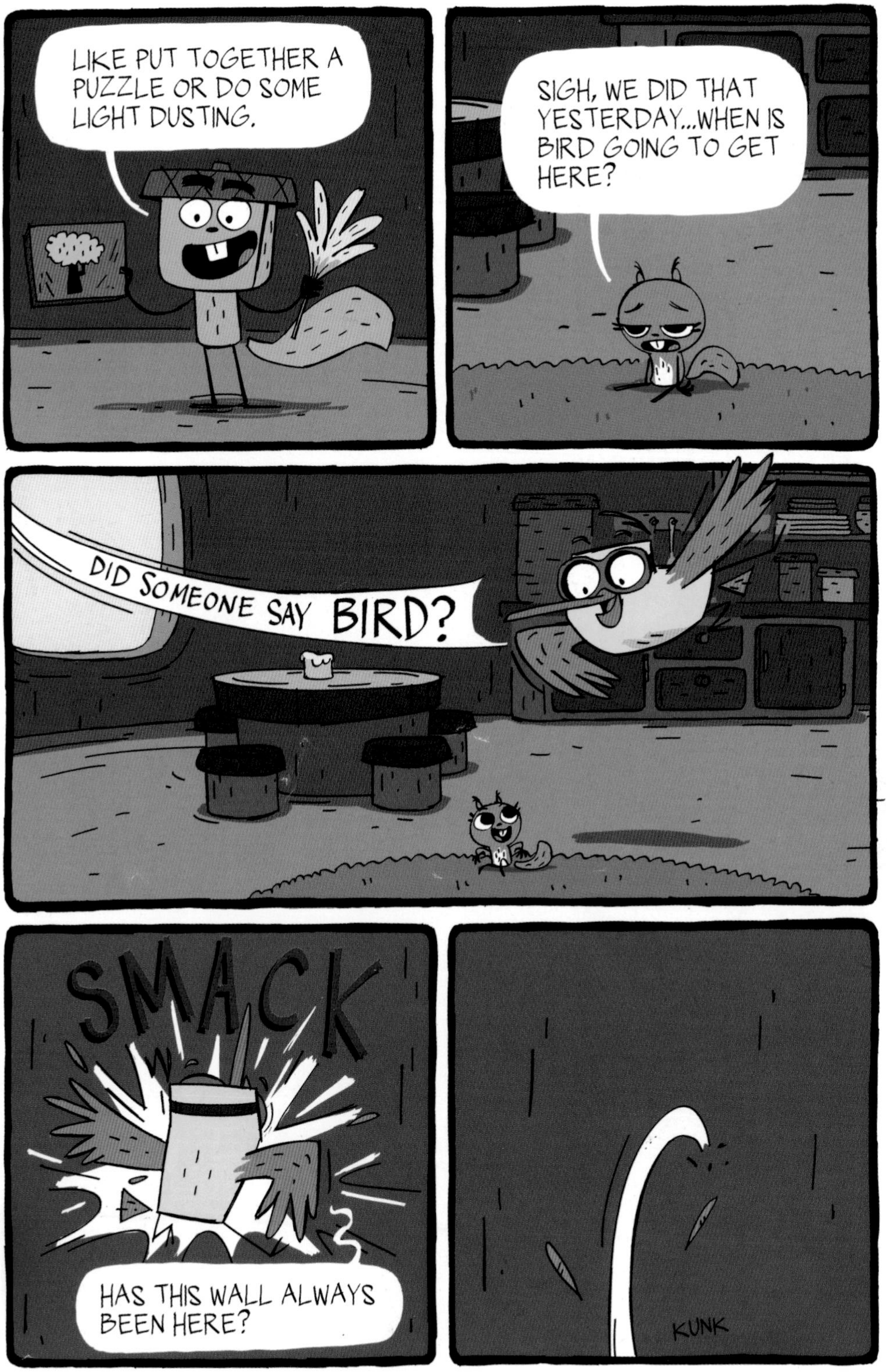
LIKE PUT TOGETHER A PUZZLE OR DO SOME LIGHT DUSTING.
SIGH, WE DID THAT YESTERDAY...WHEN IS BIRD GOING TO GET HERE?
DID SOMEONE SAY BIRD?
SMACK
HAS THIS WALL ALWAYS BEEN HERE?
KUNK

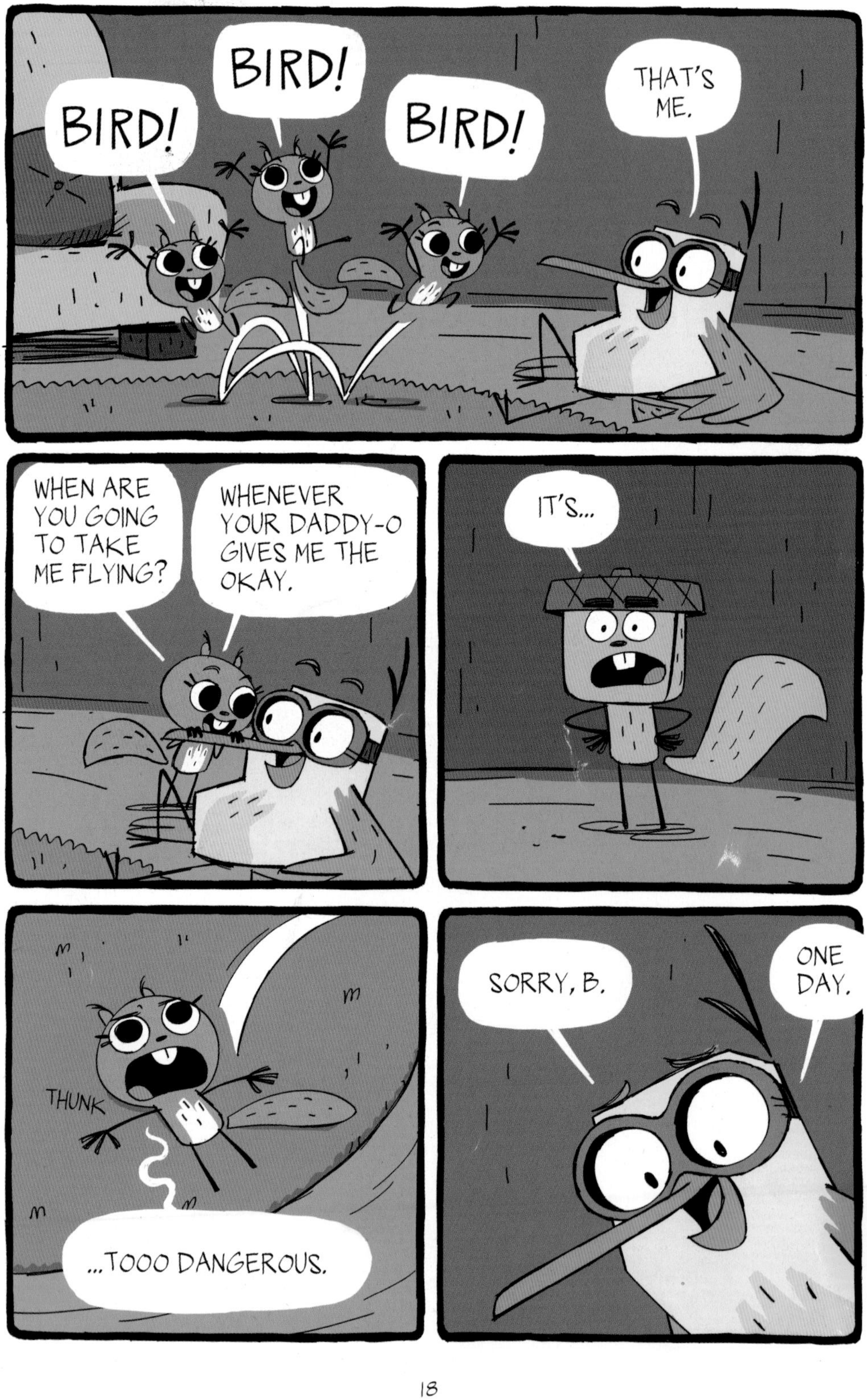
BIRD!
BIRD!
BIRD!
THAT'S ME.
WHEN ARE YOU GOING TO TAKE ME FLYING?
WHENEVER YOUR DADDY-O GIVES ME THE OKAY.
IT'S...
THUNK
...TOOO DANGEROUS.
SORRY, B.
ONE DAY.

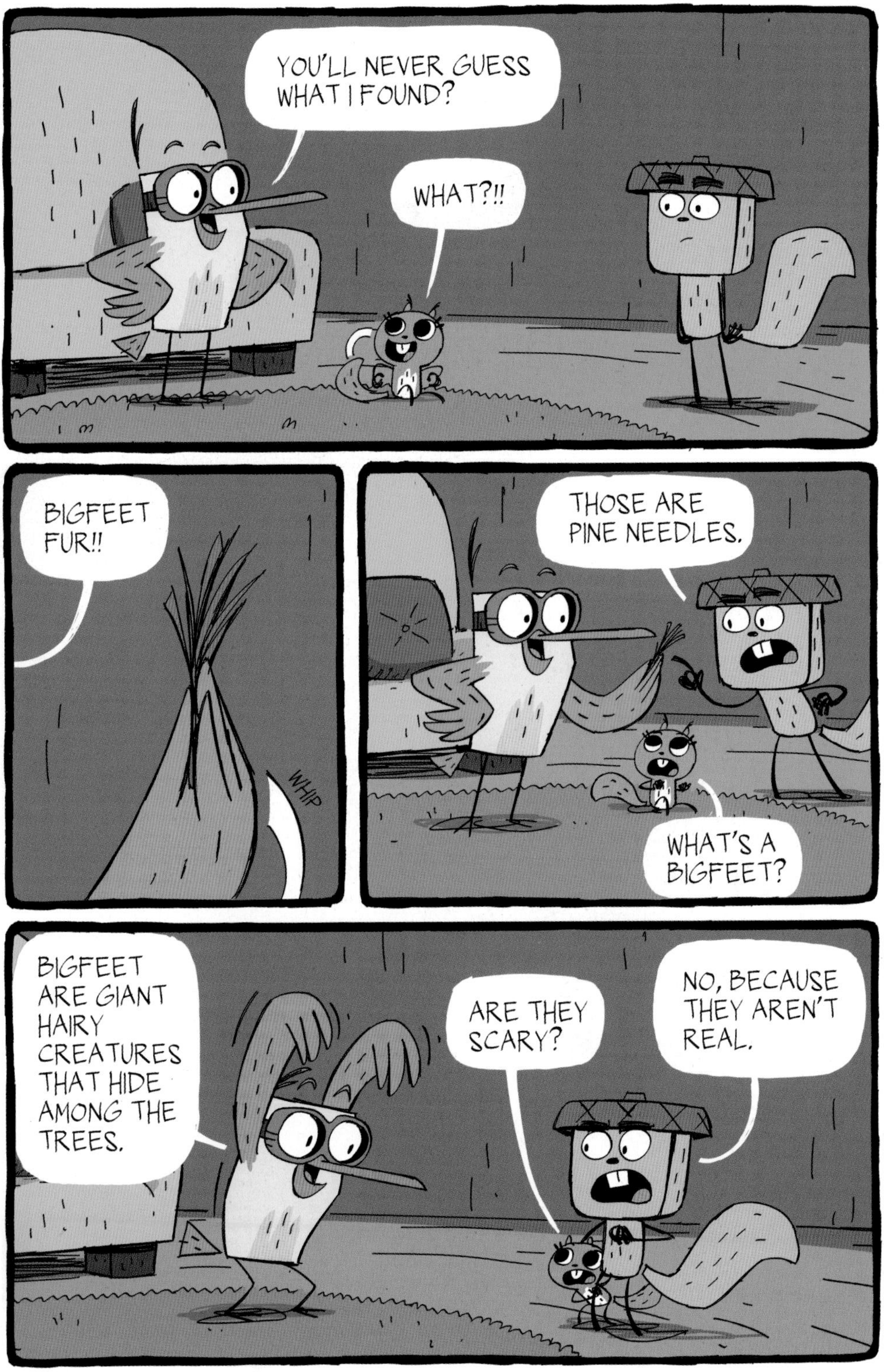
YOU'LL NEVER GUESS WHAT I FOUND?
WHAT?!!
BIGFEET FUR!!
WHIP
THOSE ARE PINE NEEDLES.
WHAT'S A BIGFEET?
BIGFEET ARE GIANT HAIRY CREATURES THAT HIDE AMONG THE TREES.
ARE THEY SCARY?
NO, BECAUSE THEY AREN'T REAL.

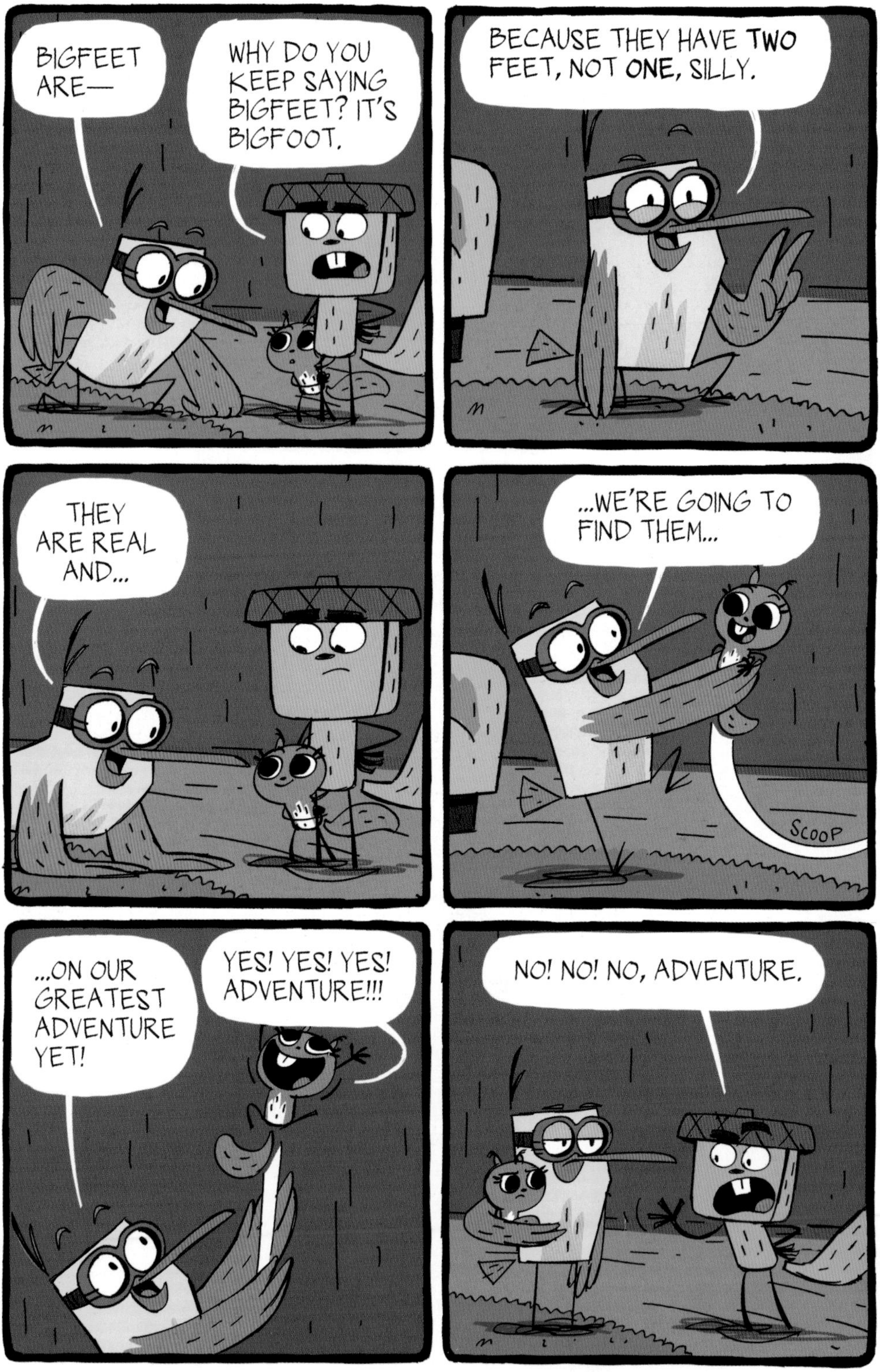
BIGFEET ARE—
WHY DO YOU KEEP SAYING BIGFEET? IT'S BIGFOOT.
BECAUSE THEY HAVE **TWO** FEET, NOT **ONE**, SILLY.
THEY ARE REAL AND...
...WE'RE GOING TO FIND THEM...
SCOOP
...ON OUR GREATEST ADVENTURE YET!
YES! YES! YES! ADVENTURE!!!
NO! NO! NO, ADVENTURE.

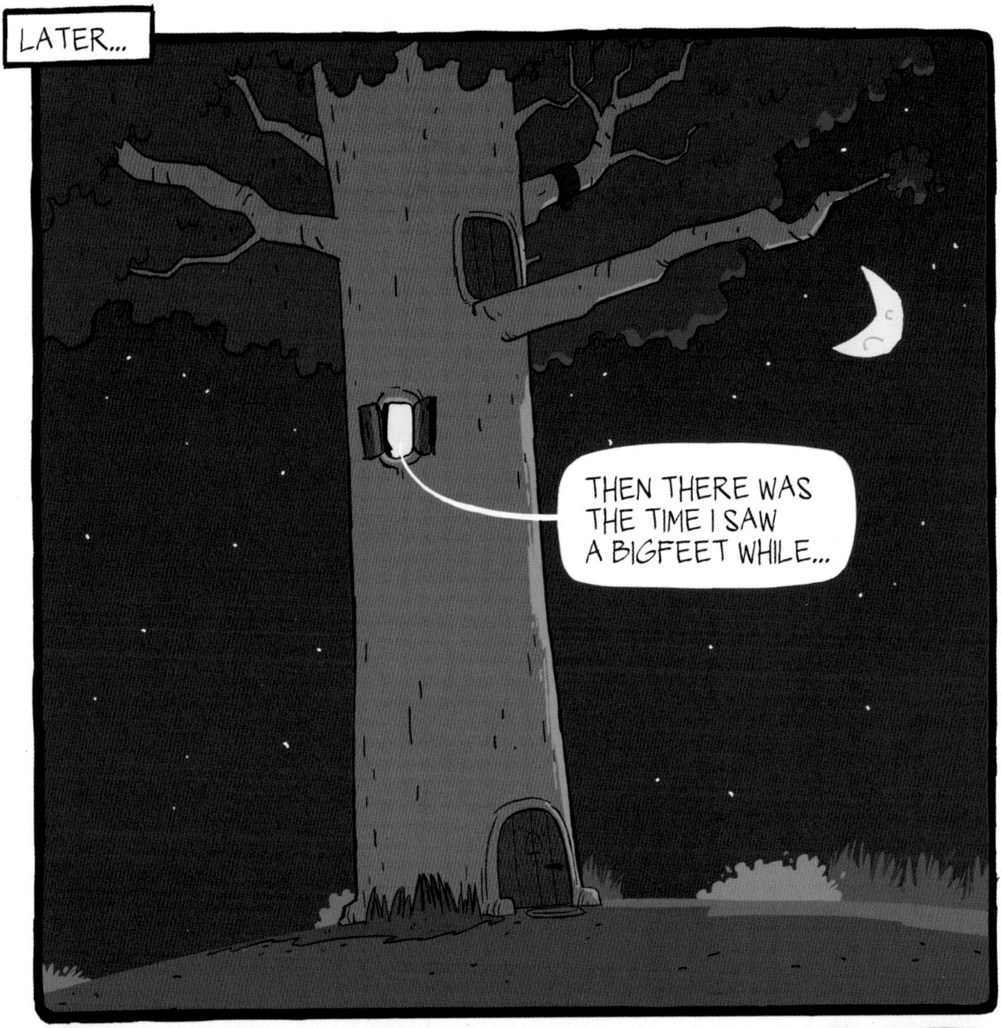
LATER...
THEN THERE WAS THE TIME I SAW A BIGFEET WHILE...

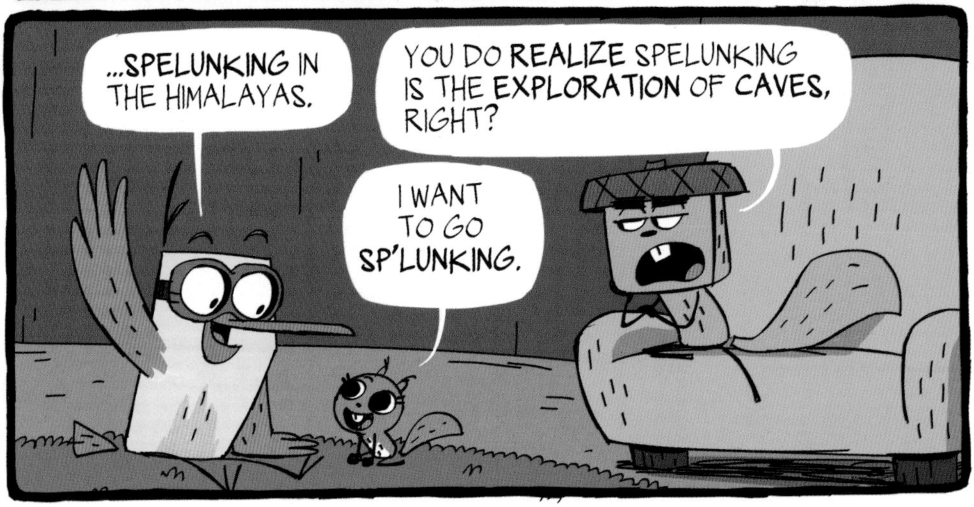
...**SPELUNKING** IN THE HIMALAYAS.
YOU DO **REALIZE** SPELUNKING IS THE **EXPLORATION** OF **CAVES**, RIGHT?
I WANT TO GO **SP'LUNKING.**

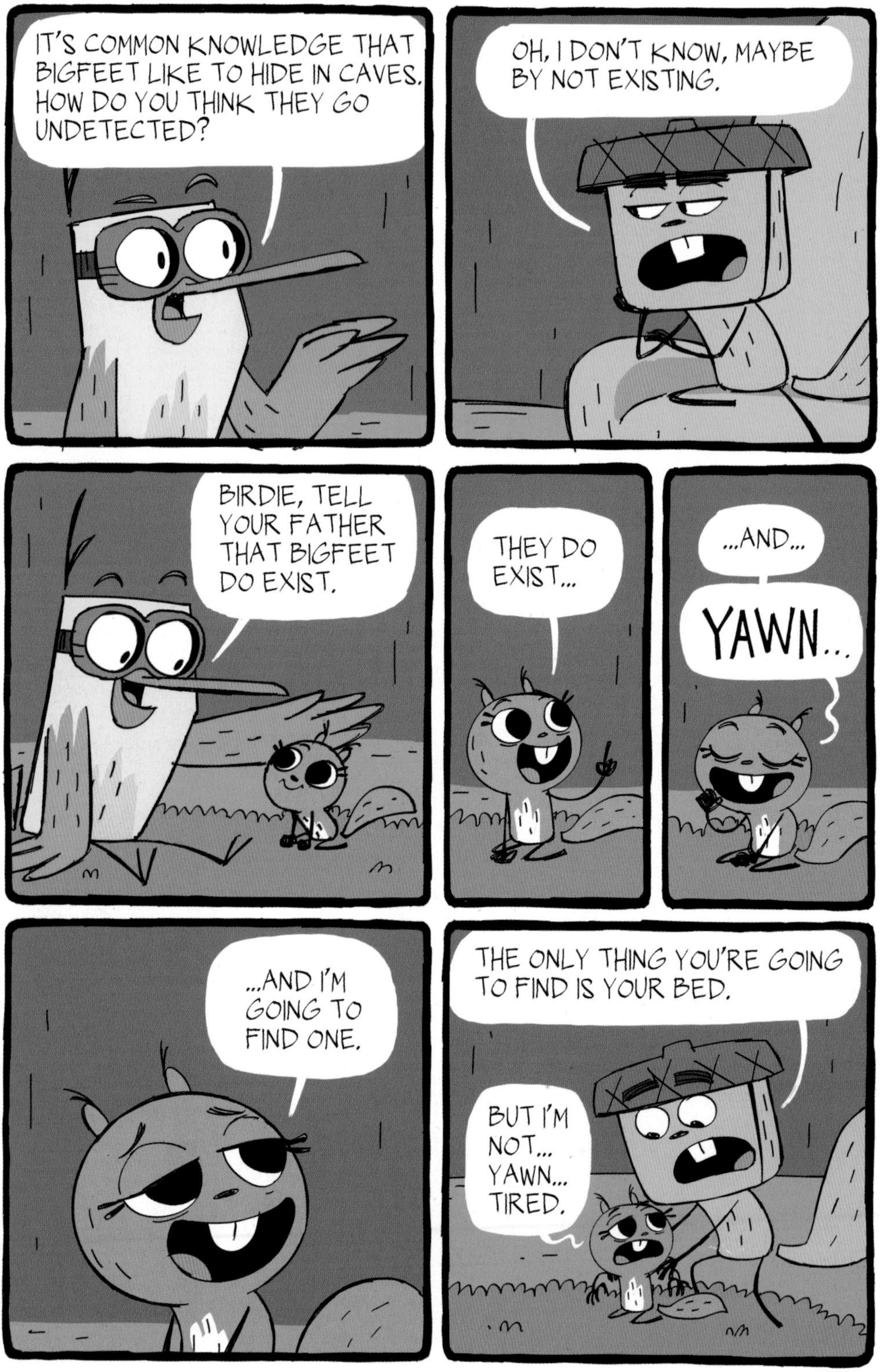
IT'S COMMON KNOWLEDGE THAT BIGFEET LIKE TO HIDE IN CAVES. HOW DO YOU THINK THEY GO UNDETECTED?
OH, I DON'T KNOW, MAYBE BY NOT EXISTING.
BIRDIE, TELL YOUR FATHER THAT BIGFEET DO EXIST.
THEY DO EXIST...
...AND...
YAWN...
...AND I'M GOING TO FIND ONE.
THE ONLY THING YOU'RE GOING TO FIND IS YOUR BED.
BUT I'M NOT... YAWN... TIRED.

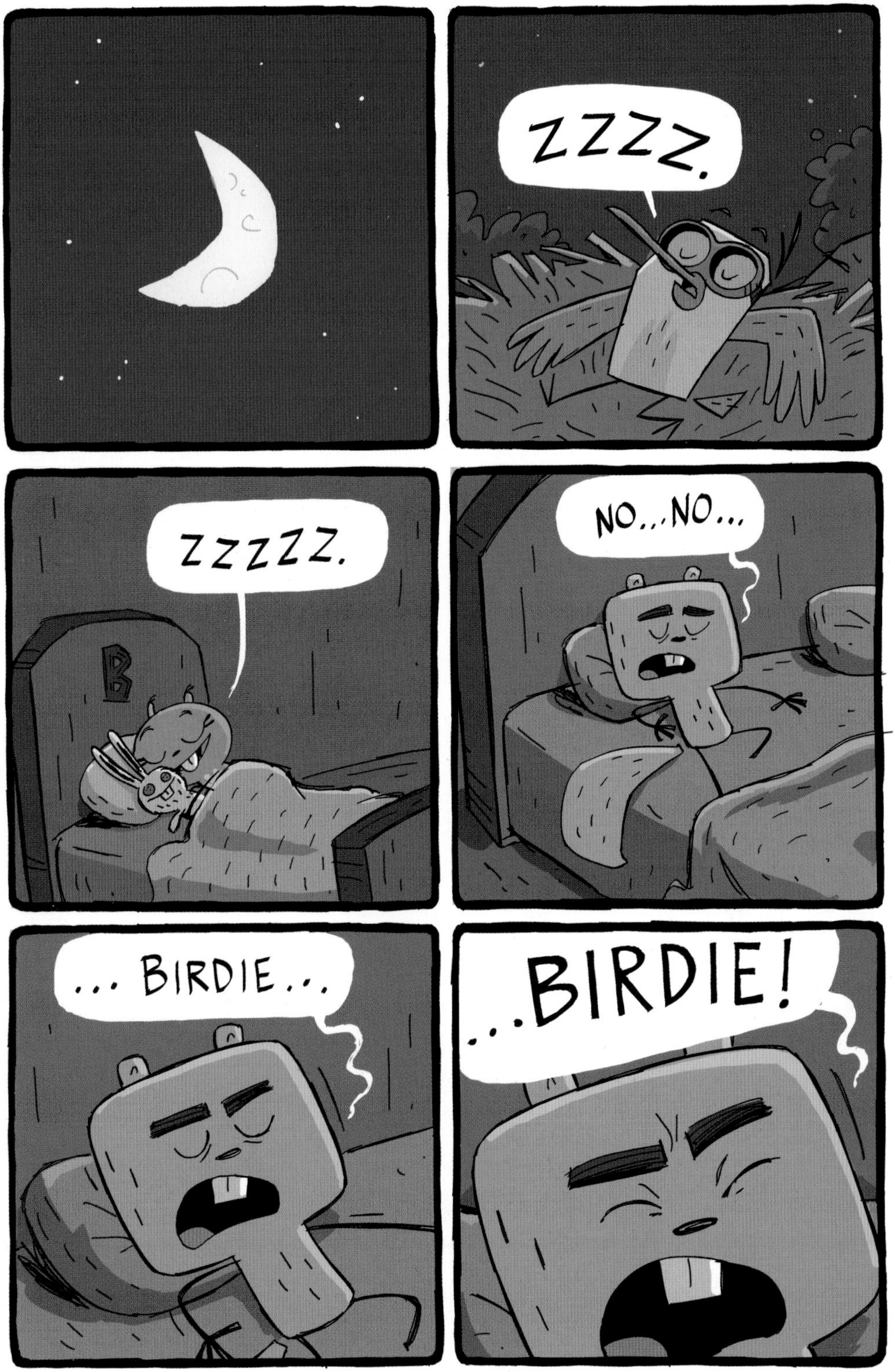
ZZZZ.
ZZZZZ.
NO...NO...
... BIRDIE...
...BIRDIE!

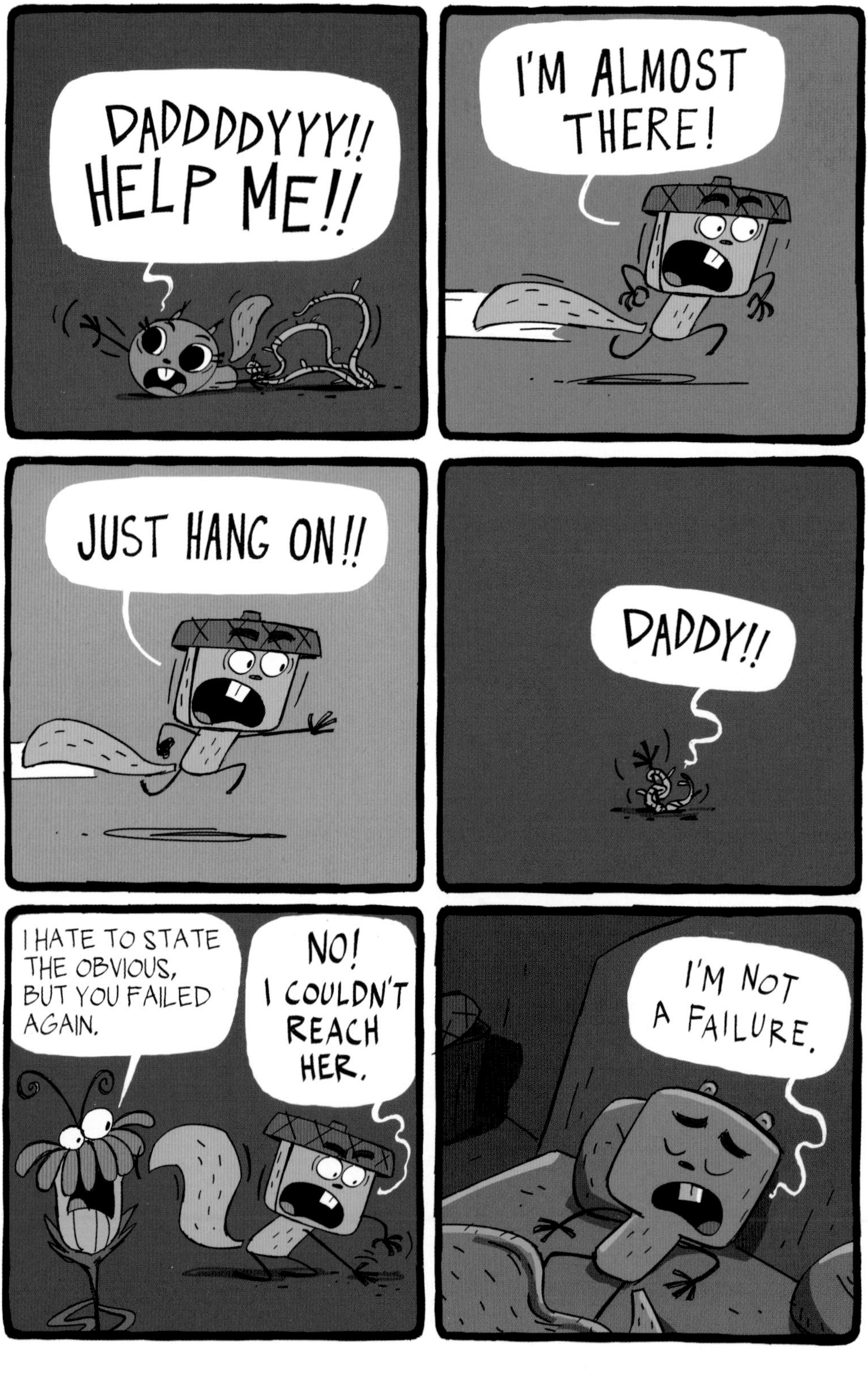
DADDDDYYY!! HELP ME!!
I'M ALMOST THERE!
JUST HANG ON!!
DADDY!!
I HATE TO STATE THE OBVIOUS, BUT YOU FAILED AGAIN.
NO! I COULDN'T REACH HER.
I'M NOT A FAILURE.

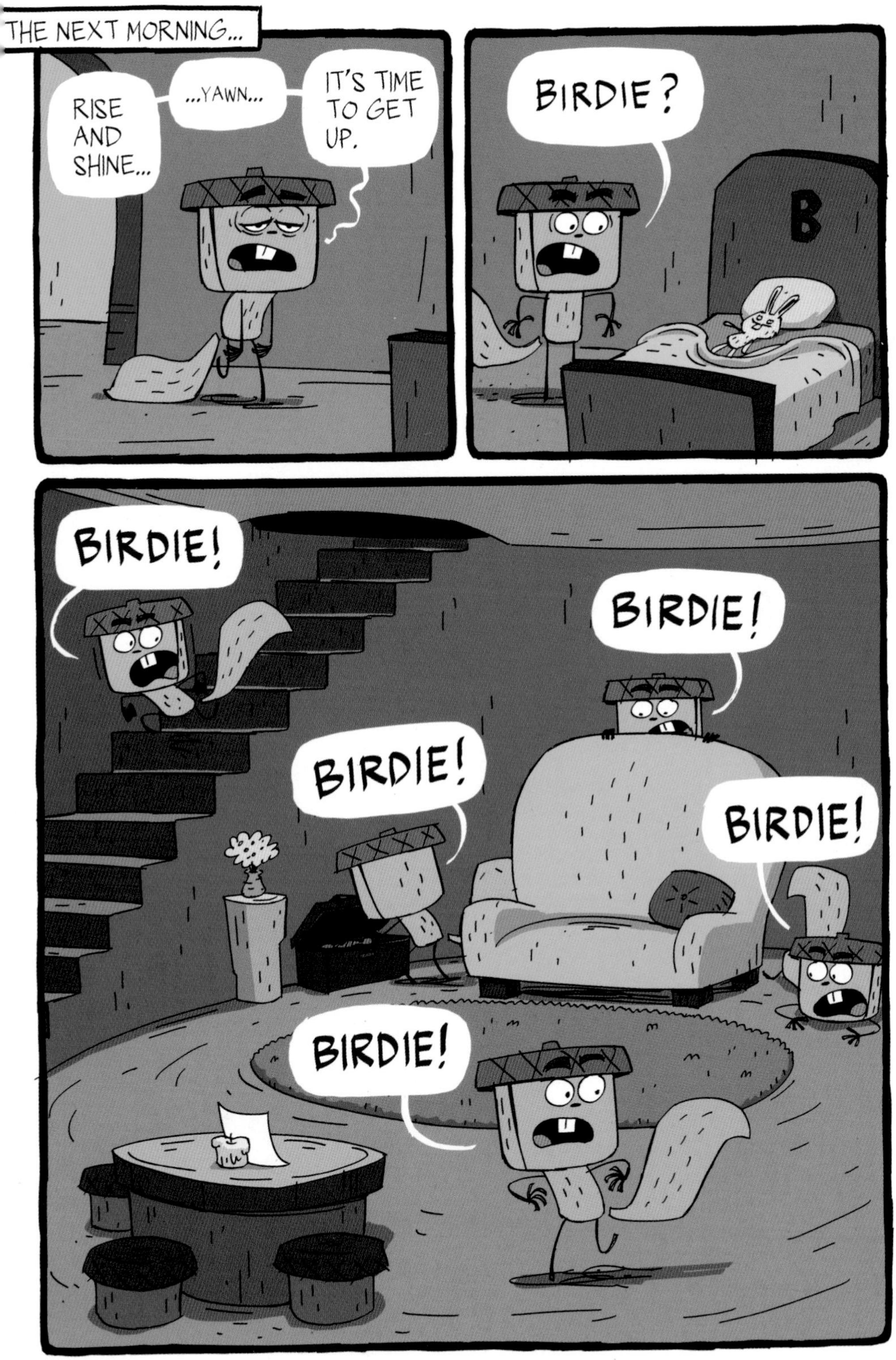
THE NEXT MORNING...
RISE AND SHINE...
...YAWN...
IT'S TIME TO GET UP.
BIRDIE?
BIRDIE!
BIRDIE!
BIRDIE!
BIRDIE!
BIRDIE!

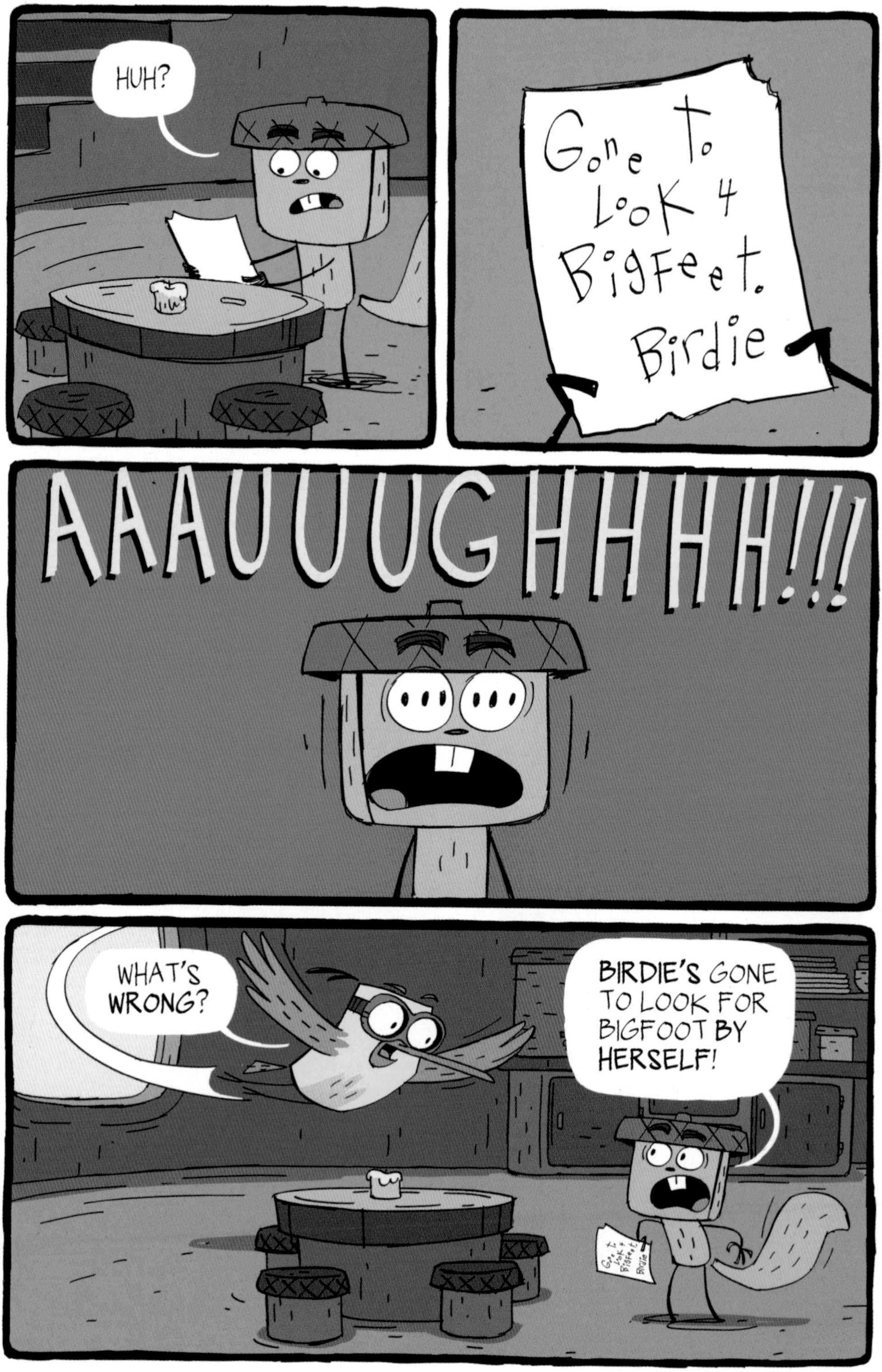
HUH?
Gone To Look 4 BigFeet. Birdie
AAAUUUGHHHH!!!
WHAT'S WRONG?
BIRDIE'S GONE TO LOOK FOR BIGFOOT BY HERSELF!

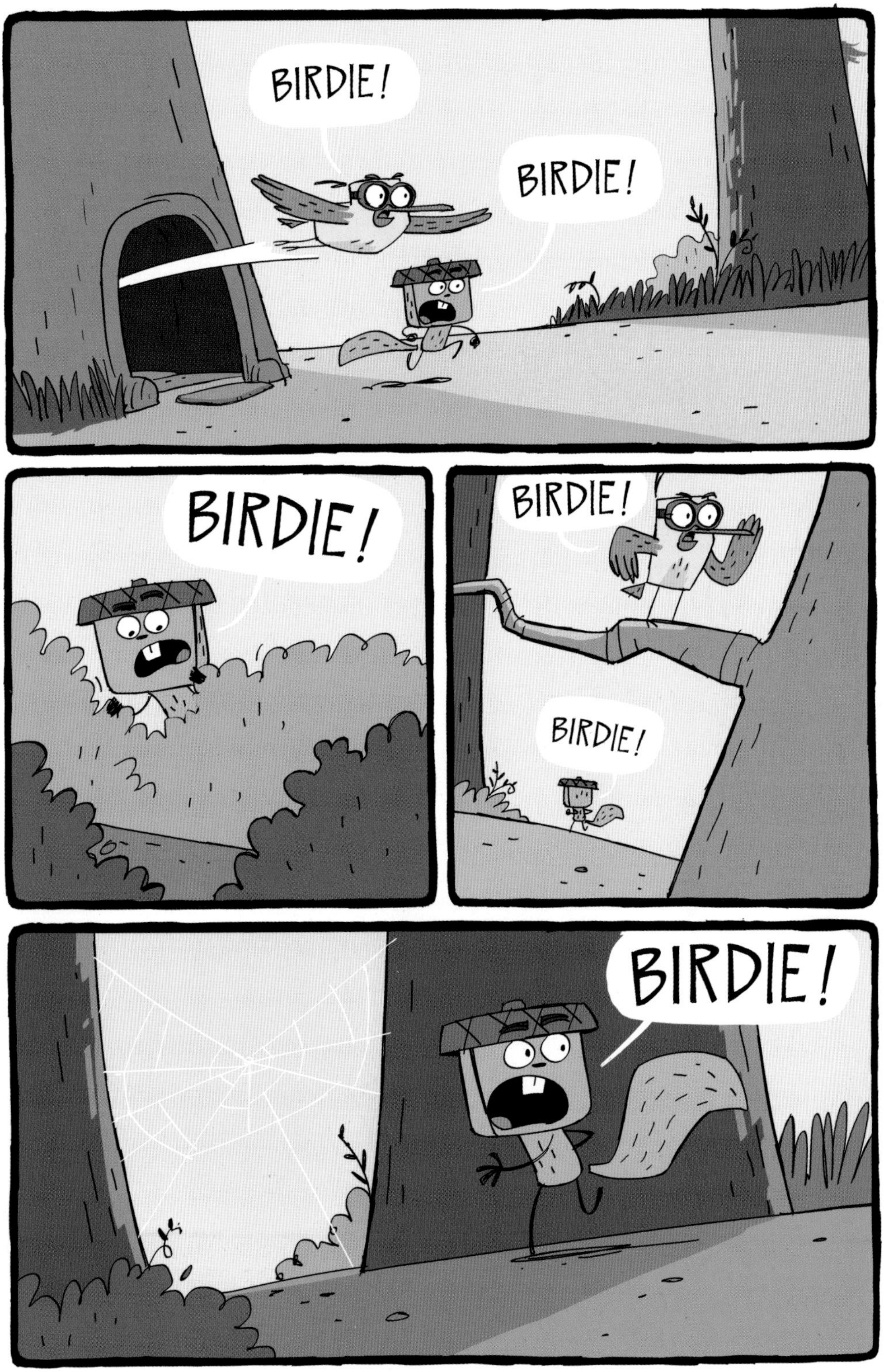
BIRDIE!
BIRDIE!
BIRDIE!
BIRDIE!
BIRDIE!
BIRDIE!

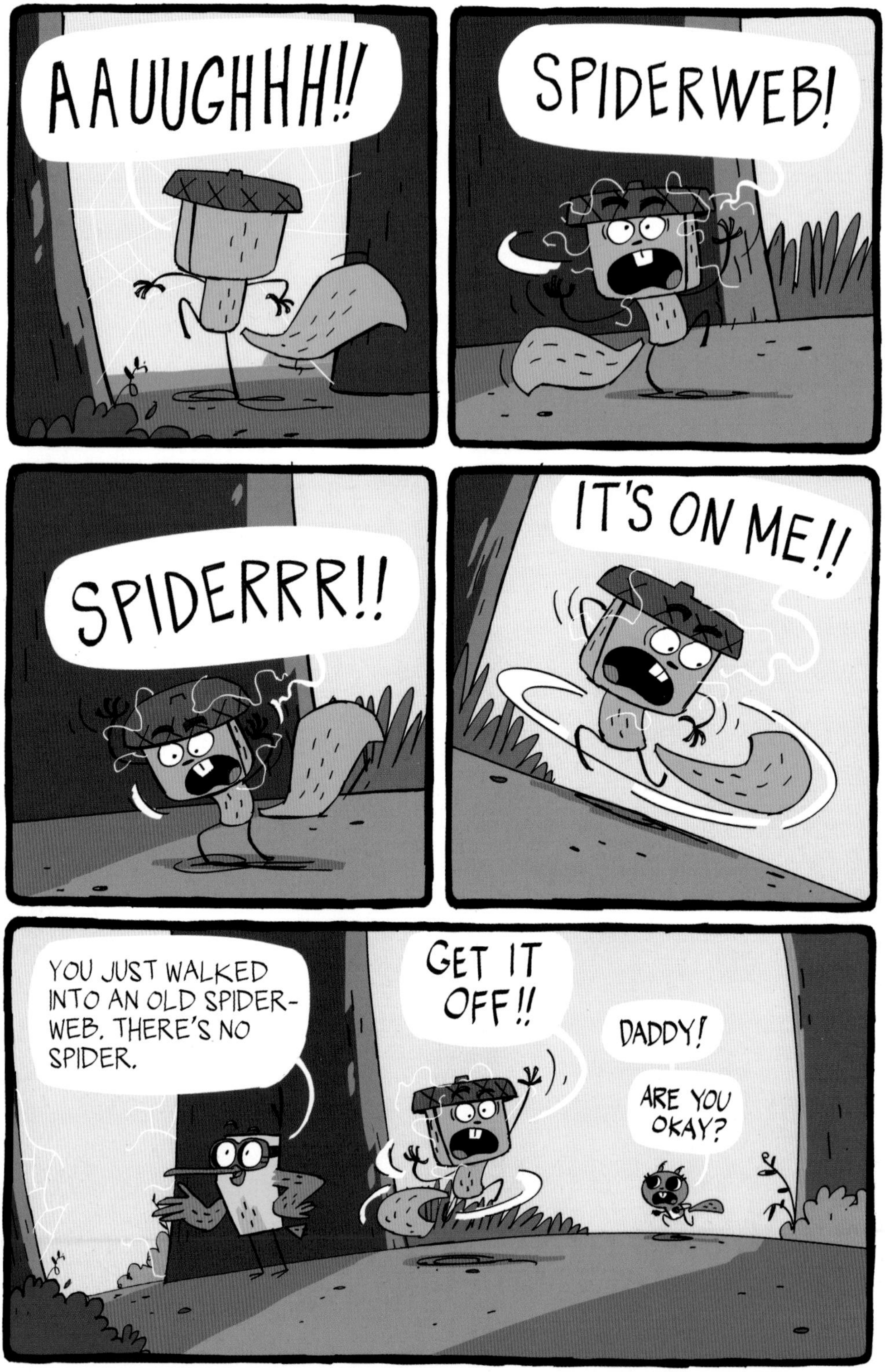
AAUUGHHH!!
SPIDERWEB!
SPIDERRRR!!
IT'S ON ME!!
YOU JUST WALKED INTO AN OLD SPIDER-WEB. THERE'S NO SPIDER.
GET IT OFF!!
DADDY!
ARE YOU OKAY?

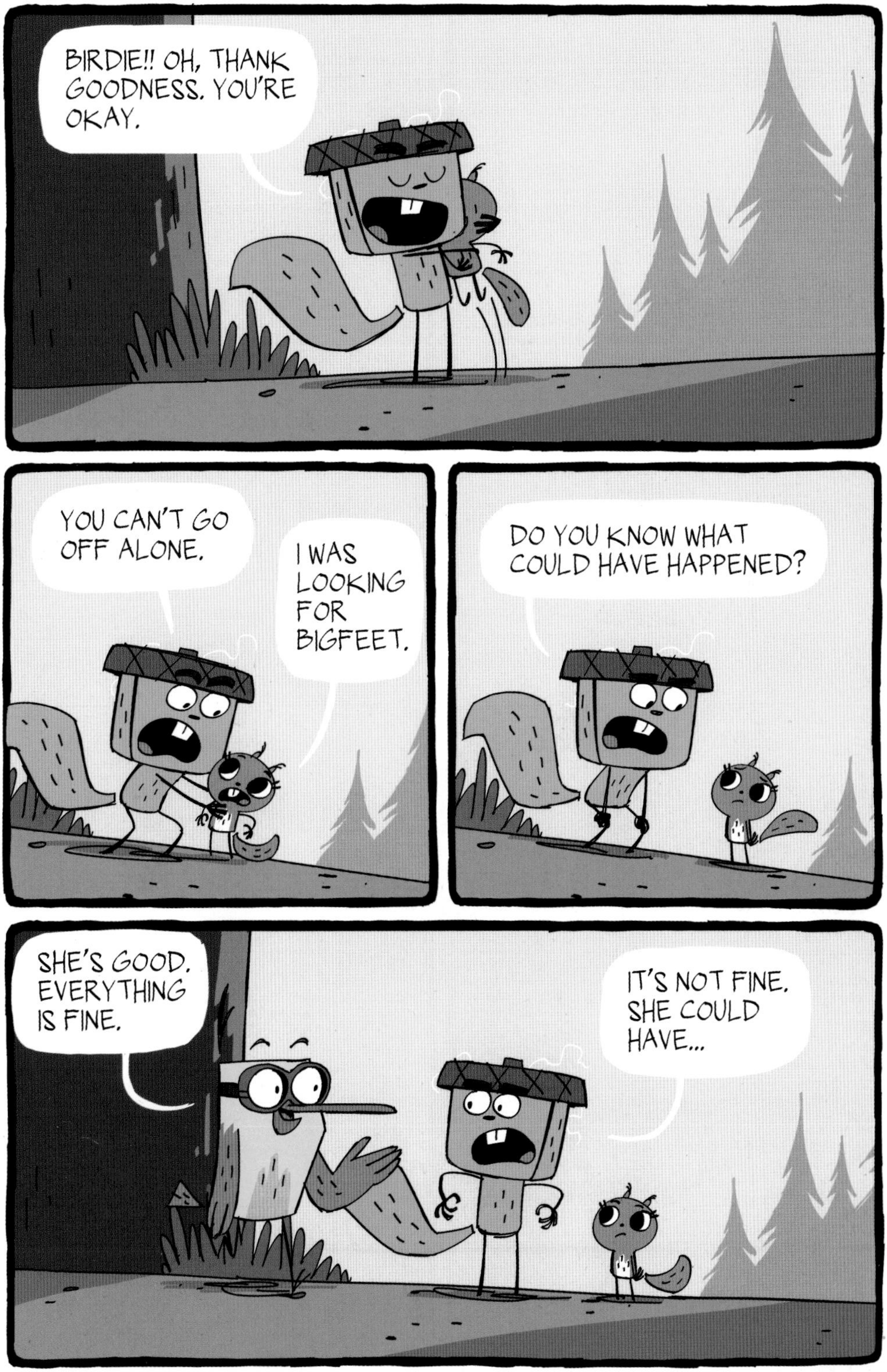
BIRDIE!! OH, THANK GOODNESS. YOU'RE OKAY.
YOU CAN'T GO OFF ALONE.
I WAS LOOKING FOR BIGFEET.
DO YOU KNOW WHAT COULD HAVE HAPPENED?
SHE'S GOOD. EVERYTHING IS FINE.
IT'S NOT FINE. SHE COULD HAVE...

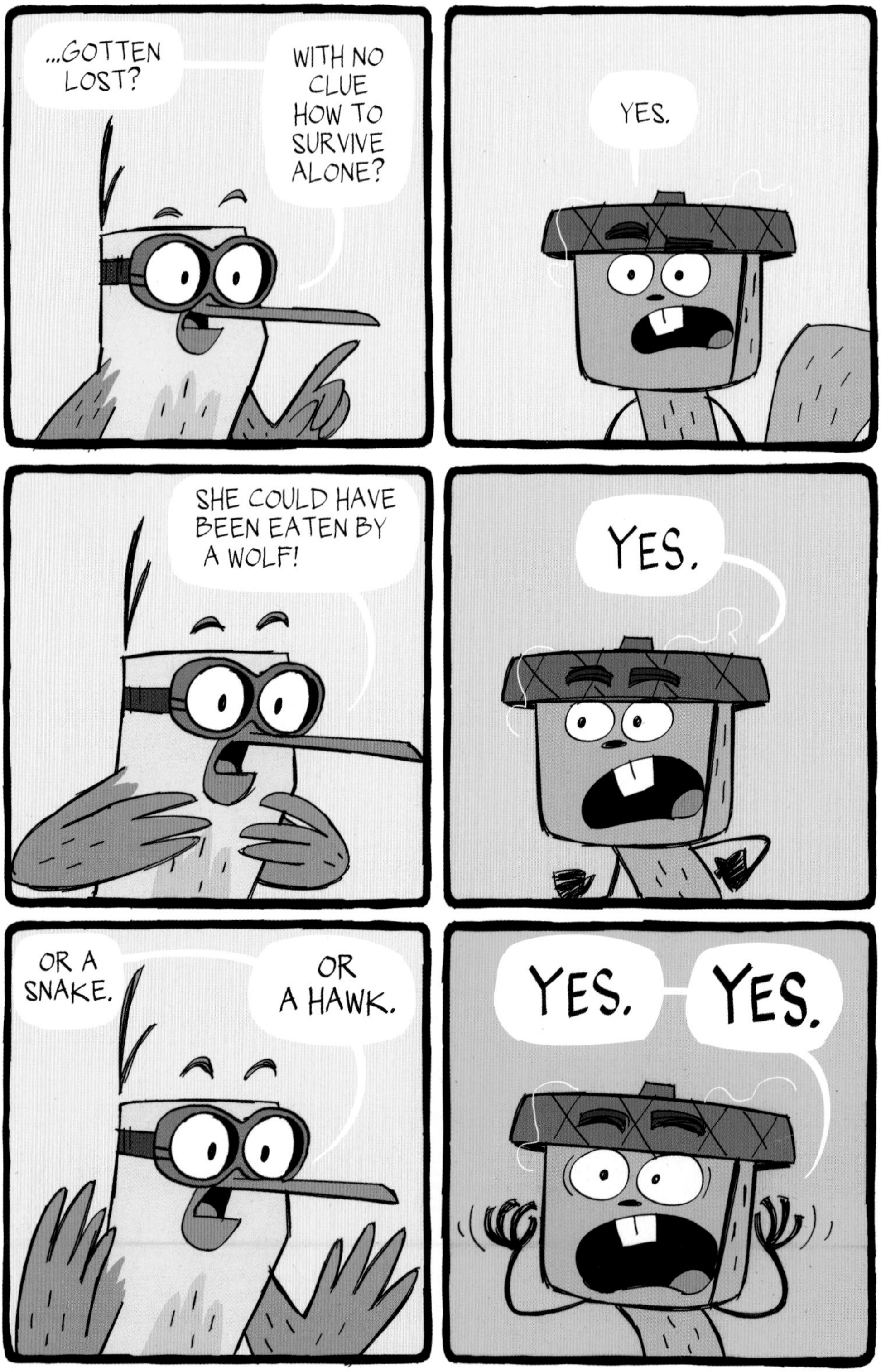
...GOTTEN LOST?
WITH NO CLUE HOW TO SURVIVE ALONE?
YES.
SHE COULD HAVE BEEN EATEN BY A WOLF!
YES.
OR A SNAKE.
OR A HAWK.
YES.
YES.

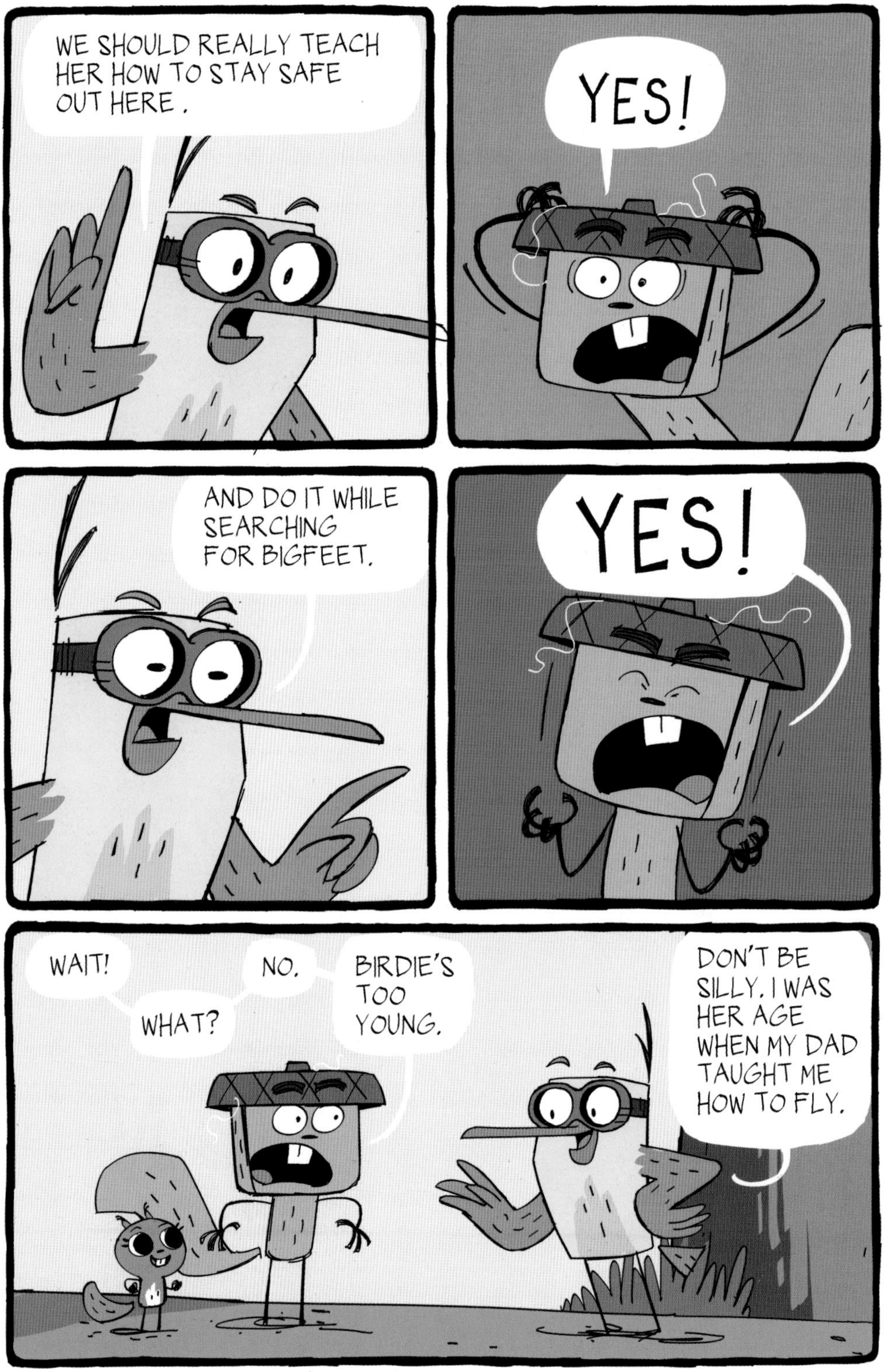
WE SHOULD REALLY TEACH HER HOW TO STAY SAFE OUT HERE.
YES!
AND DO IT WHILE SEARCHING FOR BIGFEET.
YES!
WAIT!
WHAT?
NO.
BIRDIE'S TOO YOUNG.
DON'T BE SILLY. I WAS HER AGE WHEN MY DAD TAUGHT ME HOW TO FLY.

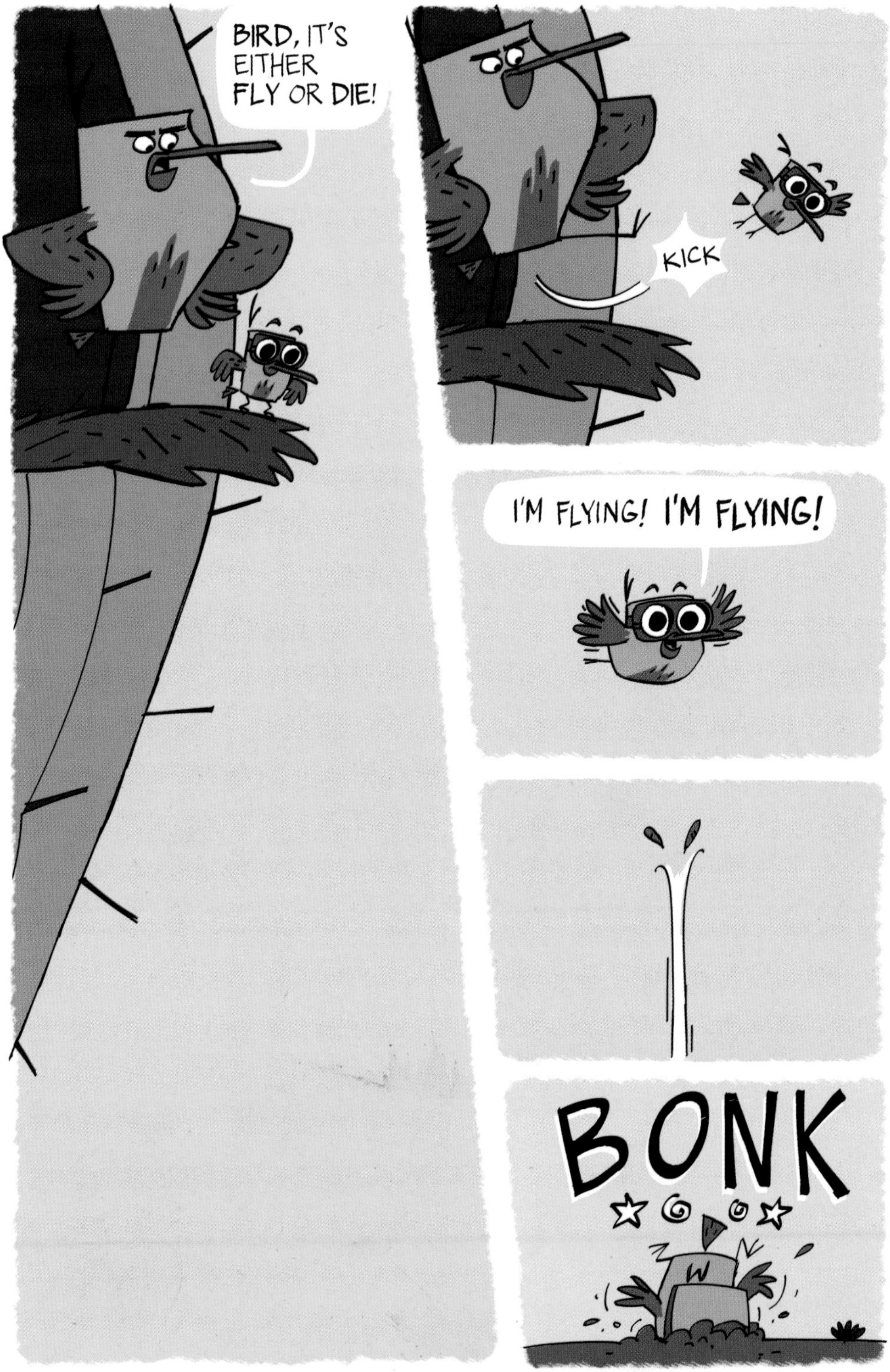
BIRD, IT'S EITHER FLY OR DIE!
KICK
I'M FLYING! I'M FLYING!
BONK
W

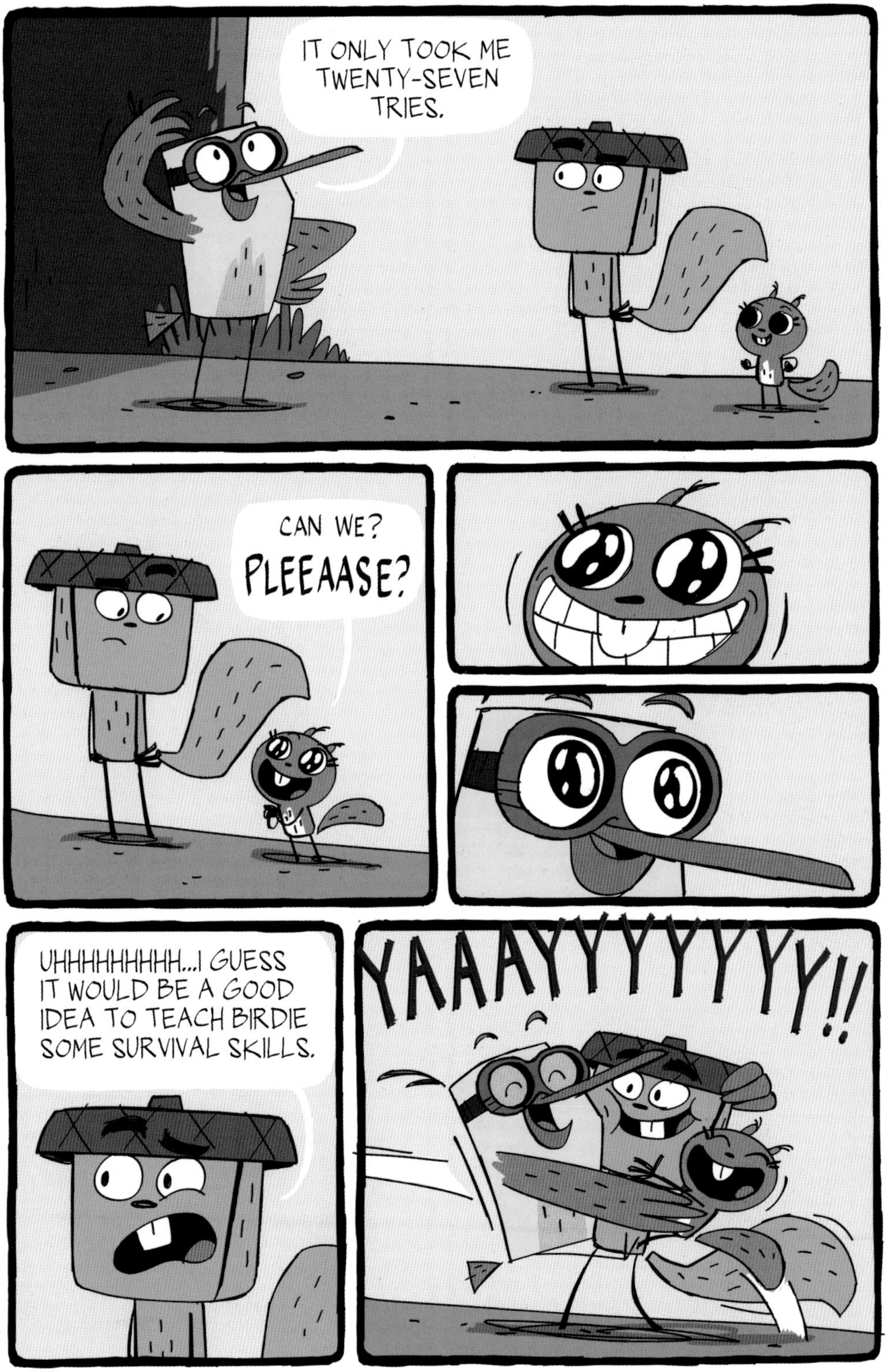
IT ONLY TOOK ME TWENTY-SEVEN TRIES.
CAN WE? PLEEAASE?
UHHHHHHHHH...I GUESS IT WOULD BE A GOOD IDEA TO TEACH BIRDIE SOME SURVIVAL SKILLS.
YAAAYYYYYYYY!!

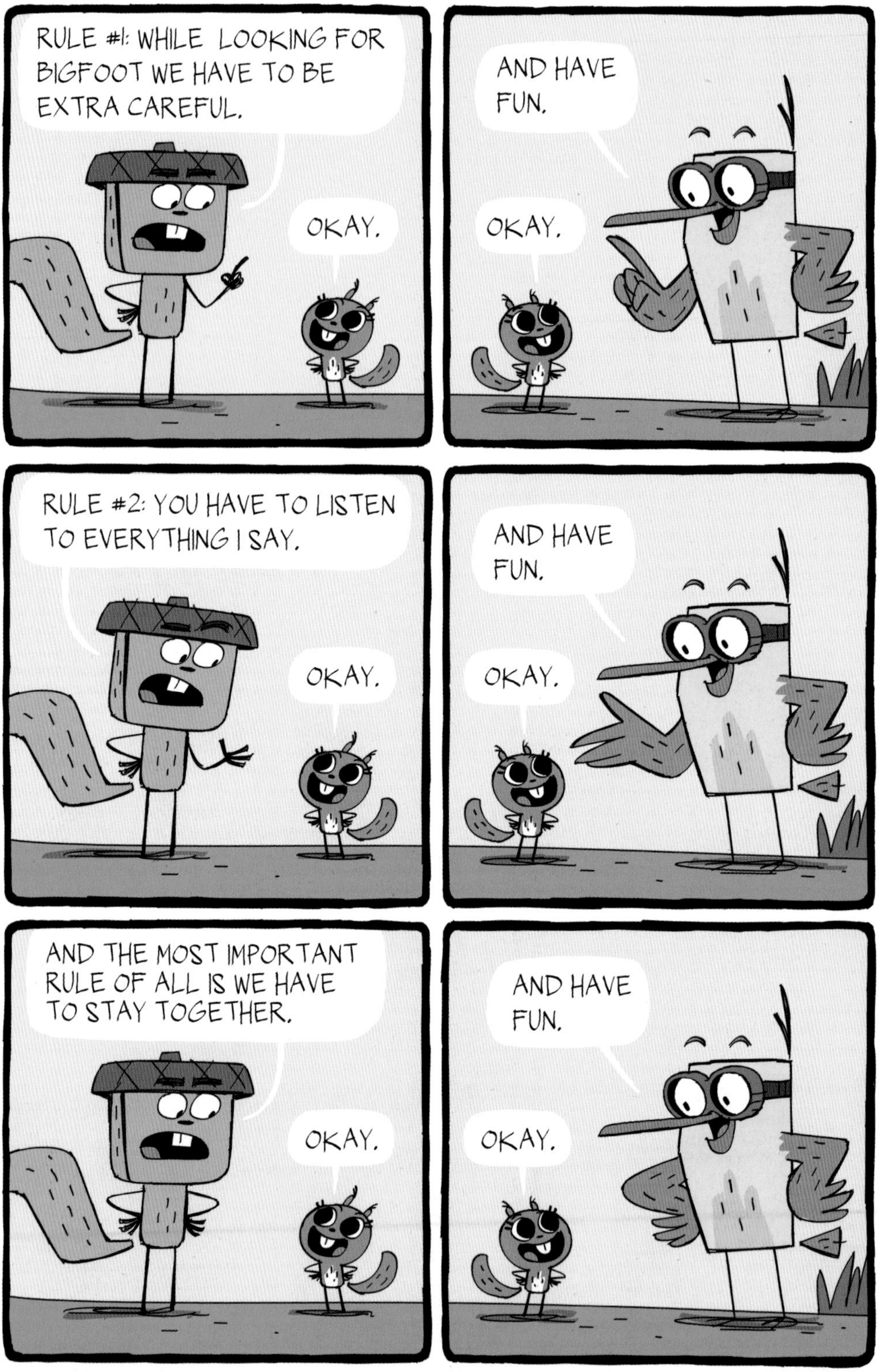
RULE #1: WHILE LOOKING FOR BIGFOOT WE HAVE TO BE EXTRA CAREFUL.
OKAY.
AND HAVE FUN.
OKAY.
RULE #2: YOU HAVE TO LISTEN TO EVERYTHING I SAY.
OKAY.
AND HAVE FUN.
OKAY.
AND THE MOST IMPORTANT RULE OF ALL IS WE HAVE TO STAY TOGETHER.
OKAY.
AND HAVE FUN.
OKAY.

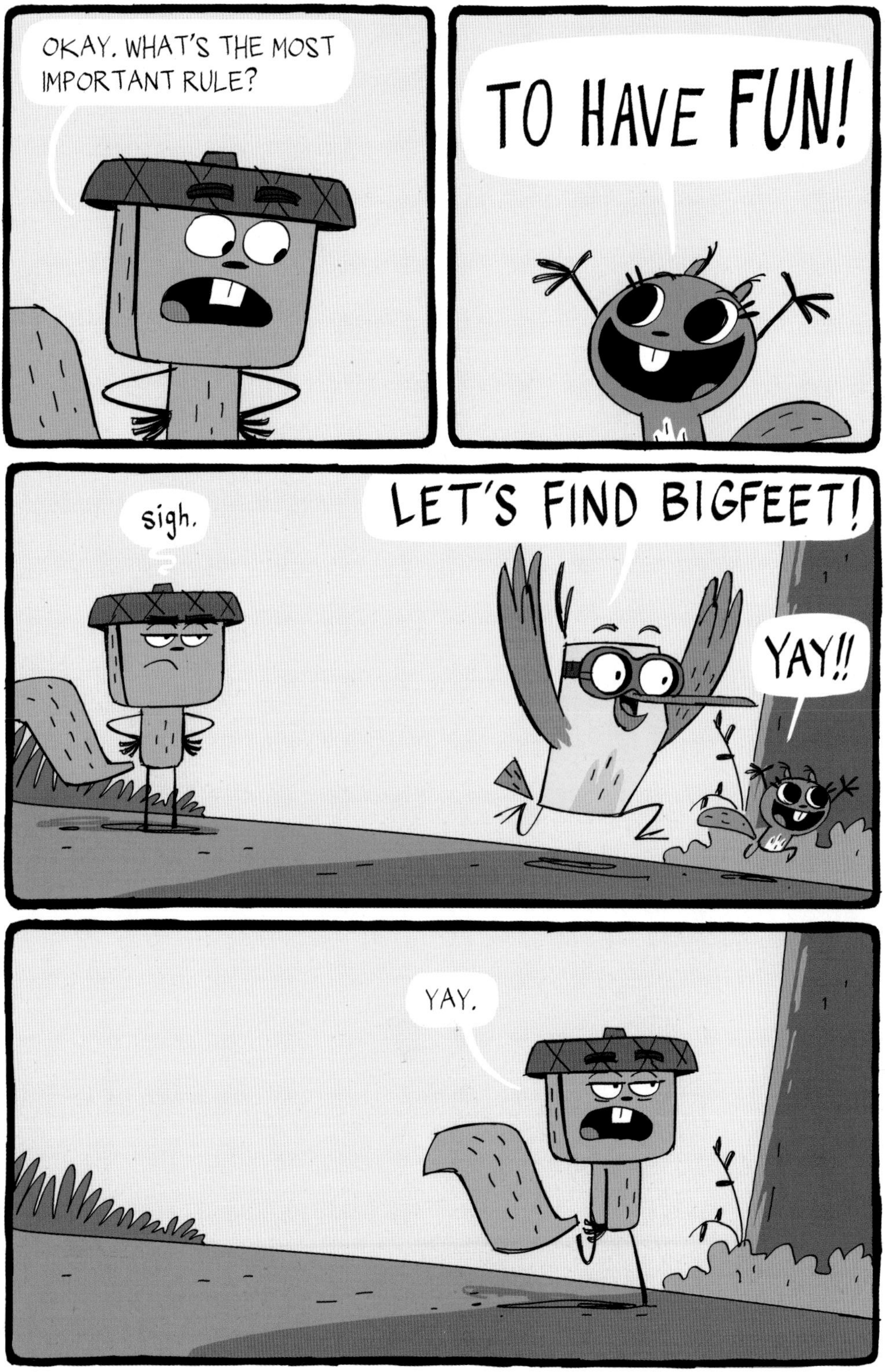
OKAY. WHAT'S THE MOST IMPORTANT RULE?
TO HAVE FUN!
sigh.
LET'S FIND BIGFEET!
YAY!!
YAY.

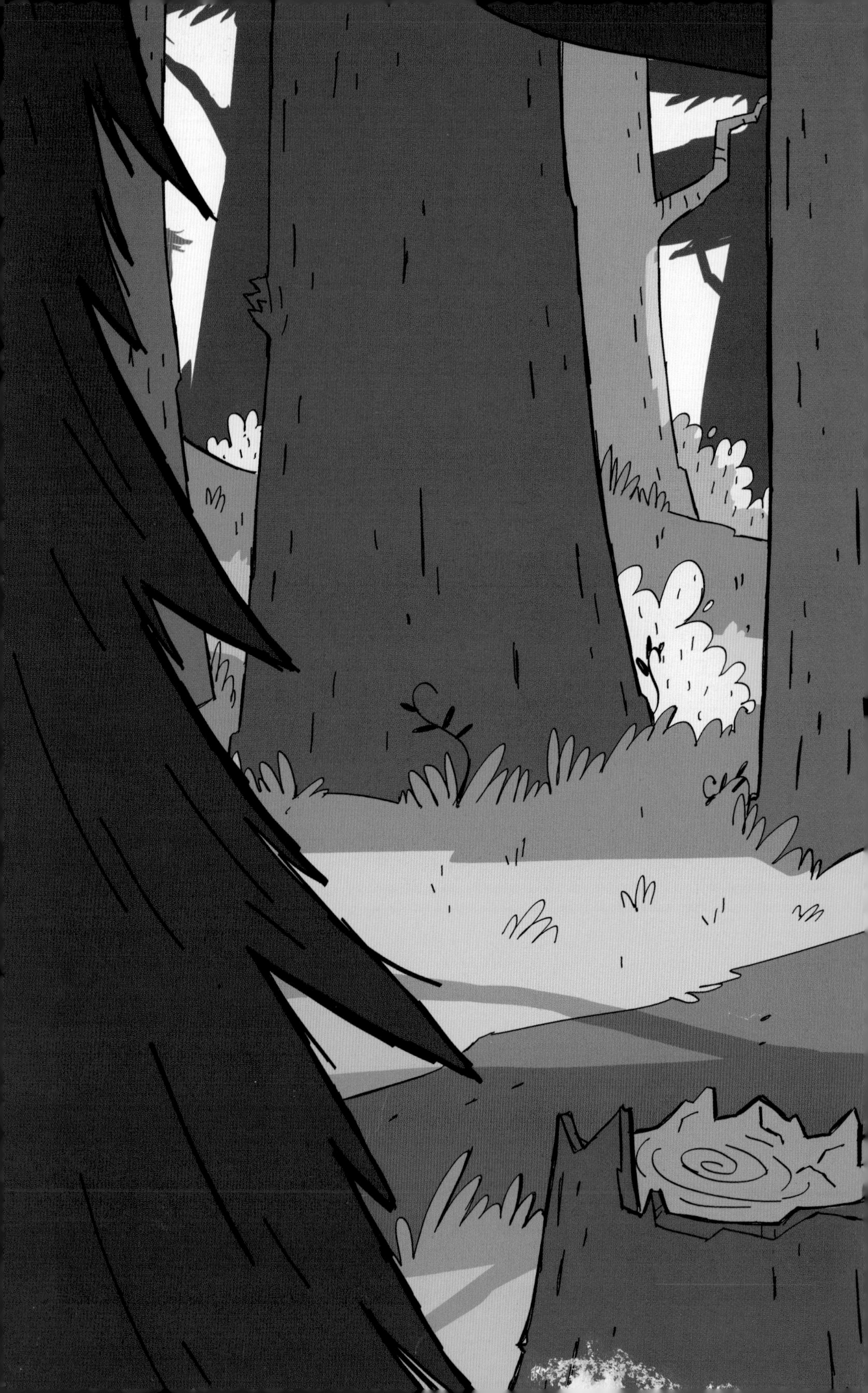

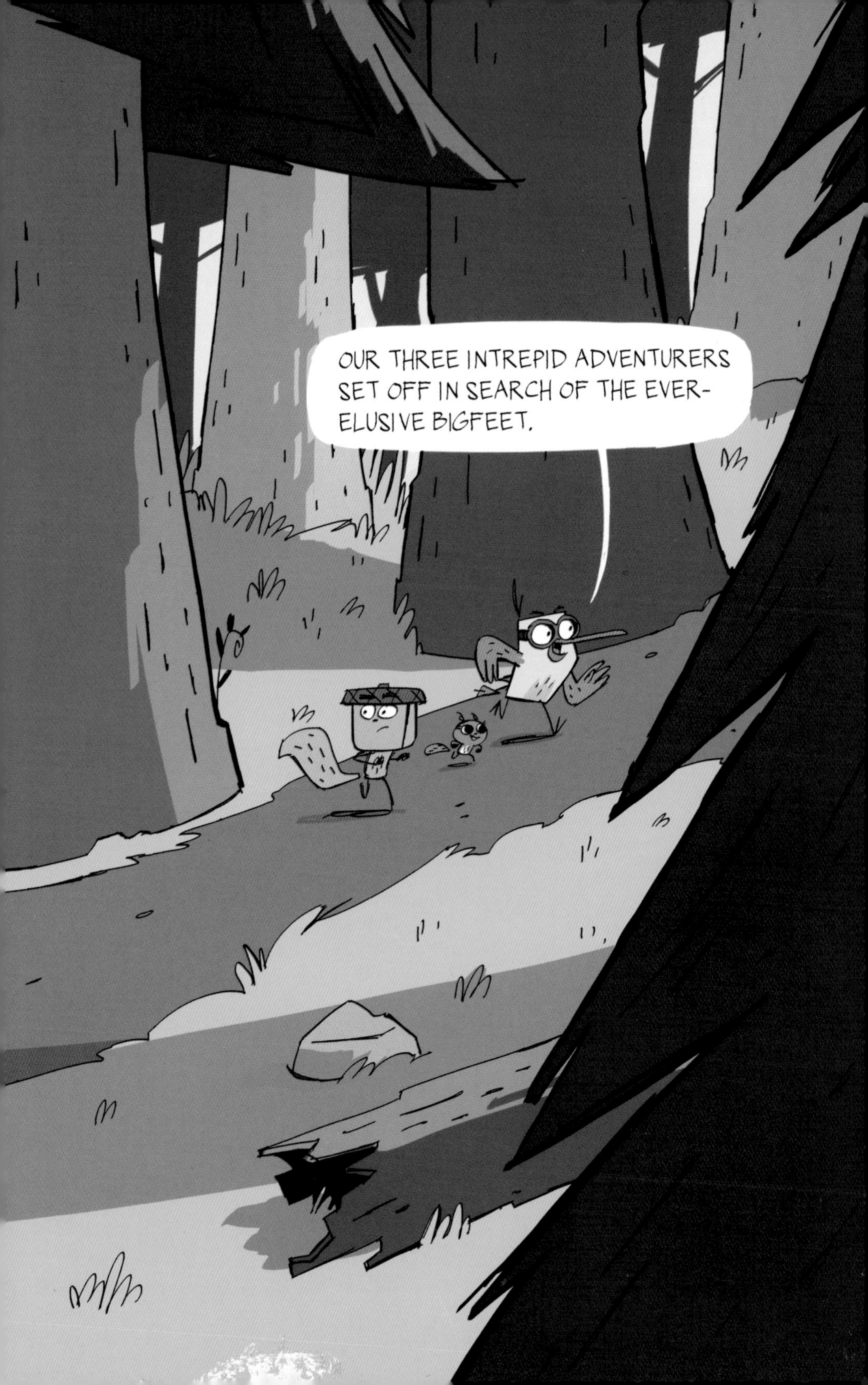
OUR THREE INTREPID ADVENTURERS SET OFF IN SEARCH OF THE EVER-ELUSIVE BIGFEET.

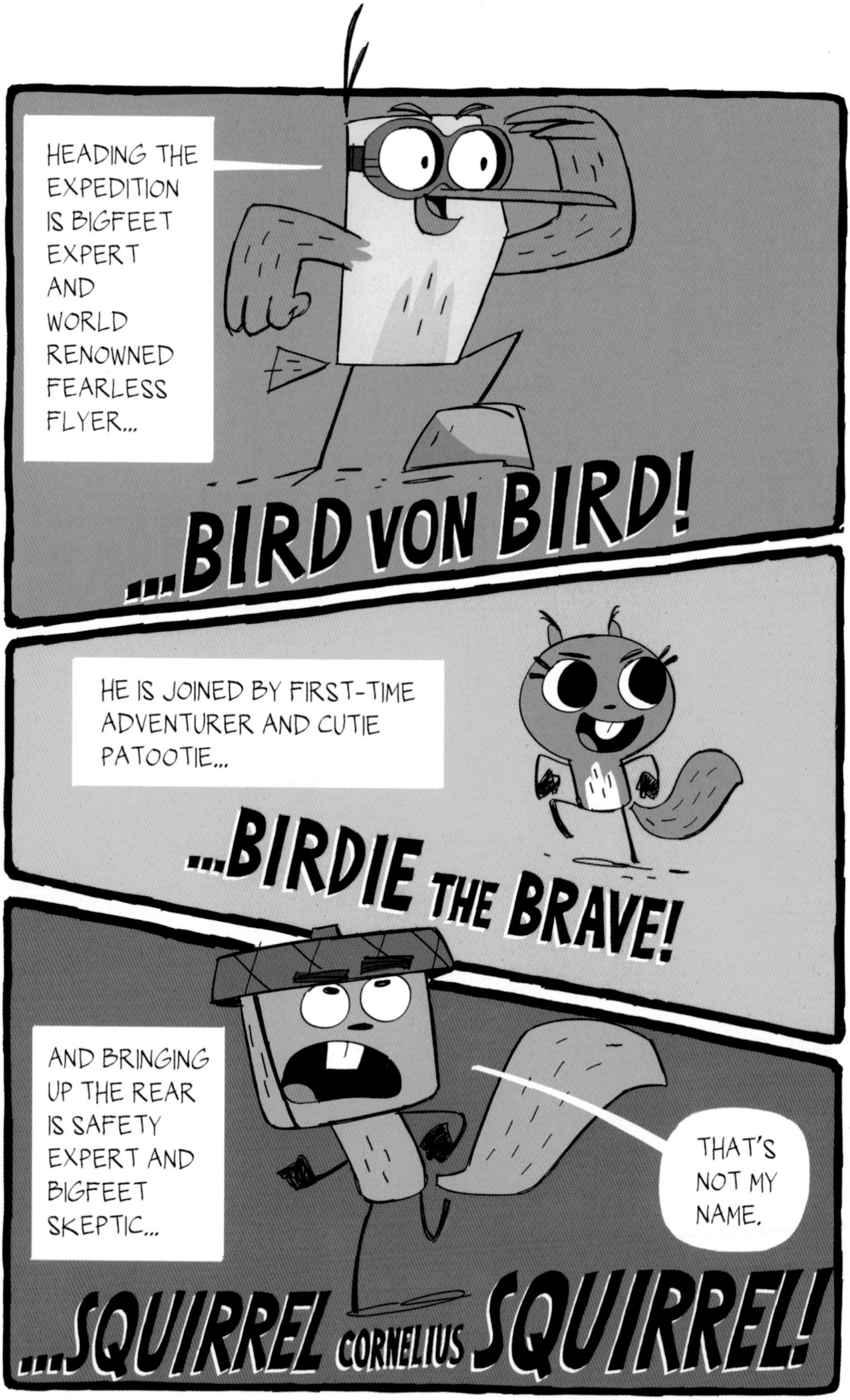
HEADING THE EXPEDITION IS BIGFEET EXPERT AND WORLD RENOWNED FEARLESS FLYER...
...BIRD VON BIRD!
HE IS JOINED BY FIRST-TIME ADVENTURER AND CUTIE PATOOTIE...
...BIRDIE THE BRAVE!
AND BRINGING UP THE REAR IS SAFETY EXPERT AND BIGFEET SKEPTIC...
THAT'S NOT MY NAME.
...SQUIRREL CORNELIUS SQUIRREL!

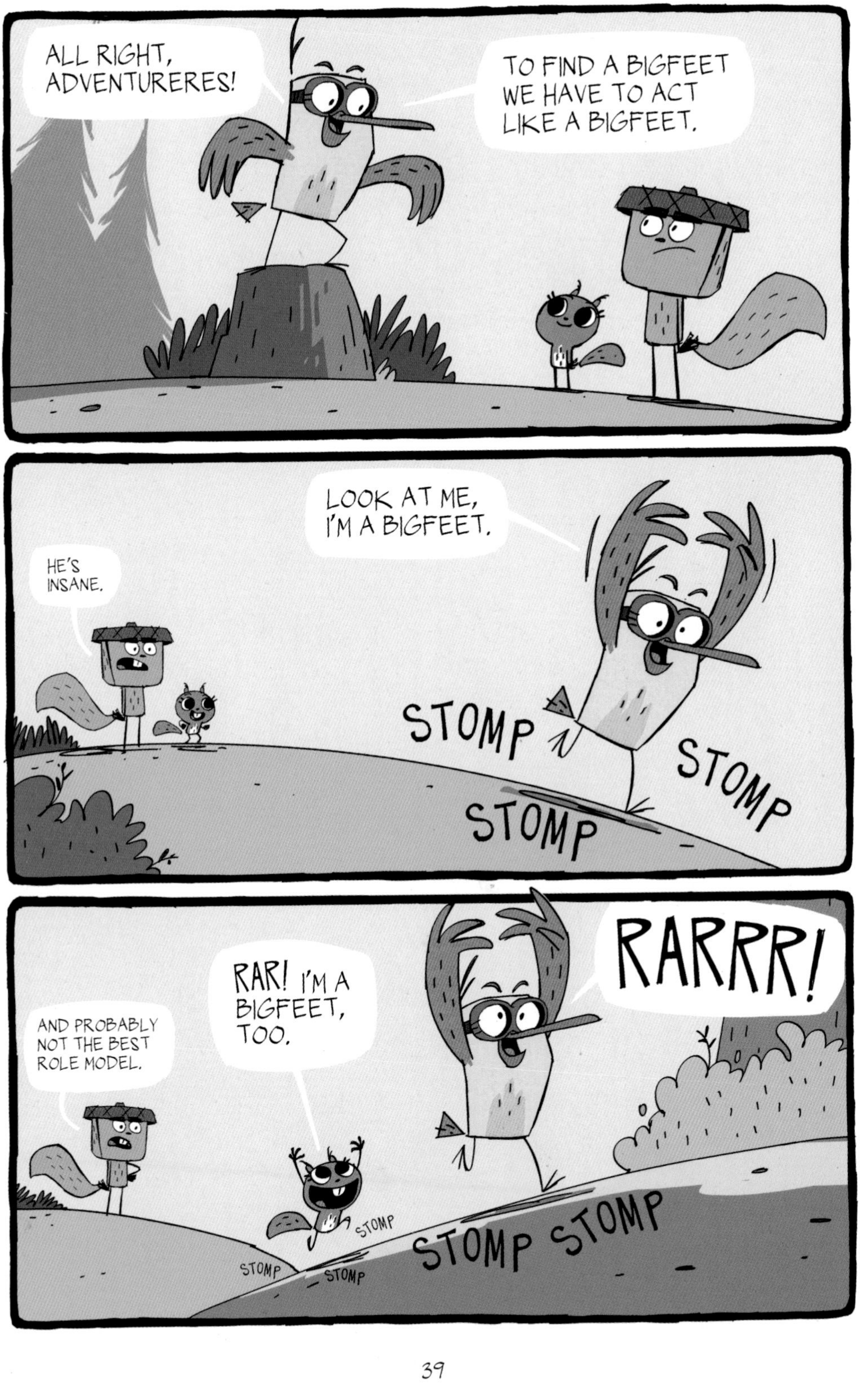
ALL RIGHT, ADVENTURERES!
TO FIND A BIGFEET WE HAVE TO ACT LIKE A BIGFEET.
HE'S INSANE.
LOOK AT ME, I'M A BIGFEET.
STOMP
STOMP
STOMP
AND PROBABLY NOT THE BEST ROLE MODEL.
RAR! I'M A BIGFEET, TOO.
RARRR!
STOMP
STOMP
STOMP
STOMP STOMP

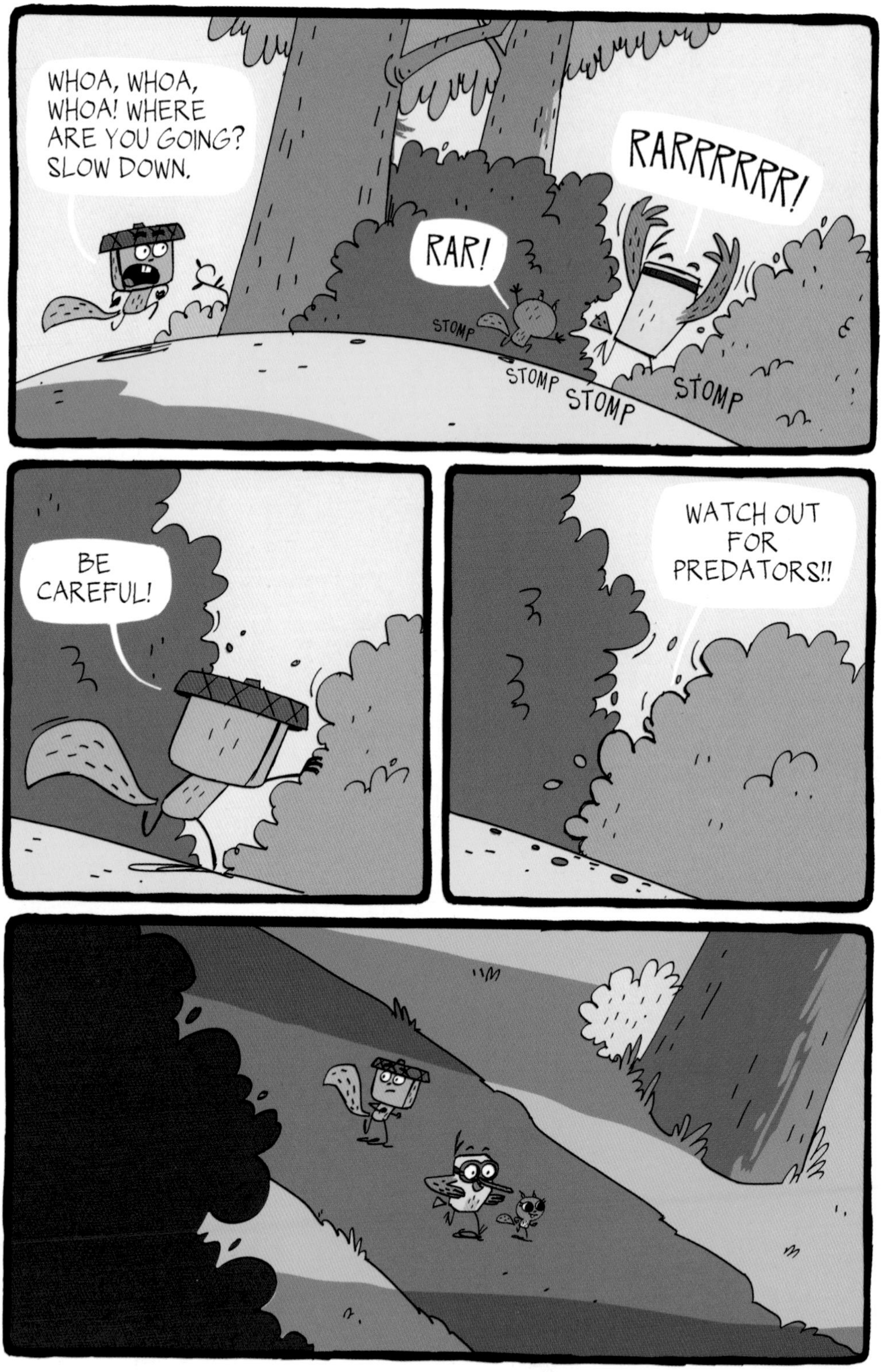
WHOA, WHOA, WHOA! WHERE ARE YOU GOING? SLOW DOWN.
RAR!
RARRRRRR!
STOMP
STOMP STOMP
STOMP
BE CAREFUL!
WATCH OUT FOR PREDATORS!!

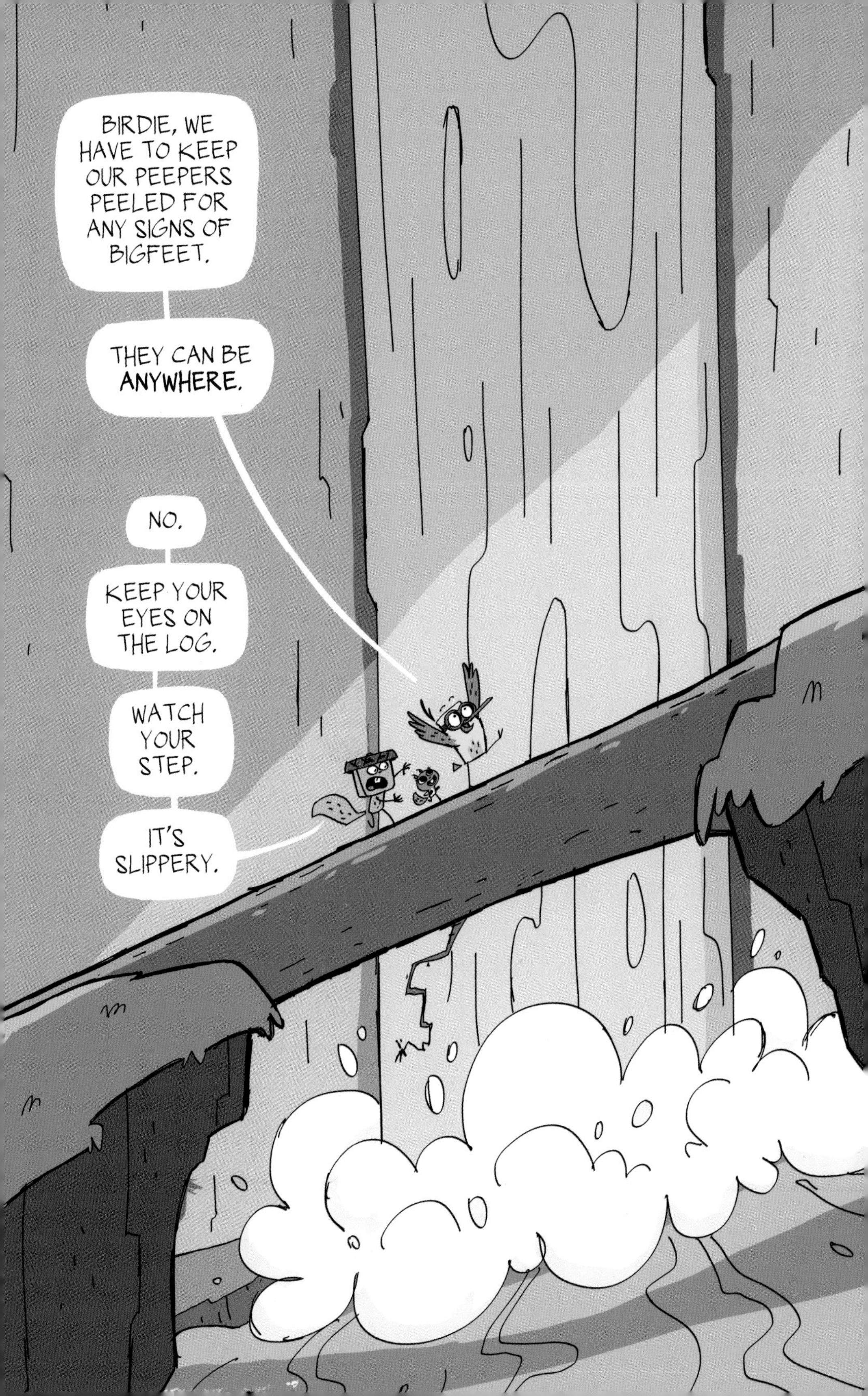
BIRDIE, WE HAVE TO KEEP OUR PEEPERS PEELED FOR ANY SIGNS OF BIGFEET.
THEY CAN BE **ANYWHERE.**
NO.
KEEP YOUR EYES ON THE LOG.
WATCH YOUR STEP.
IT'S SLIPPERY.

MOSS TENDS TO GROW ON THE NORTH SIDE OF A TREE, ISN'T THAT EXCITING?

I GUESS.

AND MOOSE ANTLERS GROW ON MOOSE.

WOW!

WEEEEEEEEEEEEEEEEEEEEEEE!!!

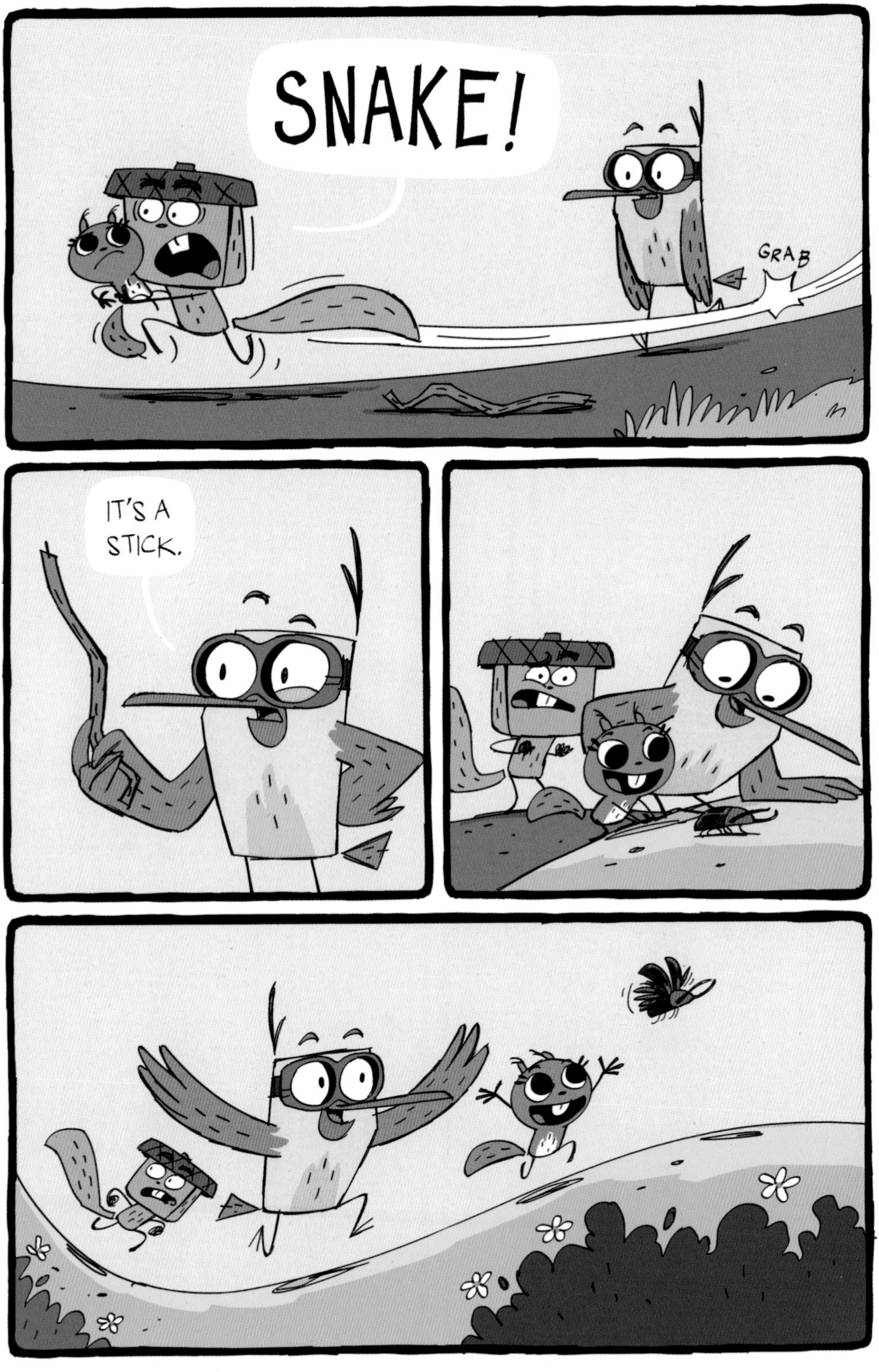
SNAKE!
GRAB
IT'S A STICK.

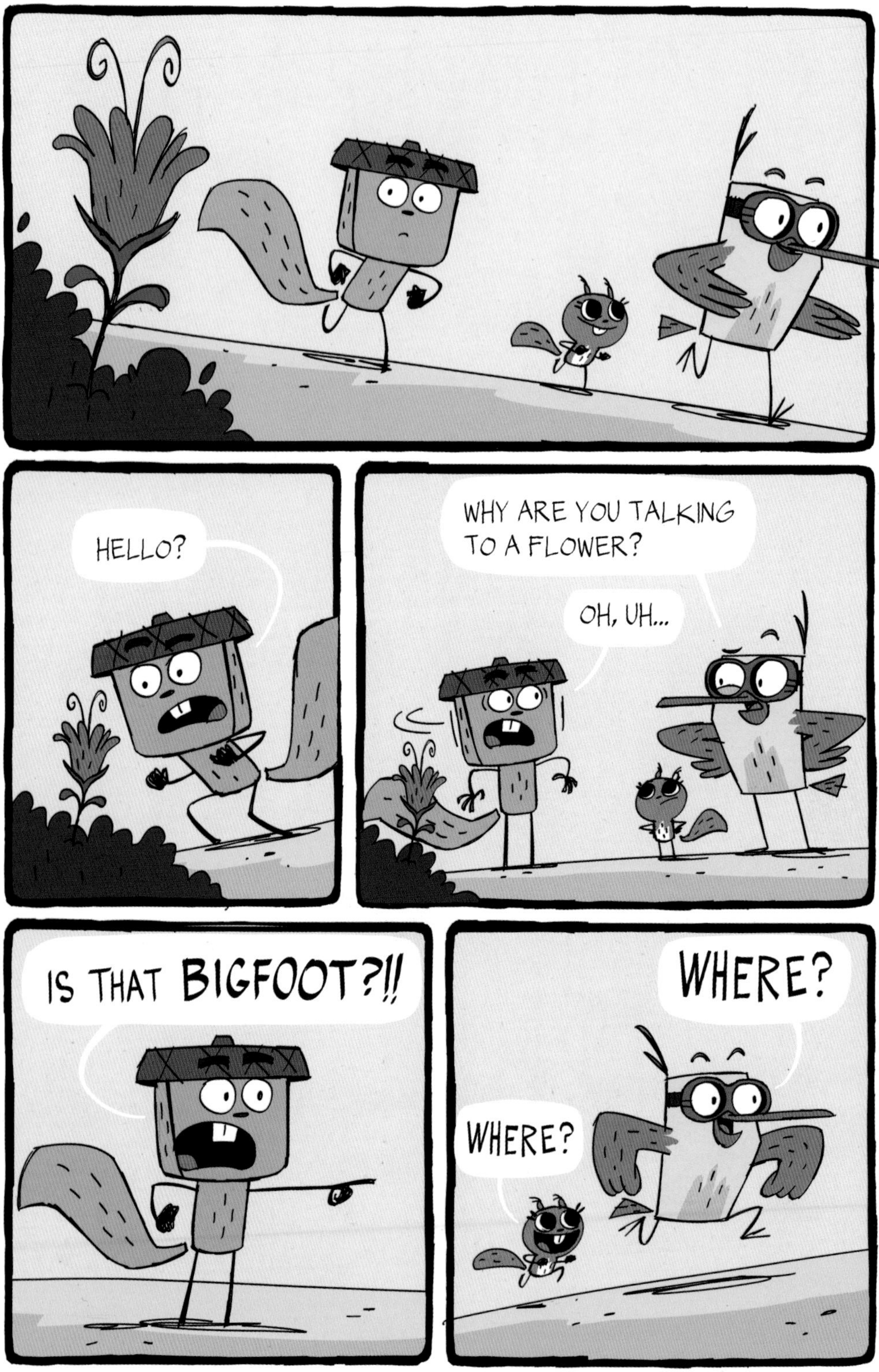
HELLO?
WHY ARE YOU TALKING TO A FLOWER?
OH, UH...
IS THAT BIGFOOT?!!
WHERE?
WHERE?

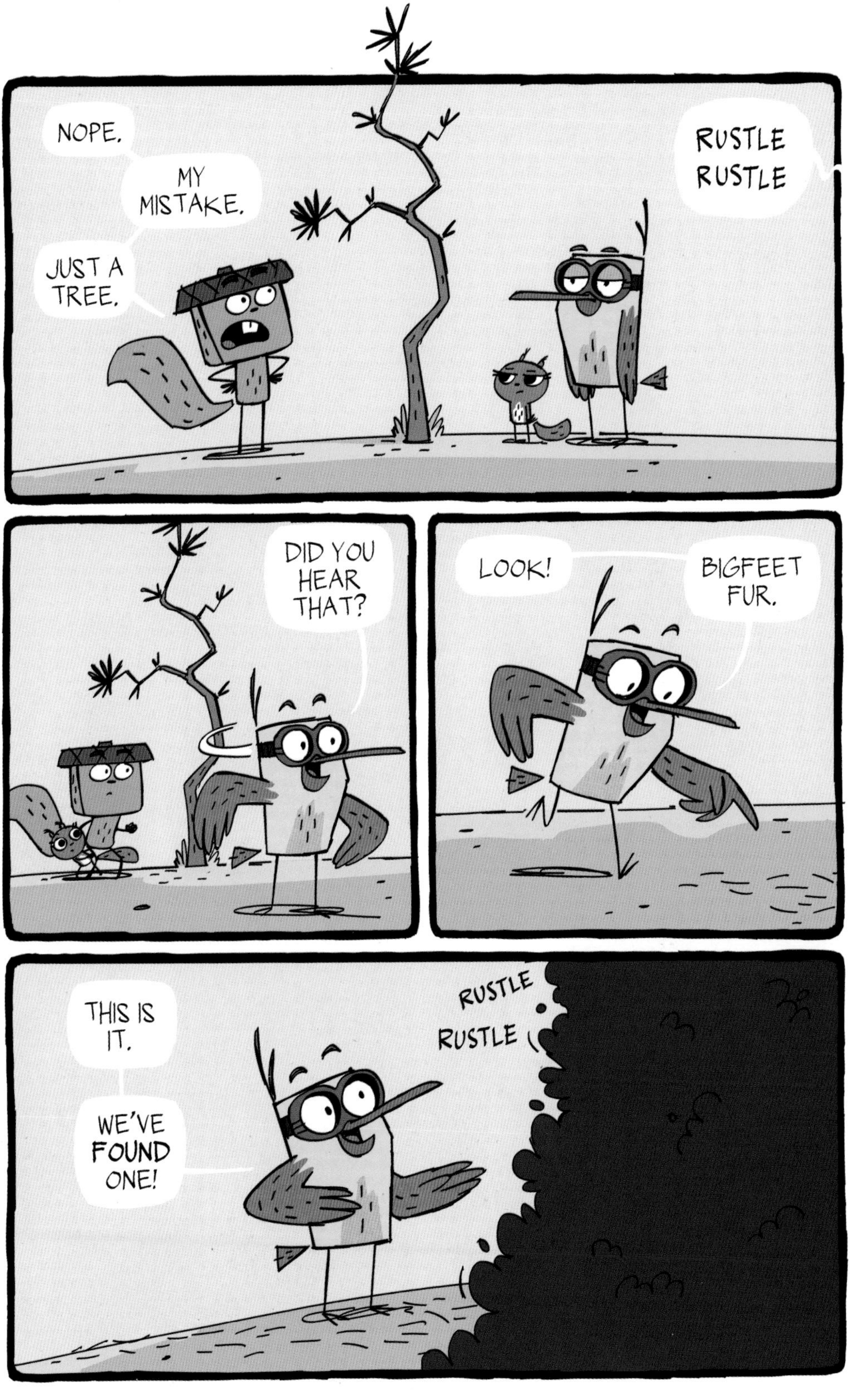
NOPE.
MY MISTAKE.
JUST A TREE.
RUSTLE RUSTLE
DID YOU HEAR THAT?
LOOK!
BIGFEET FUR.
THIS IS IT.
WE'VE **FOUND** ONE!
RUSTLE
RUSTLE

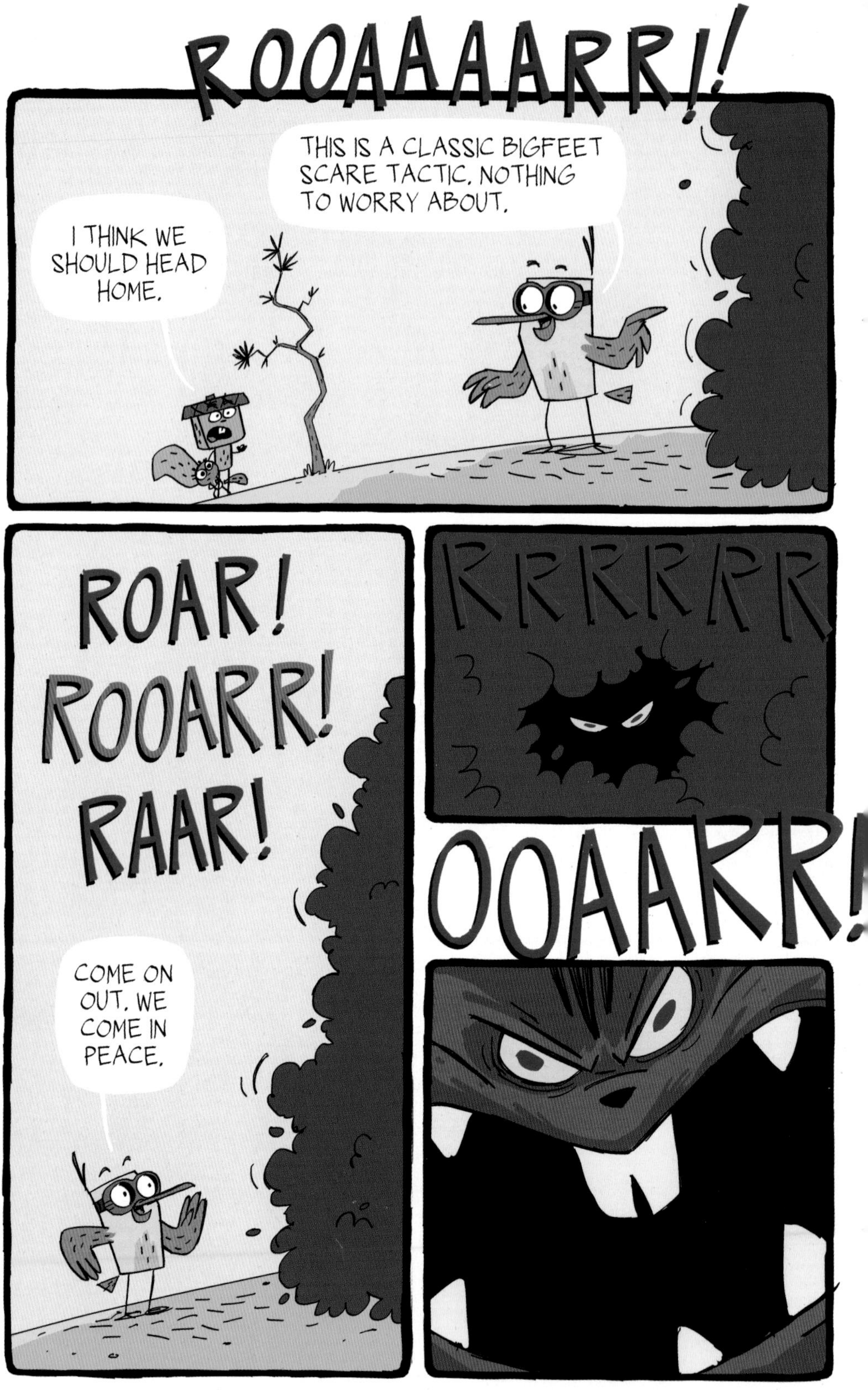
ROOAAAARR!
I THINK WE SHOULD HEAD HOME.
THIS IS A CLASSIC BIGFEET SCARE TACTIC. NOTHING TO WORRY ABOUT.
ROAR!
ROOARR!
RAAR!
COME ON OUT. WE COME IN PEACE.
RRRRRR
OOARR!

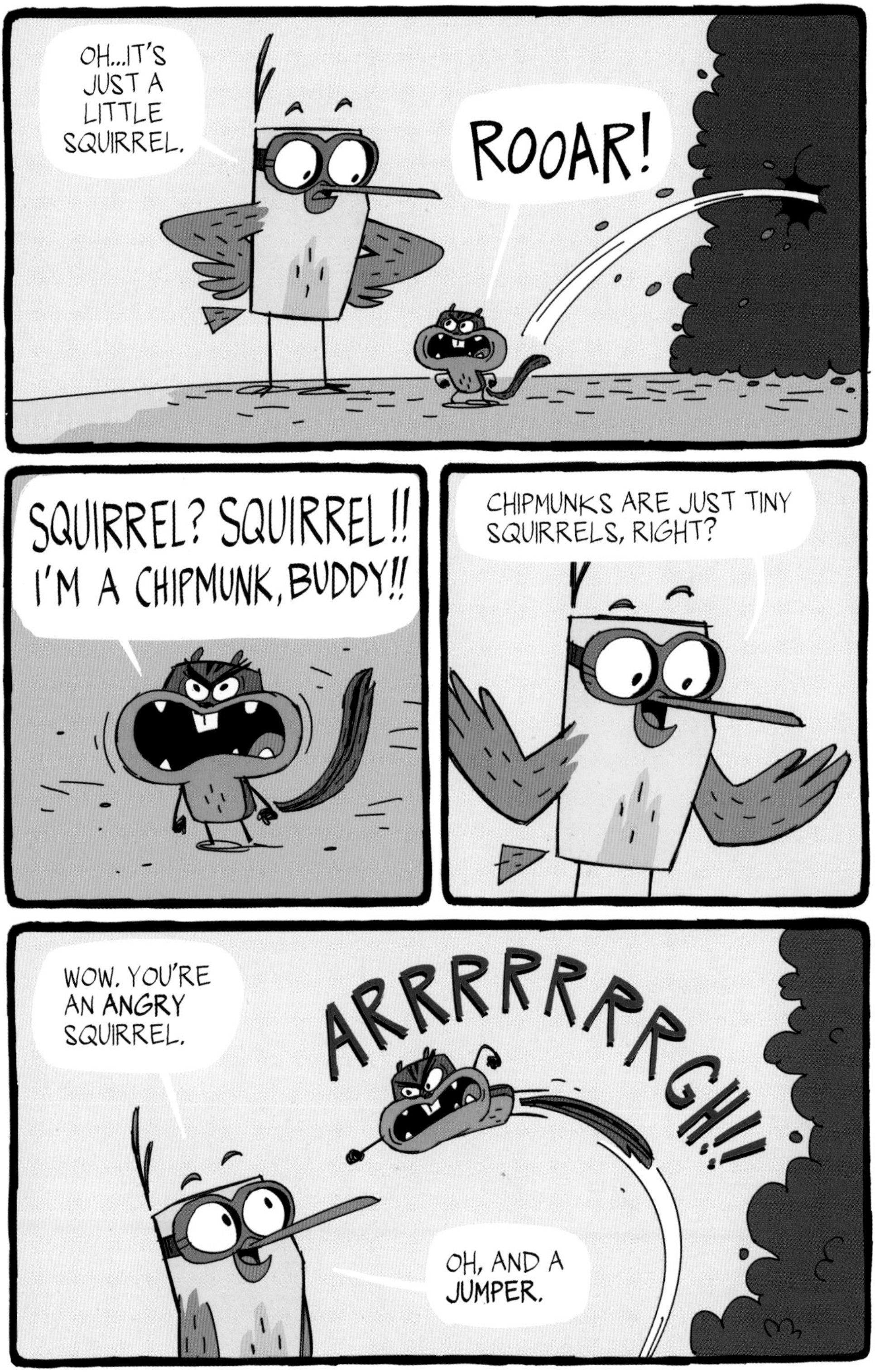
OH...IT'S JUST A LITTLE SQUIRREL.
ROOAR!
SQUIRREL? SQUIRREL!! I'M A CHIPMUNK, BUDDY!!
CHIPMUNKS ARE JUST TINY SQUIRRELS, RIGHT?
WOW. YOU'RE AN ANGRY SQUIRREL.
ARRRRRRRGH!!!
OH, AND A JUMPER.

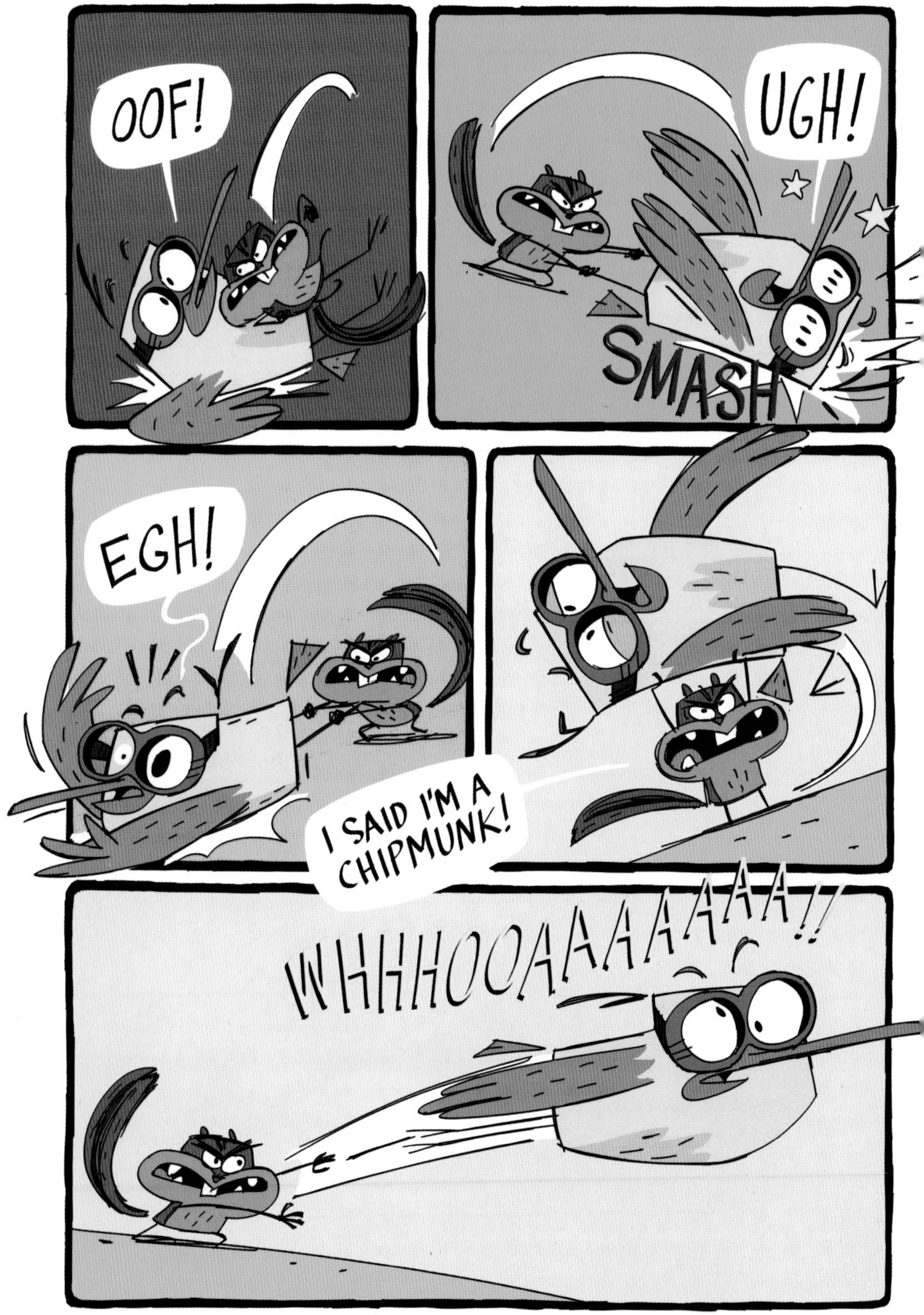
OOF!
UGH!
SMASH
EGH!
I SAID I'M A CHIPMUNK!
WHHHOOAAAAAAA!!

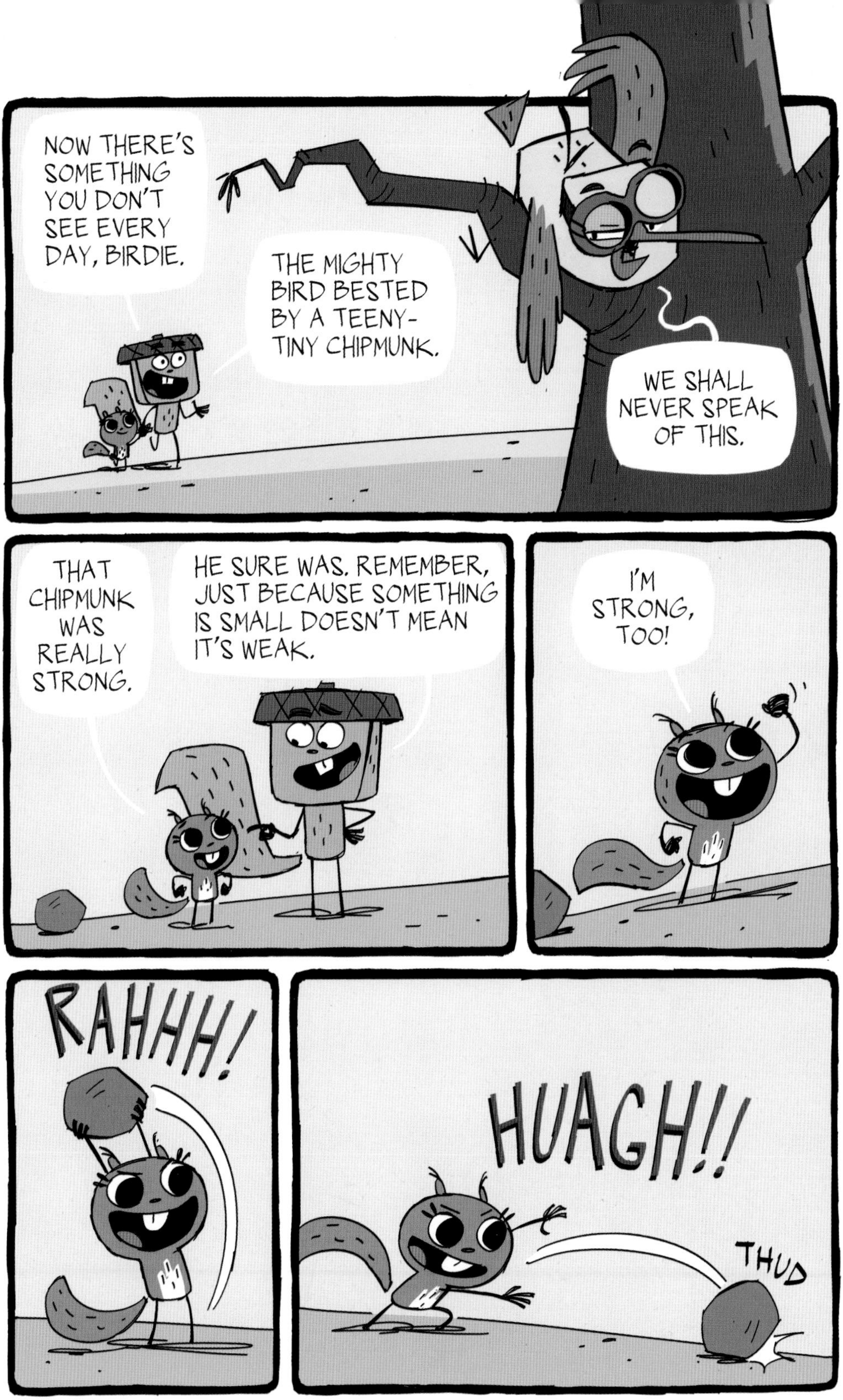

NOW THERE'S SOMETHING YOU DON'T SEE EVERY DAY, BIRDIE.
THE MIGHTY BIRD BESTED BY A TEENY-TINY CHIPMUNK.
WE SHALL NEVER SPEAK OF THIS.
THAT CHIPMUNK WAS REALLY STRONG.
HE SURE WAS. REMEMBER, JUST BECAUSE SOMETHING IS SMALL DOESN'T MEAN IT'S WEAK.
I'M STRONG, TOO!
RAHHH!
HUAGH!!
THUD

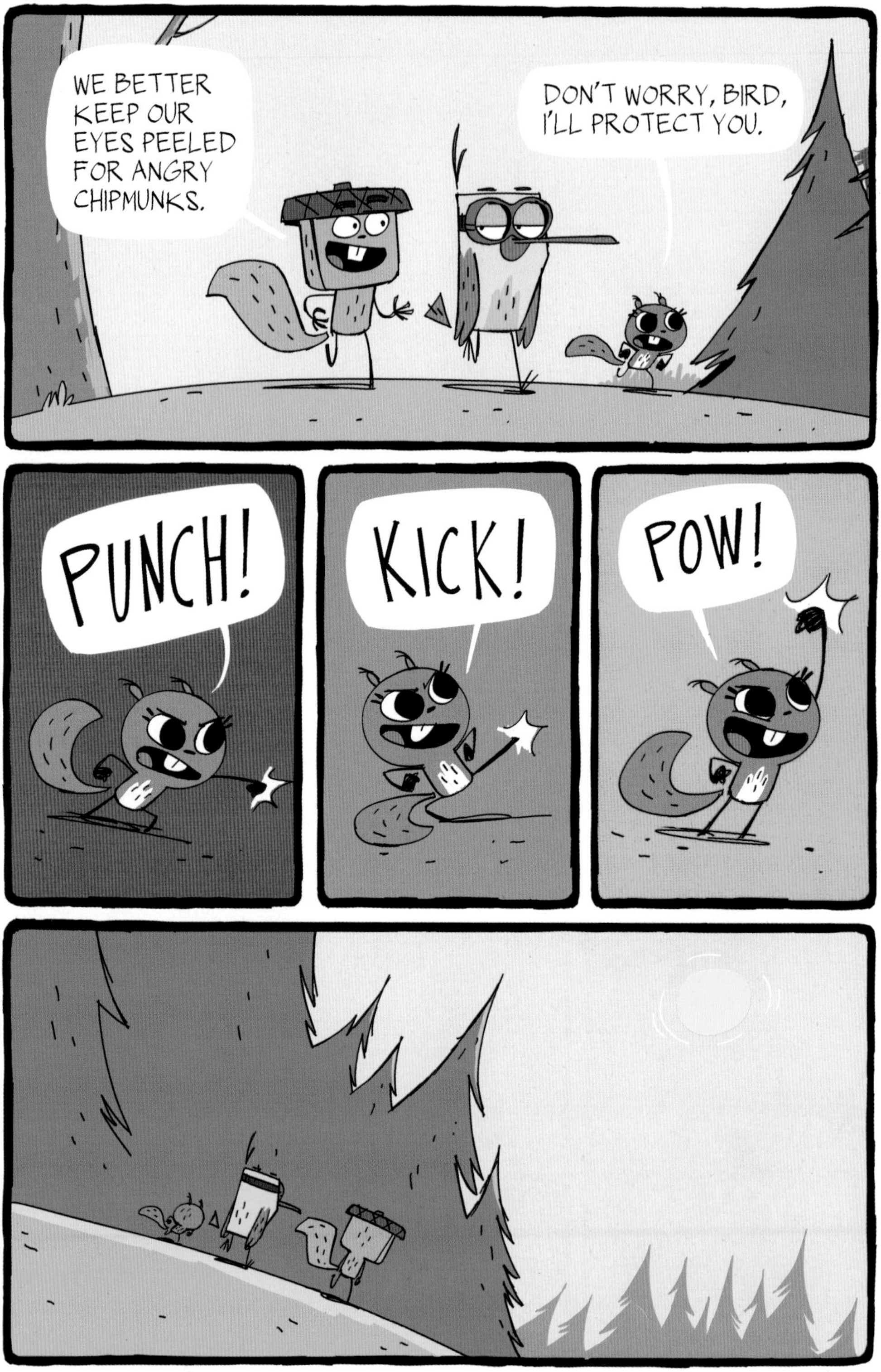
WE BETTER KEEP OUR EYES PEELED FOR ANGRY CHIPMUNKS.
DON'T WORRY, BIRD, I'LL PROTECT YOU.
PUNCH!
KICK!
POW!

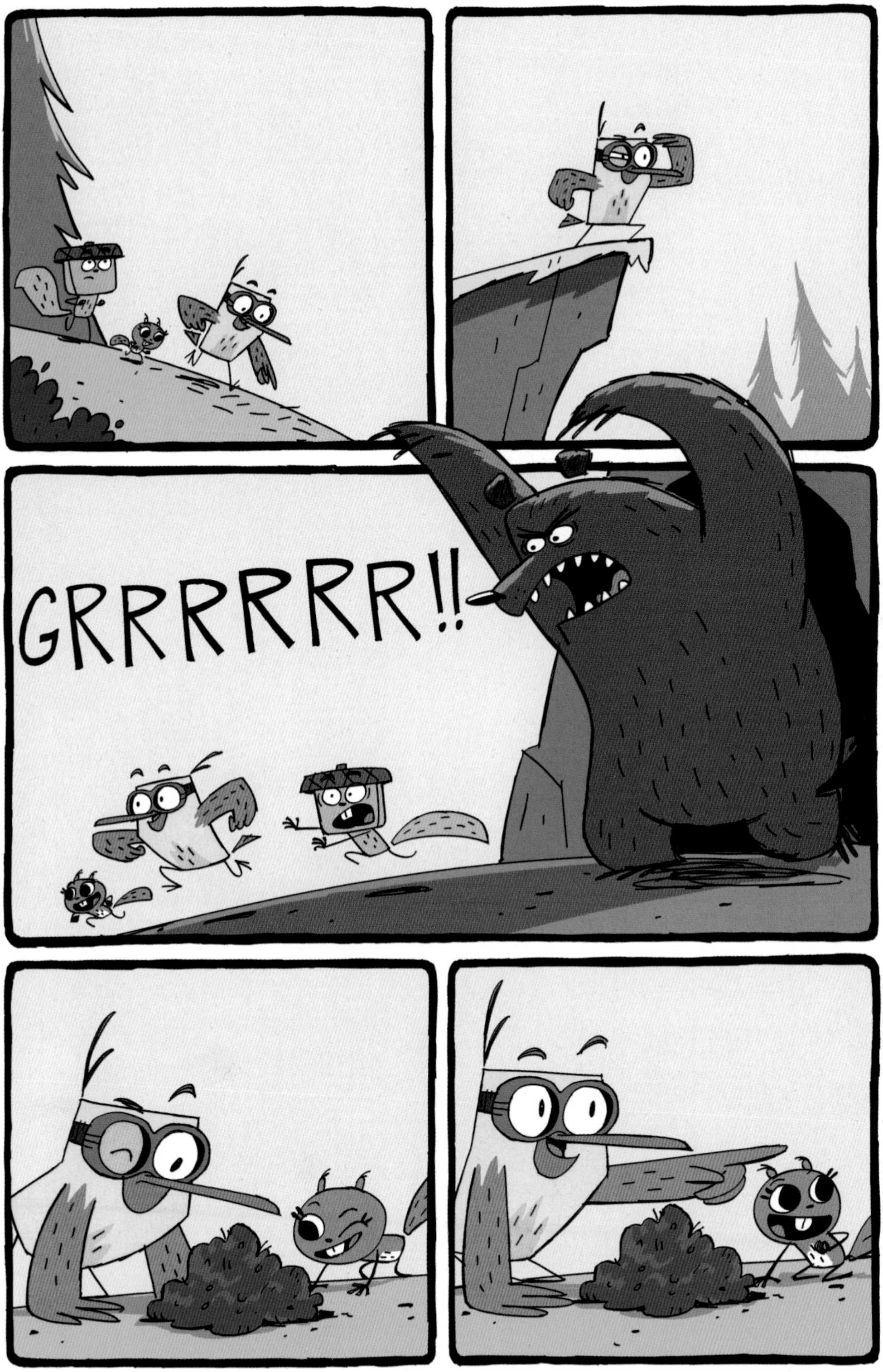
GRRRRRR!!

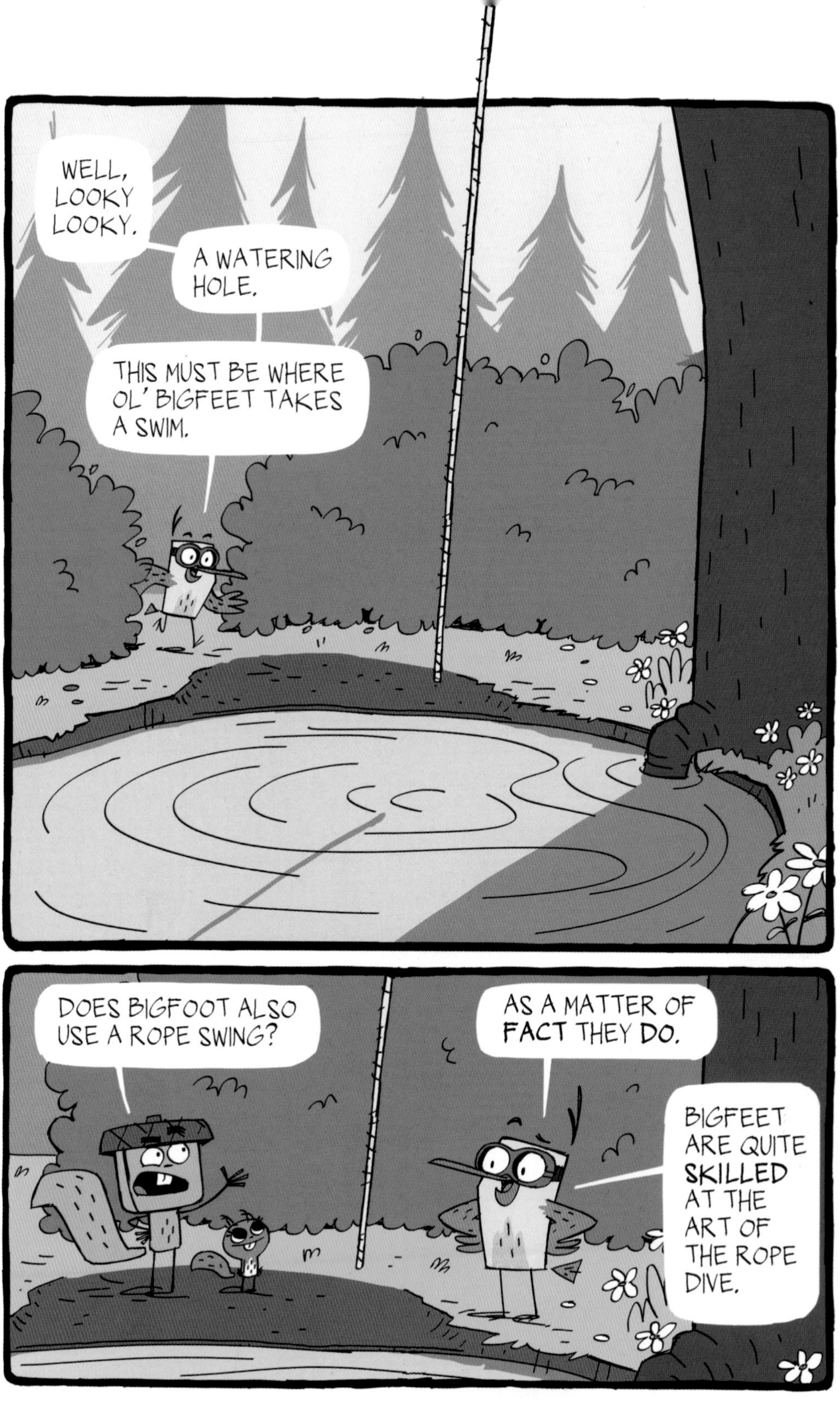
WELL, LOOKY LOOKY.
A WATERING HOLE.
THIS MUST BE WHERE OL' BIGFEET TAKES A SWIM.
DOES BIGFOOT ALSO USE A ROPE SWING?
AS A MATTER OF **FACT** THEY **DO.**
BIGFEET ARE QUITE **SKILLED** AT THE ART OF THE ROPE DIVE.

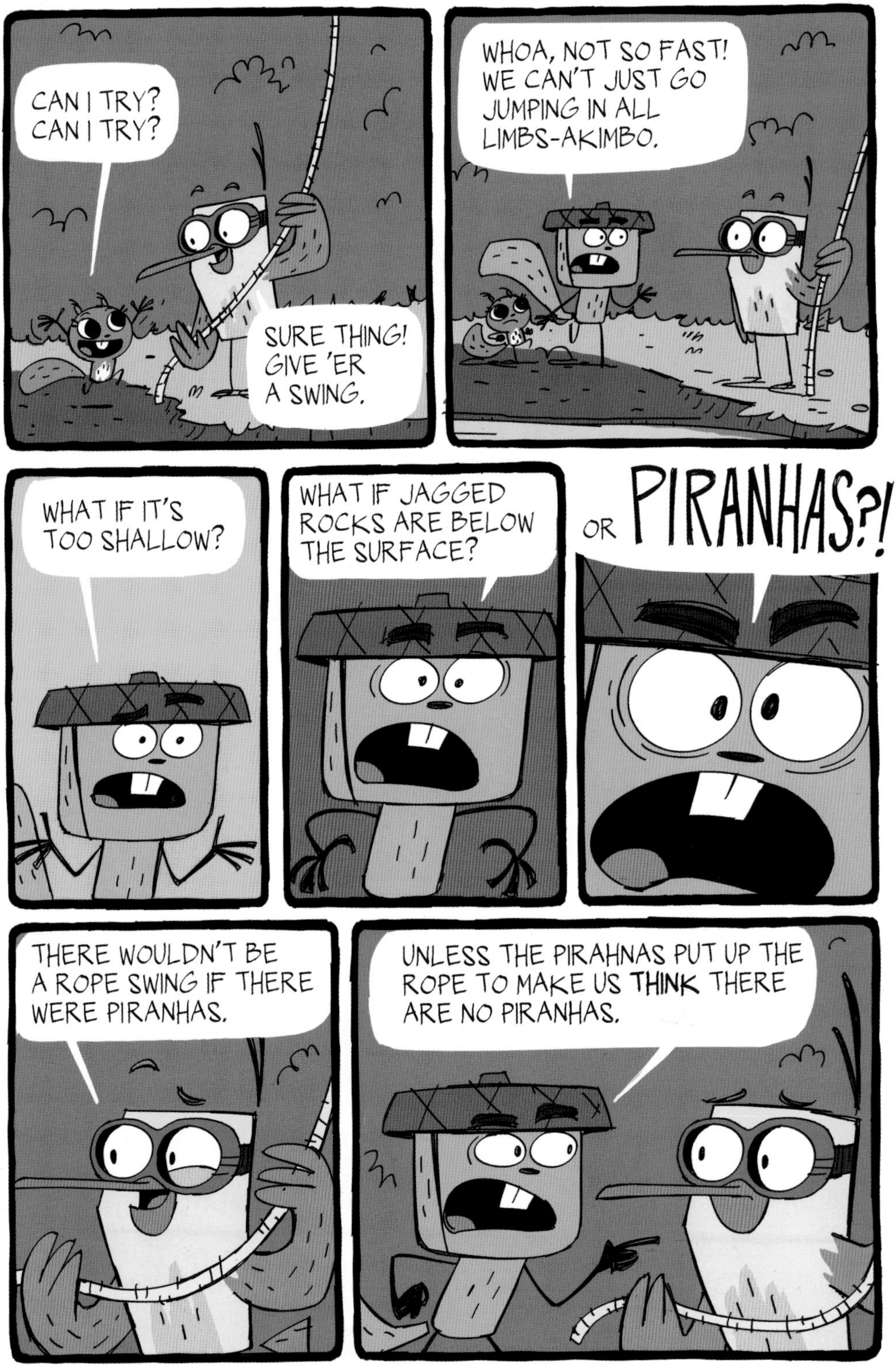
CAN I TRY? CAN I TRY?
SURE THING! GIVE 'ER A SWING.
WHOA, NOT SO FAST! WE CAN'T JUST GO JUMPING IN ALL LIMBS-AKIMBO.
WHAT IF IT'S TOO SHALLOW?
WHAT IF JAGGED ROCKS ARE BELOW THE SURFACE?
OR PIRANHAS?!
THERE WOULDN'T BE A ROPE SWING IF THERE WERE PIRANHAS.
UNLESS THE PIRAHNAS PUT UP THE ROPE TO MAKE US THINK THERE ARE NO PIRANHAS.

HMMM...

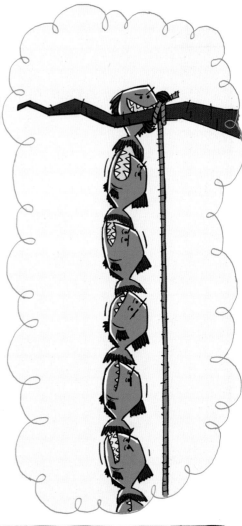

...I GUESS THAT IS A POSSIBILITY.

WHAT'S A PIRANHA?

THEY'RE FISH WITH RAZOR-SHARP TEETH AND...

ARE THEY SCARY?

...THEY'LL EAT THE FLESH RIGHT OFF YOUR BONES.

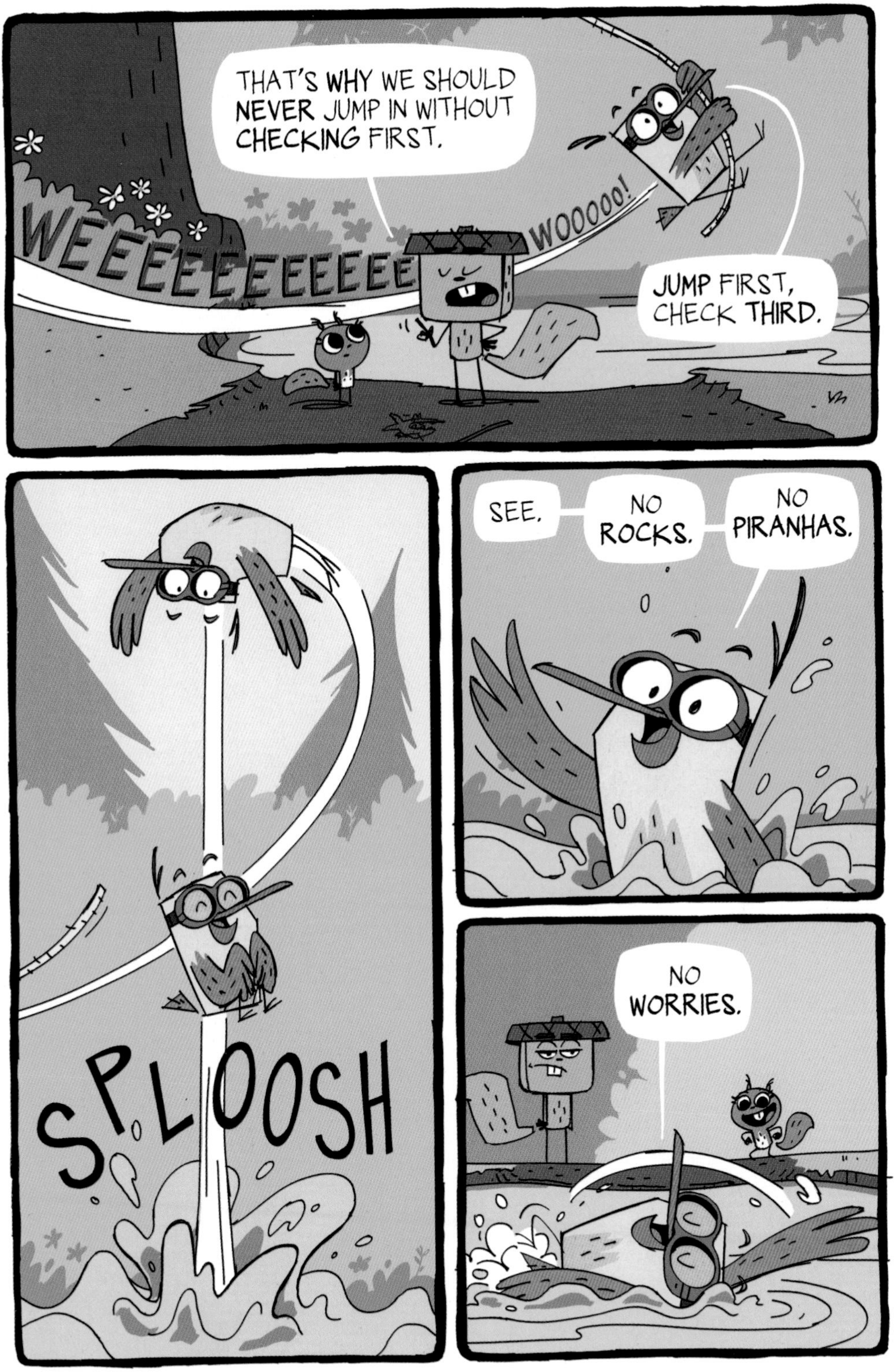
THAT'S WHY WE SHOULD NEVER JUMP IN WITHOUT CHECKING FIRST.
WEEEEEEEEEEEE
WOOOOO!
JUMP FIRST, CHECK THIRD.
SPLOOSH
SEE.
NO ROCKS.
NO PIRANHAS.
NO WORRIES.

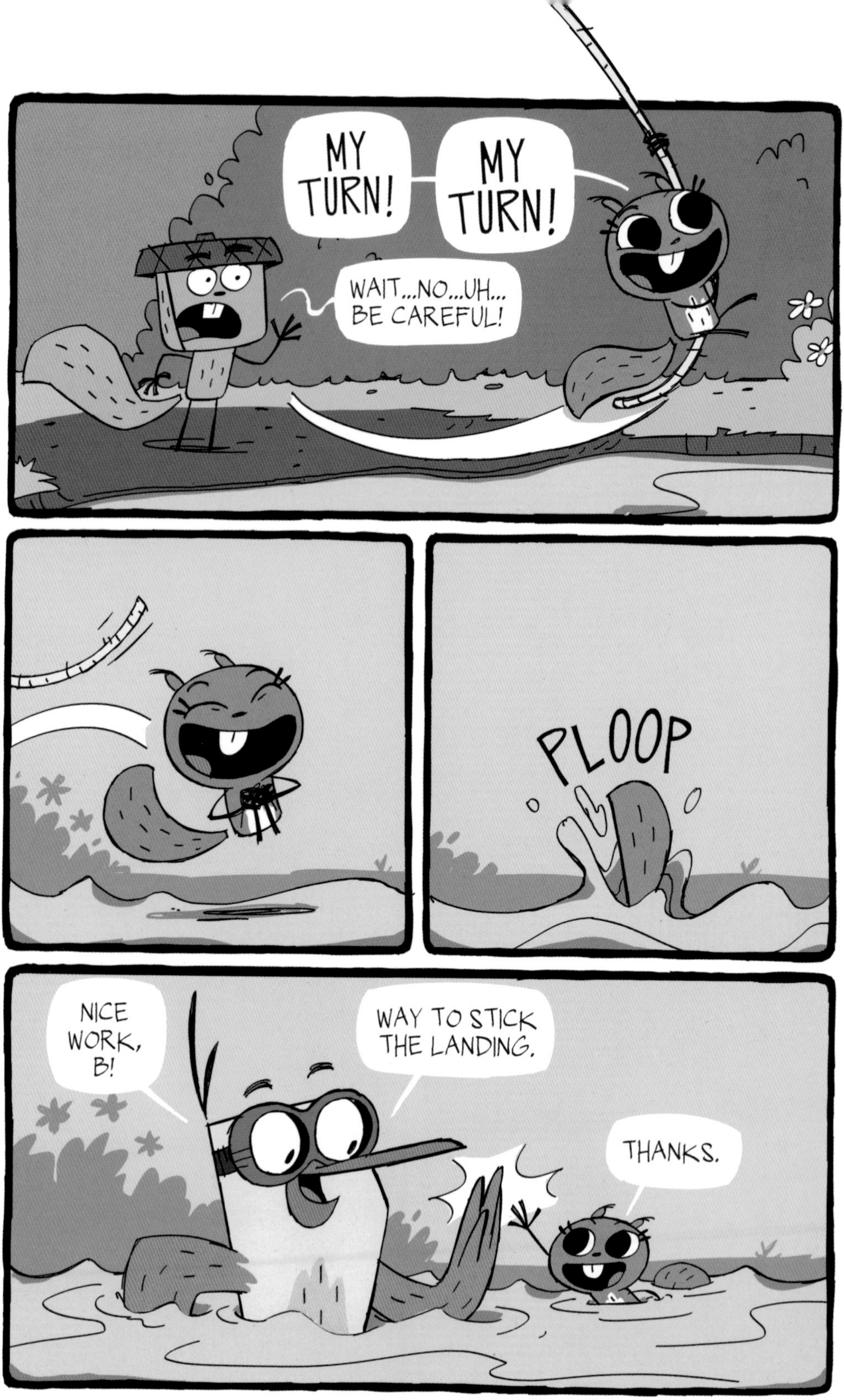
MY TURN!
MY TURN!
WAIT...NO...UH... BE CAREFUL!
PLOOP
NICE WORK, B!
WAY TO STICK THE LANDING.
THANKS.

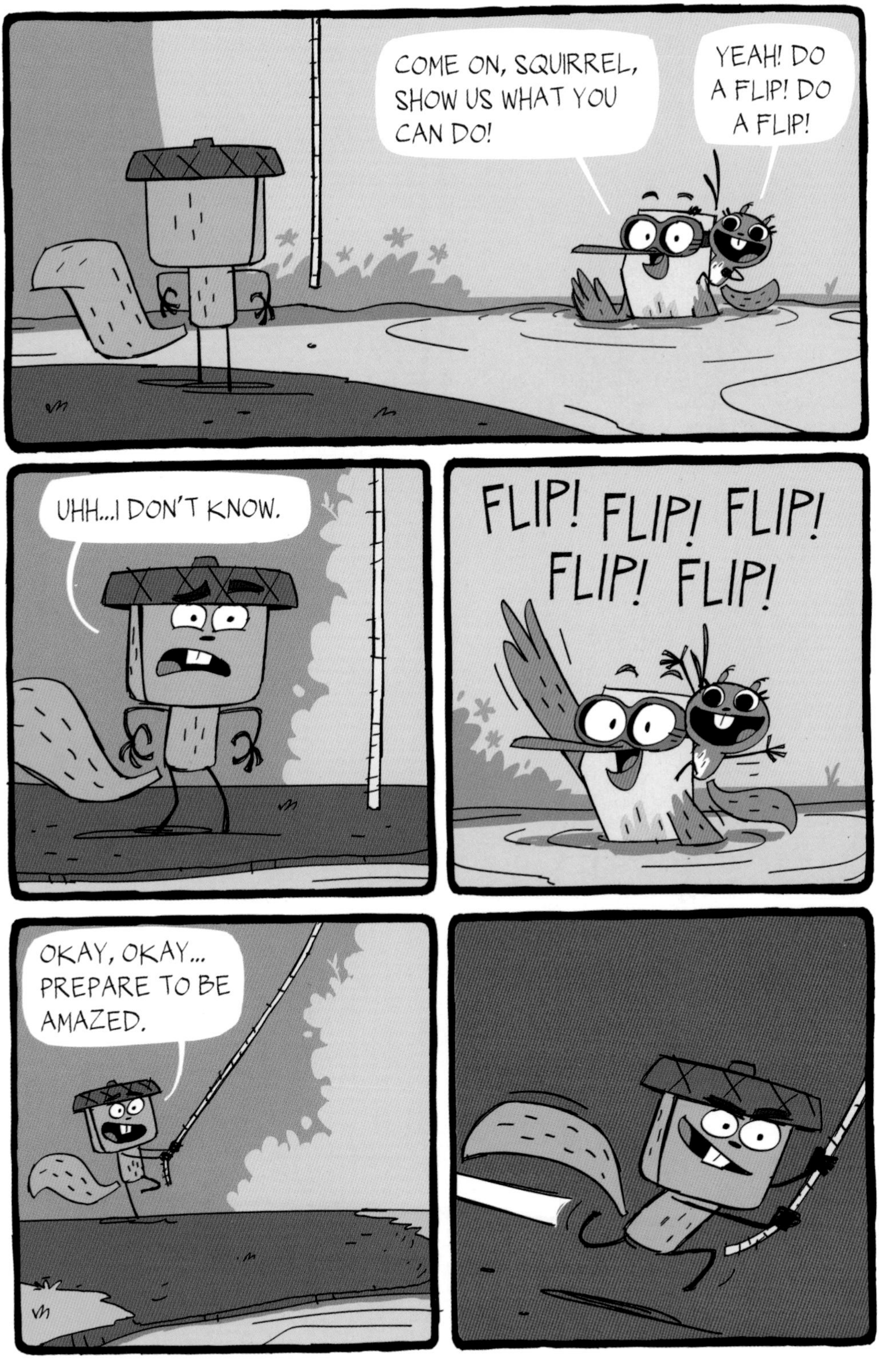
COME ON, SQUIRREL, SHOW US WHAT YOU CAN DO!
YEAH! DO A FLIP! DO A FLIP!
UHH...I DON'T KNOW.
FLIP! FLIP! FLIP! FLIP! FLIP!
OKAY, OKAY... PREPARE TO BE AMAZED.

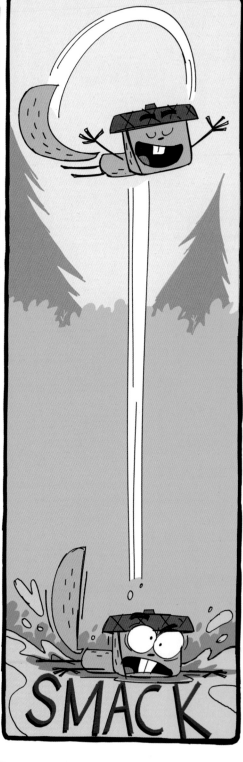

SMACK

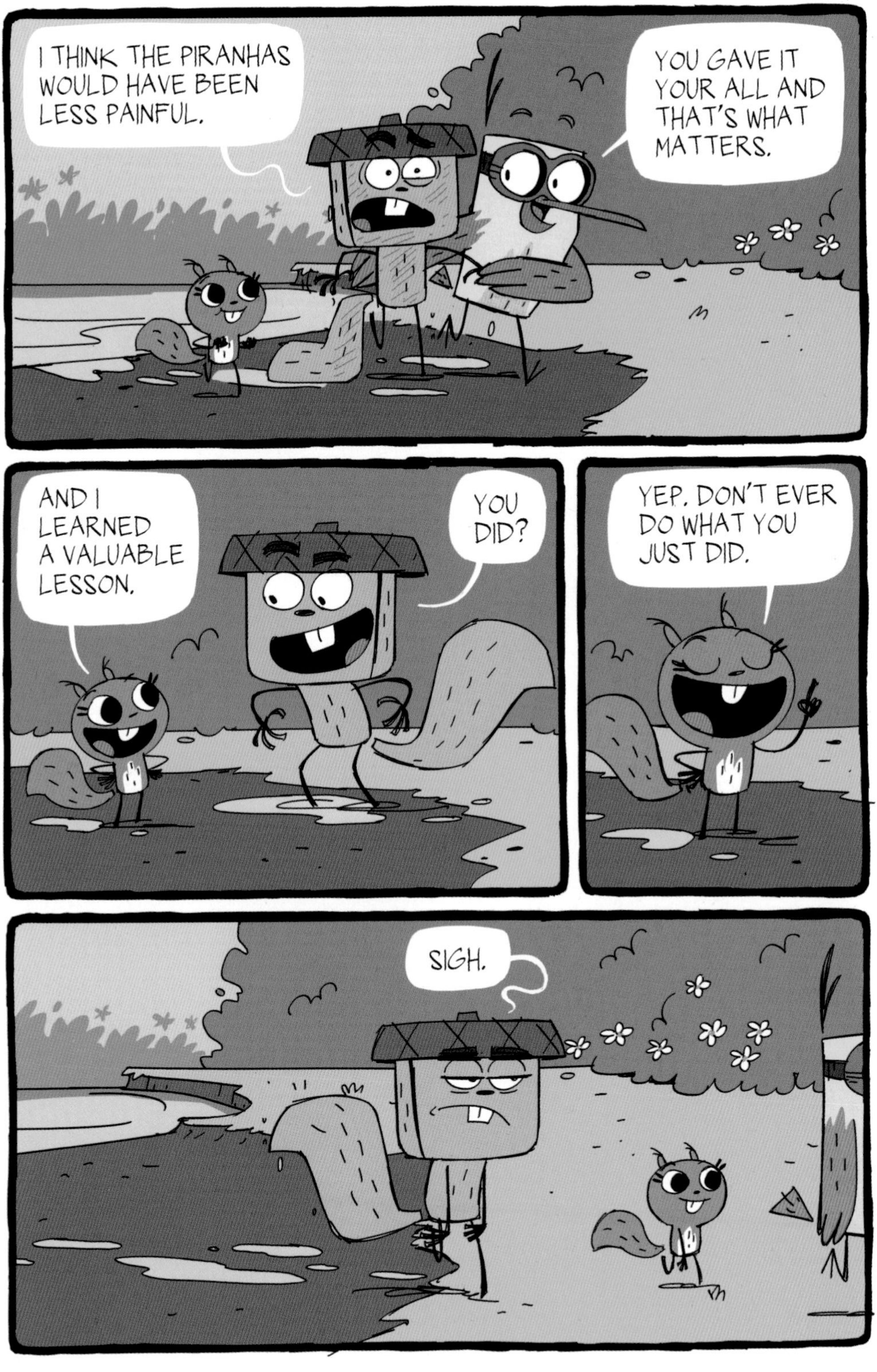
I THINK THE PIRANHAS WOULD HAVE BEEN LESS PAINFUL.
YOU GAVE IT YOUR ALL AND THAT'S WHAT MATTERS.
AND I LEARNED A VALUABLE LESSON.
YOU DID?
YEP. DON'T EVER DO WHAT YOU JUST DID.
SIGH.

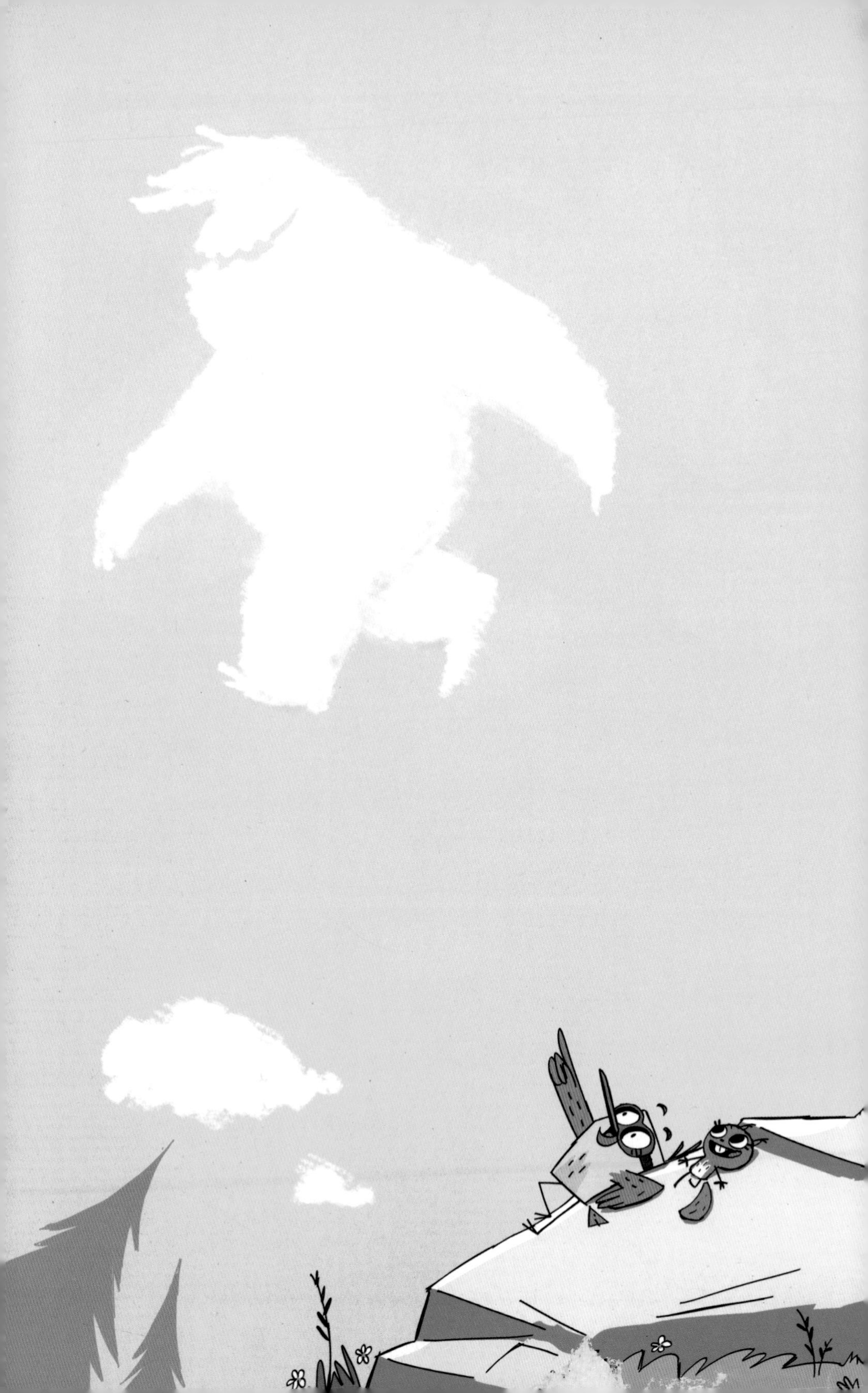

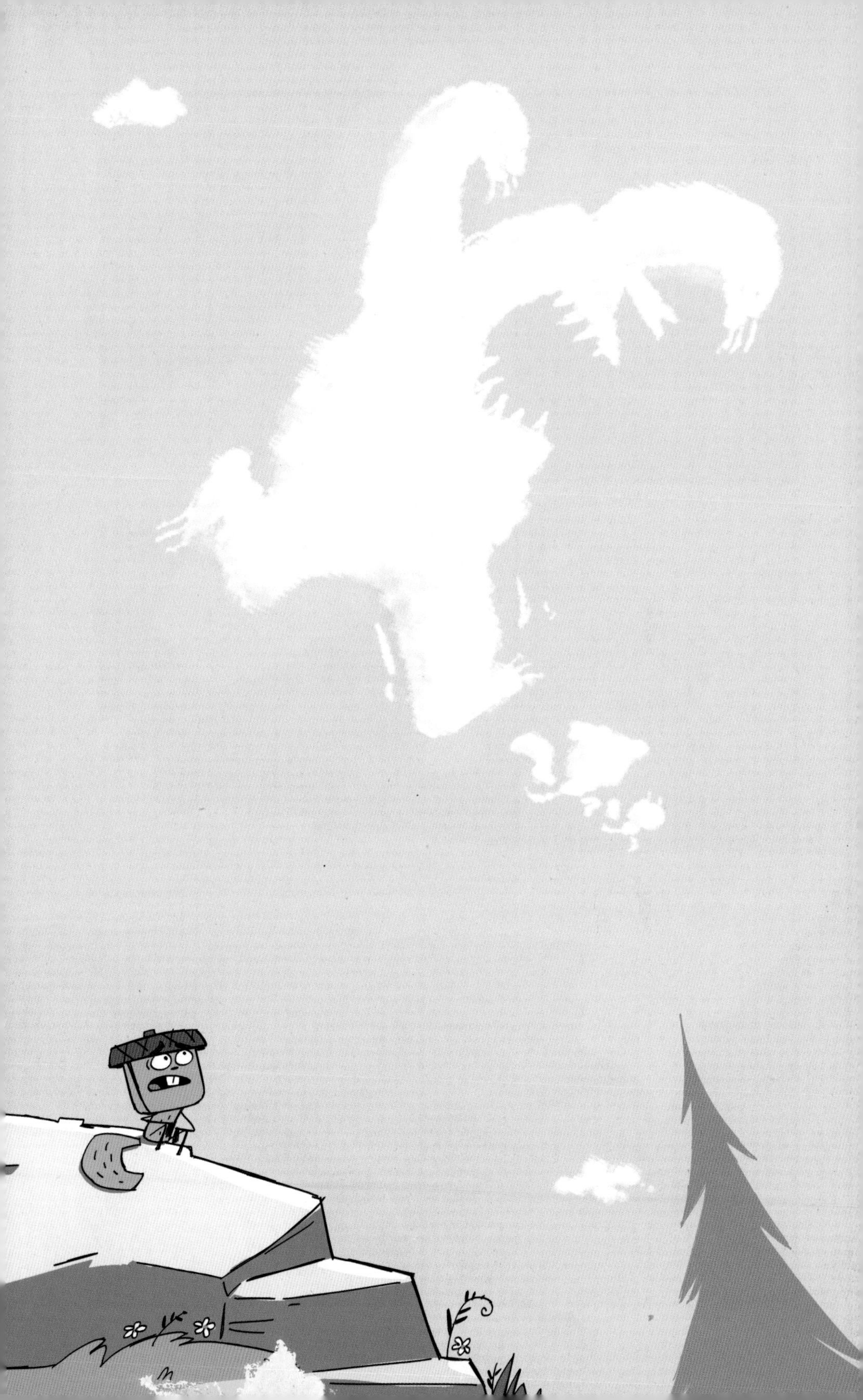

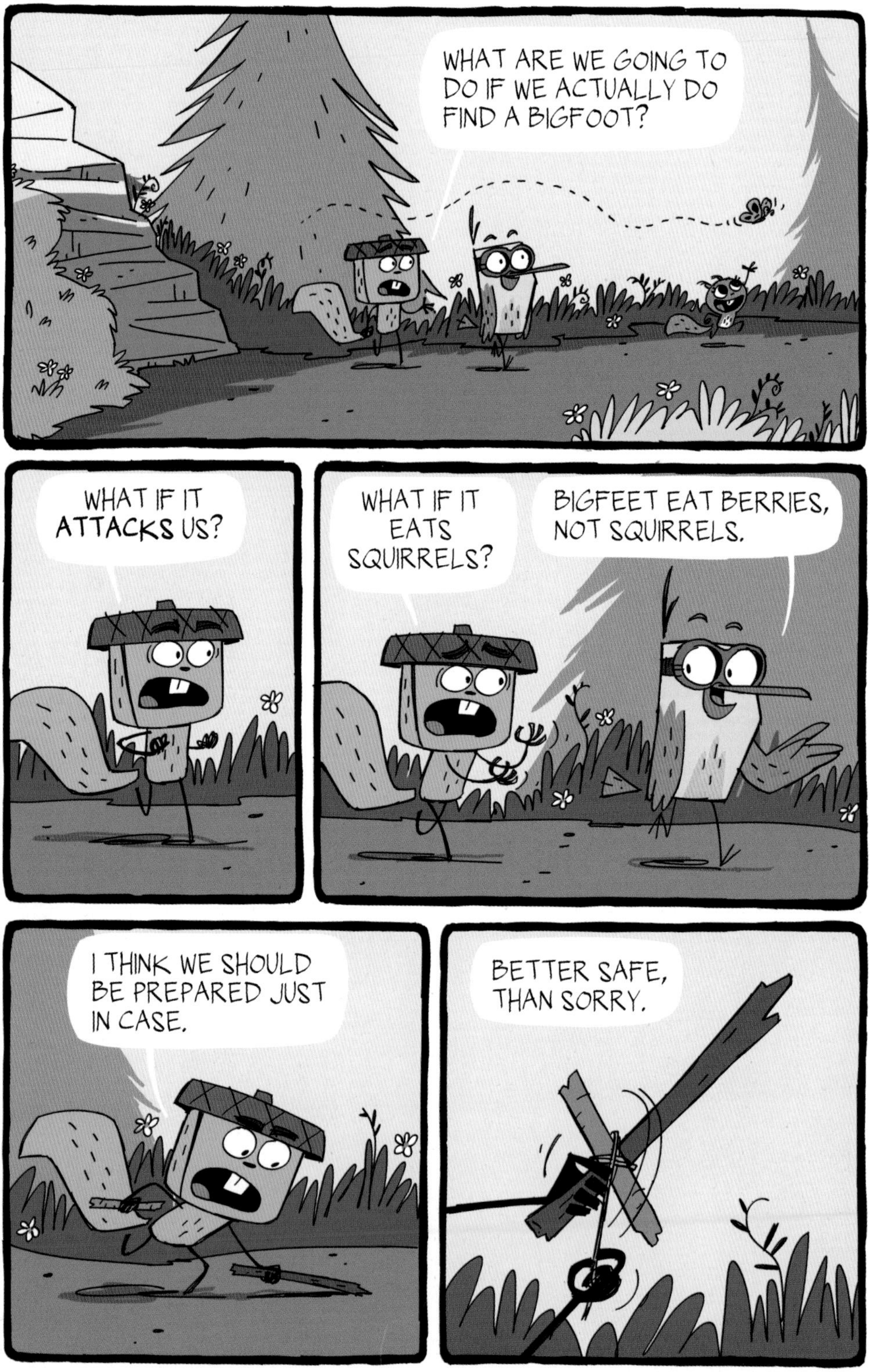
WHAT ARE WE GOING TO DO IF WE ACTUALLY DO FIND A BIGFOOT?
WHAT IF IT **ATTACKS** US?
WHAT IF IT EATS SQUIRRELS?
BIGFEET EAT BERRIES, NOT SQUIRRELS.
I THINK WE SHOULD BE PREPARED JUST IN CASE.
BETTER SAFE, THAN SORRY.

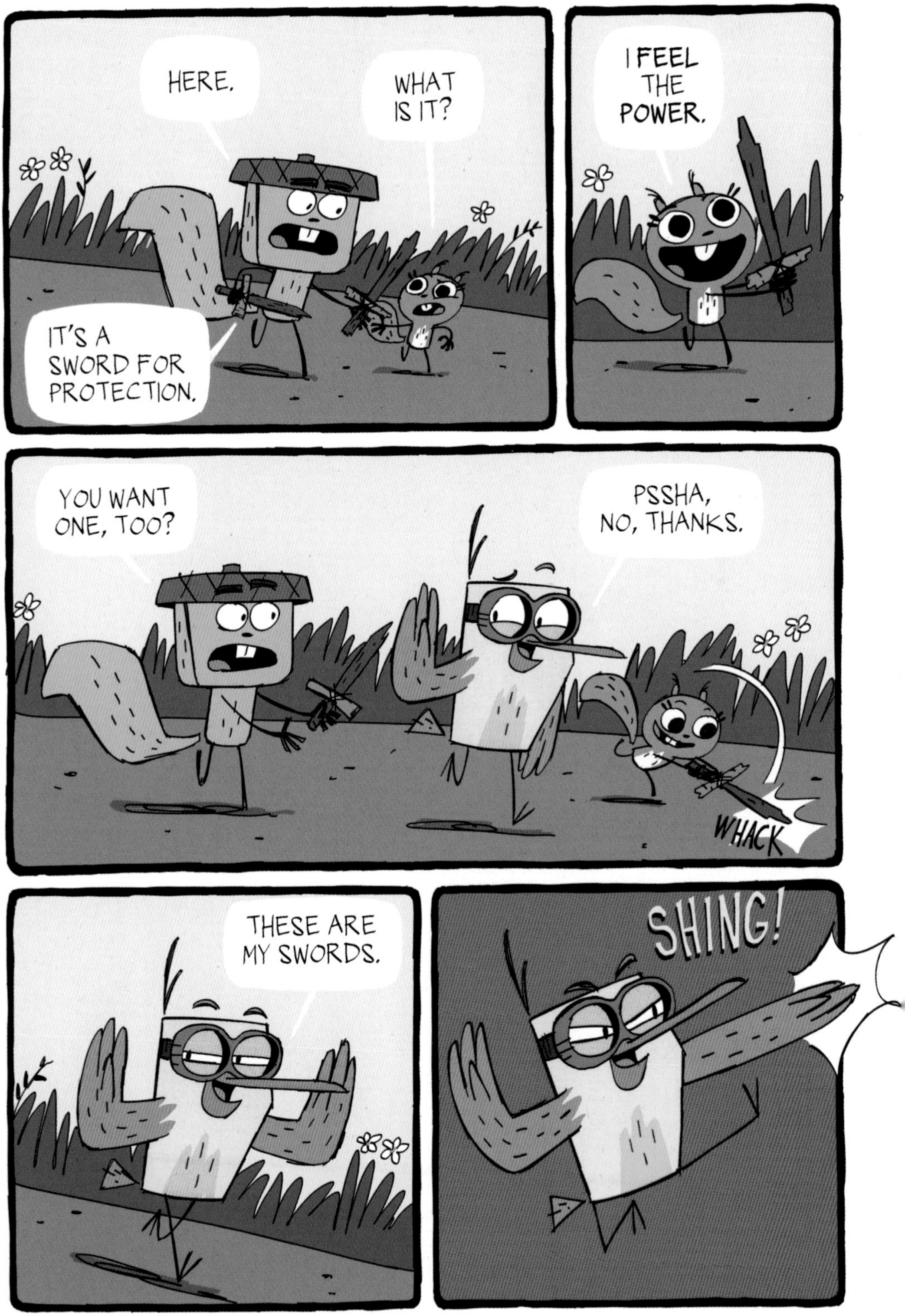
HERE.
WHAT IS IT?
IT'S A SWORD FOR PROTECTION.
I FEEL THE POWER.
YOU WANT ONE, TOO?
PSSHA, NO, THANKS.
WHACK
THESE ARE MY SWORDS.
SHING!

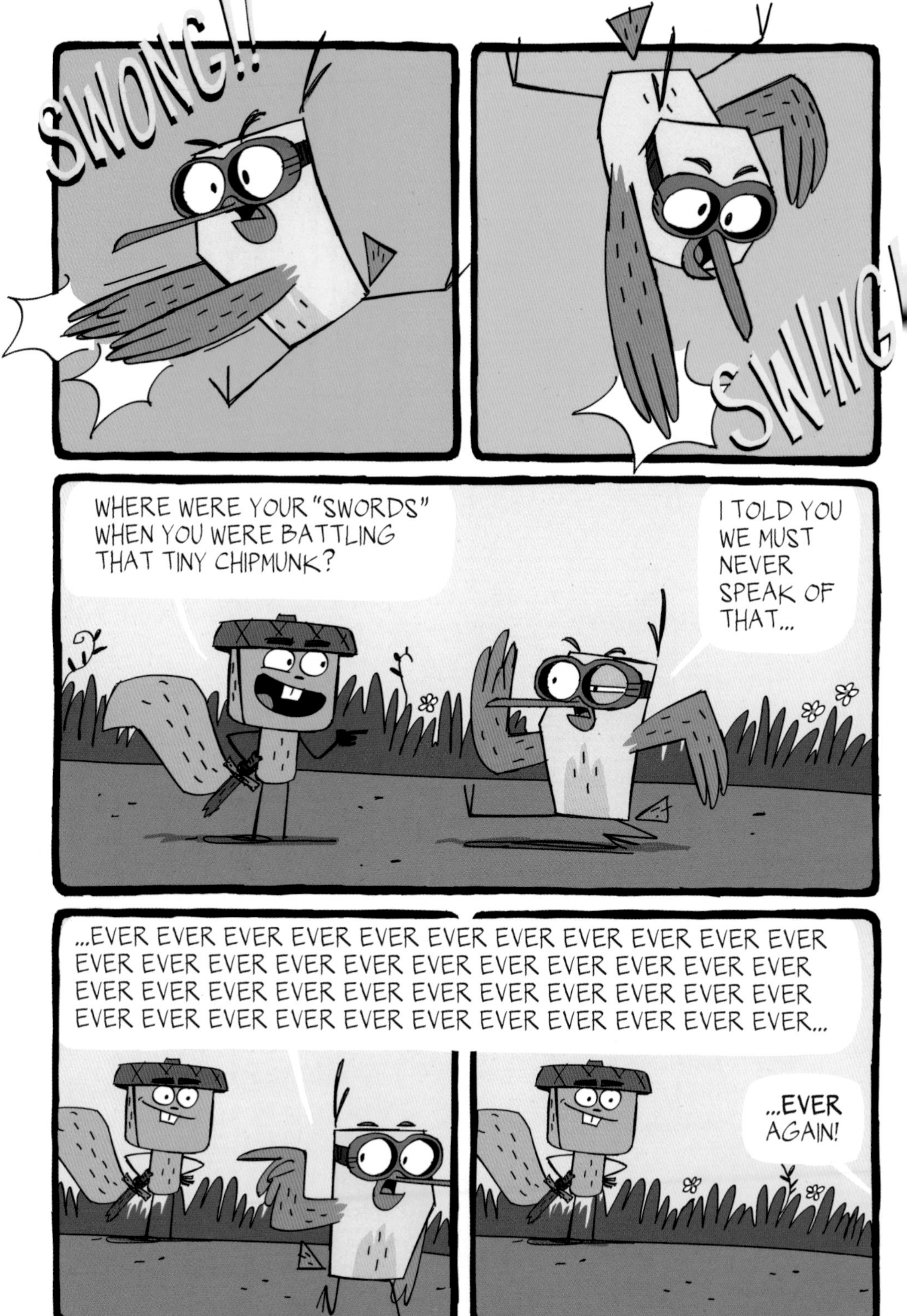
SWONG!!
SWING
WHERE WERE YOUR "SWORDS" WHEN YOU WERE BATTLING THAT TINY CHIPMUNK?
I TOLD YOU WE MUST NEVER SPEAK OF THAT...
...EVER EVER EVER EVER EVER EVER EVER EVER EVER EVER EVER EVER EVER EVER EVER EVER EVER EVER EVER EVER EVER EVER EVER EVER EVER EVER EVER EVER EVER EVER EVER EVER EVER EVER EVER EVER EVER EVER EVER EVER EVER EVER EVER EVER...
...EVER AGAIN!

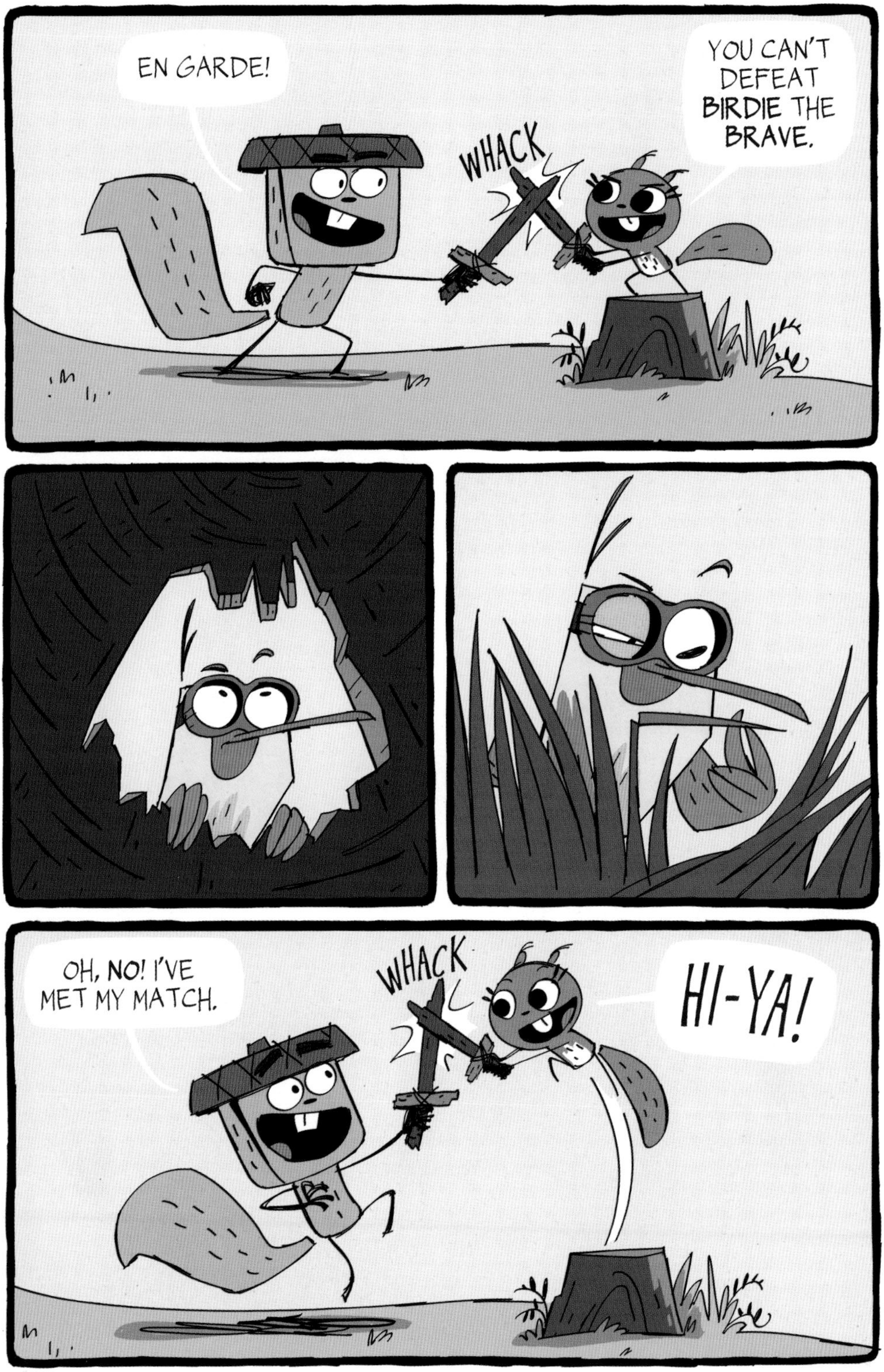
EN GARDE!
WHACK
YOU CAN'T DEFEAT BIRDIE THE BRAVE.
OH, NO! I'VE MET MY MATCH.
WHACK
HI-YA!

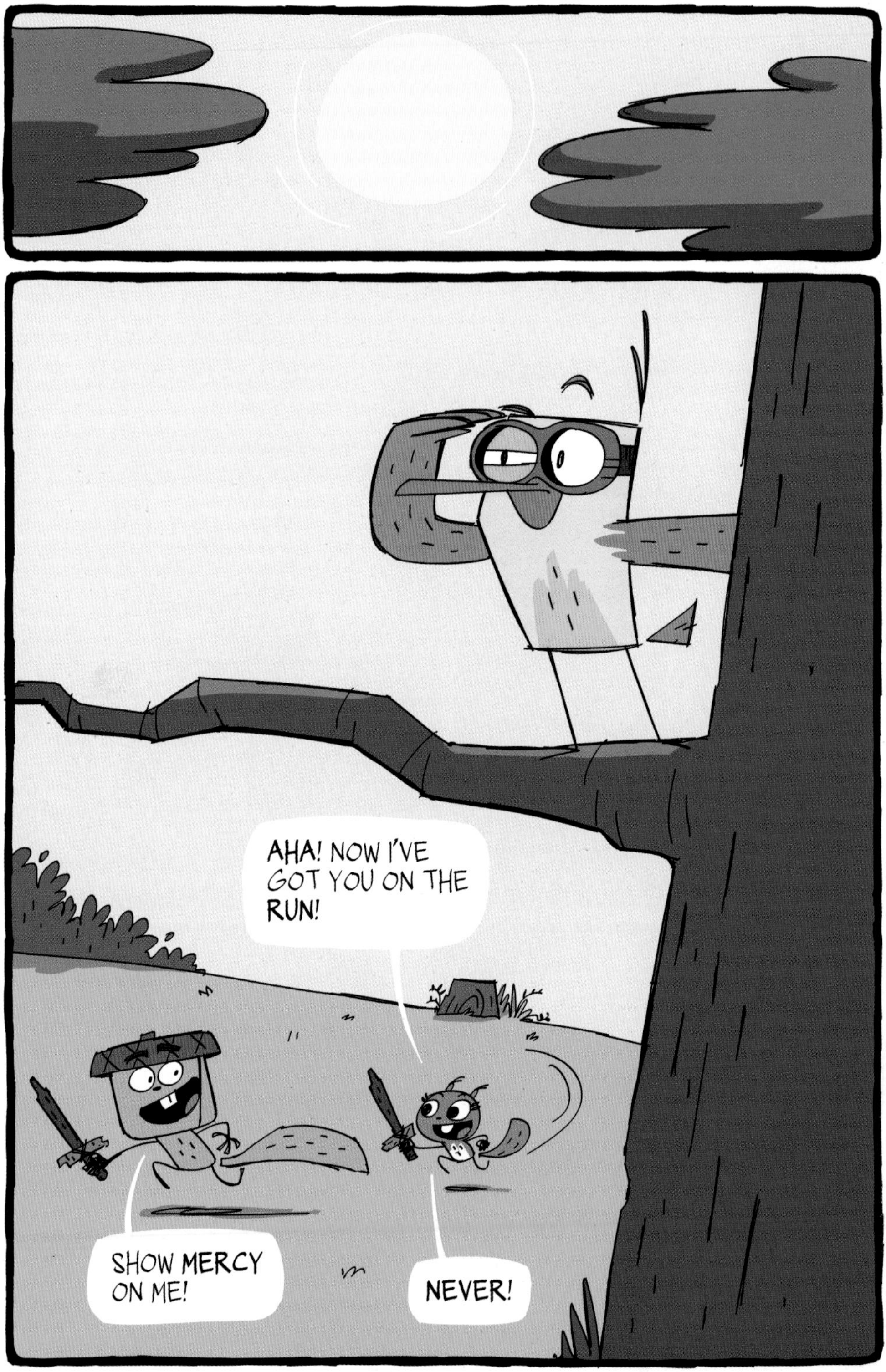
AHA! NOW I'VE GOT YOU ON THE RUN!
SHOW MERCY ON ME!
NEVER!

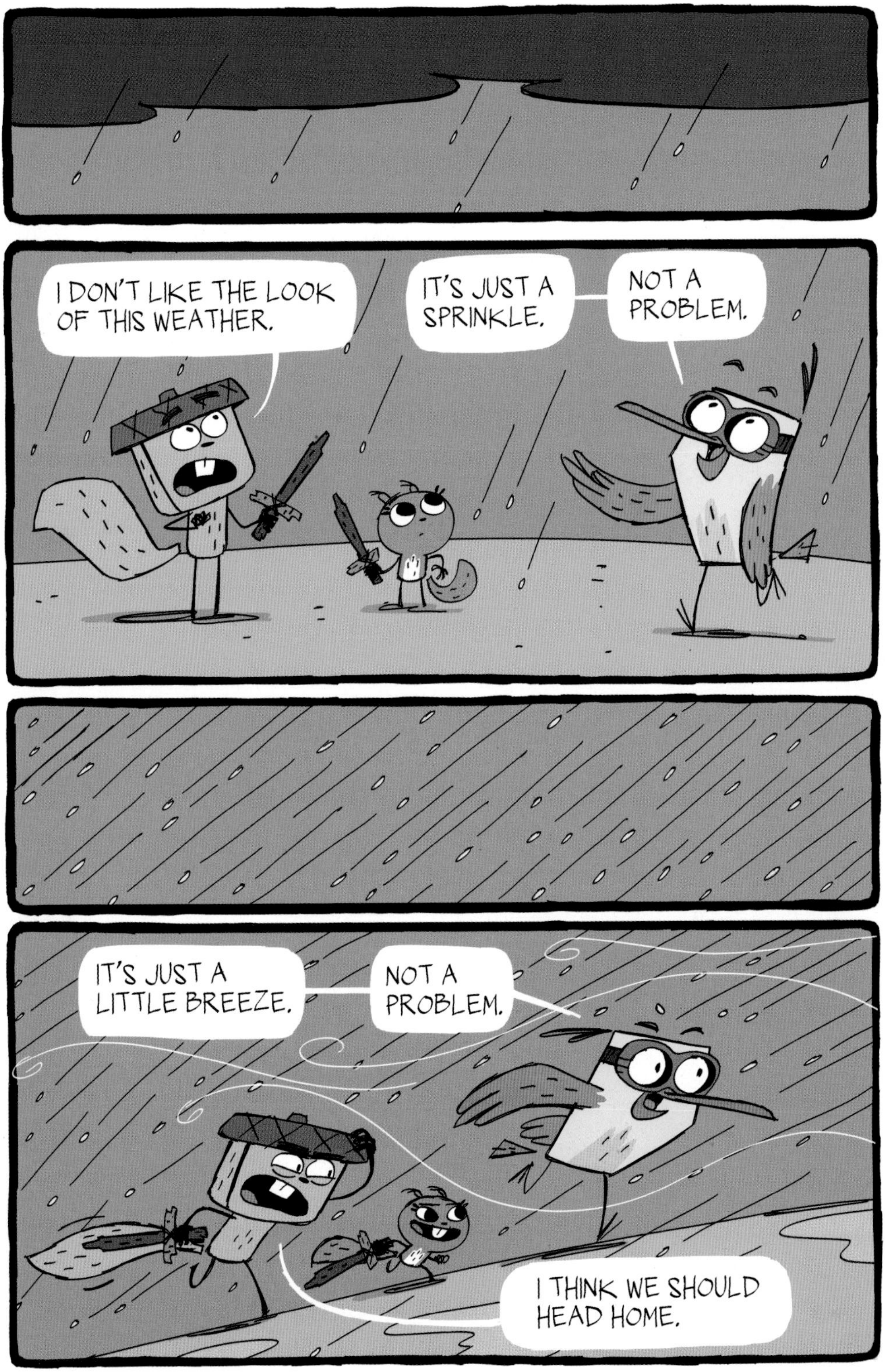
I DON'T LIKE THE LOOK OF THIS WEATHER.
IT'S JUST A SPRINKLE.
NOT A PROBLEM.
IT'S JUST A LITTLE BREEZE.
NOT A PROBLEM.
I THINK WE SHOULD HEAD HOME.

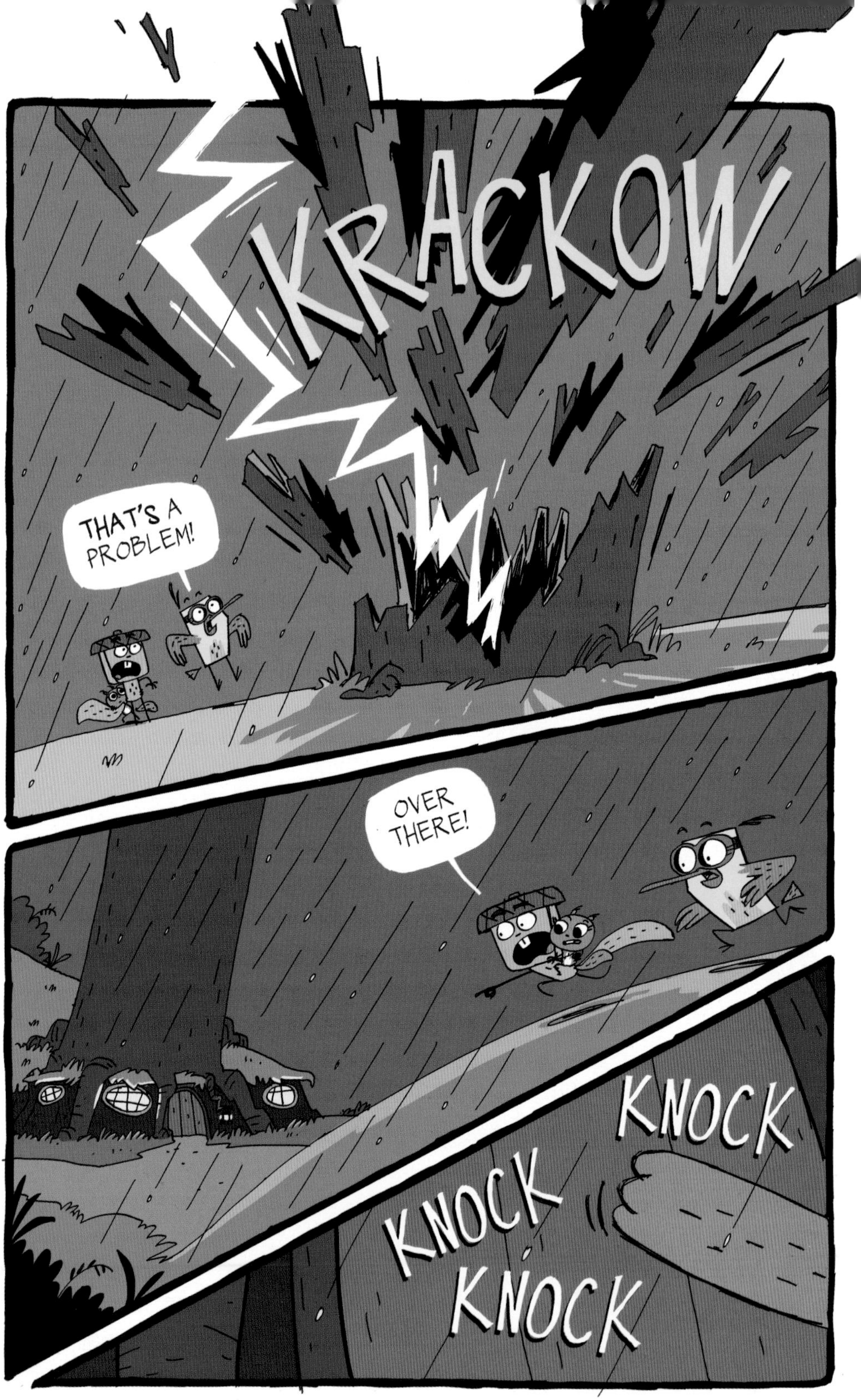
KRACKOW
THAT'S A PROBLEM!
OVER THERE!
KNOCK
KNOCK
KNOCK

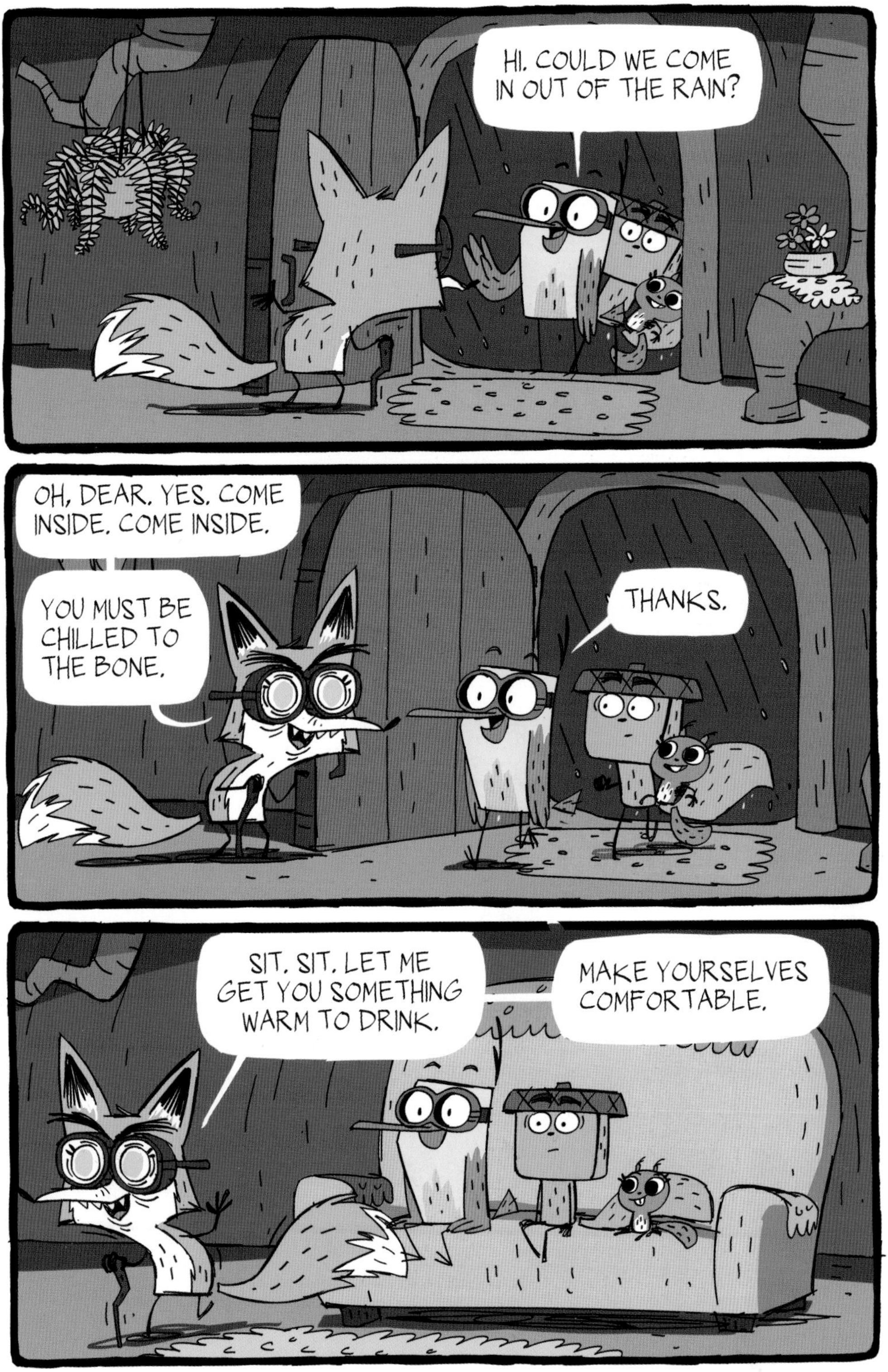
HI. COULD WE COME IN OUT OF THE RAIN?
OH, DEAR. YES. COME INSIDE. COME INSIDE.
YOU MUST BE CHILLED TO THE BONE.
THANKS.
SIT. SIT. LET ME GET YOU SOMETHING WARM TO DRINK.
MAKE YOURSELVES COMFORTABLE.

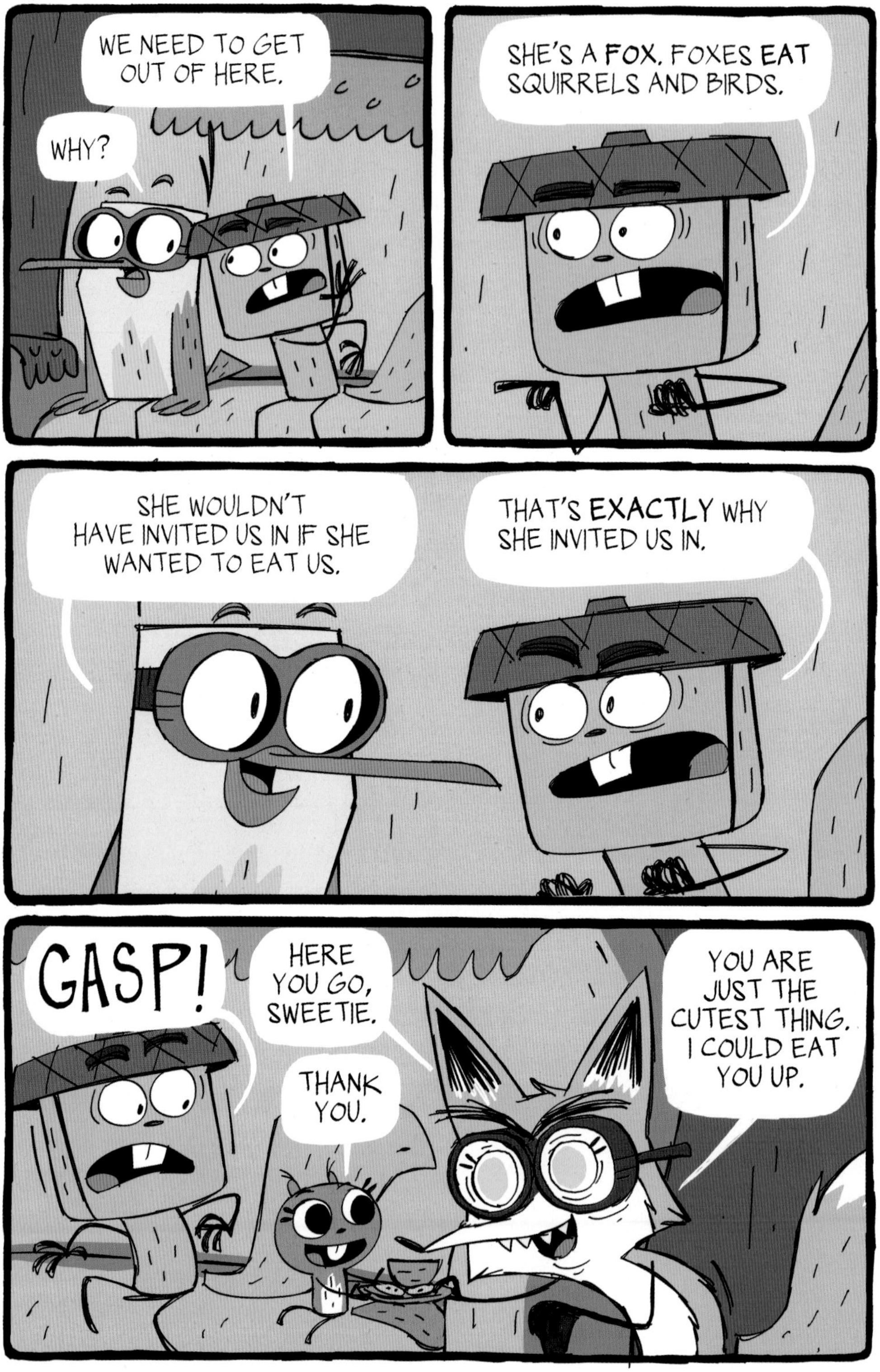
WE NEED TO GET OUT OF HERE.
WHY?
SHE'S A FOX. FOXES EAT SQUIRRELS AND BIRDS.
SHE WOULDN'T HAVE INVITED US IN IF SHE WANTED TO EAT US.
THAT'S EXACTLY WHY SHE INVITED US IN.
GASP!
HERE YOU GO, SWEETIE.
THANK YOU.
YOU ARE JUST THE CUTEST THING. I COULD EAT YOU UP.

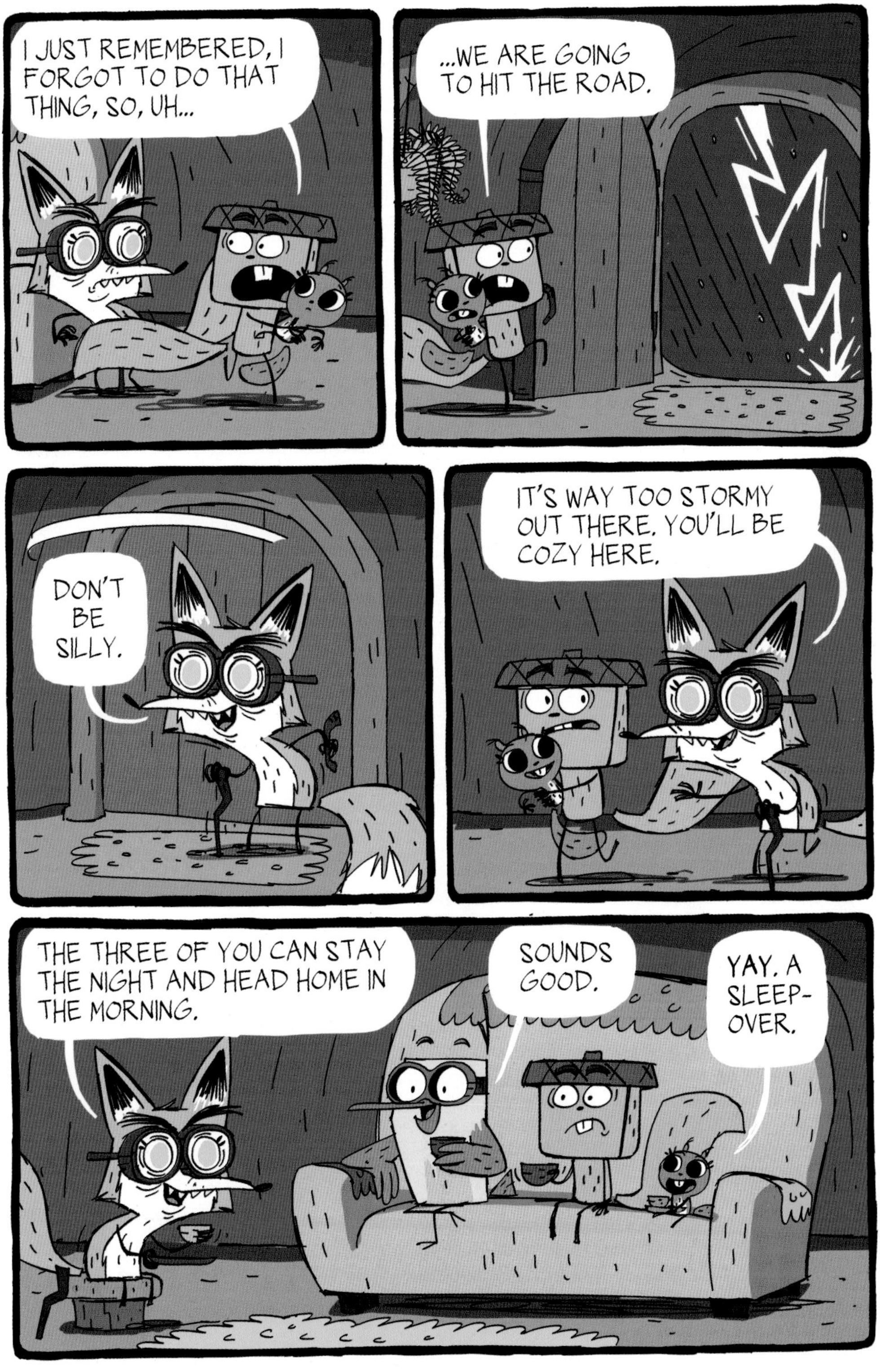
I JUST REMEMBERED, I FORGOT TO DO THAT THING, SO, UH...
...WE ARE GOING TO HIT THE ROAD.
DON'T BE SILLY.
IT'S WAY TOO STORMY OUT THERE. YOU'LL BE COZY HERE.
THE THREE OF YOU CAN STAY THE NIGHT AND HEAD HOME IN THE MORNING.
SOUNDS GOOD.
YAY. A SLEEP-OVER.

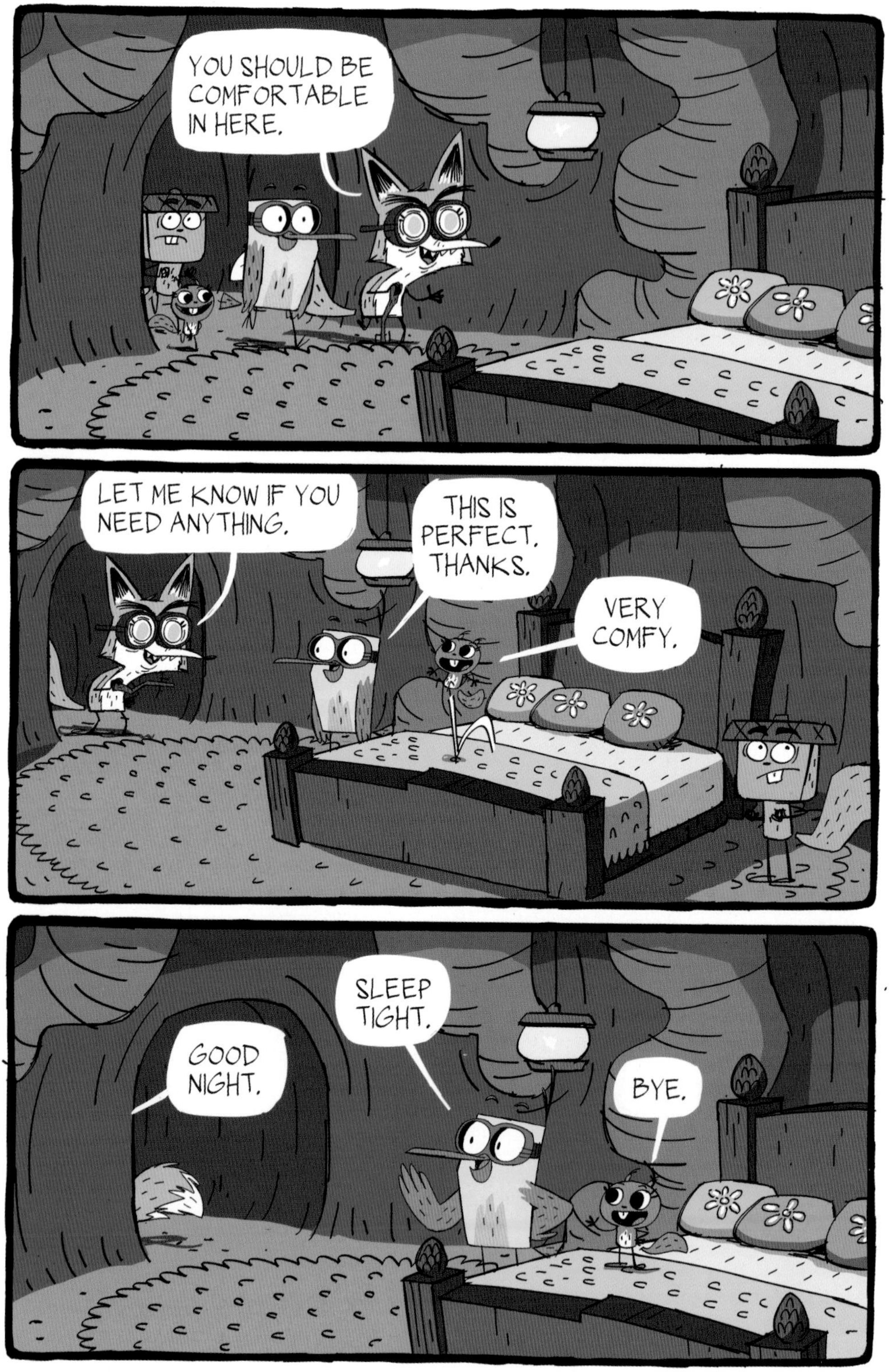
YOU SHOULD BE COMFORTABLE IN HERE.
LET ME KNOW IF YOU NEED ANYTHING.
THIS IS PERFECT. THANKS.
VERY COMFY.
GOOD NIGHT.
SLEEP TIGHT.
BYE.

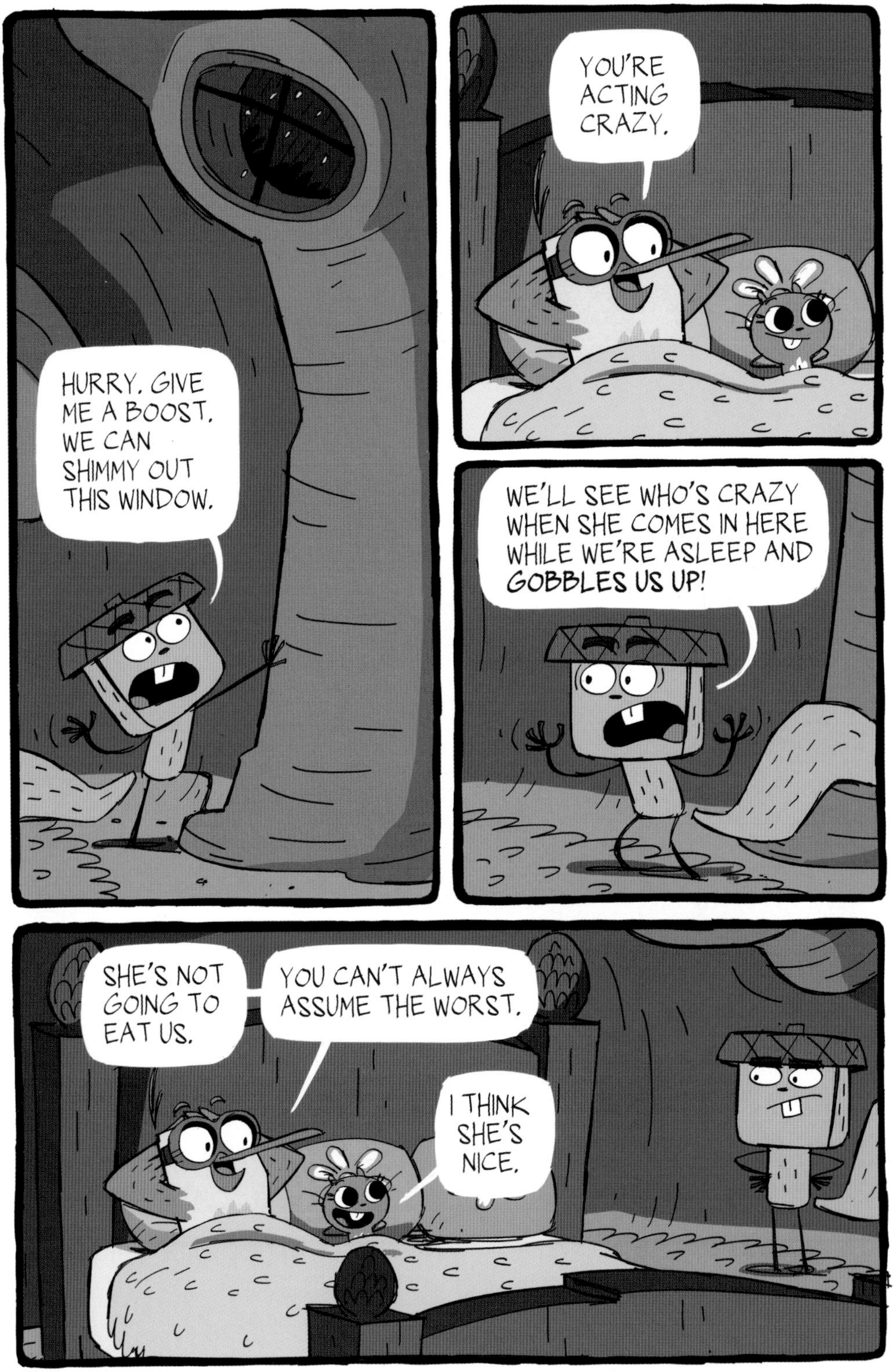
HURRY. GIVE ME A BOOST. WE CAN SHIMMY OUT THIS WINDOW.
YOU'RE ACTING CRAZY.
WE'LL SEE WHO'S CRAZY WHEN SHE COMES IN HERE WHILE WE'RE ASLEEP AND GOBBLES US UP!
SHE'S NOT GOING TO EAT US.
YOU CAN'T ALWAYS ASSUME THE WORST.
I THINK SHE'S NICE.

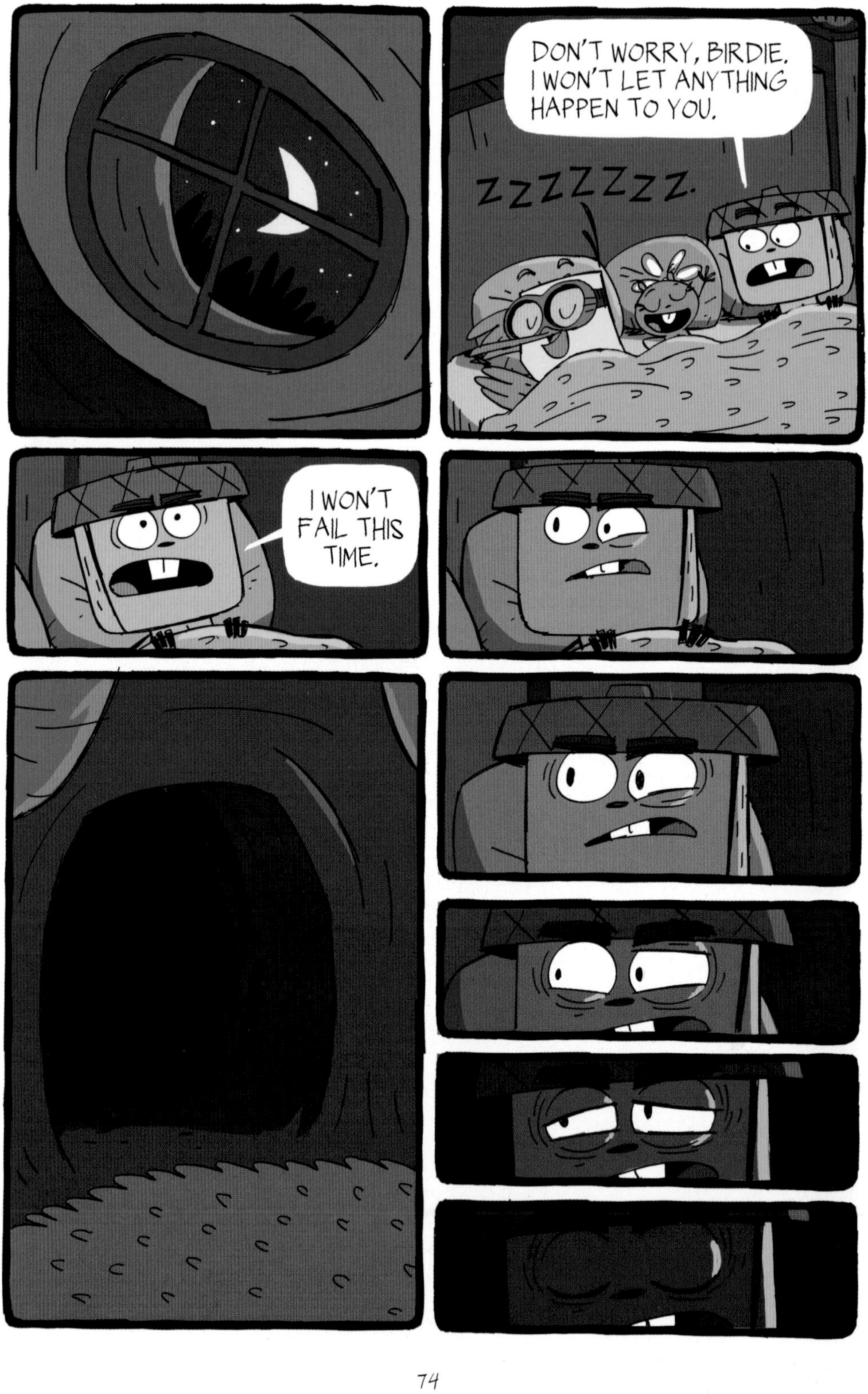
DON'T WORRY, BIRDIE. I WON'T LET ANYTHING HAPPEN TO YOU.
ZZZZZZZ.
I WON'T FAIL THIS TIME.

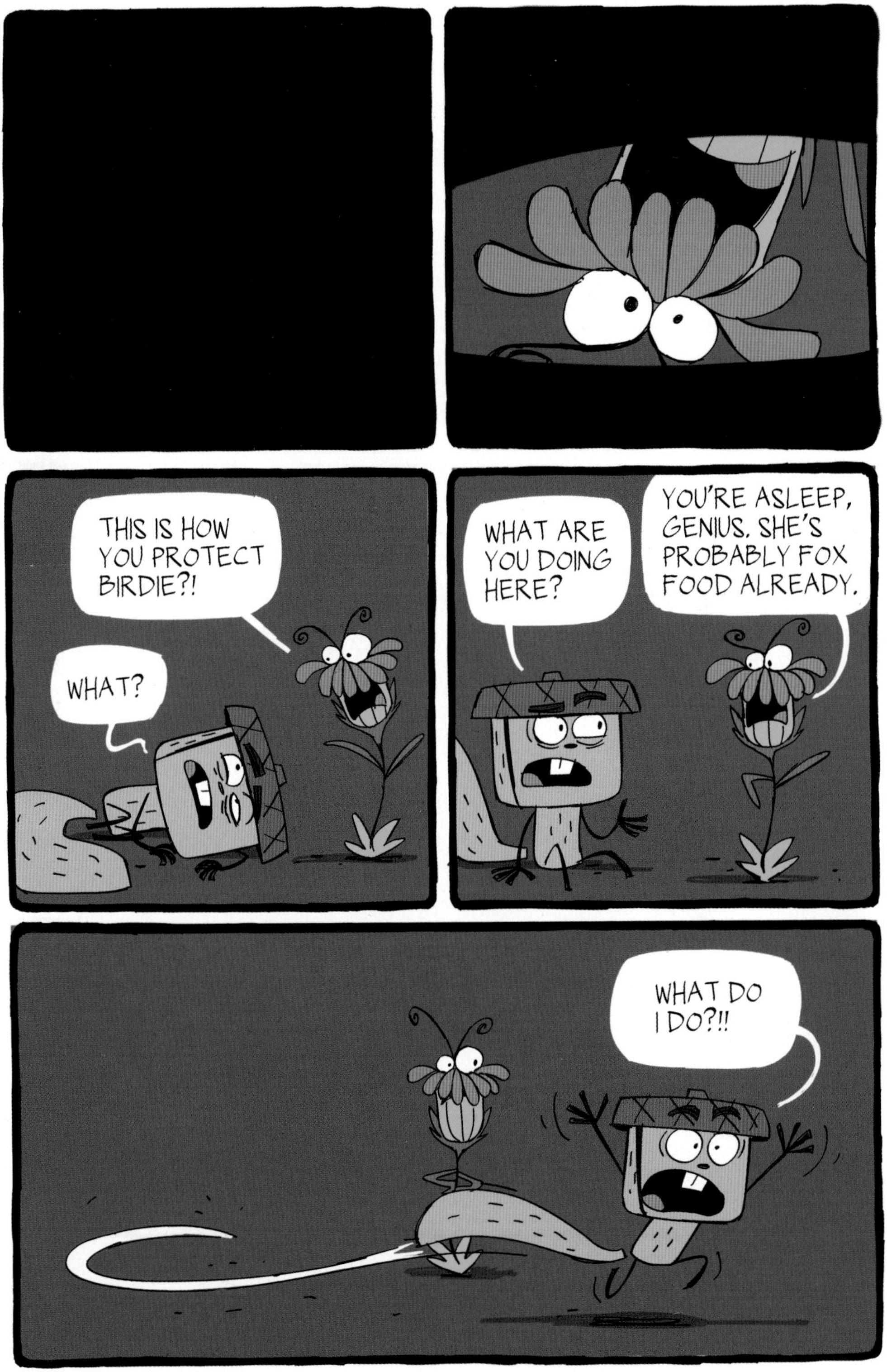
THIS IS HOW YOU PROTECT BIRDIE?!
WHAT?
WHAT ARE YOU DOING HERE?
YOU'RE ASLEEP, GENIUS. SHE'S PROBABLY FOX FOOD ALREADY.
WHAT DO I DO?!!

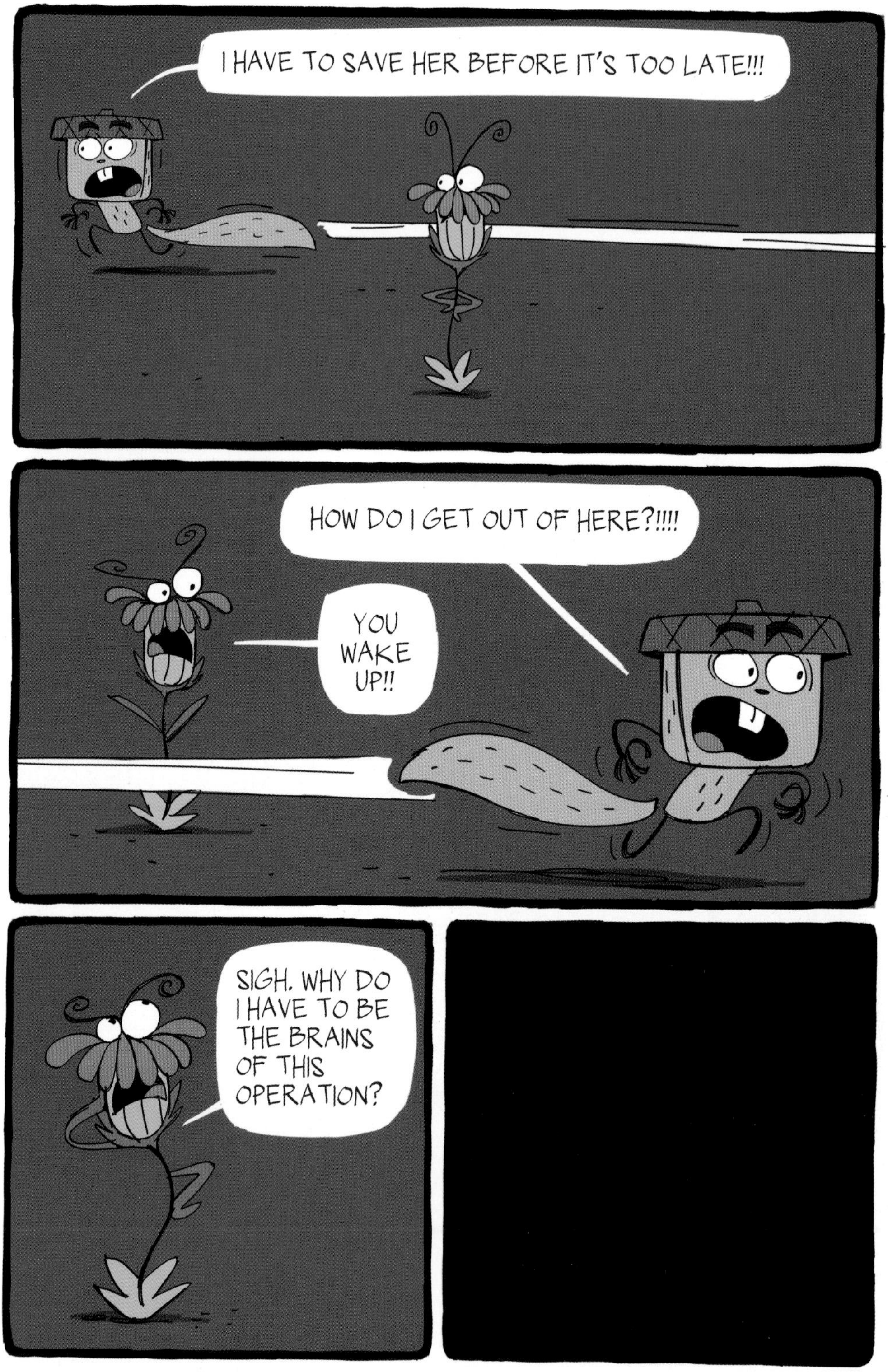
I HAVE TO SAVE HER BEFORE IT'S TOO LATE!!!
HOW DO I GET OUT OF HERE?!!!!
YOU WAKE UP!!
SIGH. WHY DO I HAVE TO BE THE BRAINS OF THIS OPERATION?

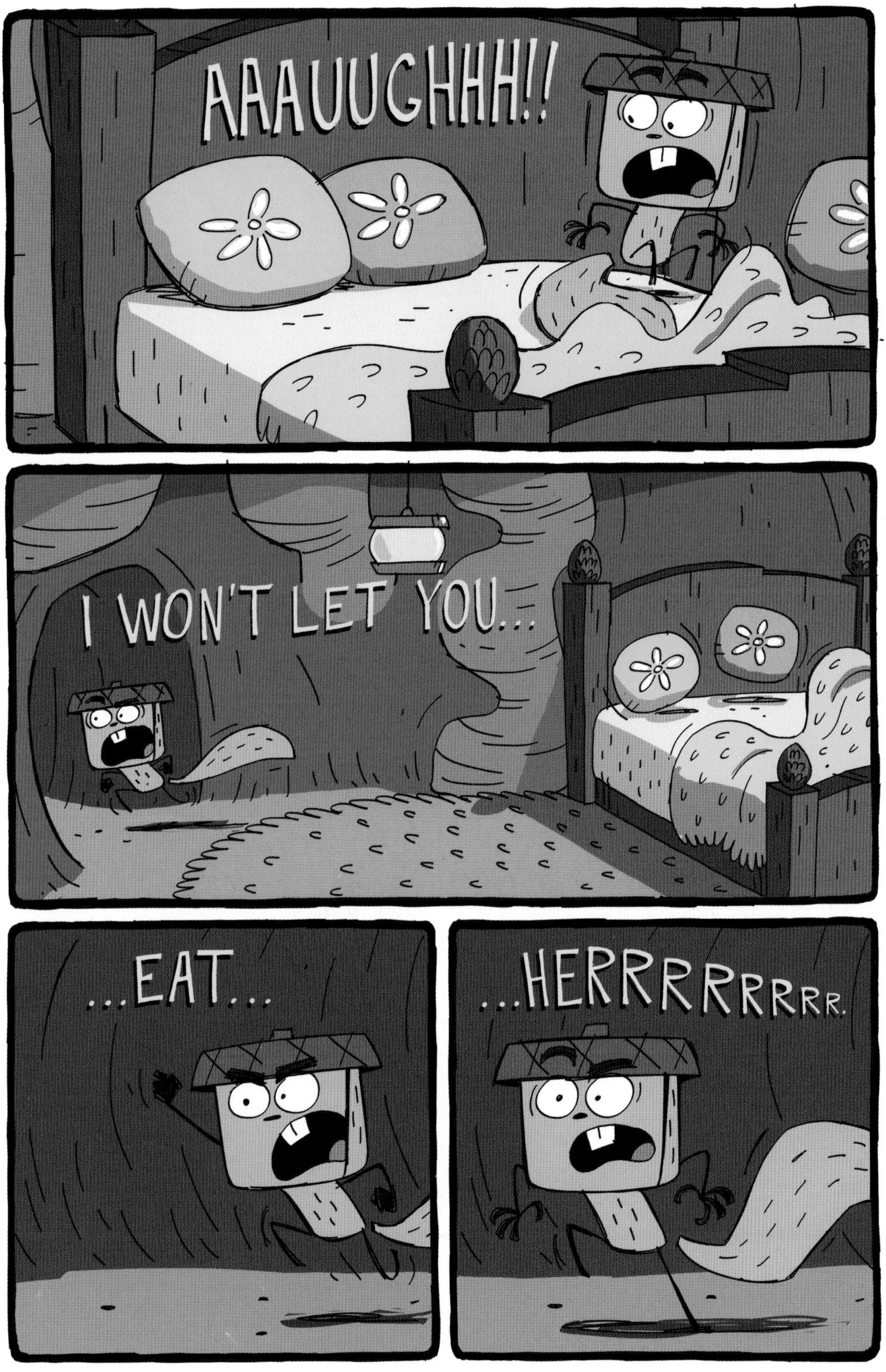
AAAUUGHHH!!
I WON'T LET YOU...
...EAT...
...HERRRRRRRR.

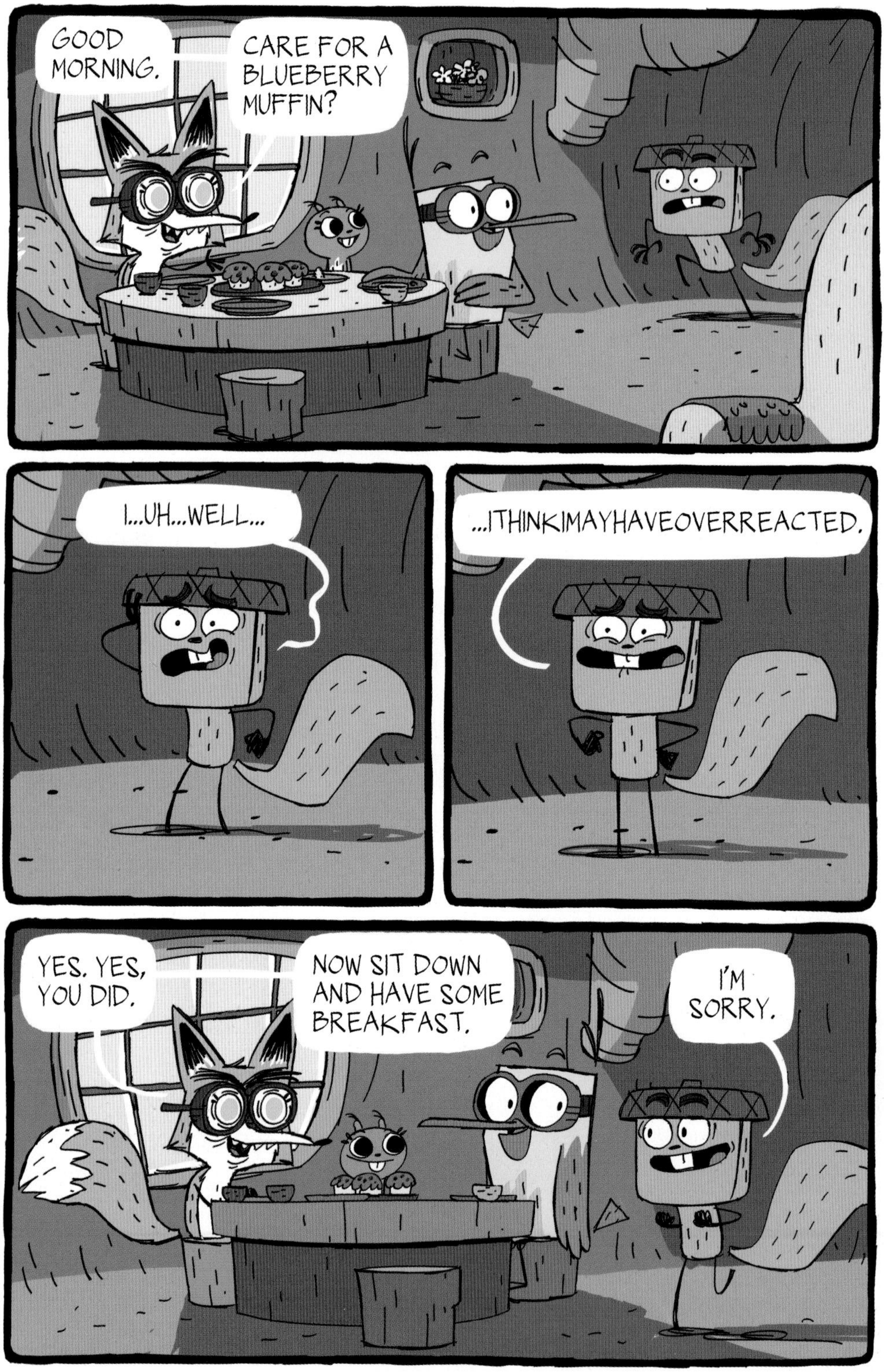
GOOD MORNING.
CARE FOR A BLUEBERRY MUFFIN?
I...UH...WELL...
...ITHINKIMAYHAVEOVERREACTED.
YES. YES, YOU DID.
NOW SIT DOWN AND HAVE SOME BREAKFAST.
I'M SORRY.

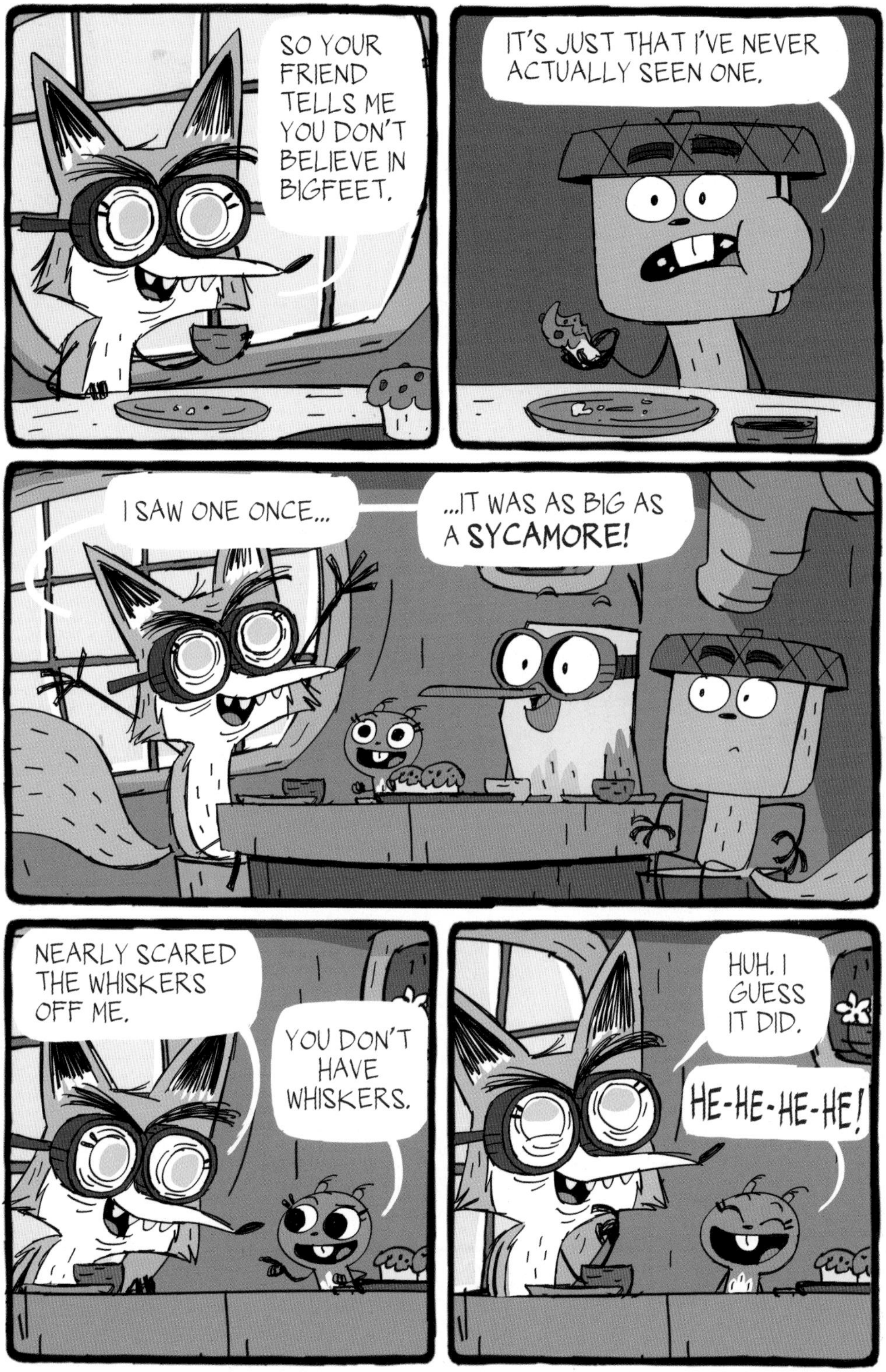
SO YOUR FRIEND TELLS ME YOU DON'T BELIEVE IN BIGFEET.
IT'S JUST THAT I'VE NEVER ACTUALLY SEEN ONE.
I SAW ONE ONCE...
...IT WAS AS BIG AS A **SYCAMORE!**
NEARLY SCARED THE WHISKERS OFF ME.
YOU DON'T HAVE WHISKERS.
HUH. I GUESS IT DID.
HE-HE-HE-HE!

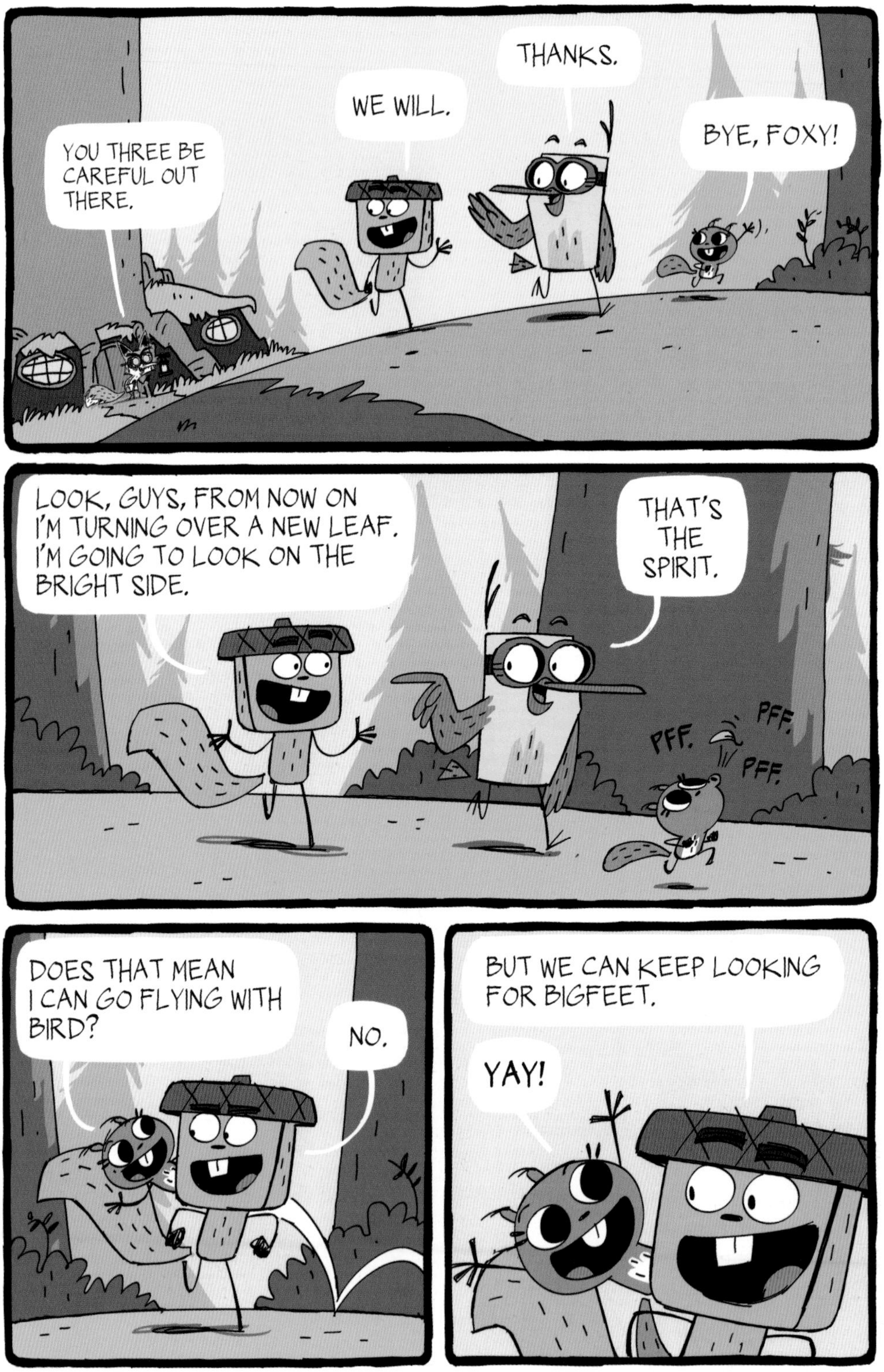
YOU THREE BE CAREFUL OUT THERE.
WE WILL.
THANKS.
BYE, FOXY!
LOOK, GUYS, FROM NOW ON I'M TURNING OVER A NEW LEAF. I'M GOING TO LOOK ON THE BRIGHT SIDE.
THAT'S THE SPIRIT.
PFF.
PFF.
PFF.
DOES THAT MEAN I CAN GO FLYING WITH BIRD?
NO.
BUT WE CAN KEEP LOOKING FOR BIGFEET.
YAY!

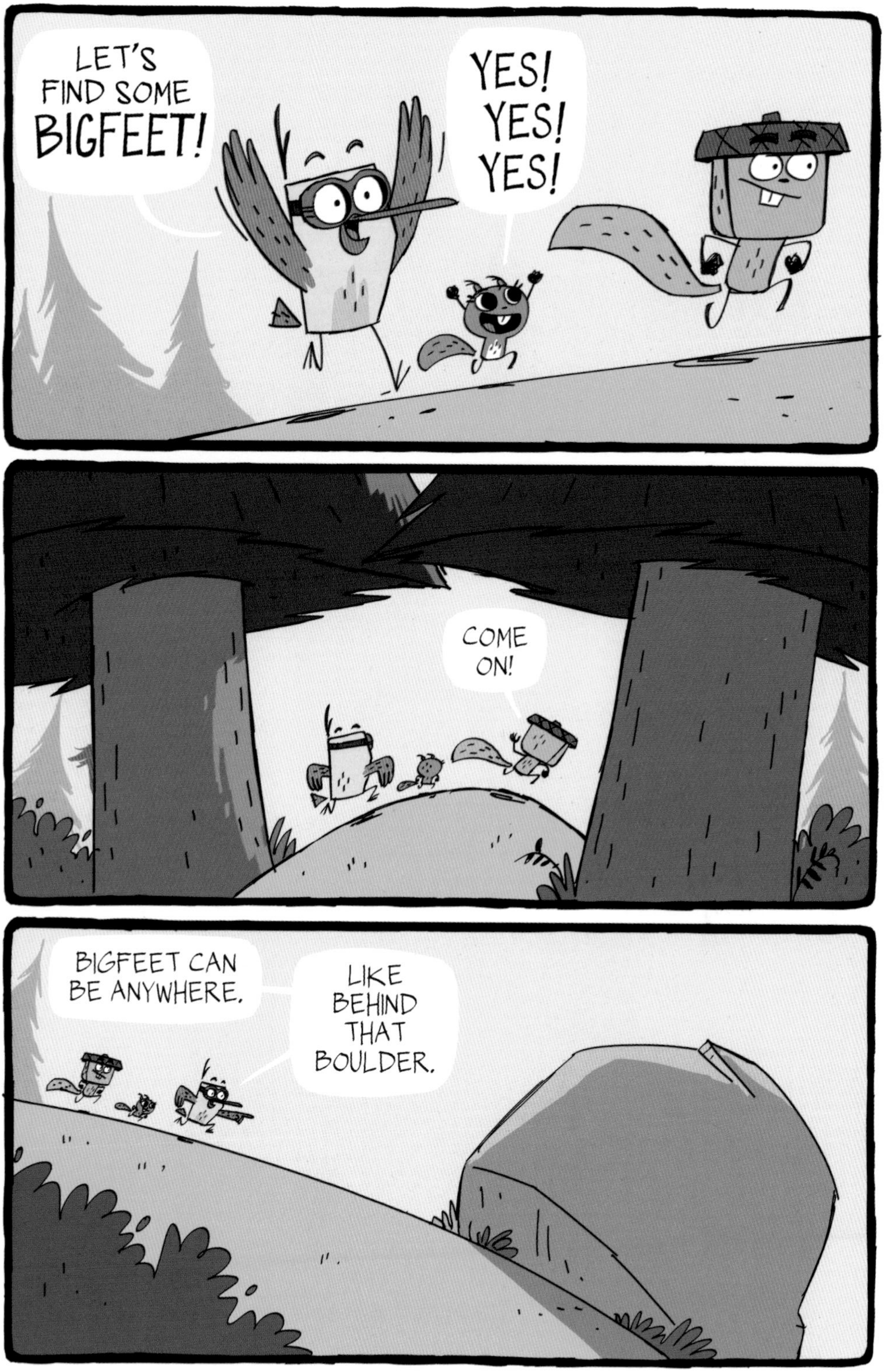
LET'S FIND SOME BIGFEET!
YES! YES! YES!
COME ON!
BIGFEET CAN BE ANYWHERE.
LIKE BEHIND THAT BOULDER.

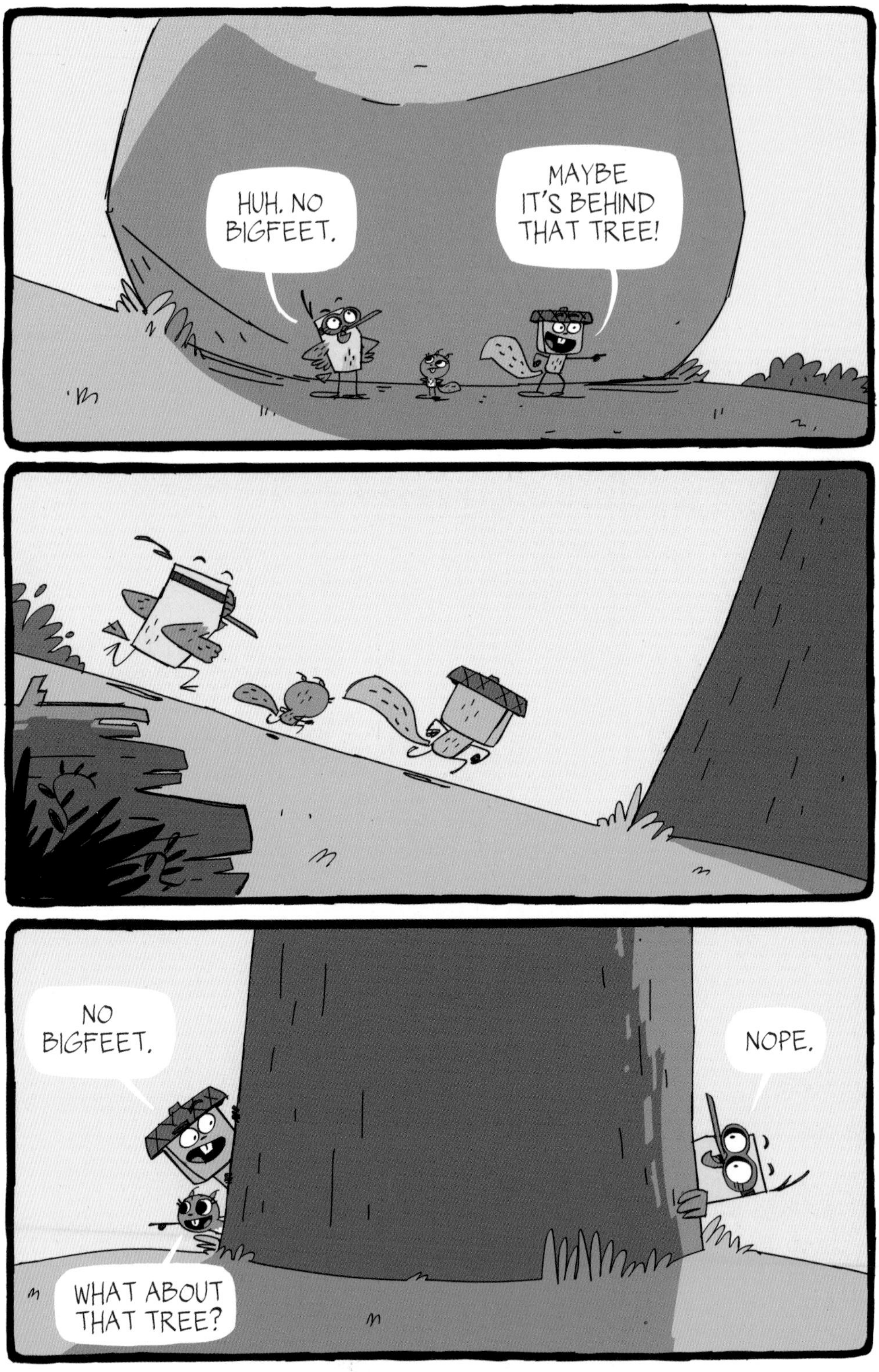
HUH. NO BIGFEET.
MAYBE IT'S BEHIND THAT TREE!
NO BIGFEET.
NOPE.
WHAT ABOUT THAT TREE?

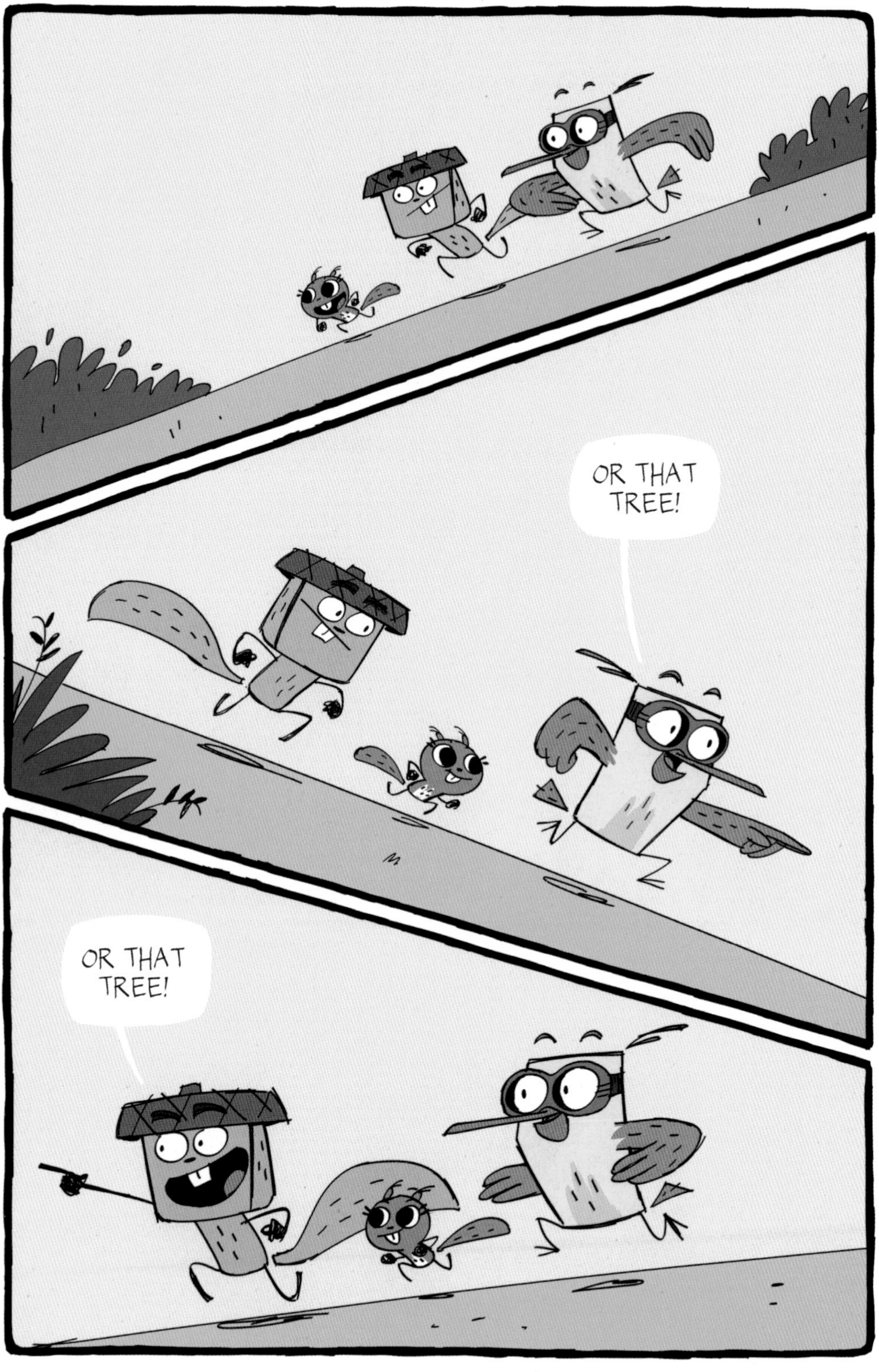

OR THAT TREE!
OR THAT TREE!

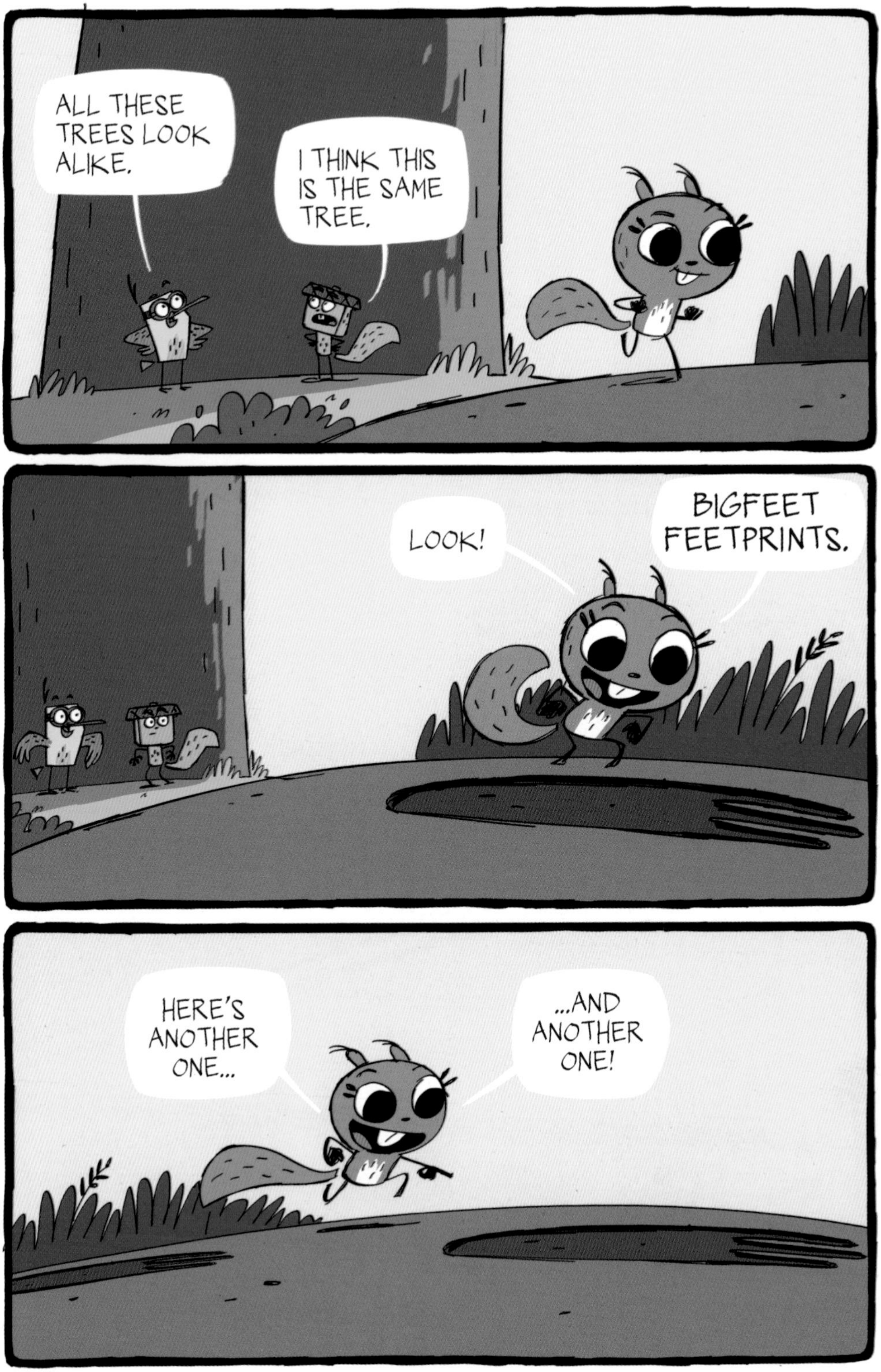
ALL THESE TREES LOOK ALIKE.
I THINK THIS IS THE SAME TREE.
LOOK!
BIGFEET FEETPRINTS.
HERE'S ANOTHER ONE...
...AND ANOTHER ONE!

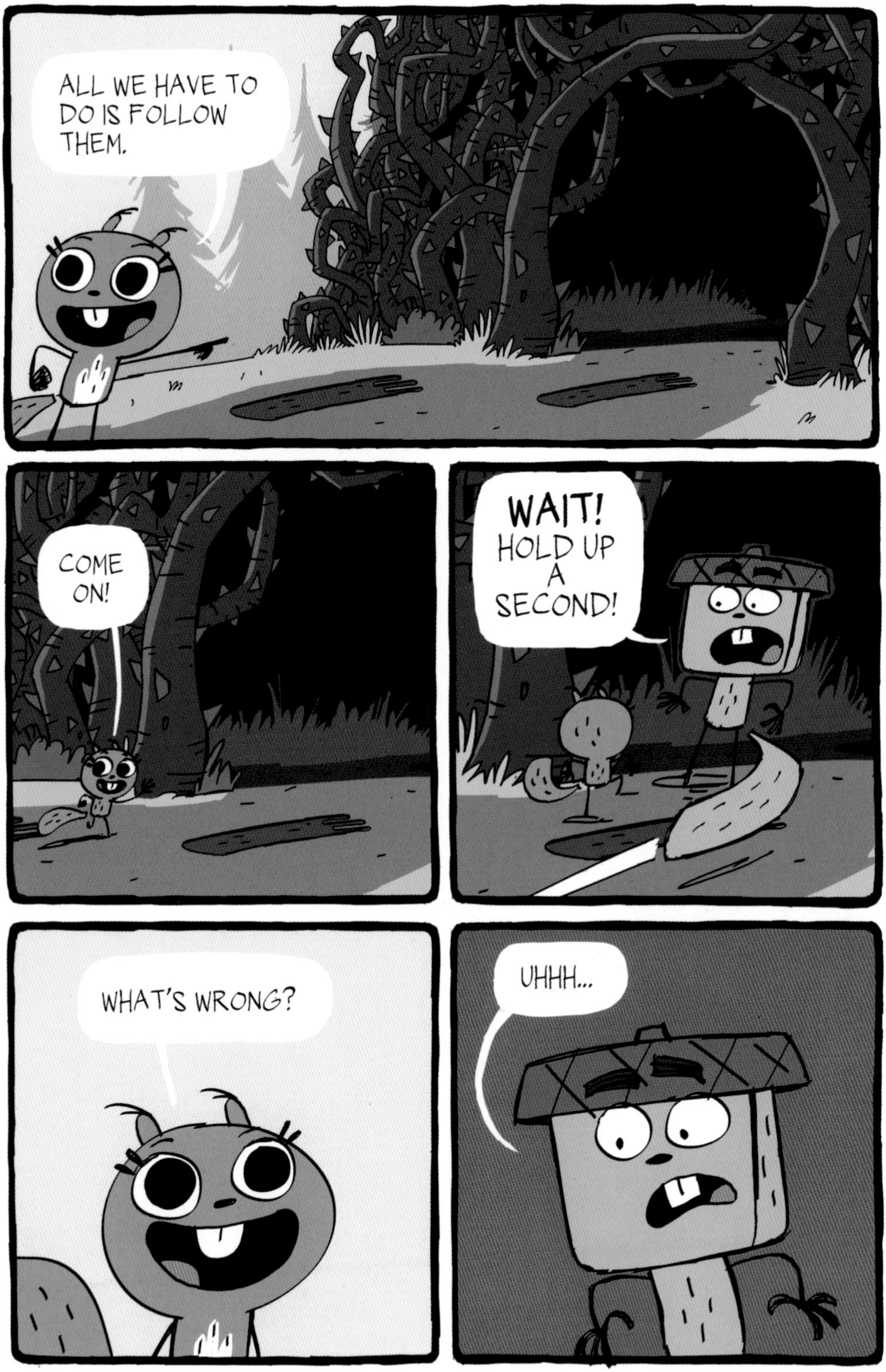
ALL WE HAVE TO DO IS FOLLOW THEM.
COME ON!
WAIT! HOLD UP A SECOND!
WHAT'S WRONG?
UHHH...

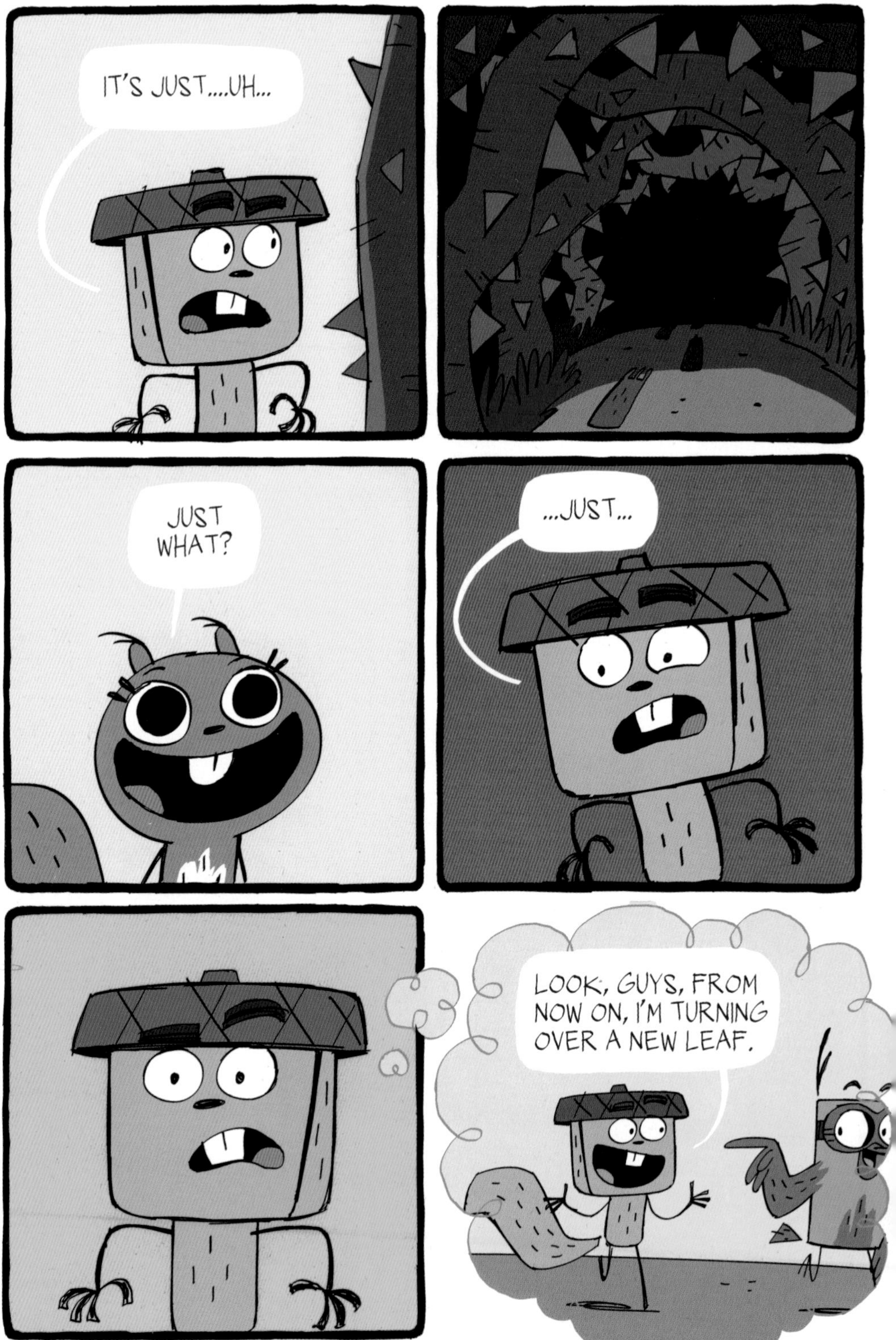
IT'S JUST....UH...
JUST WHAT?
...JUST...
LOOK, GUYS, FROM NOW ON, I'M TURNING OVER A NEW LEAF.

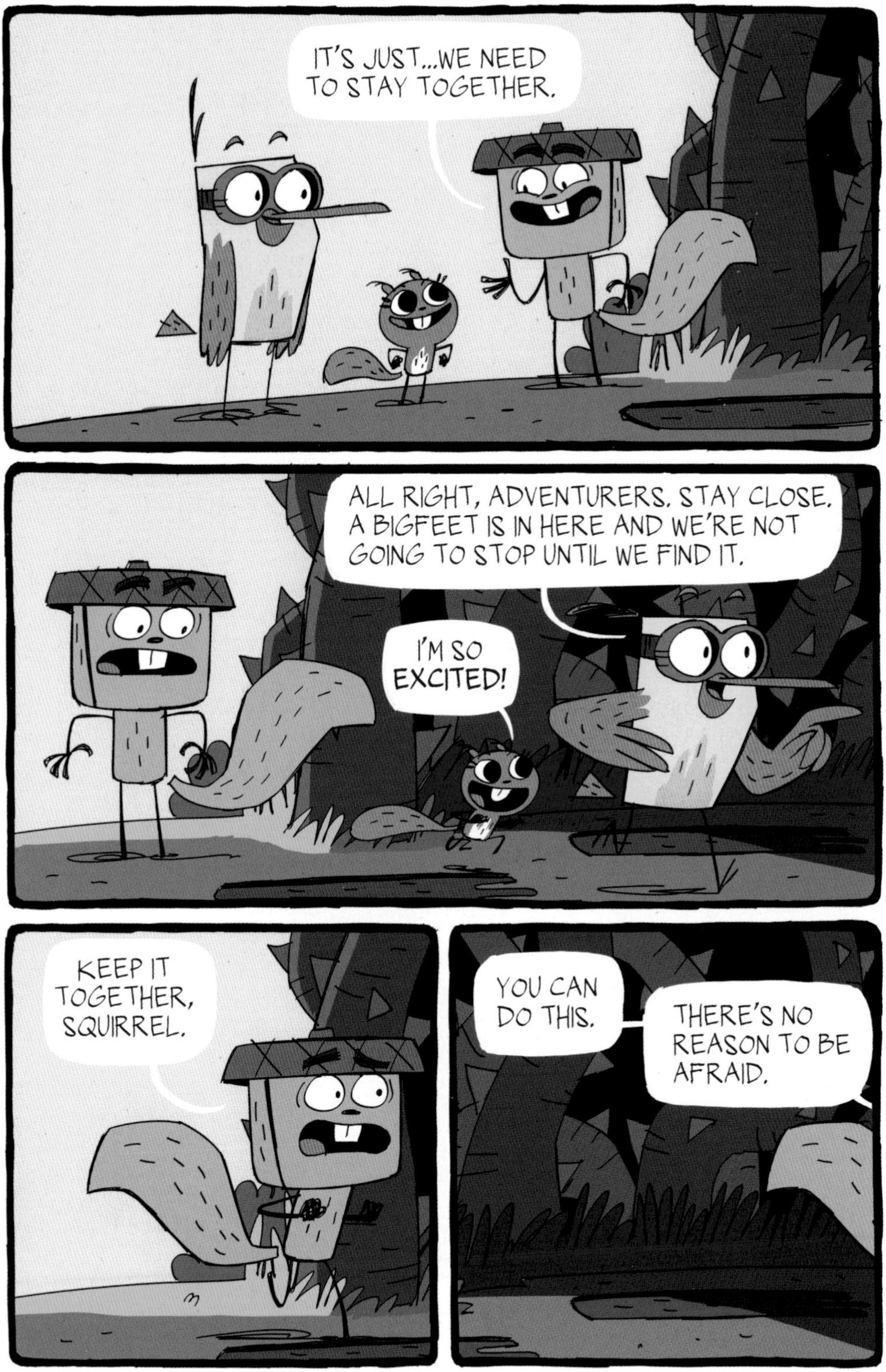
IT'S JUST...WE NEED TO STAY TOGETHER.
ALL RIGHT, ADVENTURERS. STAY CLOSE. A BIGFEET IS IN HERE AND WE'RE NOT GOING TO STOP UNTIL WE FIND IT.
I'M SO EXCITED!
KEEP IT TOGETHER, SQUIRREL.
YOU CAN DO THIS.
THERE'S NO REASON TO BE AFRAID.

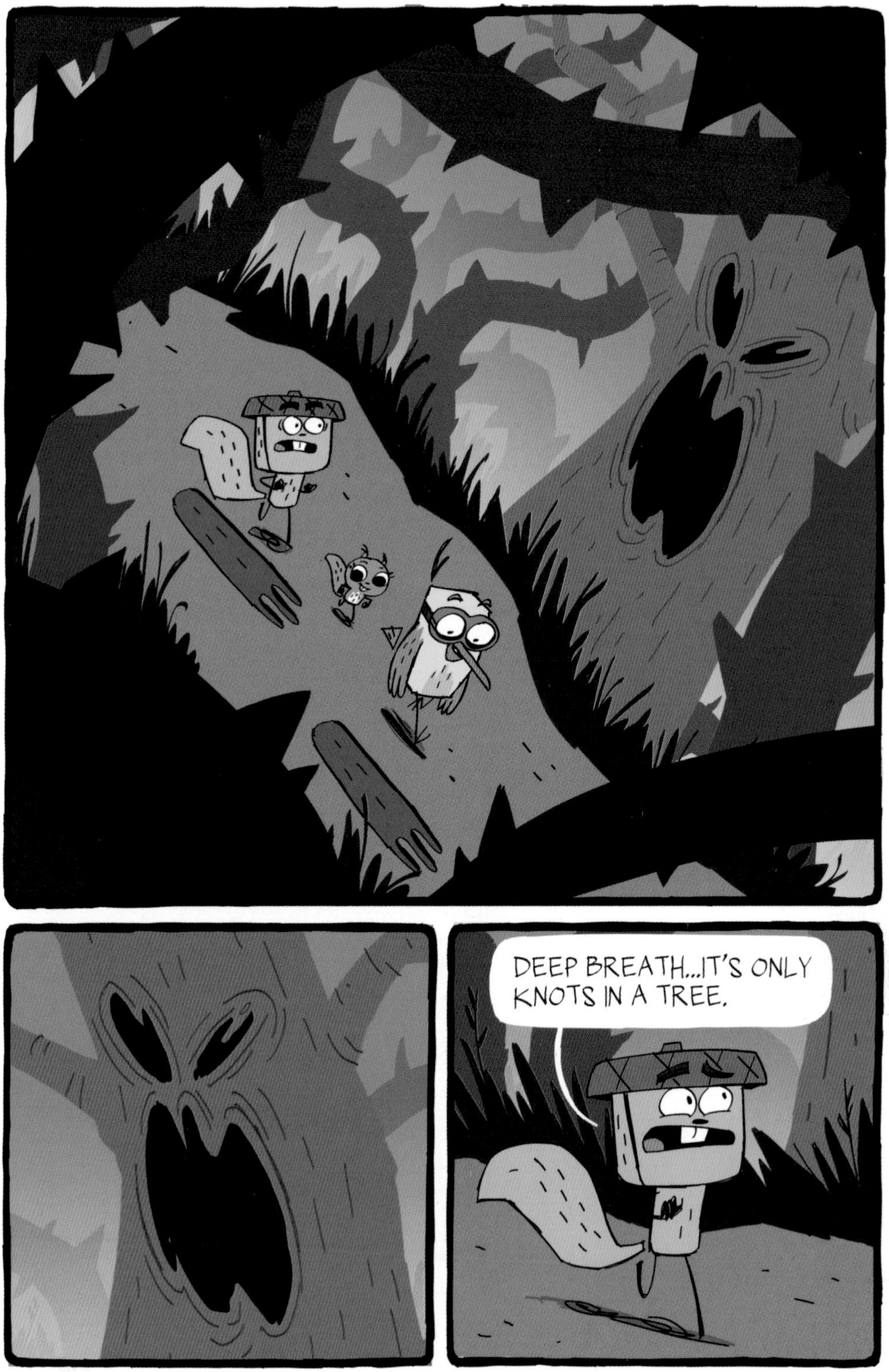
DEEP BREATH...IT'S ONLY KNOTS IN A TREE.

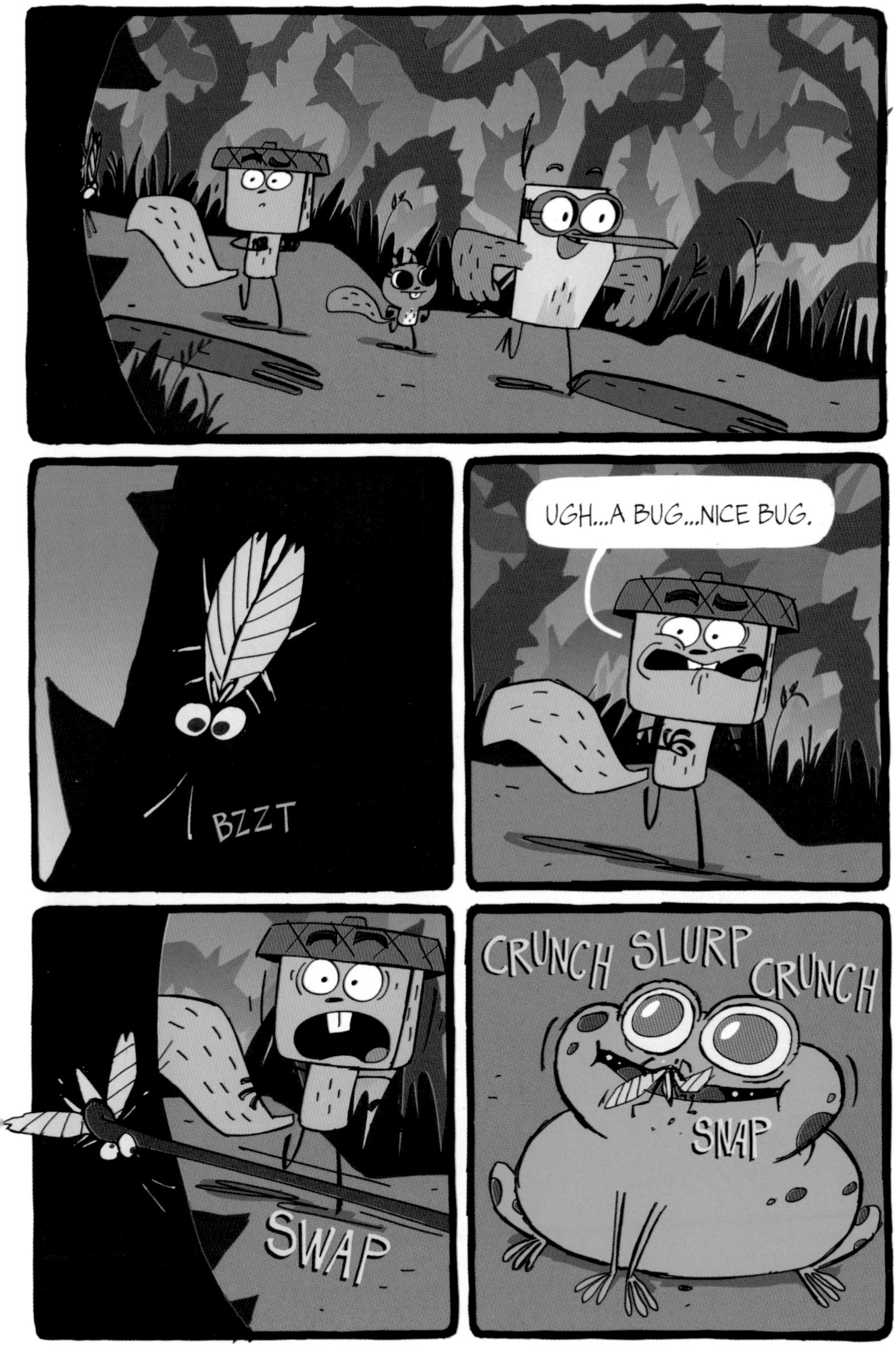
BZZT
UGH...A BUG...NICE BUG.
SWAP
CRUNCH SLURP CRUNCH
SNAP

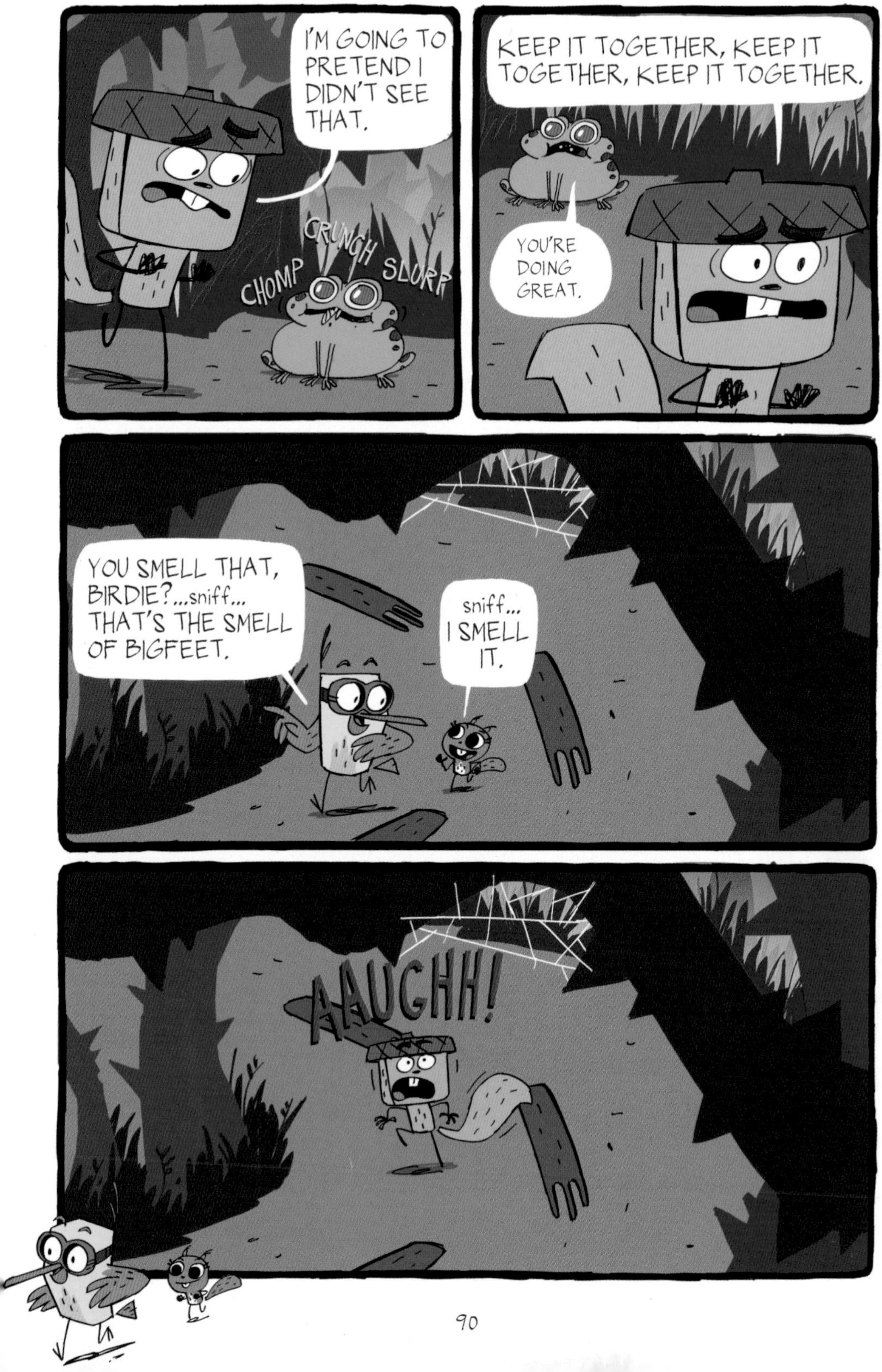
I'M GOING TO PRETEND I DIDN'T SEE THAT.
CRUNCH
CHOMP
SLURP
KEEP IT TOGETHER, KEEP IT TOGETHER, KEEP IT TOGETHER.
YOU'RE DOING GREAT.
YOU SMELL THAT, BIRDIE?...sniff... THAT'S THE SMELL OF BIGFEET.
sniff... I SMELL IT.
AAUGHH!

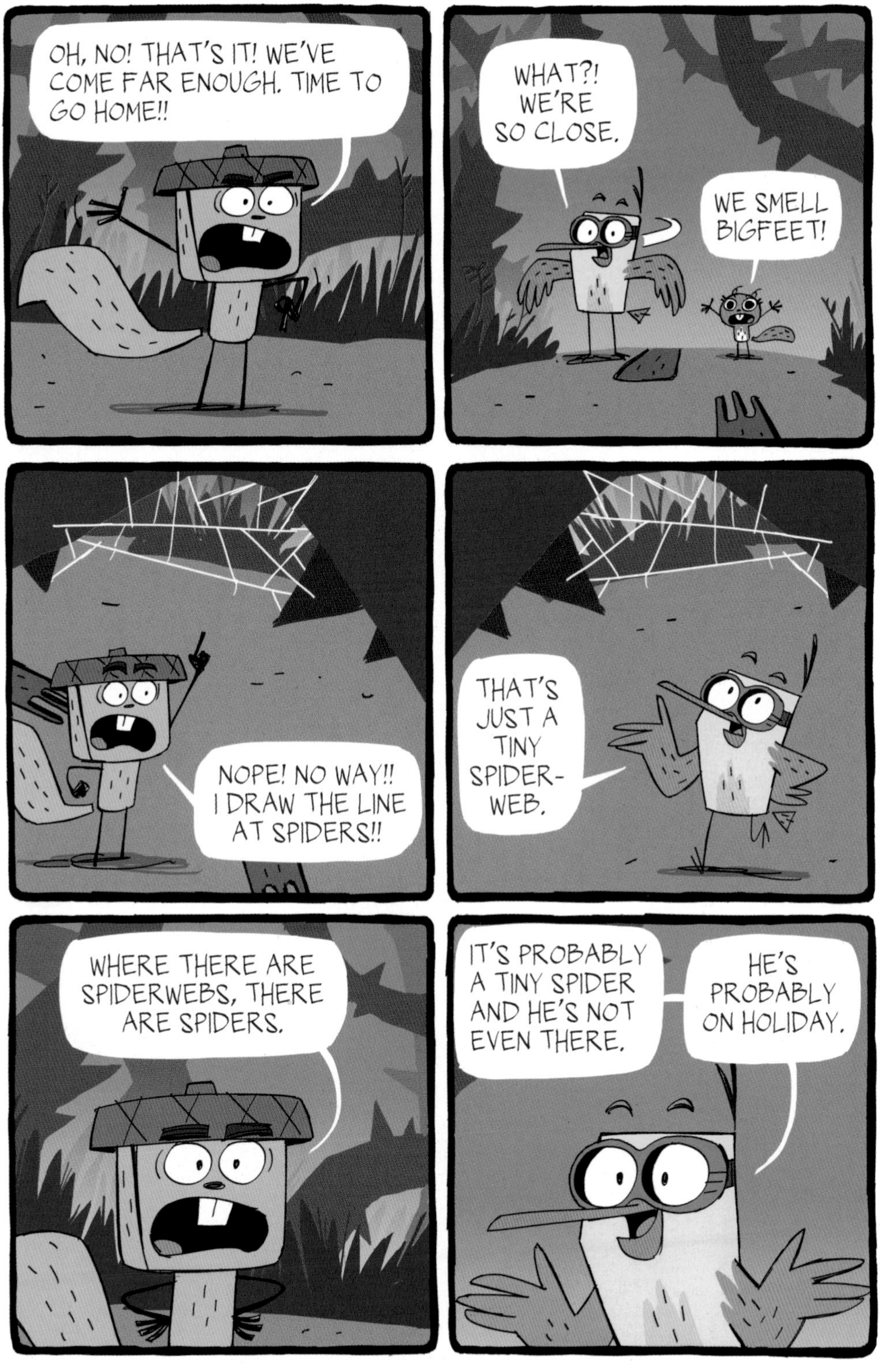
OH, NO! THAT'S IT! WE'VE COME FAR ENOUGH. TIME TO GO HOME!!
WHAT?! WE'RE SO CLOSE.
WE SMELL BIGFEET!
NOPE! NO WAY!! I DRAW THE LINE AT SPIDERS!!
THAT'S JUST A TINY SPIDER-WEB.
WHERE THERE ARE SPIDERWEBS, THERE ARE SPIDERS.
IT'S PROBABLY A TINY SPIDER AND HE'S NOT EVEN THERE.
HE'S PROBABLY ON HOLIDAY.

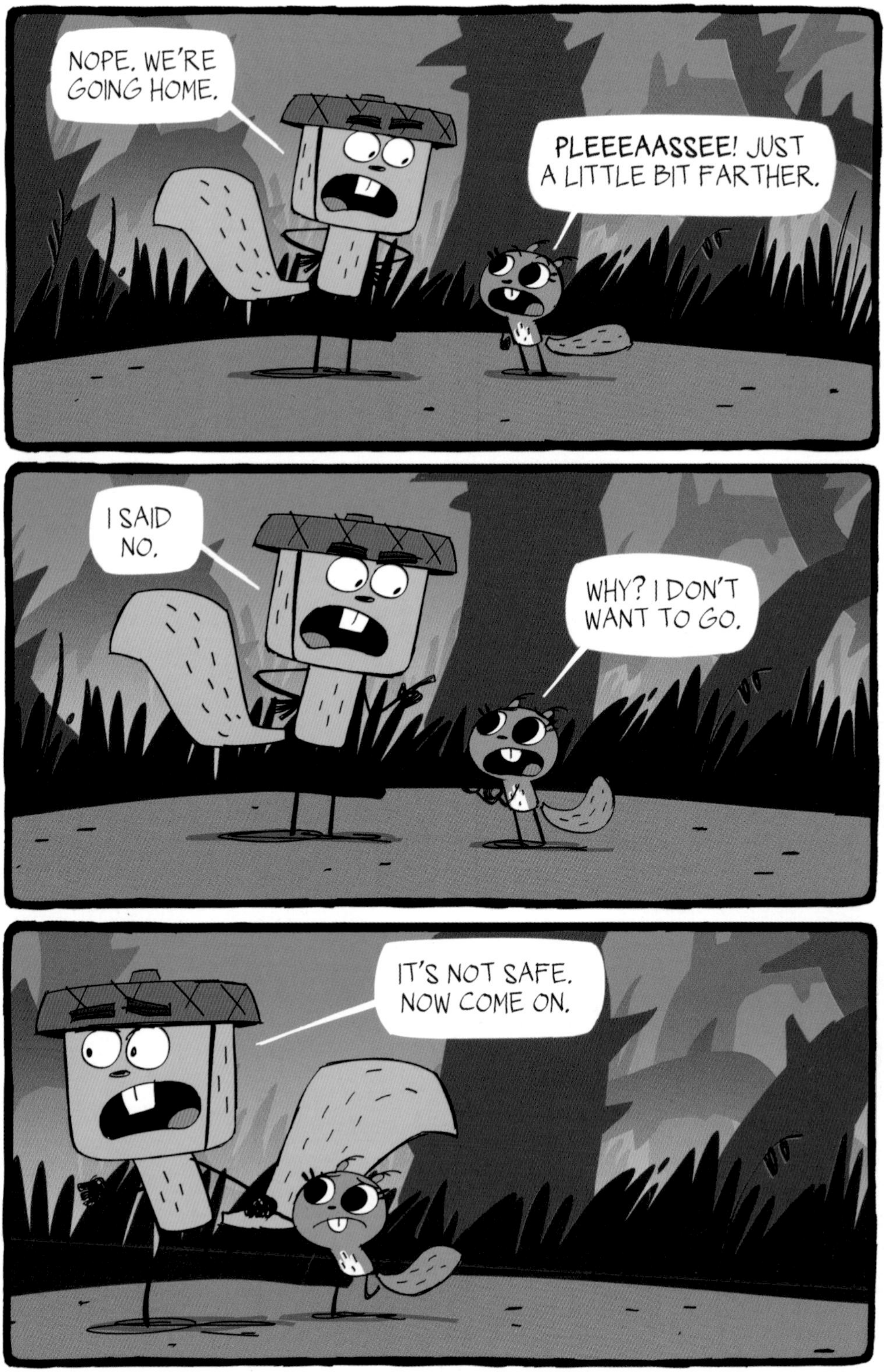
NOPE. WE'RE GOING HOME.
PLEEEAASSEE! JUST A LITTLE BIT FARTHER.
I SAID NO.
WHY? I DON'T WANT TO GO.
IT'S NOT SAFE. NOW COME ON.

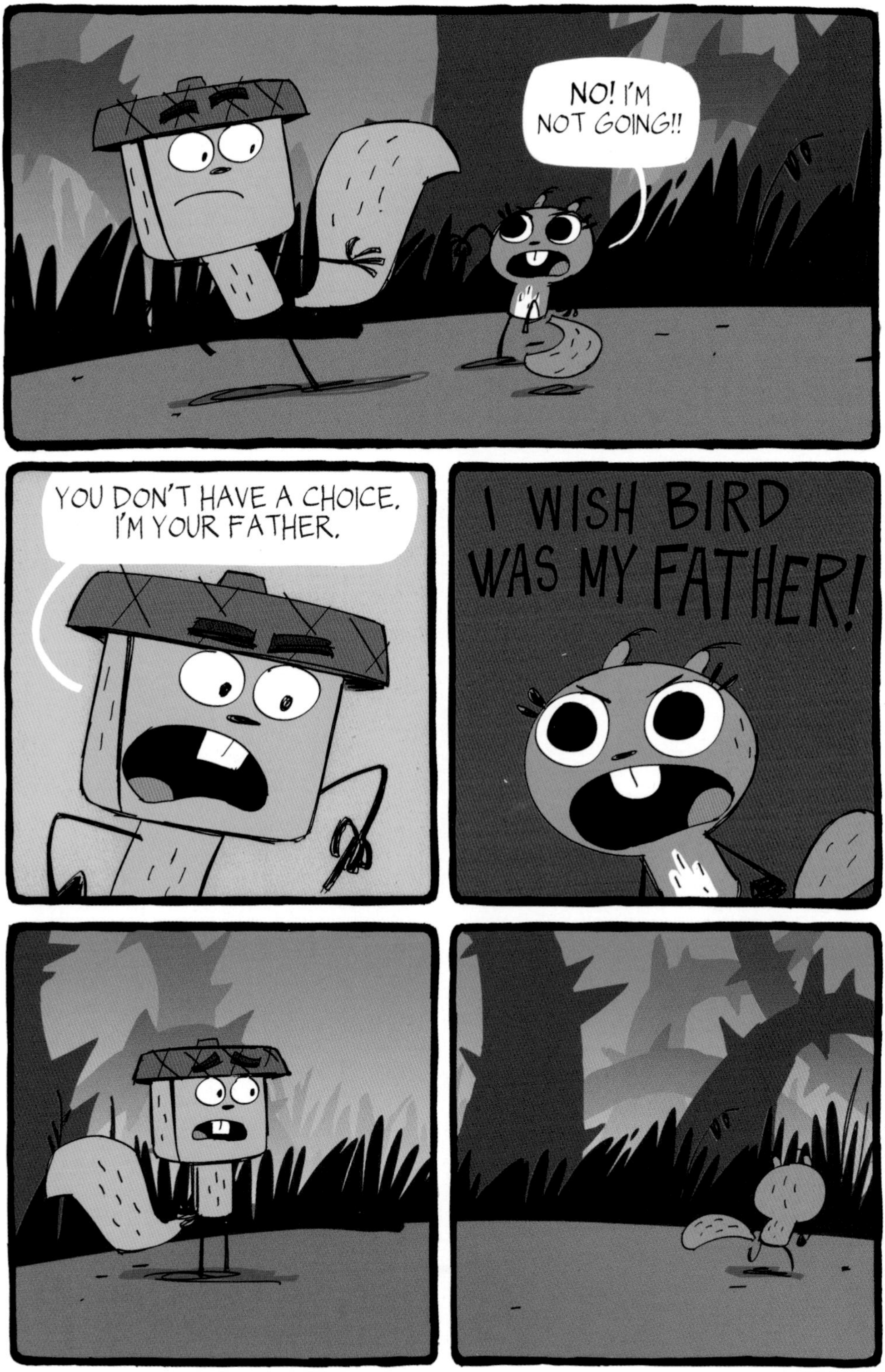
NO! I'M NOT GOING!!
YOU DON'T HAVE A CHOICE. I'M YOUR FATHER.
I WISH BIRD WAS MY FATHER!

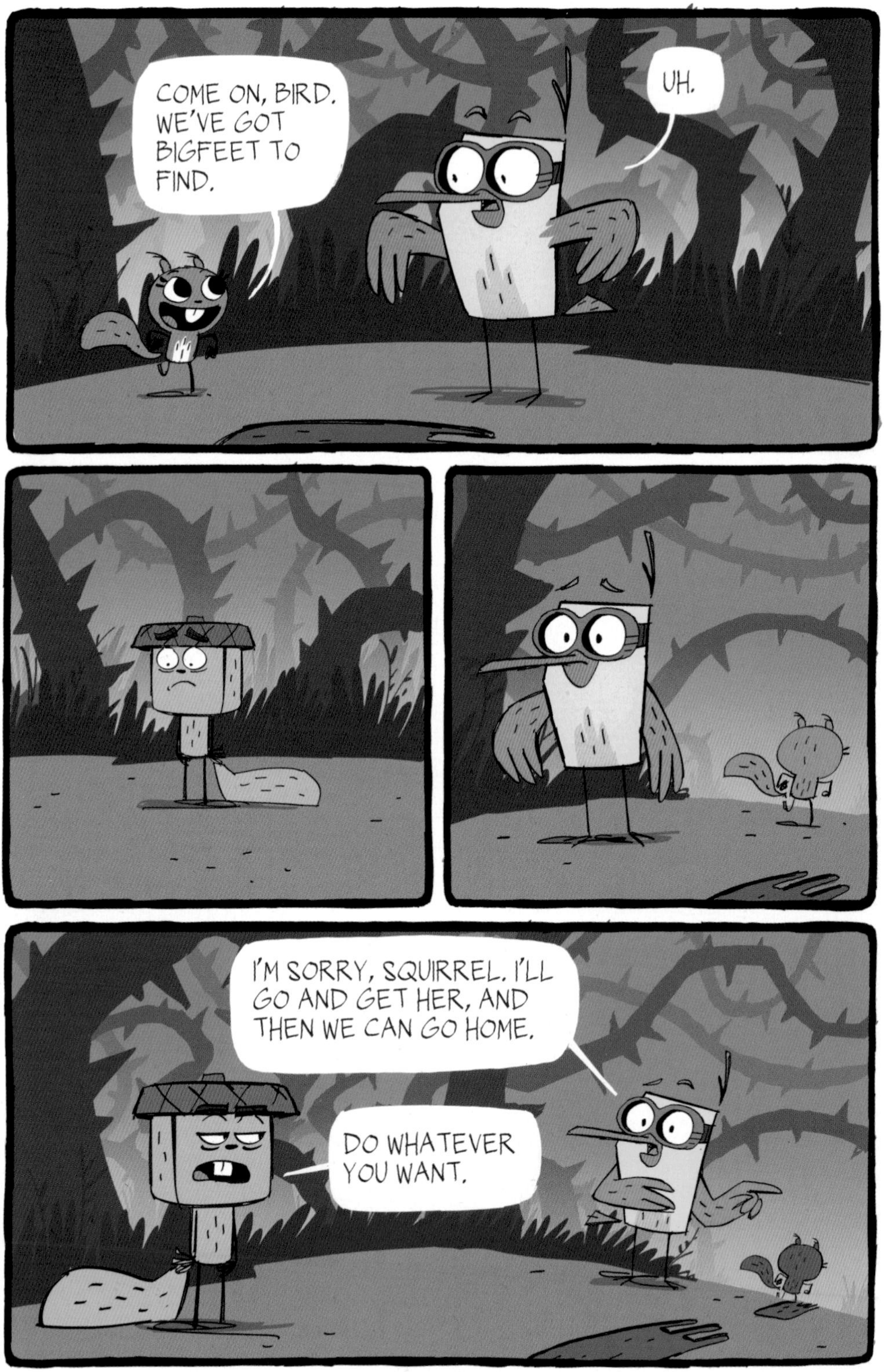
COME ON, BIRD. WE'VE GOT BIGFEET TO FIND.
UH.
I'M SORRY, SQUIRREL. I'LL GO AND GET HER, AND THEN WE CAN GO HOME.
DO WHATEVER YOU WANT.

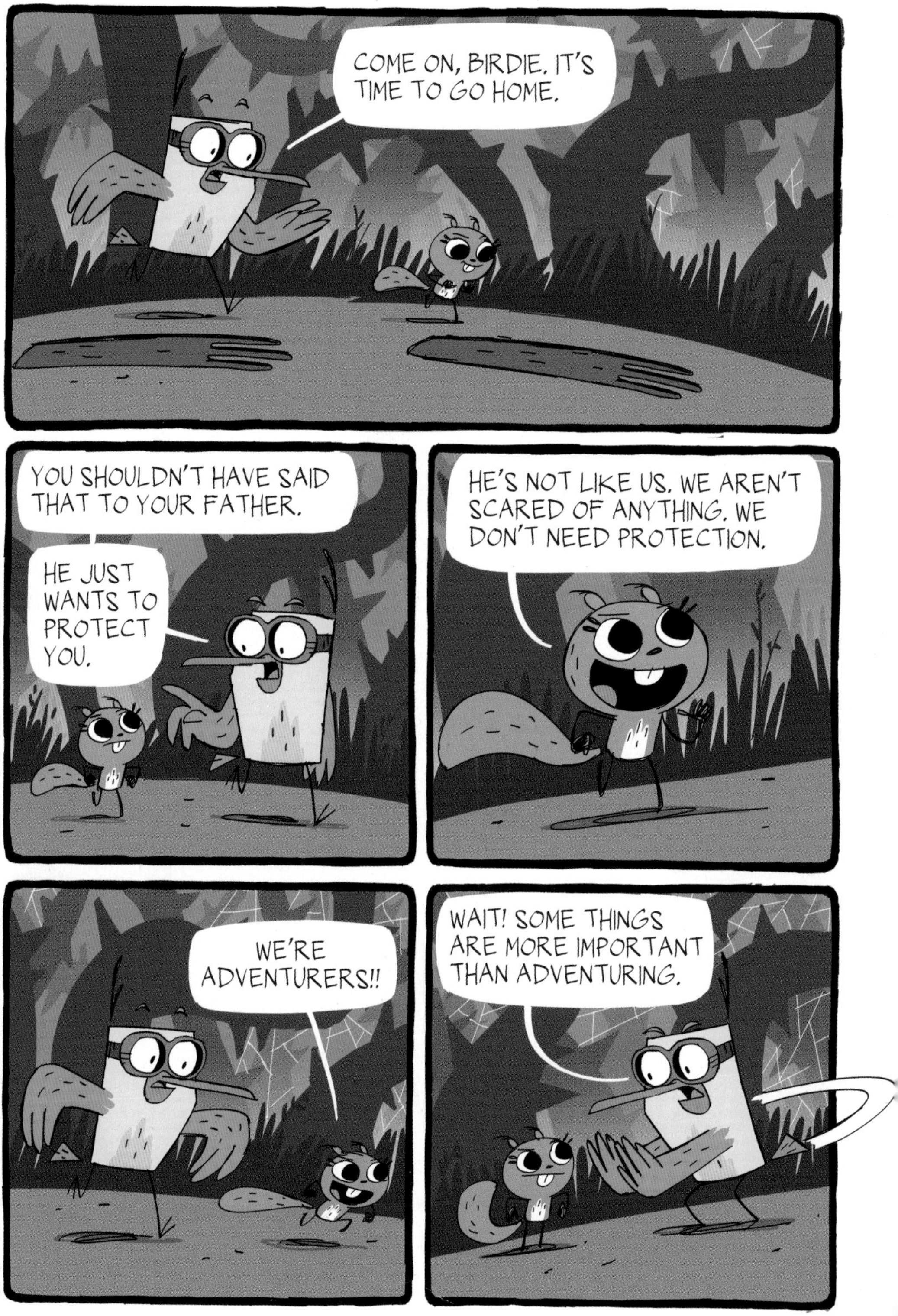
COME ON, BIRDIE. IT'S TIME TO GO HOME.
YOU SHOULDN'T HAVE SAID THAT TO YOUR FATHER.
HE JUST WANTS TO PROTECT YOU.
HE'S NOT LIKE US. WE AREN'T SCARED OF ANYTHING. WE DON'T NEED PROTECTION.
WE'RE ADVENTURERS!!
WAIT! SOME THINGS ARE MORE IMPORTANT THAN ADVENTURING.

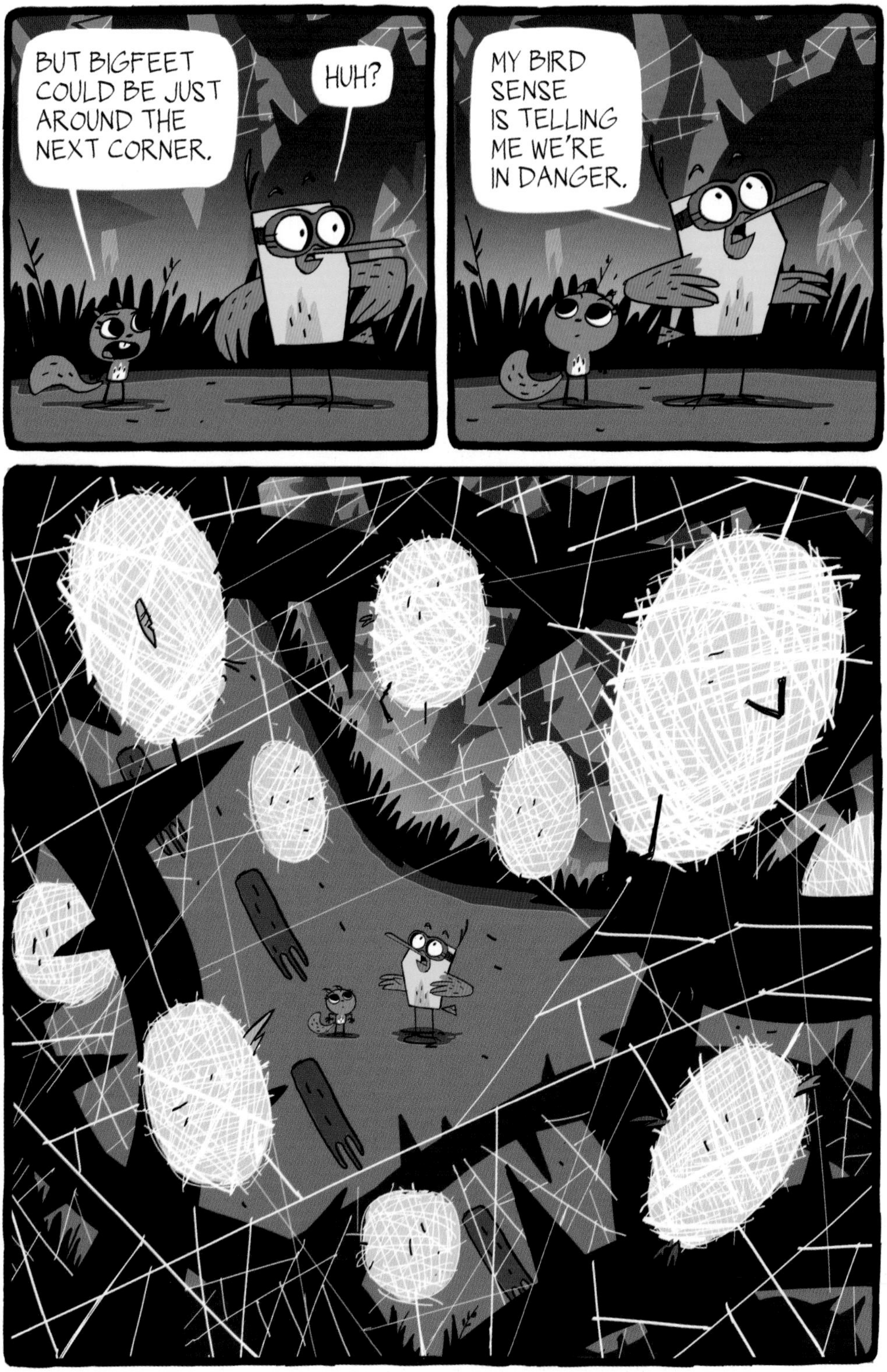
BUT BIGFEET COULD BE JUST AROUND THE NEXT CORNER.
HUH?
MY BIRD SENSE IS TELLING ME WE'RE IN DANGER.

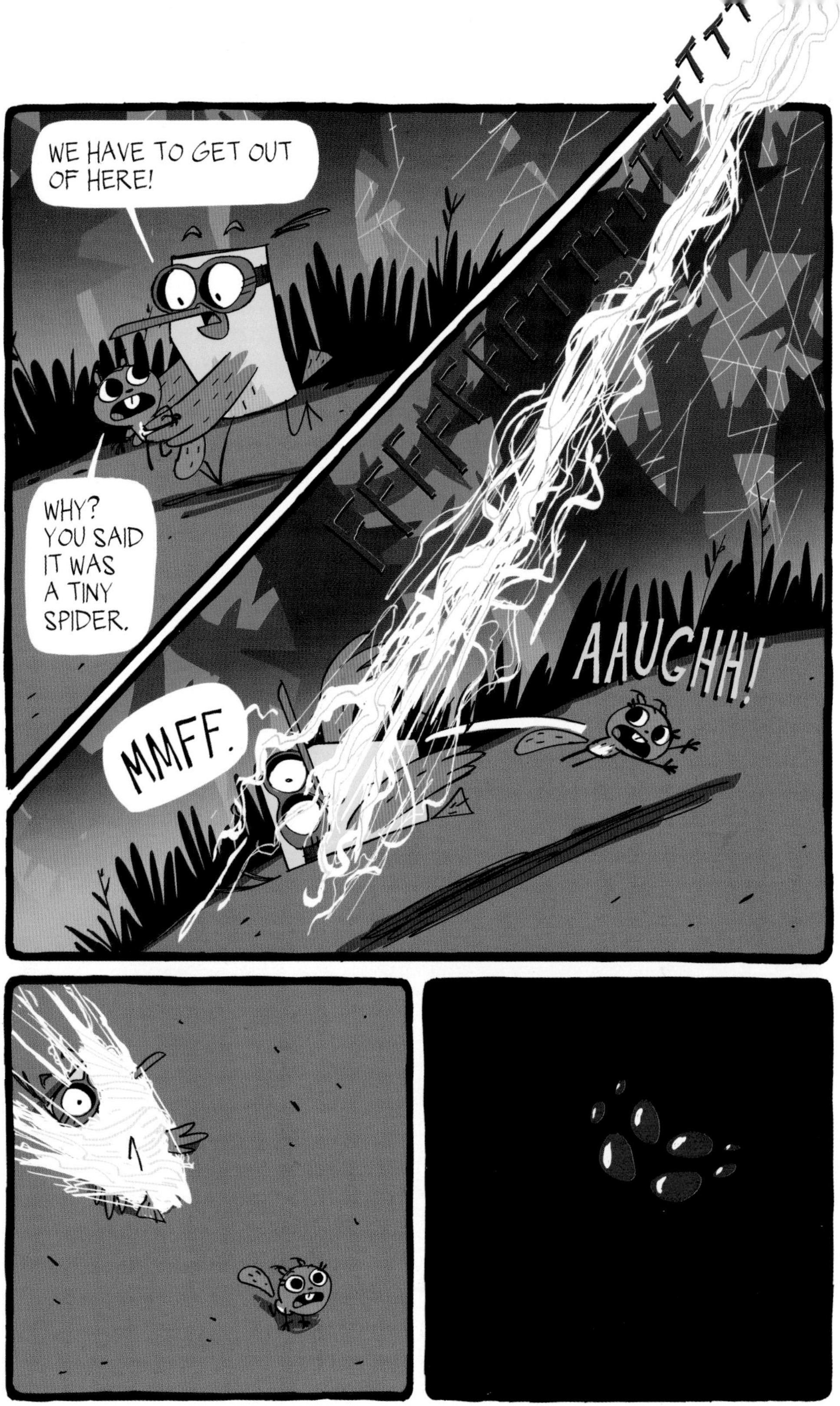
WE HAVE TO GET OUT OF HERE!
WHY? YOU SAID IT WAS A TINY SPIDER.
FFFFFFTTTTTTTTTTTT
AAUGHH!
MMFF.

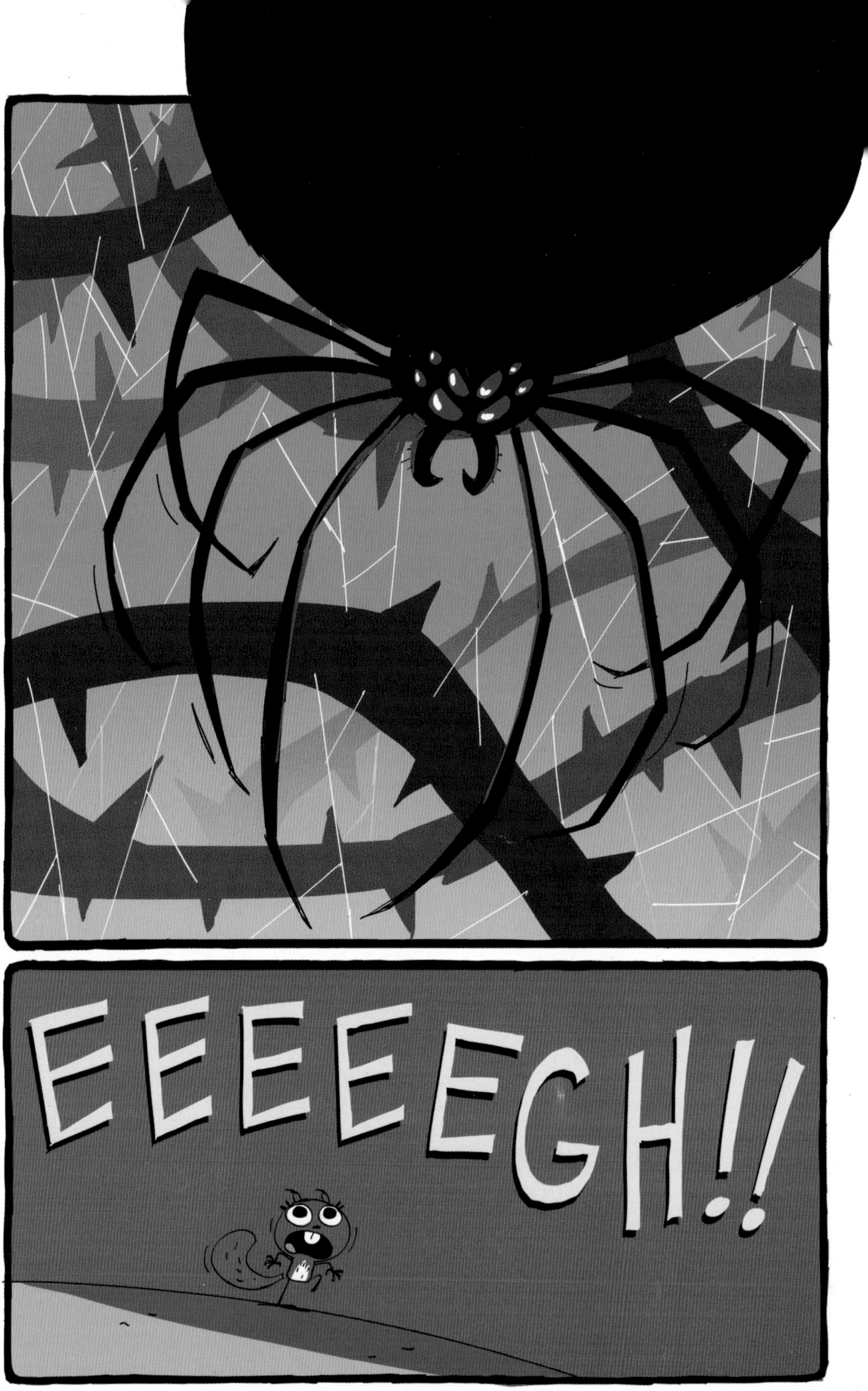
EEEEEEGH!!

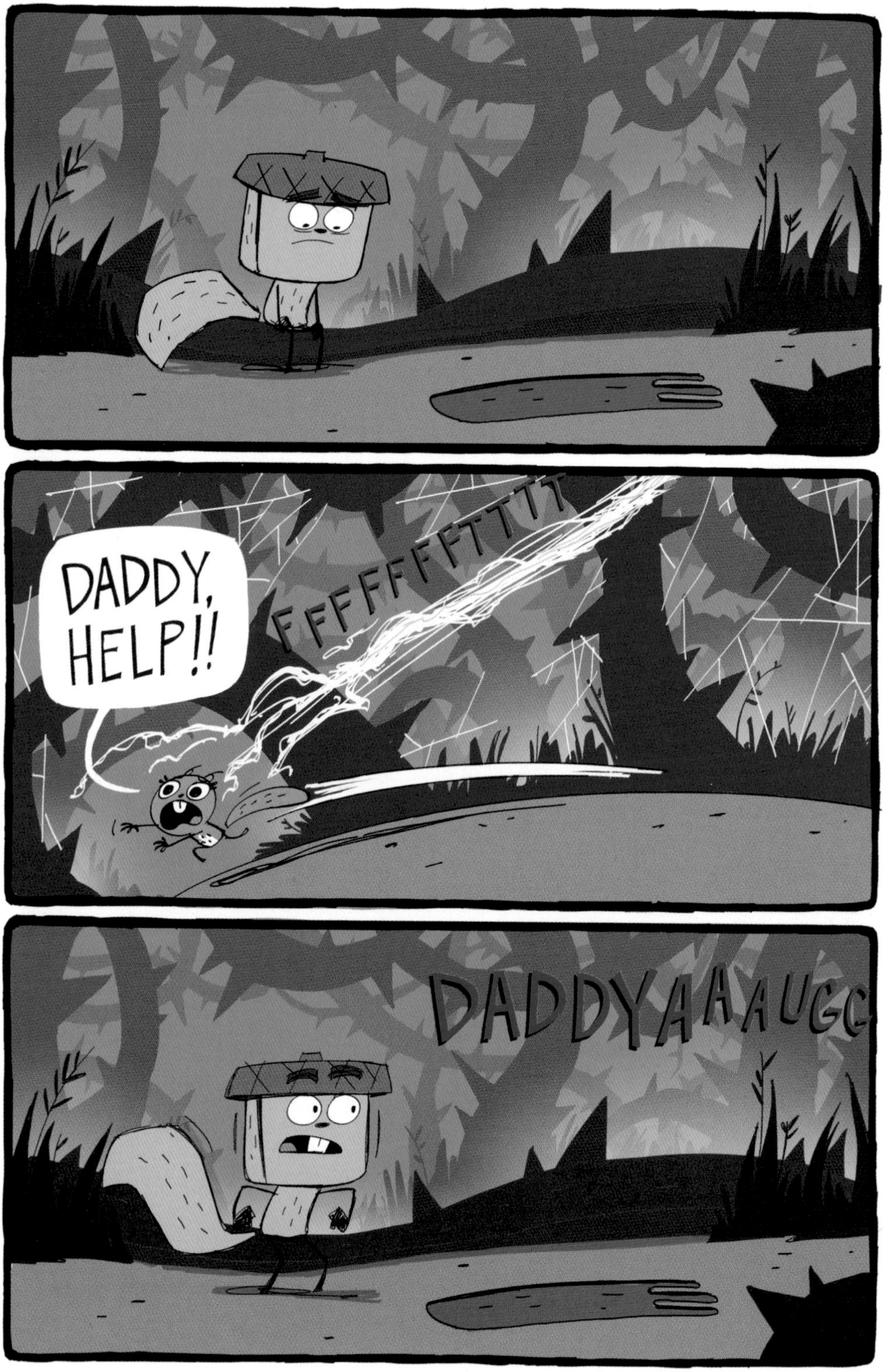
DADDY, HELP!!
FFFFFFFTTTTT
DADDYAAAUGG

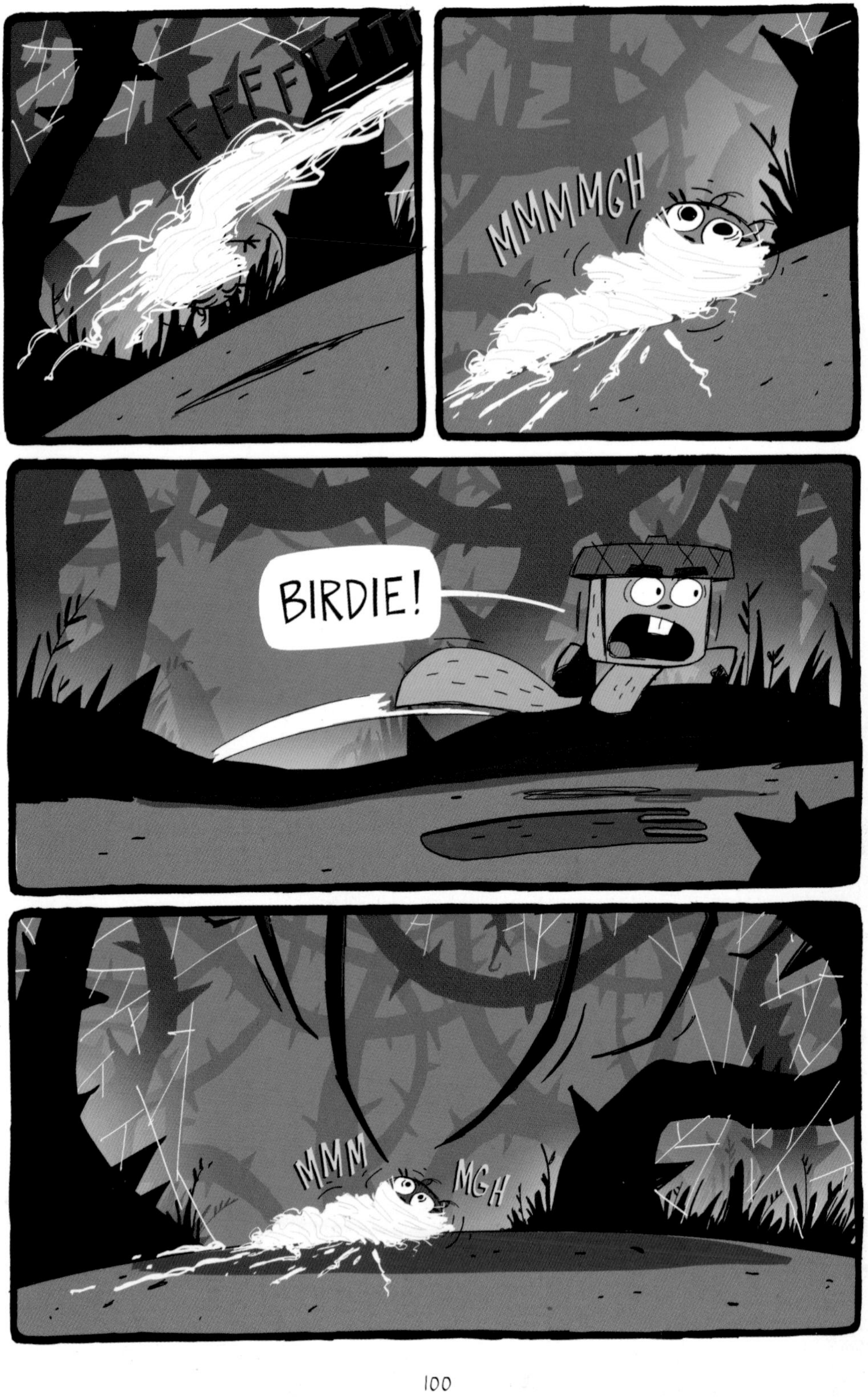
FFFFTTTTT
MMMMGH
BIRDIE!
MMM
MGH

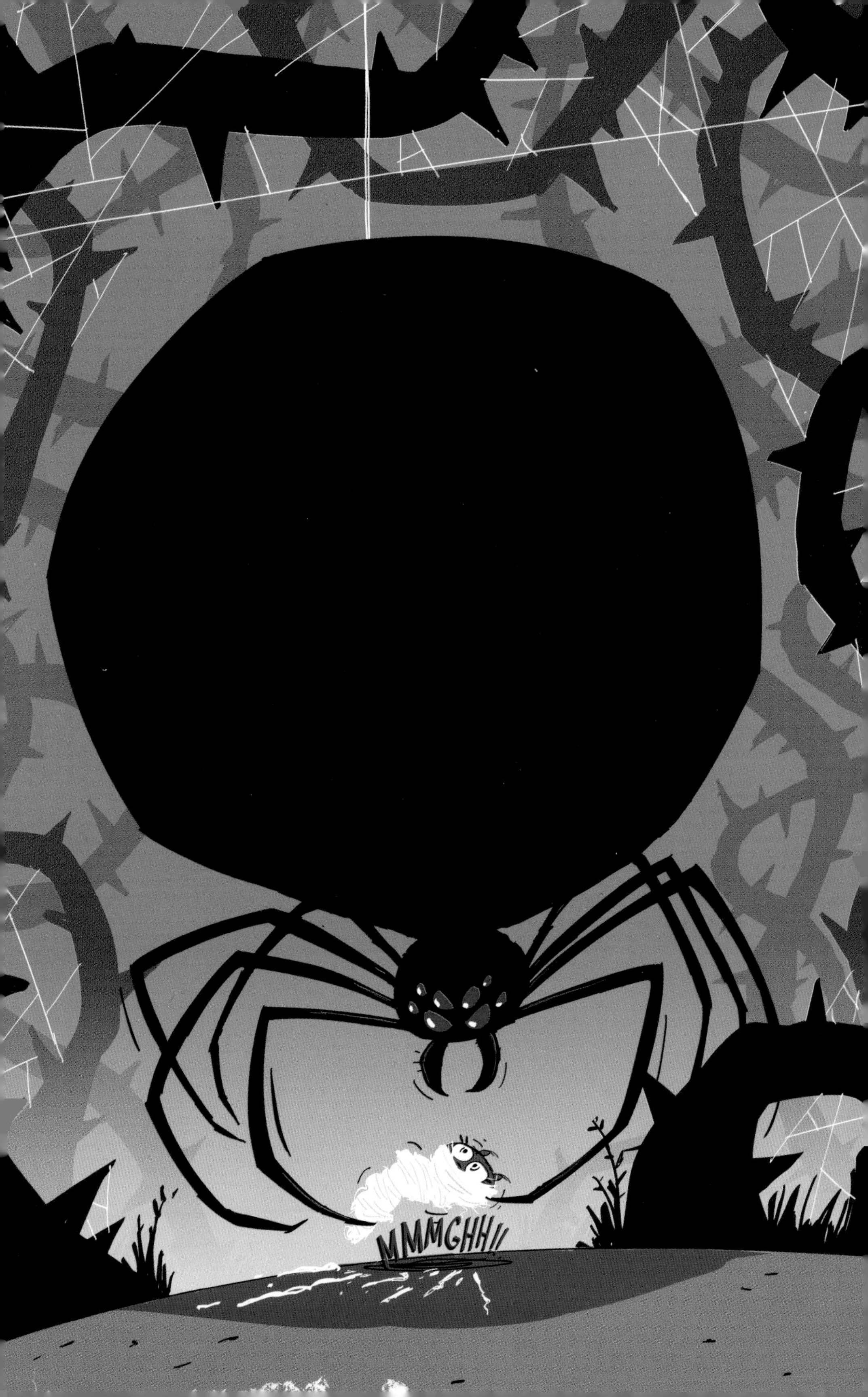
MMMGHH!!

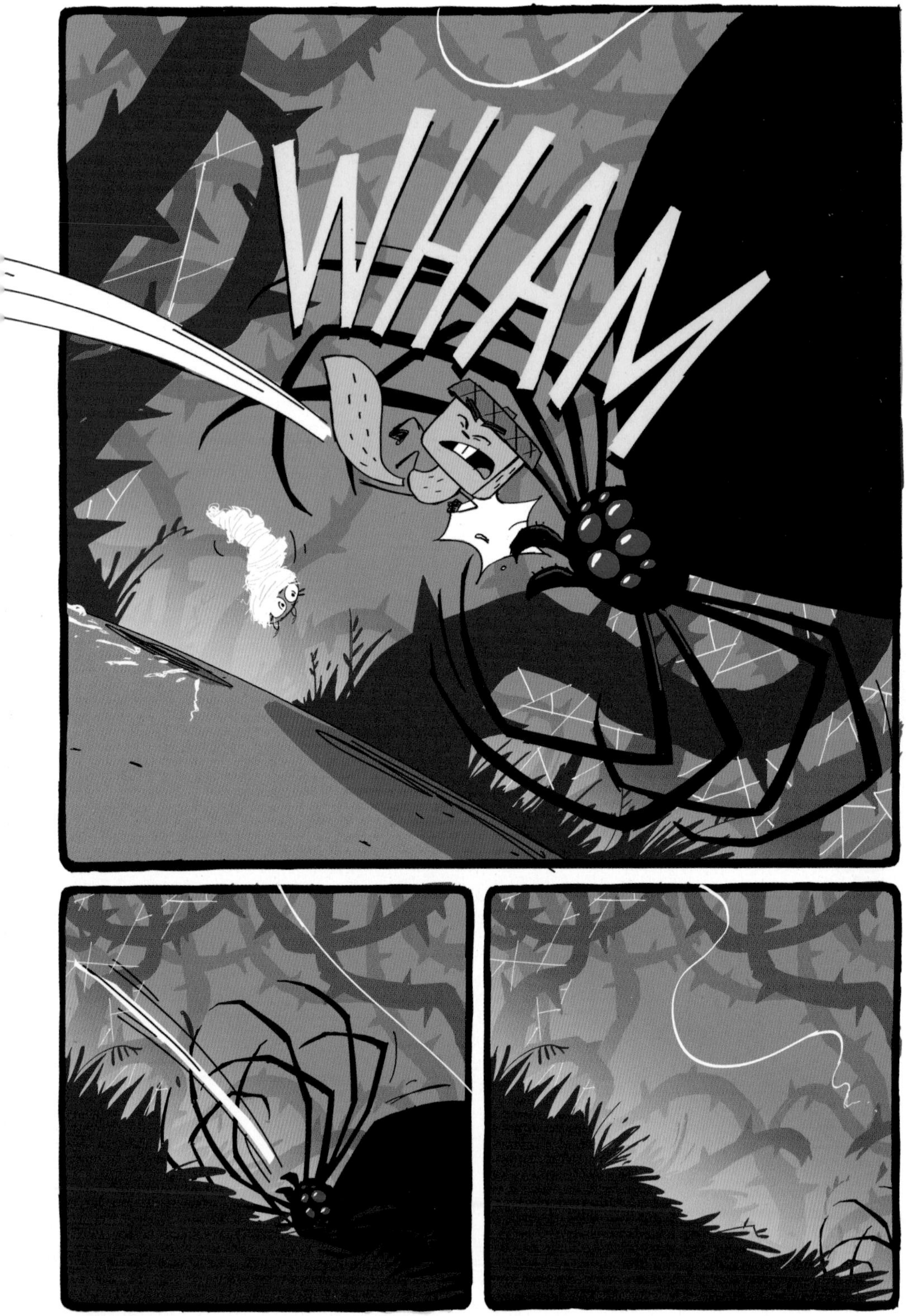
WHAM

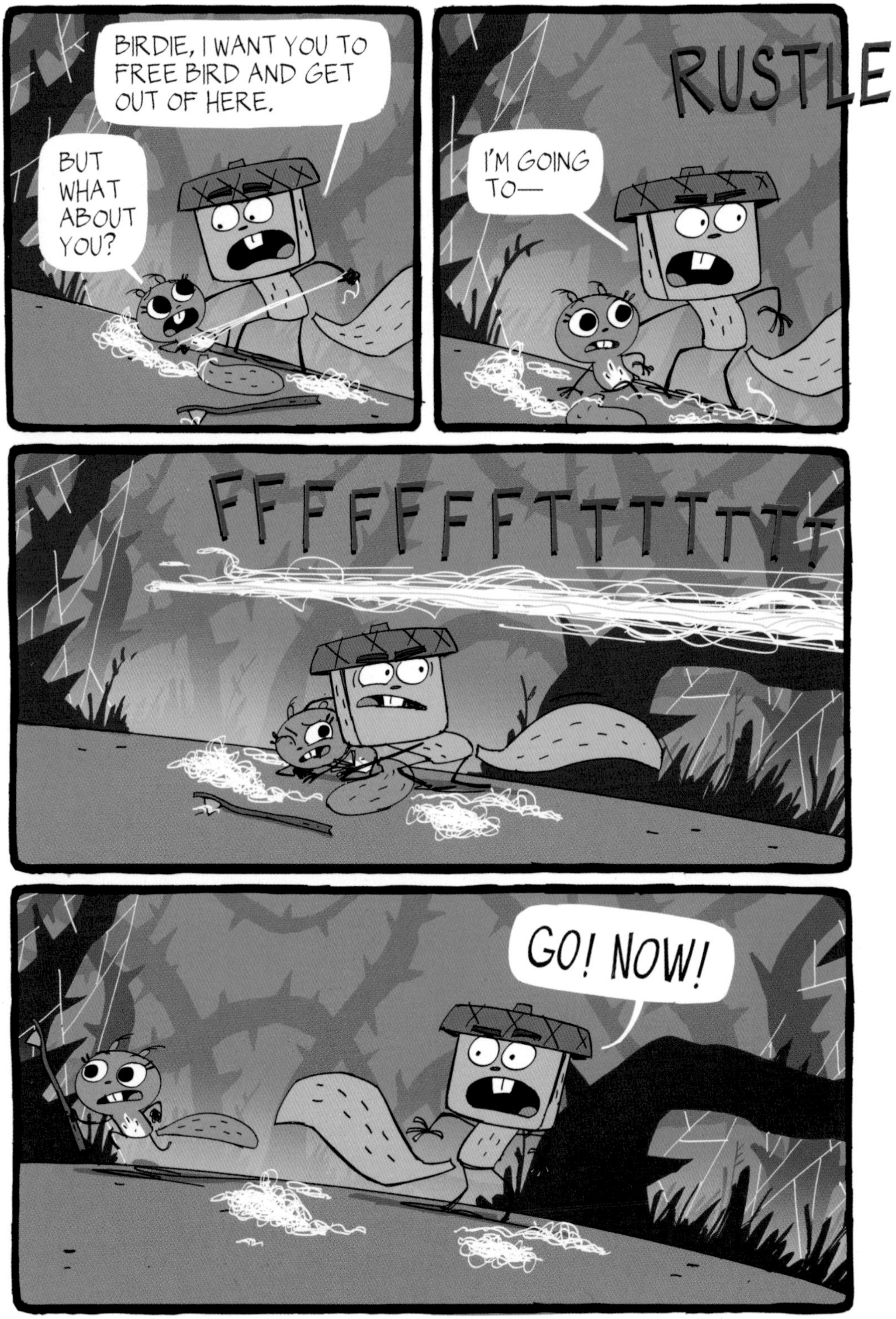
BIRDIE, I WANT YOU TO FREE BIRD AND GET OUT OF HERE.
BUT WHAT ABOUT YOU?
RUSTLE
I'M GOING TO—
FFFFFFFTTTTTTTT
GO! NOW!

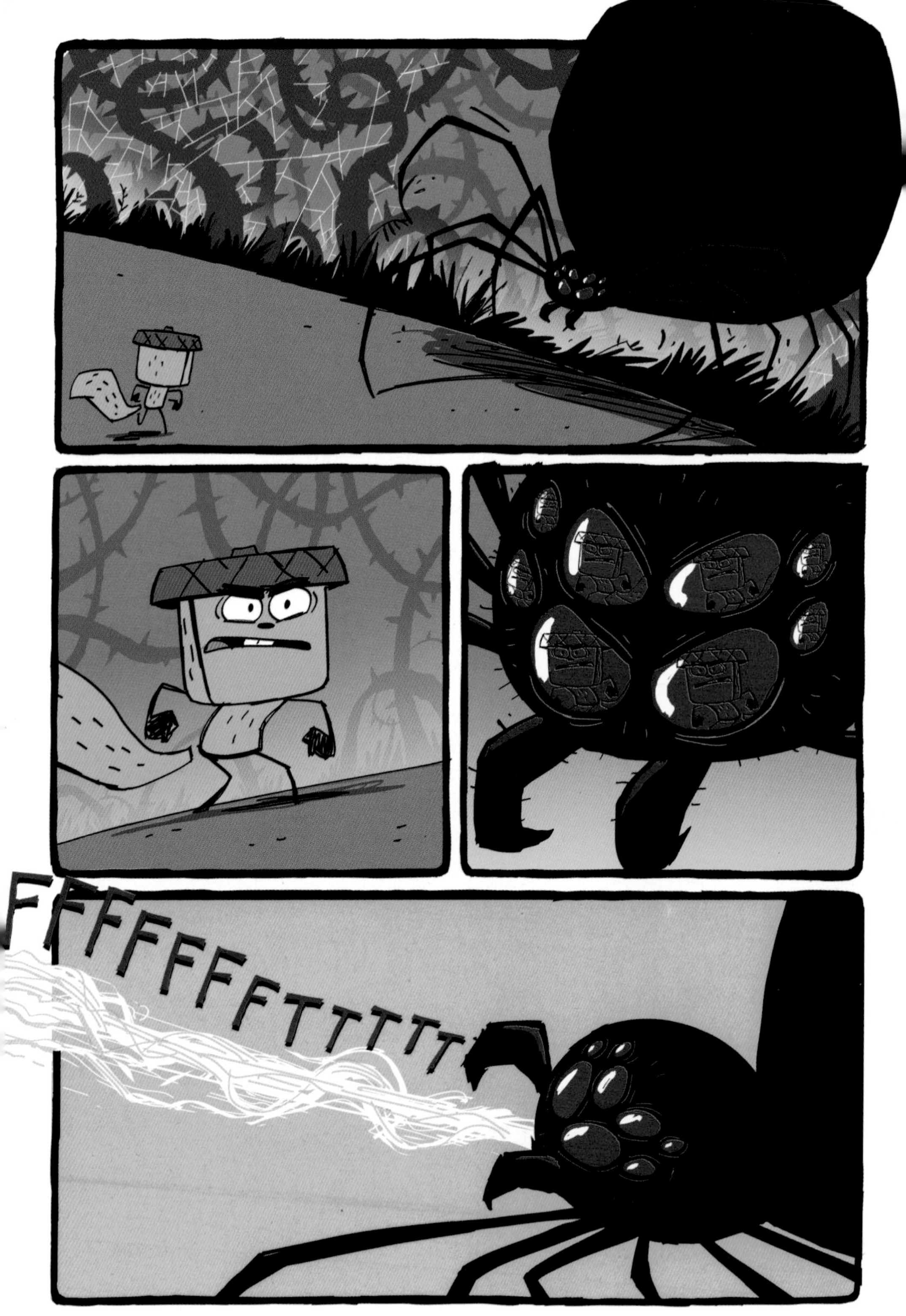
FFFFFFFFTTTTTTT

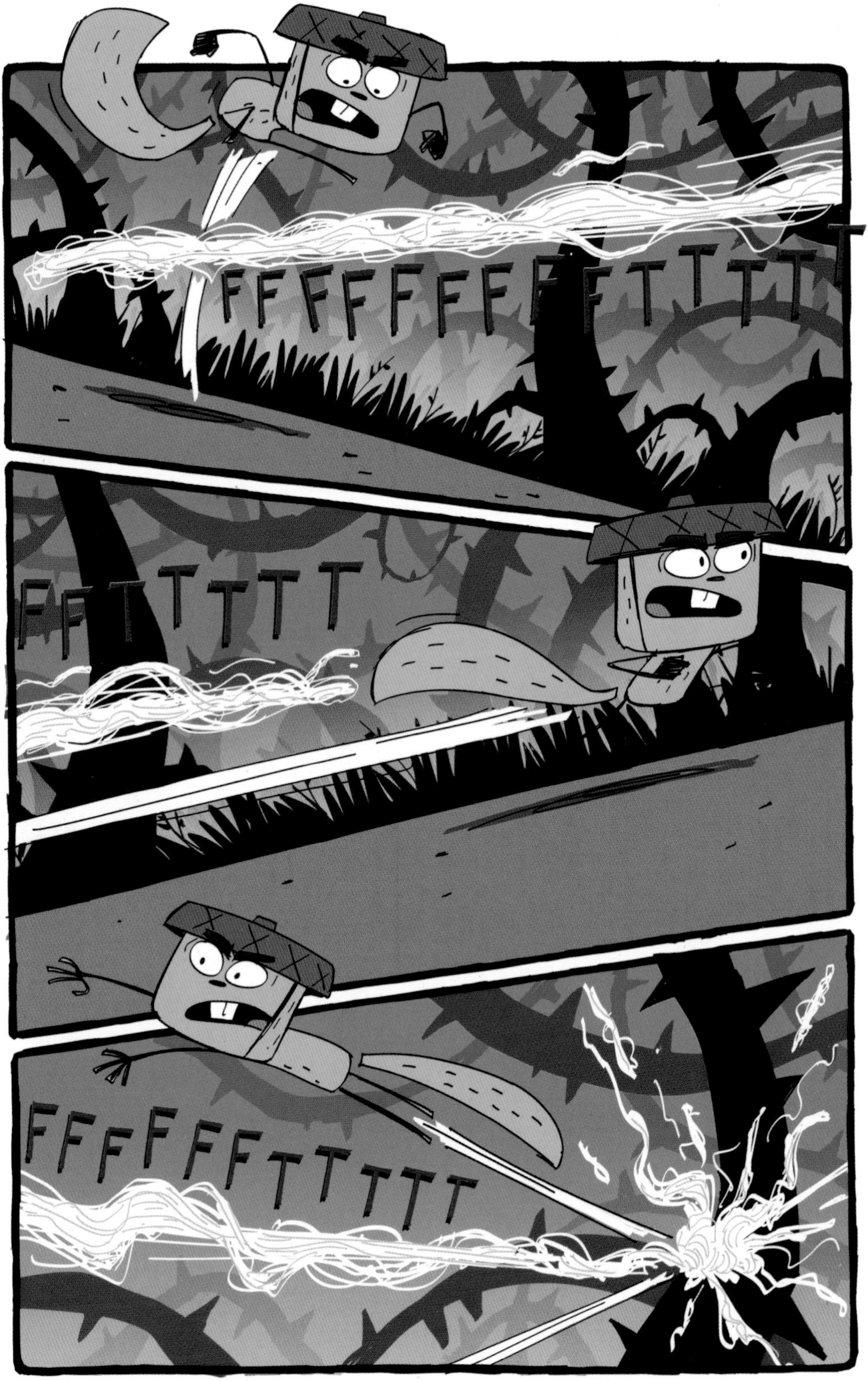
FFFFFFFFFTTTTT
FFTTTTT
FFFFFFTTTTT

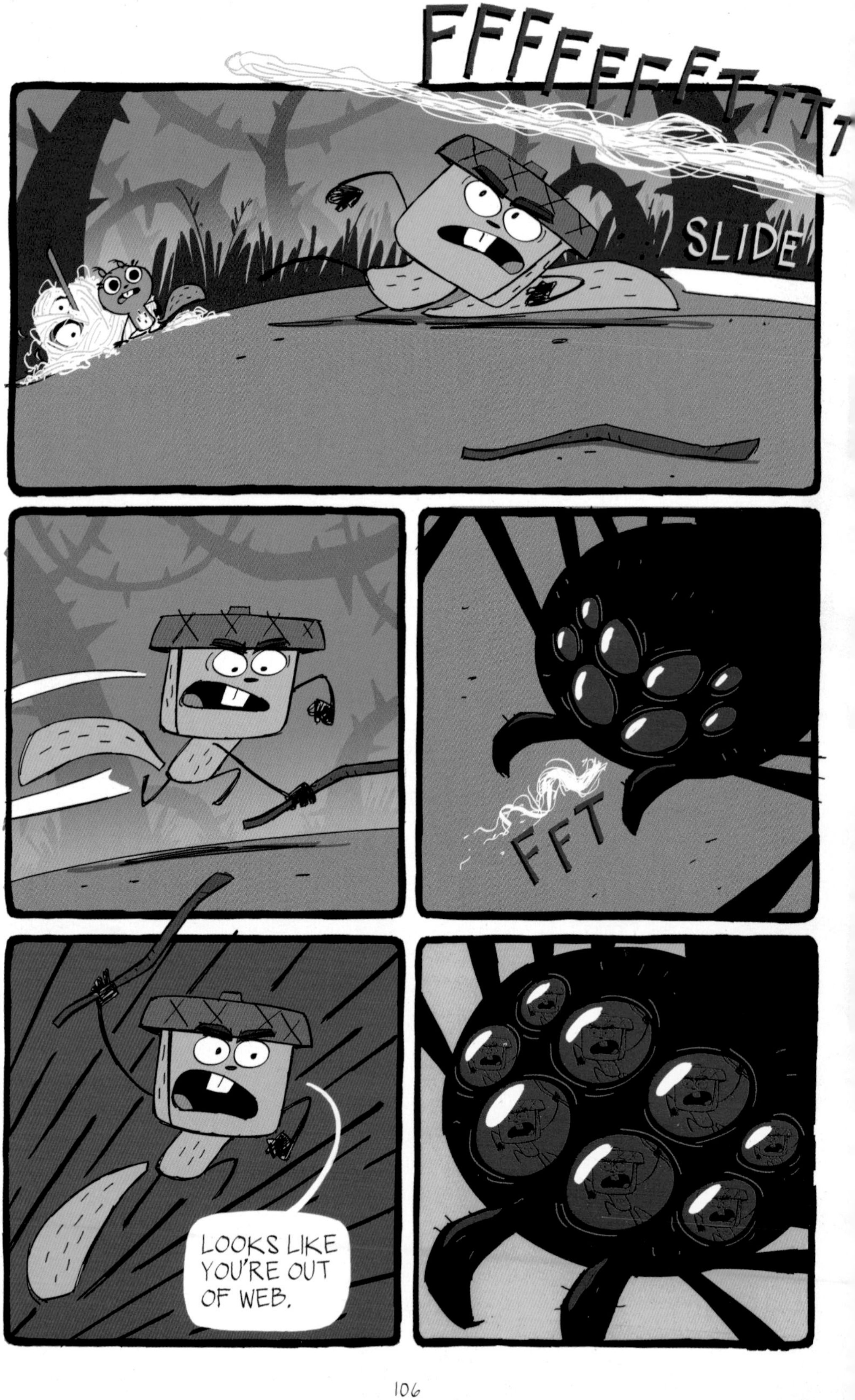
FFFFFFFTTTTT
SLIDE
FFT
LOOKS LIKE YOU'RE OUT OF WEB.

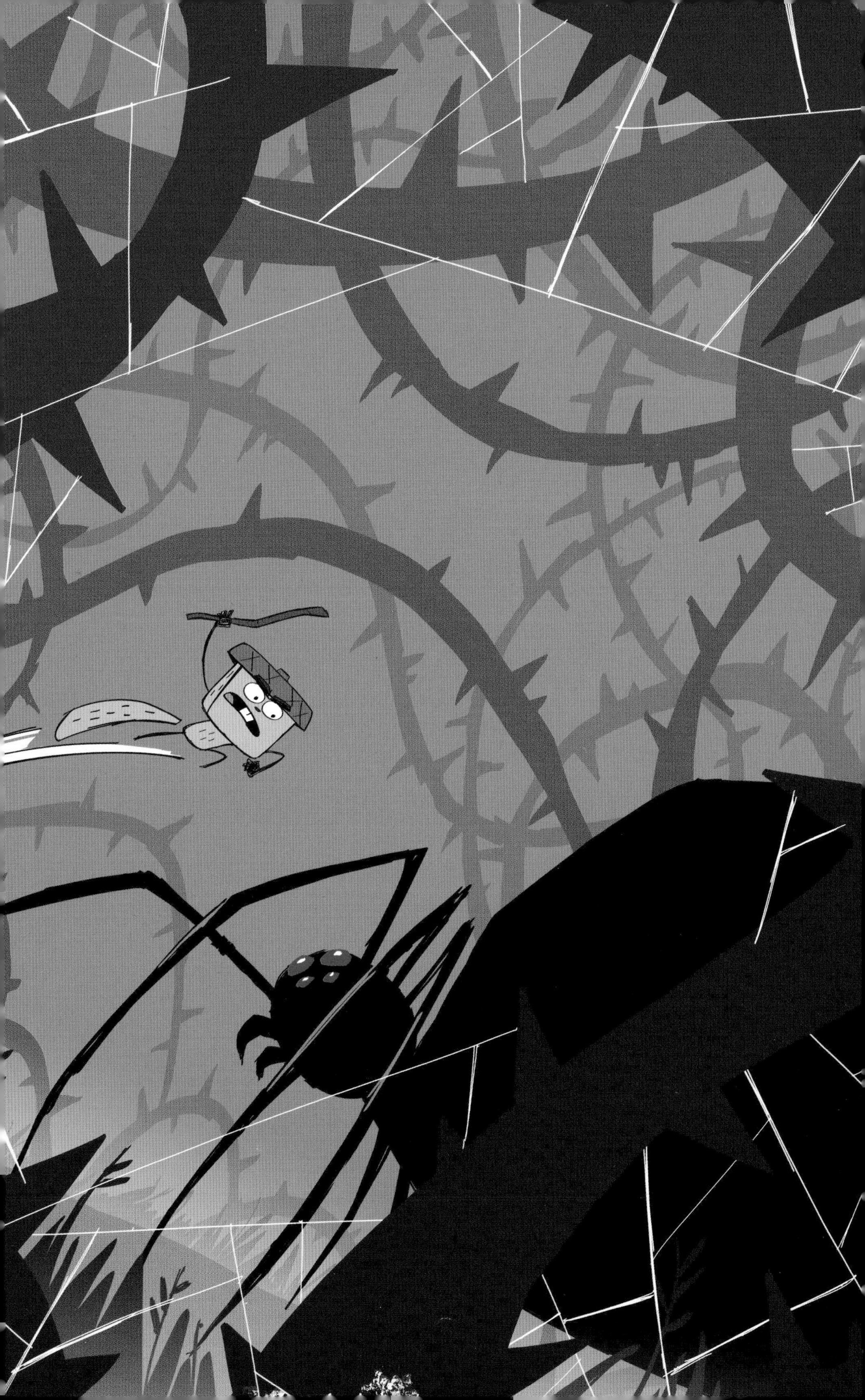

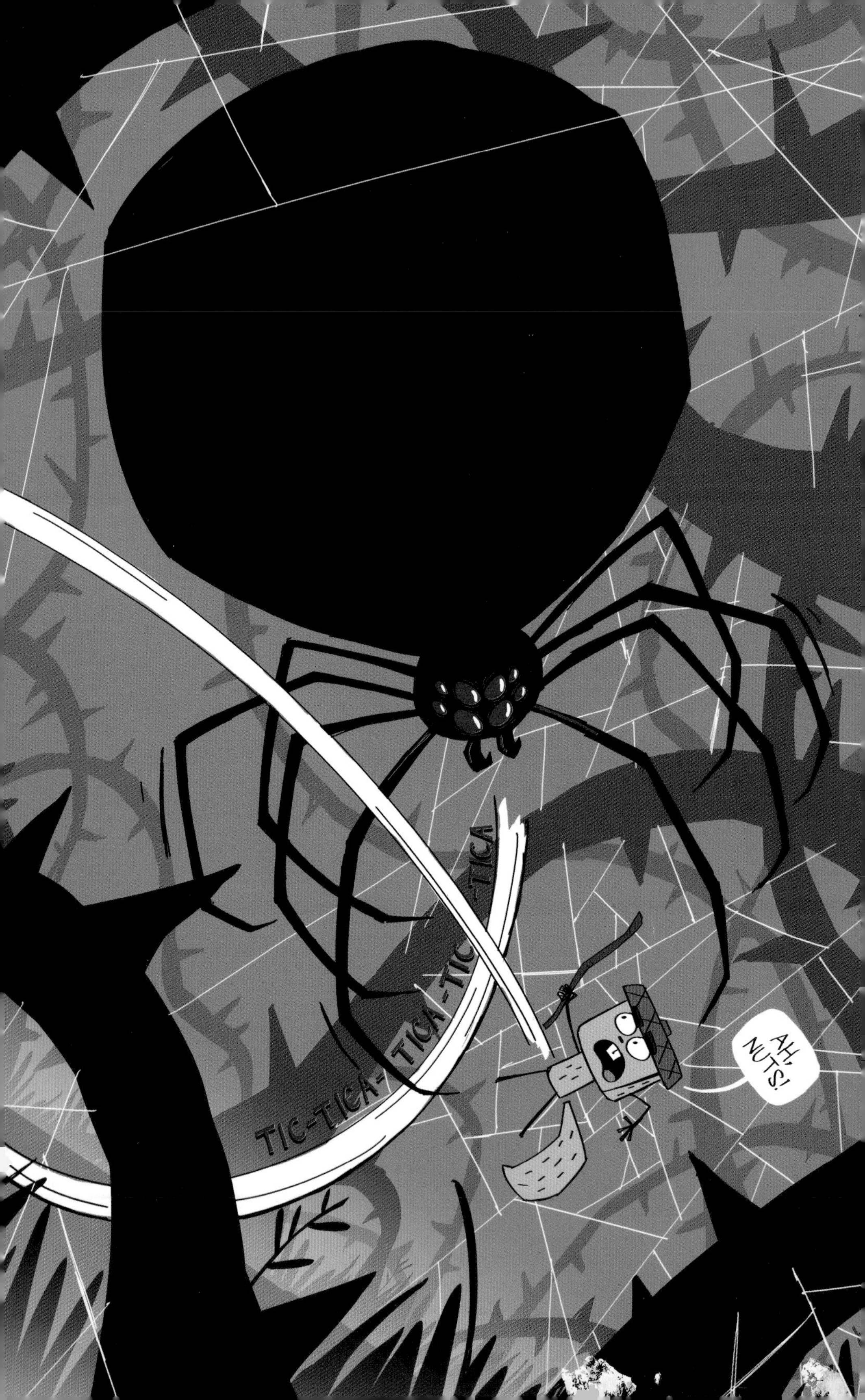
TIC-TICA-TICA-TIC-TICA
AH, NUTS!

YOU WEREN'T SUPPOSED TO MOVE.

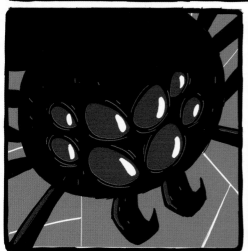

HEY!

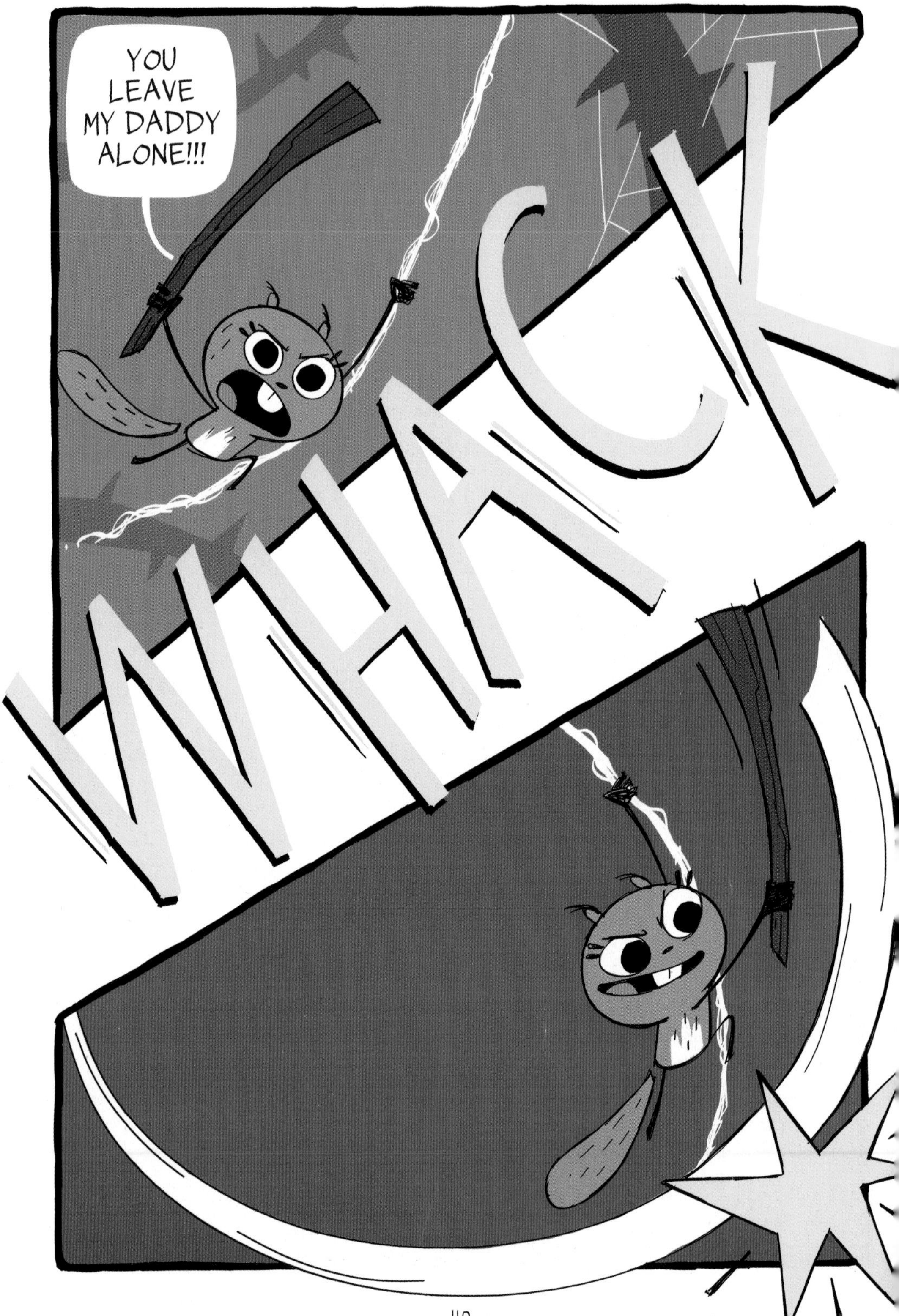
YOU LEAVE MY DADDY ALONE!!!
WHACK

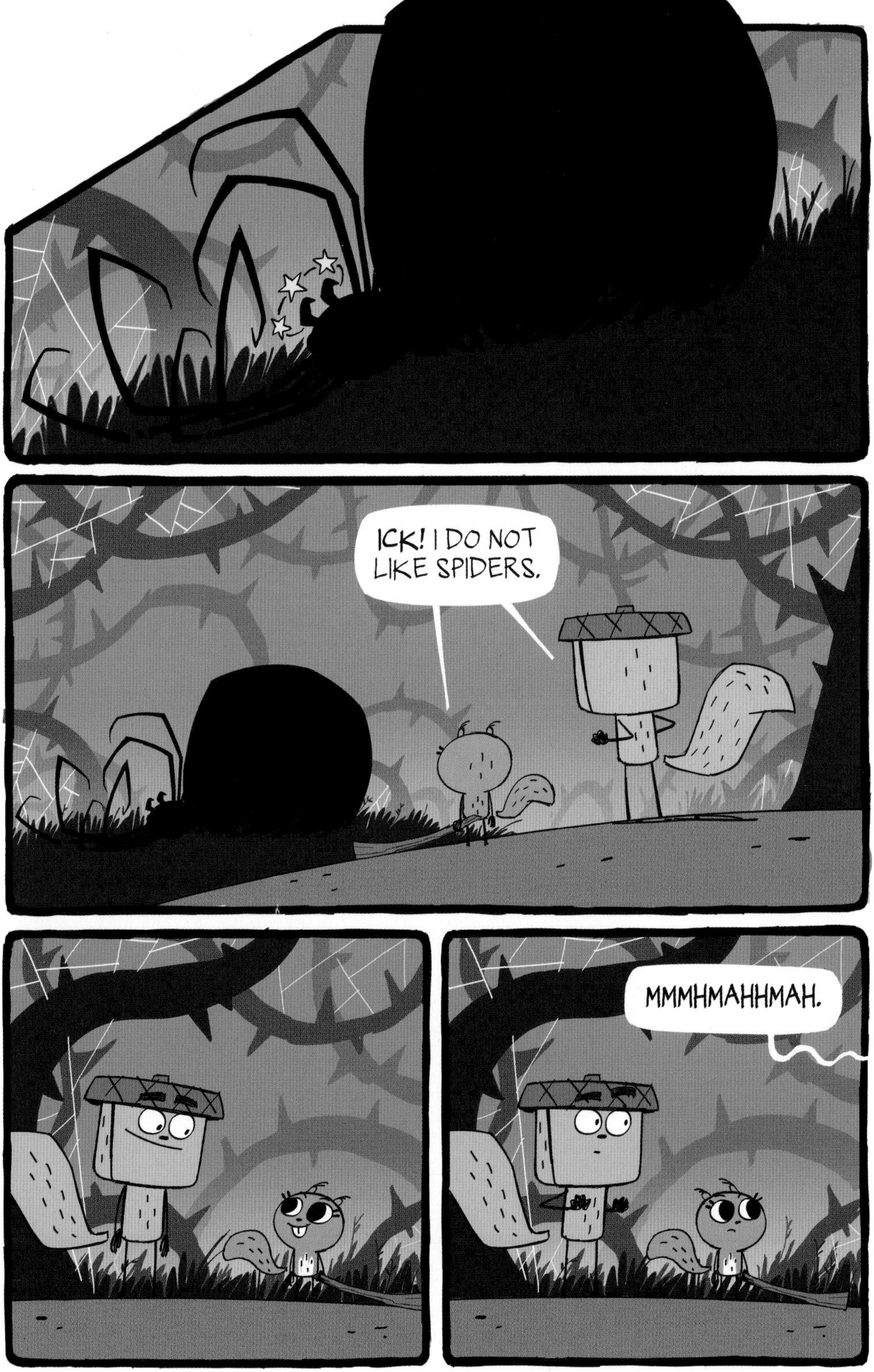
ICK! I DO NOT LIKE SPIDERS.
MMMHMAHHMAH.

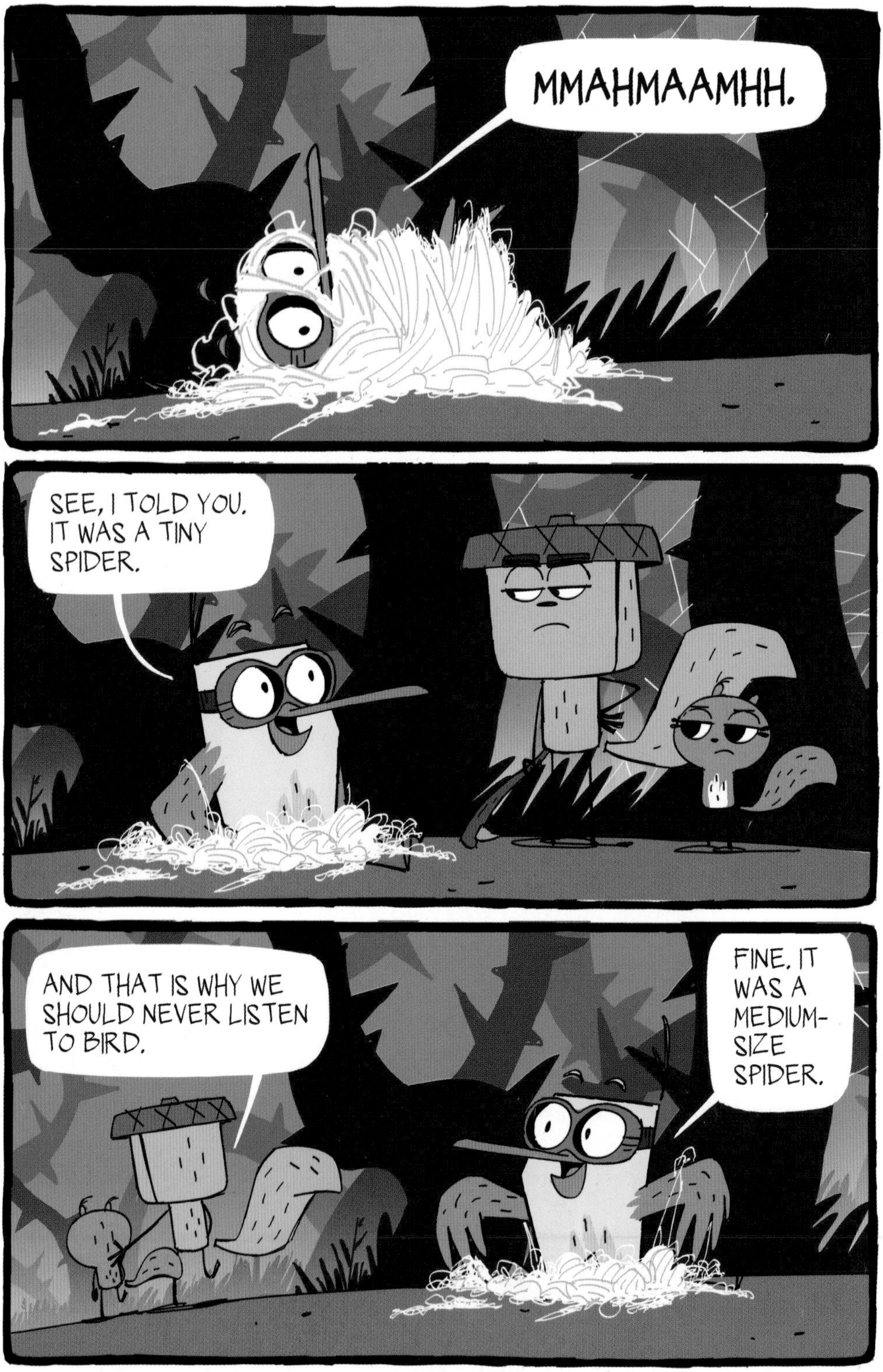
MMAHMAAMHH.
SEE, I TOLD YOU. IT WAS A TINY SPIDER.
AND THAT IS WHY WE SHOULD NEVER LISTEN TO BIRD.
FINE. IT WAS A MEDIUM-SIZE SPIDER.

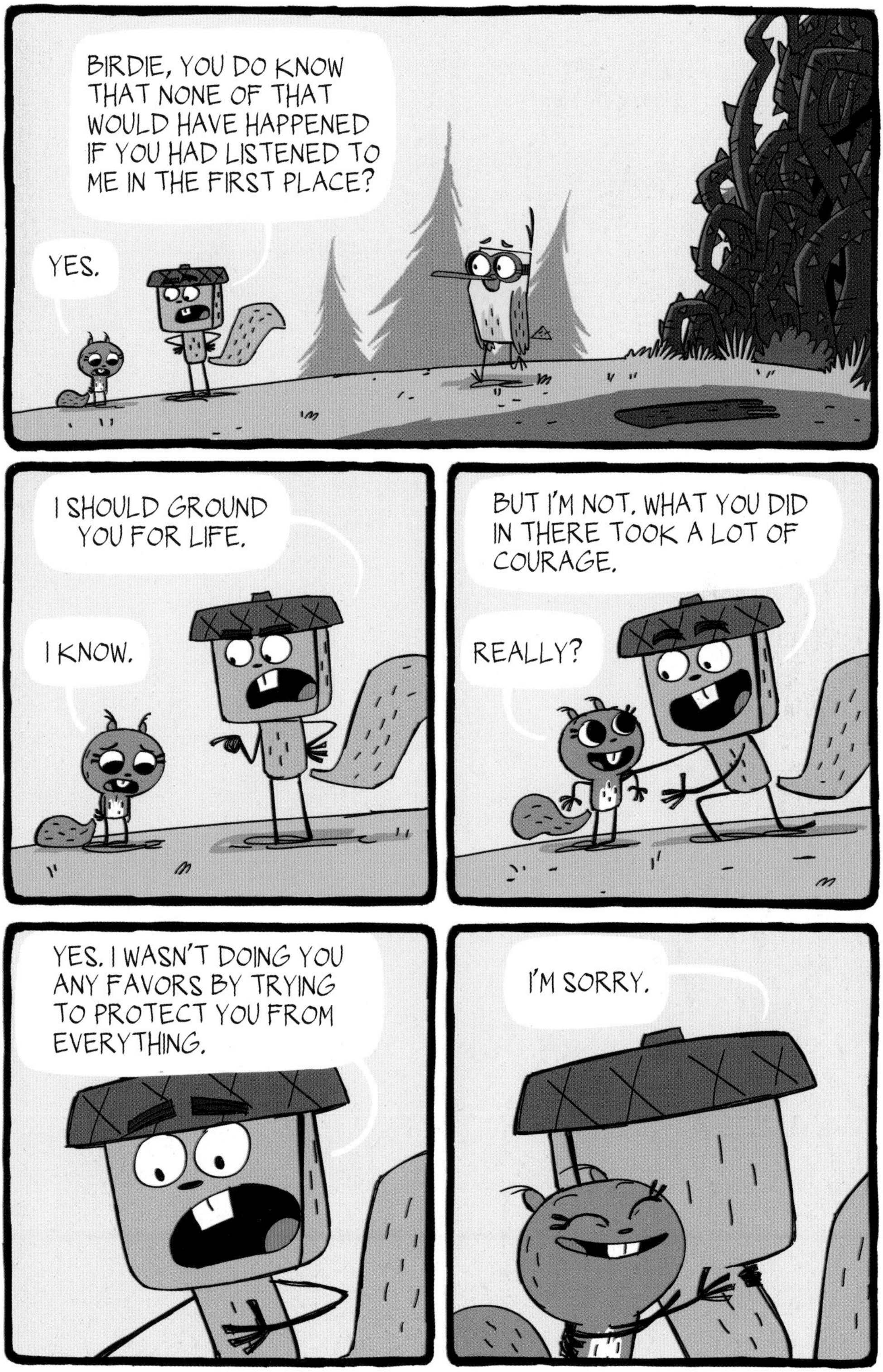
BIRDIE, YOU DO KNOW THAT NONE OF THAT WOULD HAVE HAPPENED IF YOU HAD LISTENED TO ME IN THE FIRST PLACE?
YES.
I SHOULD GROUND YOU FOR LIFE.
I KNOW.
BUT I'M NOT. WHAT YOU DID IN THERE TOOK A LOT OF COURAGE.
REALLY?
YES. I WASN'T DOING YOU ANY FAVORS BY TRYING TO PROTECT YOU FROM EVERYTHING.
I'M SORRY.

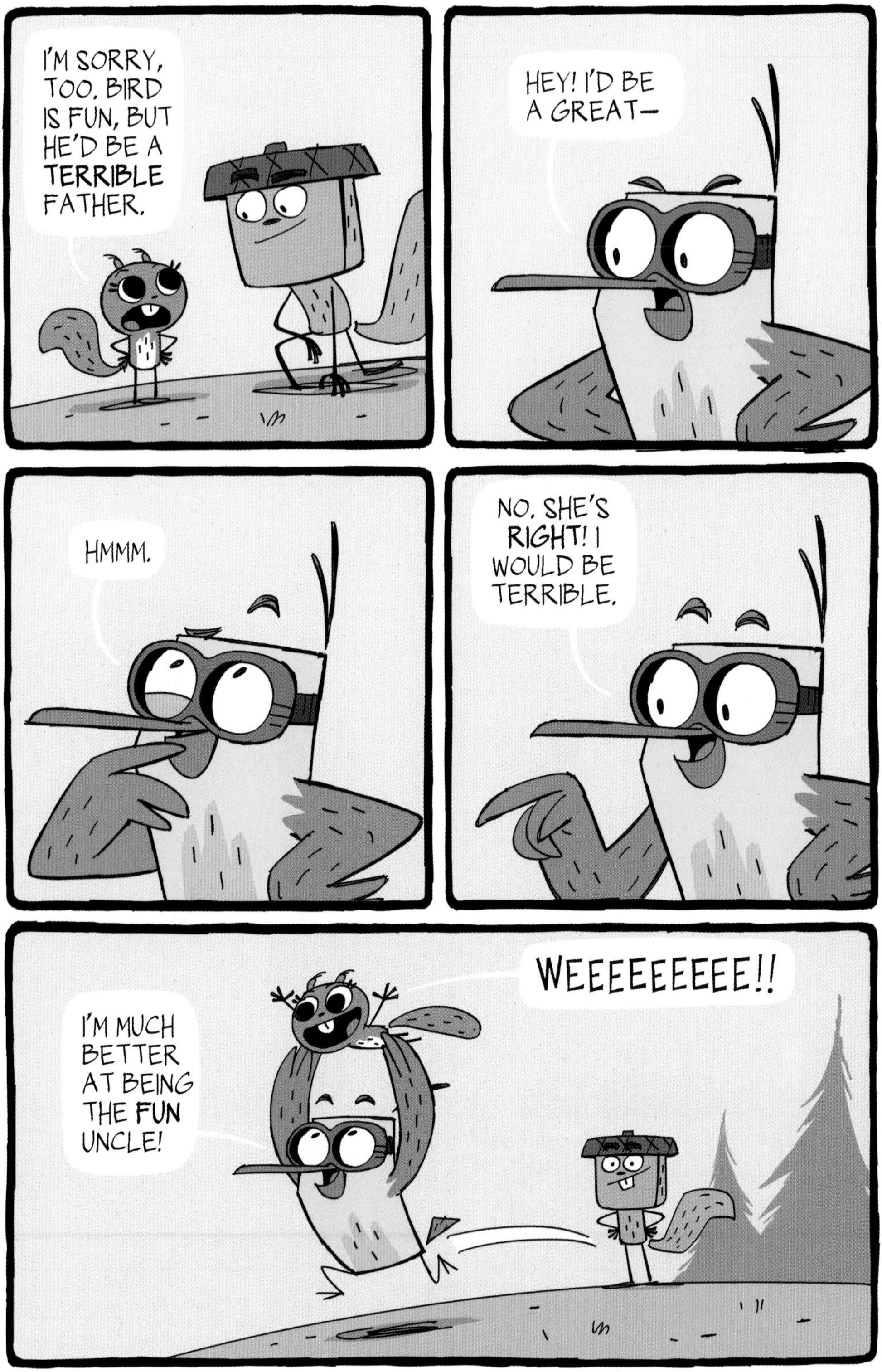
I'M SORRY, TOO. BIRD IS FUN, BUT HE'D BE A **TERRIBLE** FATHER.
HEY! I'D BE A GREAT—
HMMM.
NO. SHE'S **RIGHT**! I WOULD BE TERRIBLE.
I'M MUCH BETTER AT BEING THE **FUN** UNCLE!
WEEEEEEEEE!!

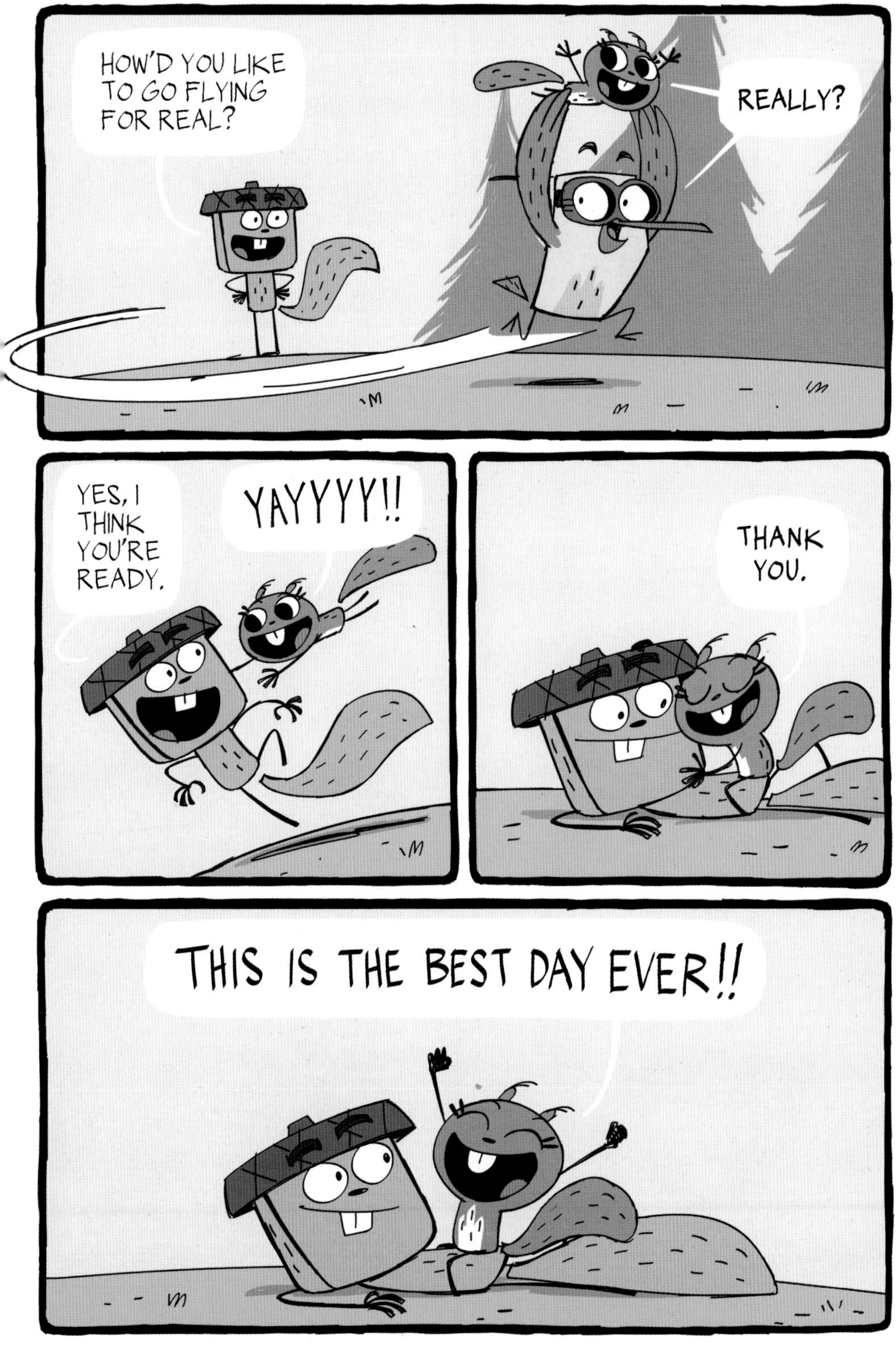
HOW'D YOU LIKE TO GO FLYING FOR REAL?
REALLY?
YES, I THINK YOU'RE READY.
YAYYYY!!
THANK YOU.
THIS IS THE BEST DAY EVER!!

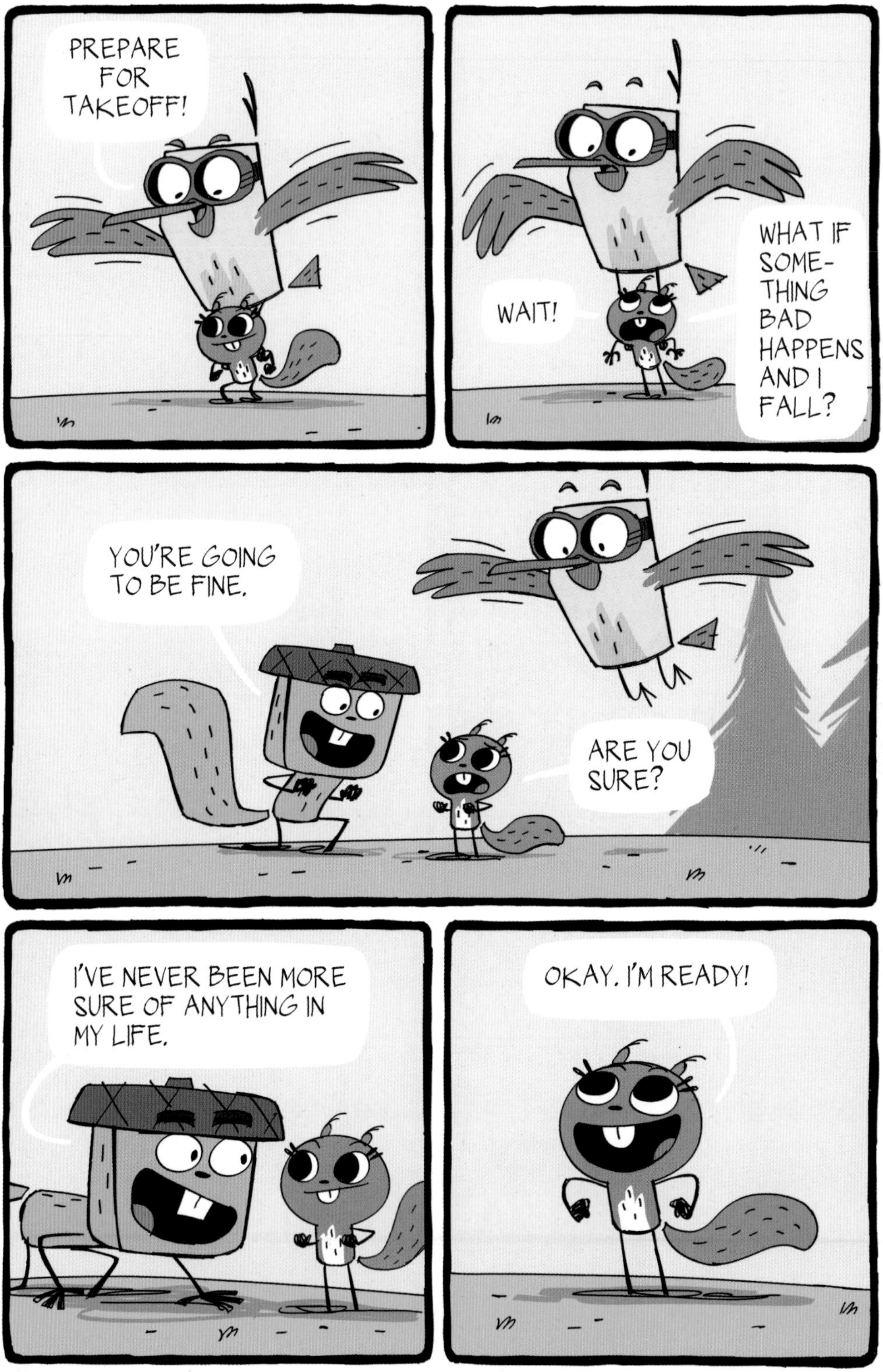
PREPARE FOR TAKEOFF!
WAIT!
WHAT IF SOME-THING BAD HAPPENS AND I FALL?
YOU'RE GOING TO BE FINE.
ARE YOU SURE?
I'VE NEVER BEEN MORE SURE OF ANYTHING IN MY LIFE.
OKAY. I'M READY!

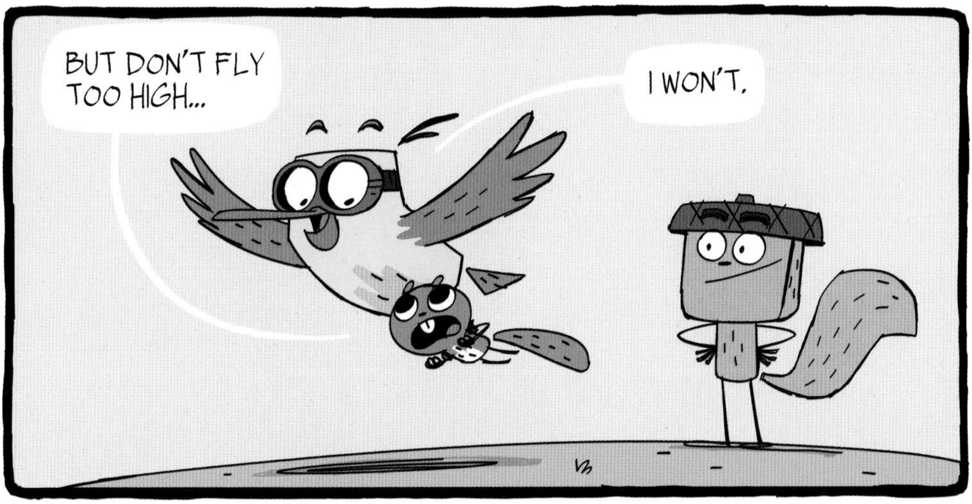
BUT DON'T FLY TOO HIGH...
I WON'T.

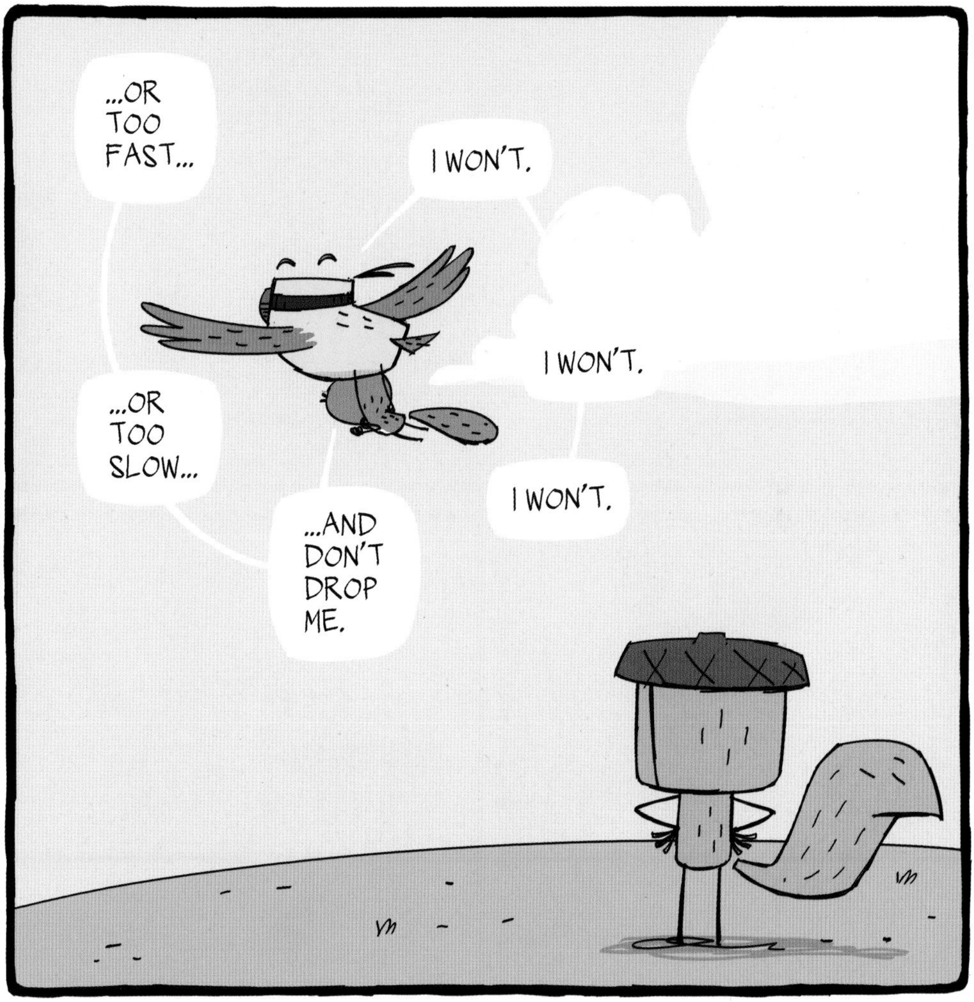
...OR TOO FAST...
I WON'T.
...OR TOO SLOW...
I WON'T.
...AND DON'T DROP ME.
I WON'T.

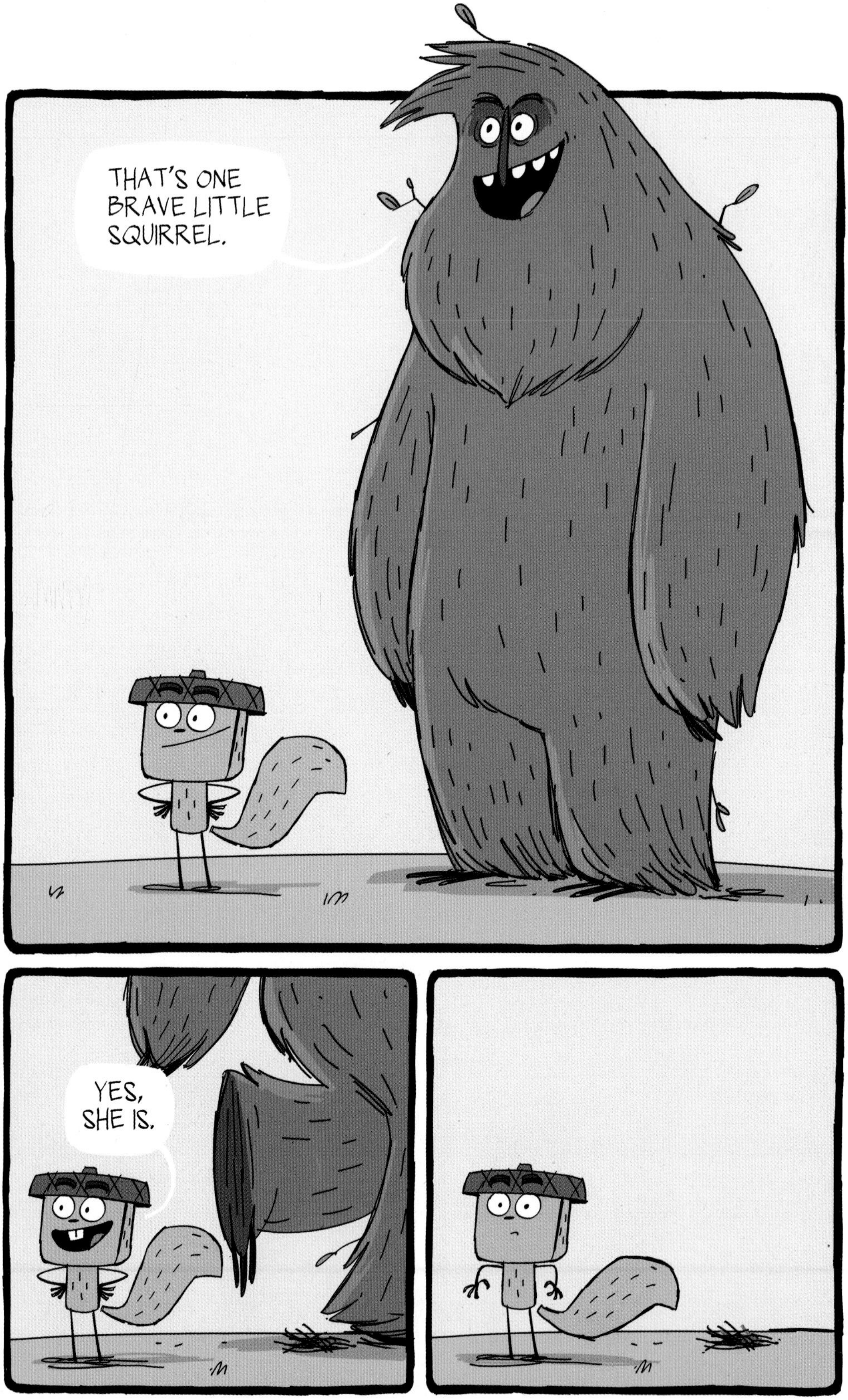
THAT'S ONE BRAVE LITTLE SQUIRREL.
YES, SHE IS.

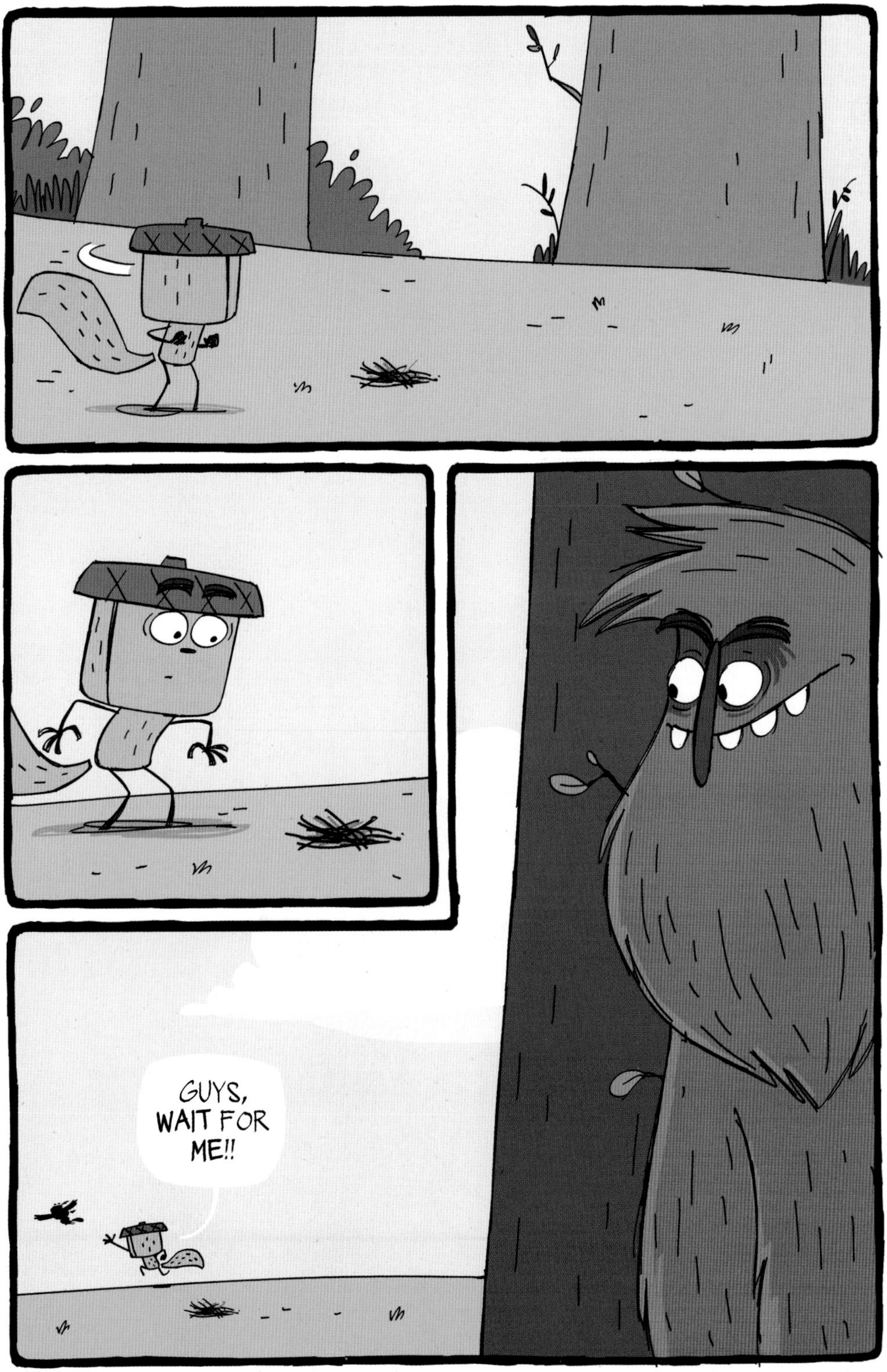
GUYS, WAIT FOR ME!!

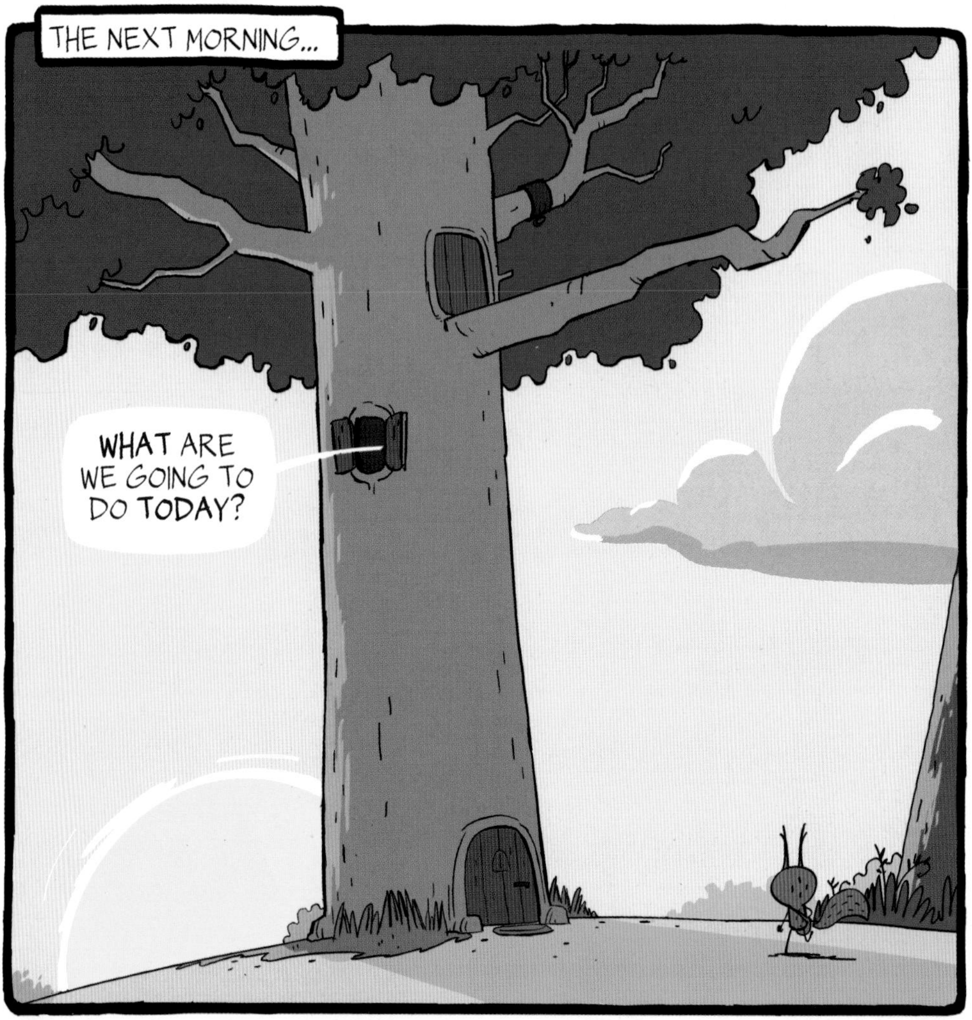
THE NEXT MORNING...
WHAT ARE WE GOING TO DO TODAY?

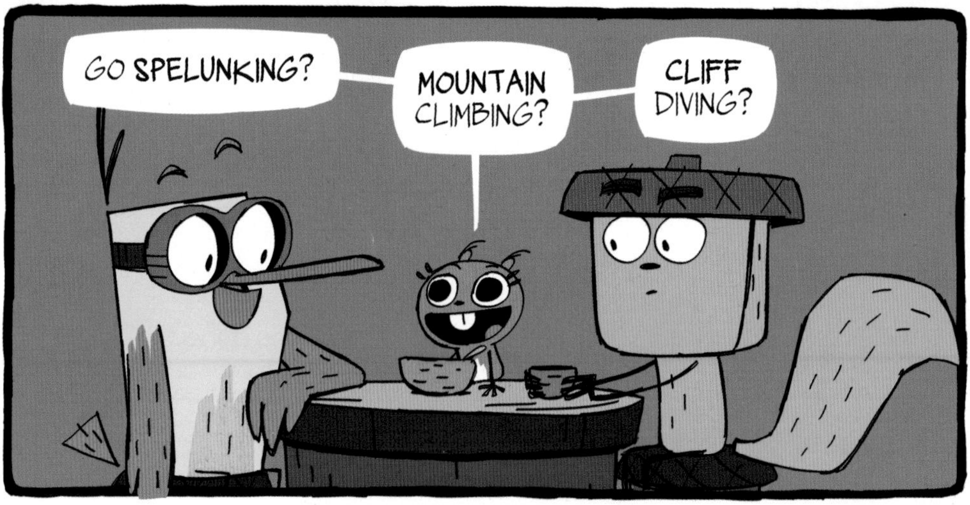
GO SPELUNKING?
MOUNTAIN CLIMBING?
CLIFF DIVING?

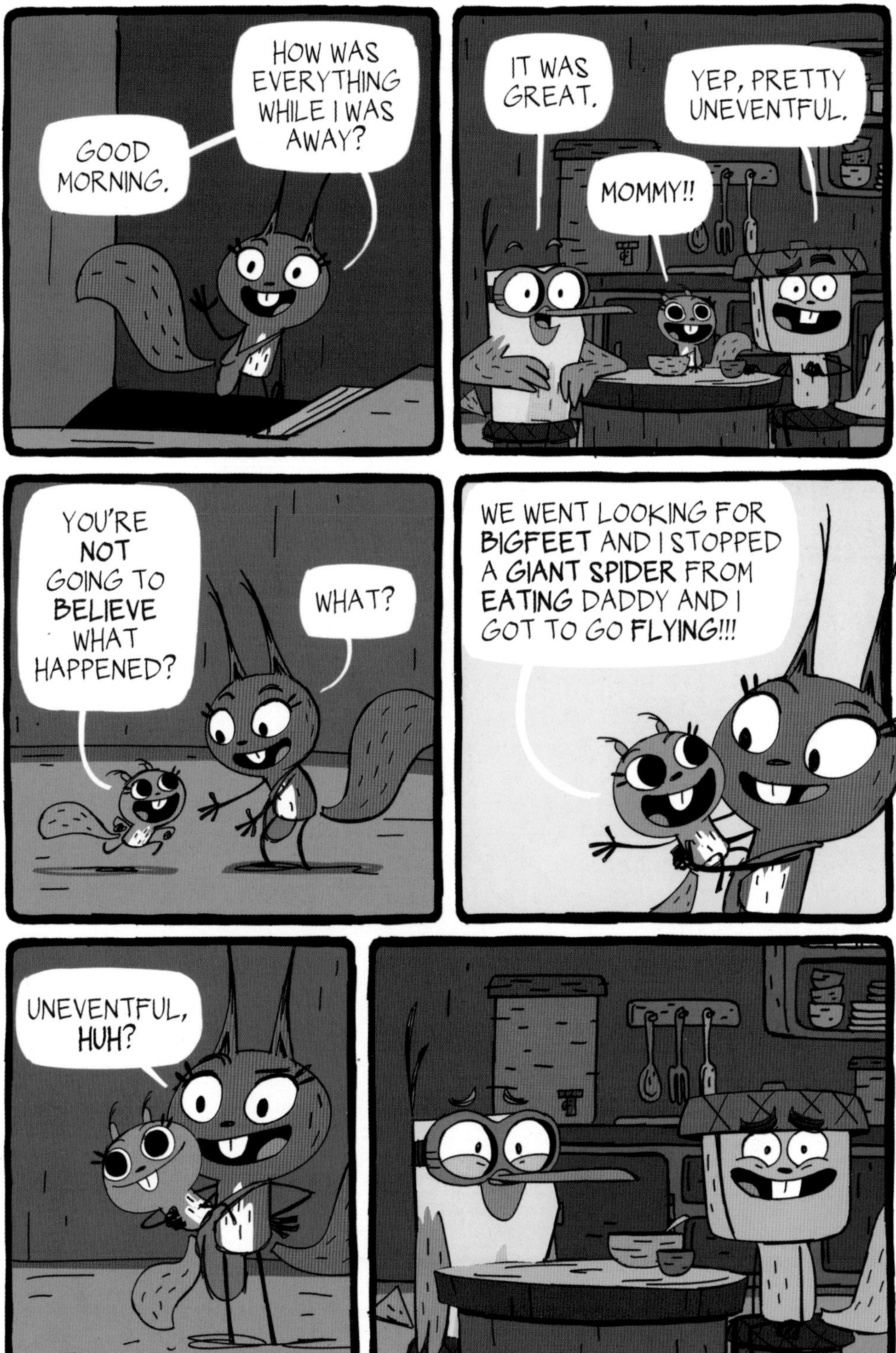
GOOD MORNING.
HOW WAS EVERYTHING WHILE I WAS AWAY?
IT WAS GREAT.
YEP, PRETTY UNEVENTFUL.
MOMMY!!
YOU'RE NOT GOING TO BELIEVE WHAT HAPPENED?
WHAT?
WE WENT LOOKING FOR BIGFEET AND I STOPPED A GIANT SPIDER FROM EATING DADDY AND I GOT TO GO FLYING!!!
UNEVENTFUL, HUH?

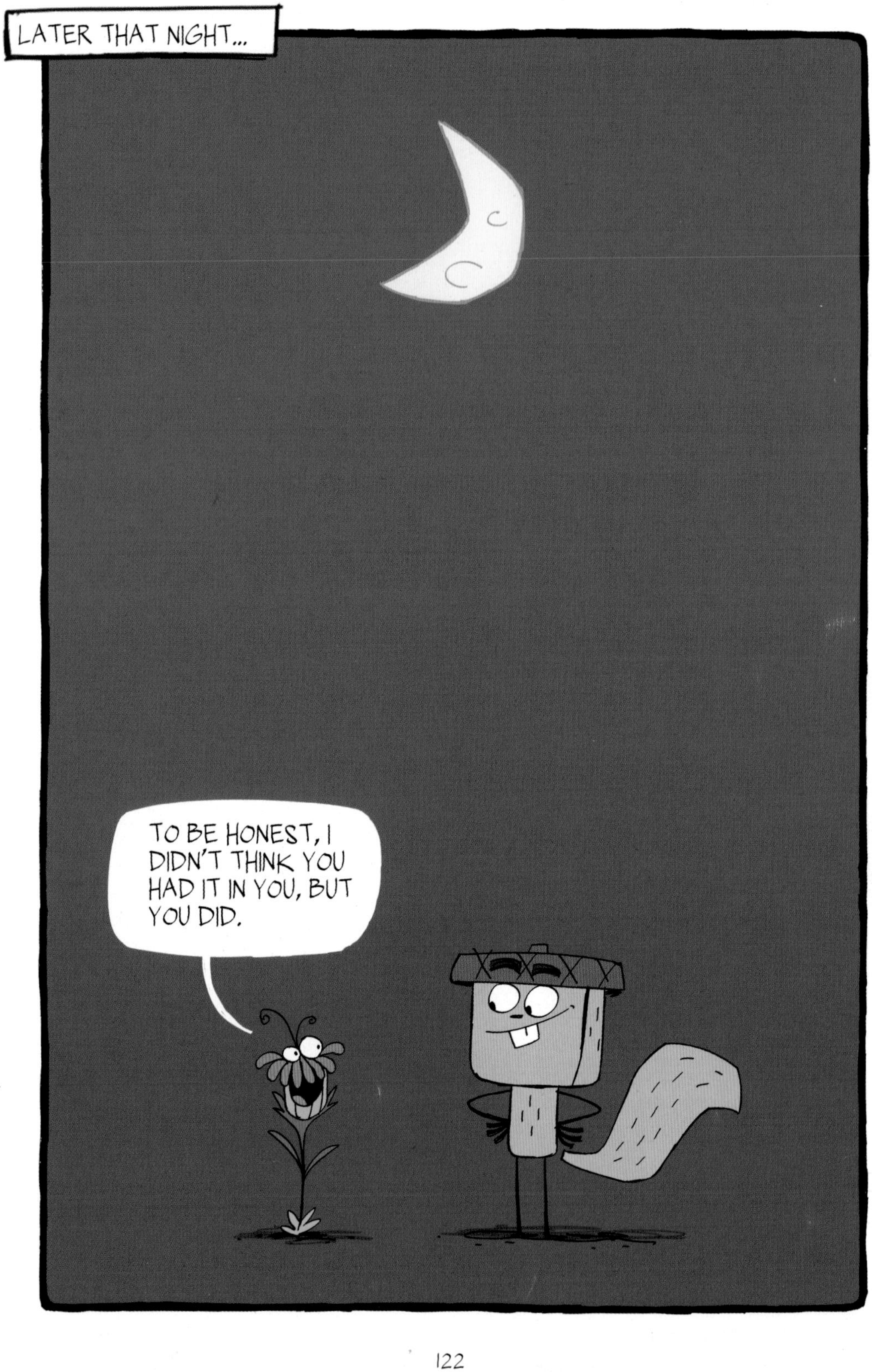
LATER THAT NIGHT...
TO BE HONEST, I DIDN'T THINK YOU HAD IT IN YOU, BUT YOU DID.

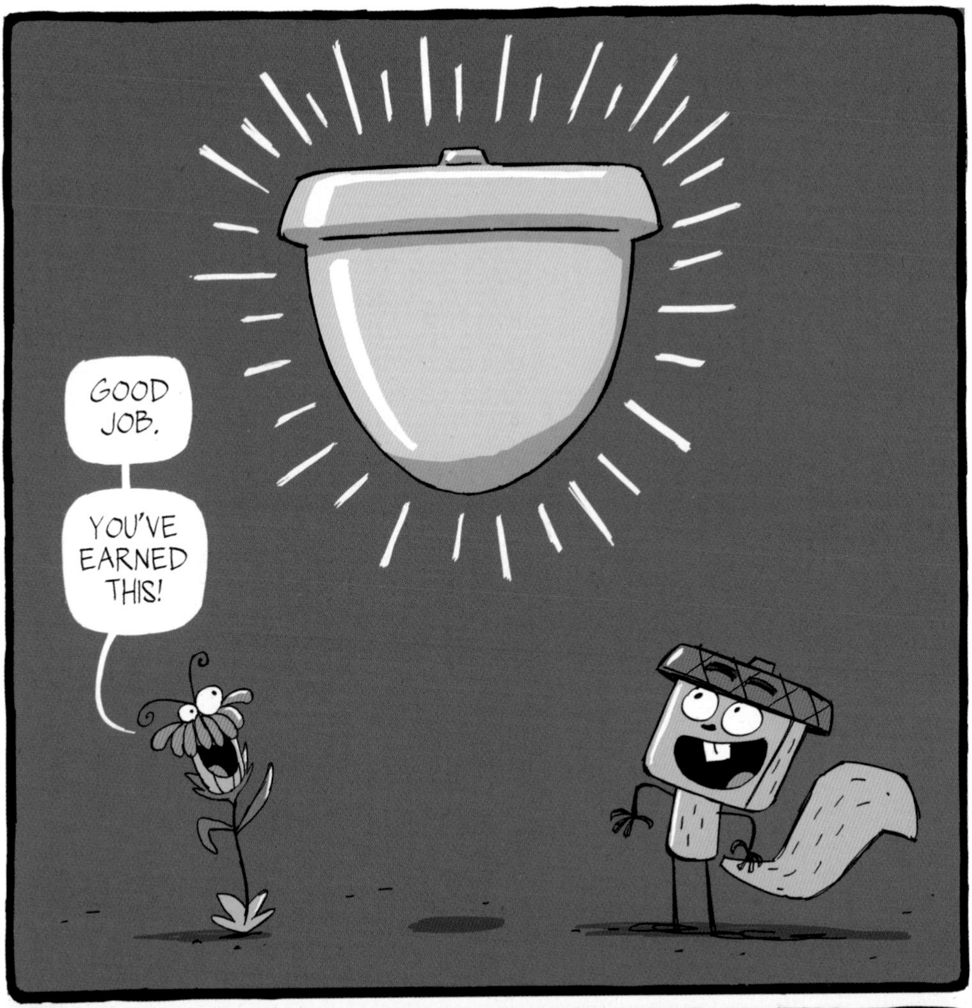
GOOD JOB.
YOU'VE EARNED THIS!
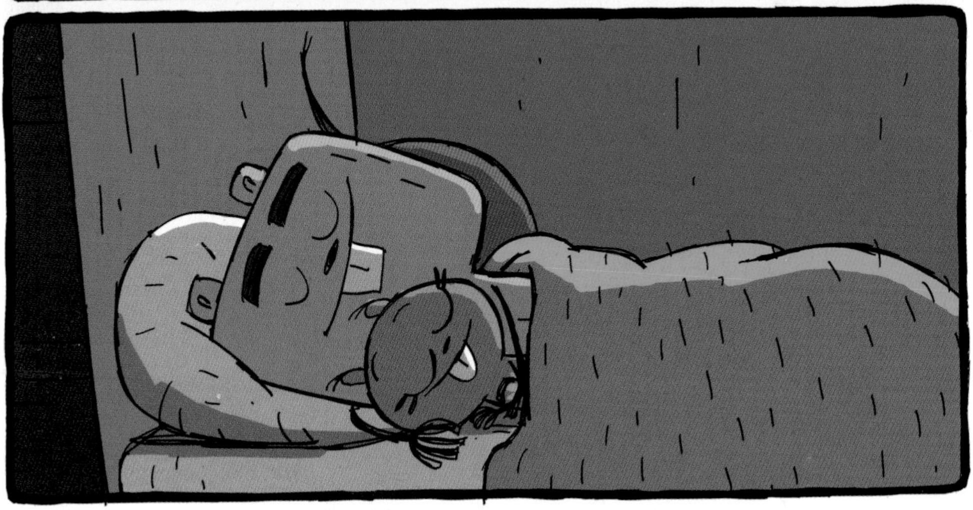

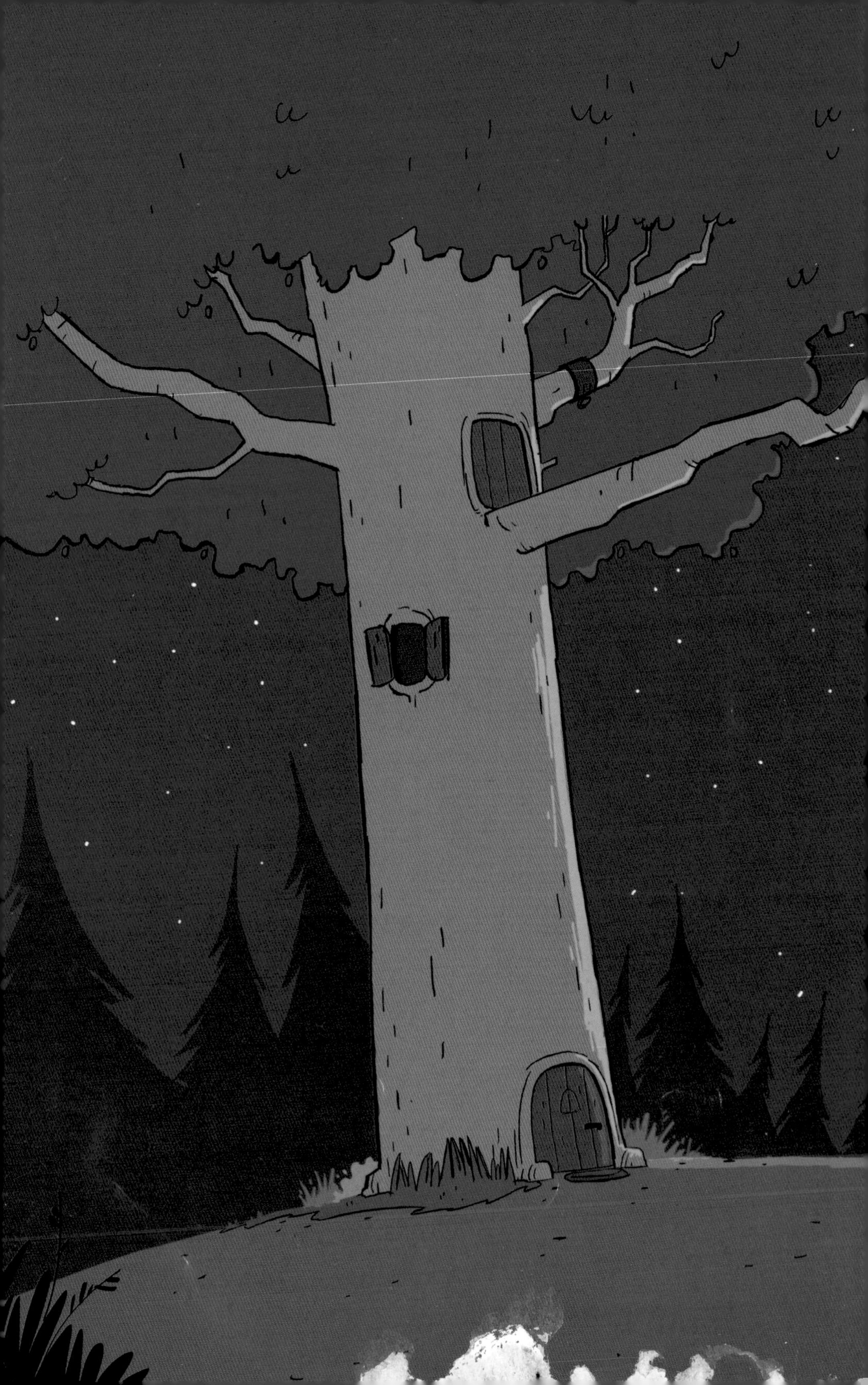

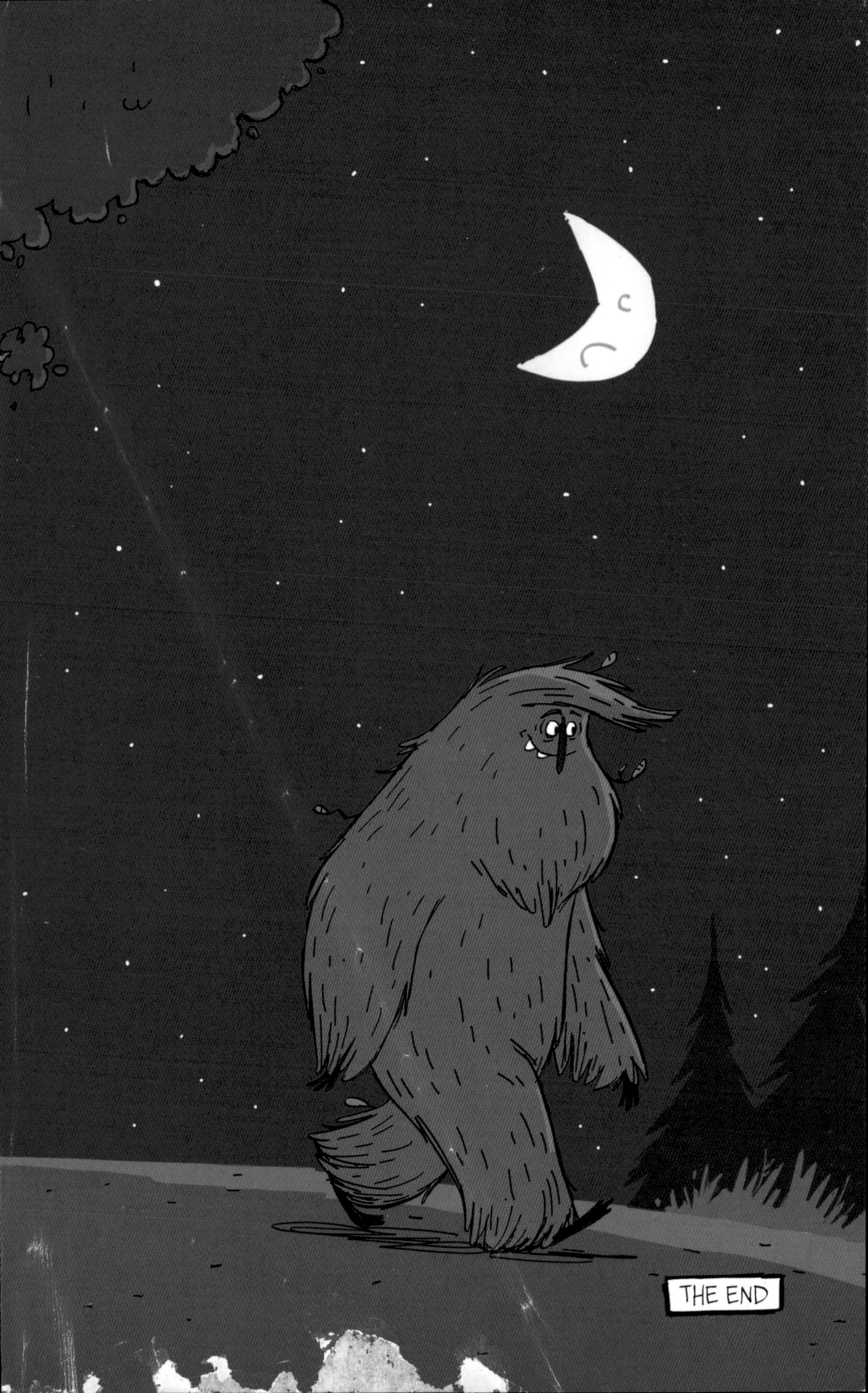
THE END

DON'T STOP HERE! THERE'S MORE BIRD & SQUIRREL ADVENTURES TO CATCH UP ON!

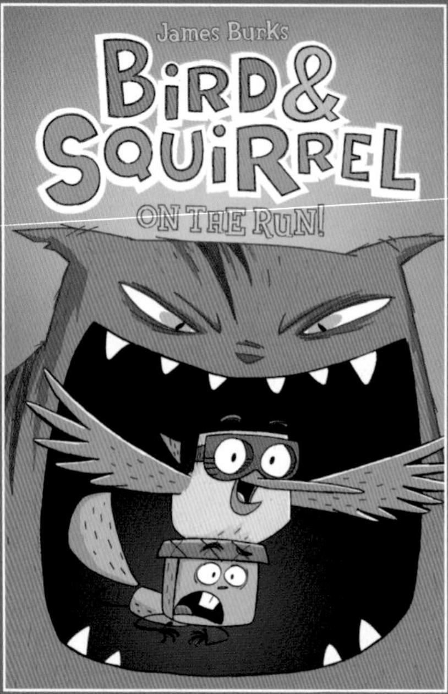
James Burks
Bird & Squirrel
On the Run!

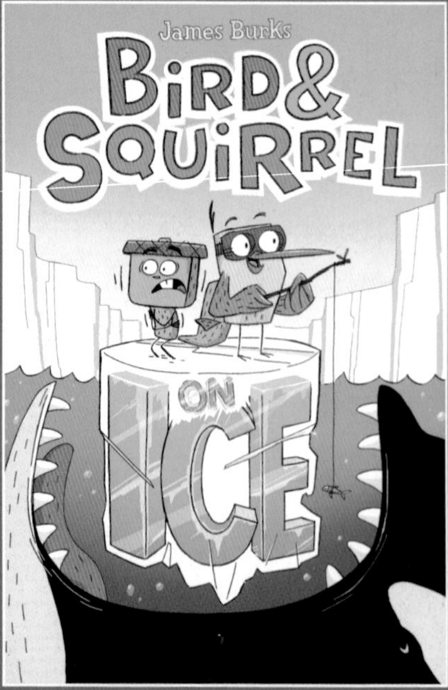
James Burks
Bird & Squirrel
On Ice

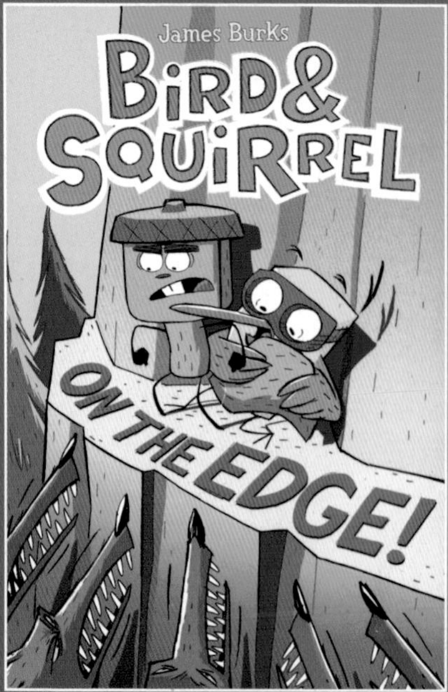
James Burks
Bird & Squirrel
On the Edge!

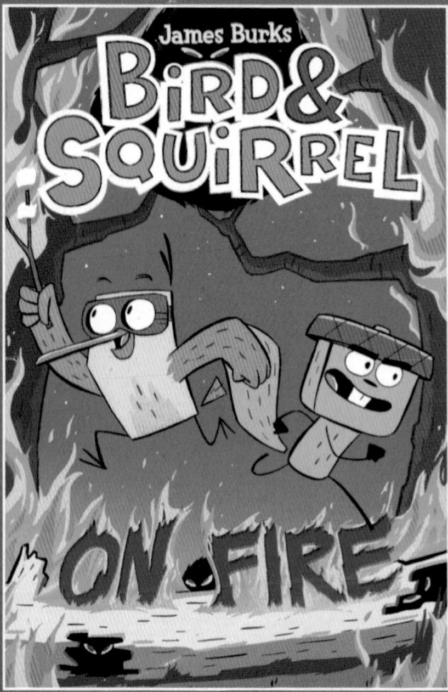
James Burks
Bird & Squirrel
On Fire